FORTRESS OF RADIANCE

FORTRESS OF RADIANCE

MARC ALAN EDELHEIT

This book is a work of fiction. Names, characters, places, and incidents are either the product of the author's imagination or are used fictitiously. Any resemblance to actual persons, living or dead, or to actual events or locales is entirely coincidental.

Fortress of Radiance, The Karus Saga, Book Two

First Edition

I wish to thank my agent, Andrea Hurst, for her invaluable support and assistance. I would also like to thank my beta readers, who suffered through several early drafts. My betas: Jon Cockes, Nicolas Weiss, Melinda Vallem, Paul Klebaur, James Doak, David Cheever, Bruce Heaven, Erin Penny, April Faas, Rodney Gigone, Brandon Purcell, Tim Adams, Paul Bersoux, Phillip Broom, David Houston, Sheldon Levy, Michael Hetts, Walker Graham, Bill Schnippert, Jan McClintock, Jonathan Parkin, Spencer Morris, Jimmy McAfee, Rusty Juban, Marshall Clowers, Joel Rainey. I would also like to take a moment to thank my loving wife, who sacrificed many an evening and weekend to allow me to work on my writing.

Editing Assistance by Hannah Streetman, Audrey Mackaman

Cover Art by Piero Mng (Gianpiero Mangialardi)

Cover Formatting by Telemachus Press

Agented by Andrea Hurst & Associates

http://maenovels.com/

TABLE OF CONTENTS

Author's note:

I hope you enjoy *Fortress of Radiance* and a sincere thank you for your purchase.

Best regards,

Marc Alan Edelheit, author and your tour guide to the worlds of Tannis and Istros

PROLOGUE

Amarra's feet bounced painfully along the paving stone as two soldiers, each gripping an arm, dragged her roughly from the temple. Their callused hands gripping her arms hurt.

The King waited, an enraged look upon his mustached face. He wore the midnight black robe that he used when he went amongst his people. A thin gold circlet rested upon his head, the sides of which disappeared into his long salt-and-pepper hair.

The soldiers released her at the foot of the King, then stepped back.

"Please," Amarra begged, gripping the rich fabric of the King's robe as she knelt in the street before him. A protective cordon of soldiers, backs to Amarra and the King, had formed into a half-moon around them. Their shields were presented outward toward the forming crowd, swords at the ready.

The crowd howled and screamed as they pressed against the shields. One soldier was shoved backward a step. Without hesitation, he lashed out with his sword. A scream was almost immediately followed by a body hitting the ground. The soldier stepped over the man he had just killed and resumed his position. The crowd quieted and nervously took a step back and away from the line of King's Guard.

The King did not turn to look. Instead his gaze was focused over Amarra, back at the temple. Six men wearing the holy robes of the priesthood were dragged forth and forced to kneel just before the steps that led up into the temple. Behind each stood a soldier.

A rock flew from the crowd and landed near one of the priests with a crack as it impacted the paving stones. Amarra, glancing back, saw that the priest did not even flinch.

The King looked down his nose upon Amarra. She saw his cold and calculating eyes. She had seen such looks before, usually directed at others. Returning his gaze, Amarra shuddered in fear and for a moment questioned her choice. She only wavered, then bit her lip and offered up a silent prayer.

"Please don't do this." Her voice was as calm as she could manage. "They are your subjects too and have done nothing to you."

"Done nothing to me?" her father hissed, anger coloring his cheeks. "How can you say that? How dare you make such a statement?"

"Please, they mean only to help, to serve."

The King's face hardened. A muscle twitched in his jaw. "Hear me—"

"You have defiled yourself." A look of disgust washed over his face. "And now you beg like a common supplicant? You are unworthy to share our family name. Your mother would be sickened if she could see you now."

"Father." She was not sure what she could say. The paving stone felt hard against her knees. If only he understood what was in her heart.

"You have betrayed me, and our house."

"Never!" Amarra tugged on the robes. "I ... I would never do that. I just believe, with all my heart and soul. Is that so wrong?"

"These filthy men have corrupted you," her father said coldly, with a glance at the priests–turned-prisoners. "They have turned your heart from me, and for that they shall pay the ultimate price."

"No, Father." Tears stung her eyes. "Please don't do this. I still love you."

"Lies," the King exploded. He kicked her hard in the chest. She fell backward, her head connecting painfully with the paving stone. Pulling herself to her hands and knees, she struggled to breathe. Her father kicked her roughly again, booted foot catching her painfully in the ribs. She collapsed, rolling onto her side.

He reached down to grab her long, dark hair by the base of her neck and dragged Amarra back to her knees. The King, his face mottled by rage, backhanded Amarra. White hot pain exploded from the point of contact. For a moment, she lost all sense. Her vision swam as he yanked her head back so she looked directly into his face.

Fear flooded Amarra's being as he locked eyes with her. She gave an involuntary shudder.

"You ungrateful bitch. They have lied to you. Why are you unable to see that? I thought I raised you better than this, but it appears you are simply too stupid to understand that." He spat into her face before pointing at the kneeling priests. "Their god is a lie."

"No, he is not," she said, tears of pain stinging her eyes. "I have felt him fill the dreadful emptiness inside me. You must listen to me. He has spoken to me. He shall save us all, and is sending aid."

The King eyed her coldly for a moment and then reached down and wiped some of the spit off of her cheek. A shadow of tenderness passed over his face. Amarra thought she recognized a glimpse of her old father. But it was gone in a flash.

"It is all a lie," he said again, "as are your protestations of love."

She started to reply. He backhanded her again. The blow landed viciously upon her cheek. She felt a hot wetness on her neck and saw blood drip down her arm.

"For the sake of your dead mother," the King hissed, "I shall give you one last chance. Recant, and I may even spare these vile men a death most foul."

Amarra glanced over to the kneeling priests. One raised his head, just enough to make eye contact. Father Lohert's eyes were filled with concern. He had spent long hours tutoring her in the faith. He was one of the kindest men she had ever known. The concern was not for himself, but for her. With a sickening feeling, she realized she had brought this misfortune upon them. The priest nodded ever so slightly, and then lowered his forehead back to the paving stone.

Amarra felt even more wretched, for she understood Father Lohert's meaning. He had given her permission to recant. She could save herself.

Was it a lie, then? Her eyes flicked from the kneeling priests to her father and his towering rage. Her eyes traveled back to the priests and then to the great temple she had come to love visiting. Massive white marble columns ran completely around the building. The columns were impossibly thick and supported an arched roof high above. The building was grand, beautiful, and awe-inspiring, just as it should be, for this temple honored a god deserving of worship. It had never failed to lift her heart, until this very moment. Was it all a lie?

No, it could not be. She could not do it. She had given herself over to her god. It was not something she could undo. Amarra believed.

She closed her eyes for a moment and offered up a silent prayer. No matter what happened, she resolved to stand strong and true to not only herself, but to her god. She felt a sense of calm settle over her, almost as if a comforting arm had been placed around her shoulders.

Scripture abruptly came to mind, and the words spilled from her mouth before she could stop them.

"Despite evil men, let us hold to the hope, for she who promised is faithful."

Her father's eyes narrowed dangerously.

The sense of calm slipped from her, replaced by a deep, cold fear.

"When we leave this place," he said, leaning down, "you, my dear, will be left behind, forgotten, just like this city will someday be." He was so close she could feel the heat of his breath upon her neck.

Amarra stared back at him, appalled. She coughed, tasting copper. Bloody spittle ran down her chin and onto her soiled, torn dress.

"No."

"Oh yes." He pulled her closer and lowered his voice to a soft whisper. "You have committed a crime most foul and have joined with these evil men. You are no longer my daughter, but you are still of the blood. As such, you will be treated differently."

He released her hair, and she fell back to her hands and knees. The King stood, gaze lingering upon the priests. He then looked back down on Amarra.

"I will not be cursed by the true gods for the killing of the fruit of my loin. You will not be killed by my hand, nor by one of my servants. I think it quite fitting, really. You will be left to rot, as your soul has. You will be locked up for eternity, wrapped only in your false faith for comfort." A grim smile split his face. "I wonder if you will last long enough for the Horde to arrive? Perhaps I shall leave you sufficient food and permit them to deal with your faith." He took a step from her, then glanced back. "Save us, will he? Let's see your god save you."

"No." Tears spilled down her face. "You don't understand. The—"

"Oh, but I do," he said, and then turned to one of the officers of his guard. "Take her away and throw her into the Morning Cell."

"Yes, my lord," the officer said. He nodded to the two soldiers who had been standing just behind Amarra. Strong hands seized each arm and dragged her roughly to her feet. The crowd behind the cordon of soldiers roared their approval. She attempted to pull free, but one of the soldiers drove a fist into her stomach, forcing the air once again from her lungs. Amarra collapsed in their arms. She gagged for air as they started dragging her away.

Still struggling to breathe, Amarra turned her head to look back. Her eyes were upon the man who had raised her. As a little girl he had once been kindly to her, kissing the hurts and showering not only love but great affection upon her. This man had changed from the one she had known. Time, and the current trials and troubles of her people, had done that.

In the place of her father now stood the King of Carthum—a man of desperation, unimaginable terror, and cruelty.

Why had she not seen it before?

"Stake them out as a warning to other false clerics," the King said to the same officer, gesturing toward the prostrated priests. "I want their deaths to be slow, and painful."

Amarra's heart cried out with the injustice. Her eyes were upon her father as she was dragged away, feet bouncing off of the ancient, uneven paving stones. She struggled once again to free herself, but it was no good. The hands upon her arms were not only bruising, but just too strong. The last thing she heard before being pulled into the enraged crowd was her father issuing a further order.

"Bring this vile monument to a false god down."

CHAPTER ONE
THE PRESENT

K arus glanced over as Amarra gave a gasp and started awake, a sheen of sweat on her brow. It was as if she had awoken from a nightmare. She had dozed off on the reclining couch he had moved into his office. She blinked, rubbing her eyes and sitting up. Amarra stretched, arching her back. She ran a hand through her long, black hair before looking over at him. She flashed him an uneasy smile and then glanced away.

"Bad dream?" Karus asked in Common, setting down the silver stylus on the ornate wooden desk. Along with it, he slid aside the wax tablet he had been making notes on and leaned back on the stool, deciding he was done with work for the moment.

Amarra looked over at him and chewed her lip.

"Tell me," Karus said again.

"It is nothing," Amarra said, standing. She went to the balcony and looked down on the overgrown gardens behind the palace. Her face was flushed, and she wrung her hands. Karus stood up, pushing the stool out of the way with the back of his sandaled foot. He walked over to her and placed his hand on her shoulder. She glanced over at him, then returned her gaze outward. He followed her eyes down into the gardens.

Two dragons, one dark green and the other a deep red, lay next to one another, so close that they almost touched. The green dragon, Kordem, was curled up, his head tucked beneath a wing. The other, Cyln'phax, lay on her side, her long neck stretched out and her head bent around and nearly upside down. An eye opened and studied them for a lazy moment before closing.

Both dragons were huge, perhaps more than a hundred fifty feet from head to tail. He shook his head at the incredible creatures just below. The dragons were covered with thick, armored scales and large spikes that ran down their backs. Even their stomachs were covered in scales that looked tougher than plate armor. The scales reflected the sunlight with an almost metallic quality.

The two dragons were not only beautiful, but fearsome. Besides rows of long, sharp, serrated teeth, each foot held claws that were longer than a man had a right to be tall. They looked incredibly strong, and that did not include their ability to breathe fire, which Karus had witnessed first-hand just a few days before when Cyln'phax had attacked the creature of evil in the High Father's temple.

The early morning sun shone downward onto the garden. Like some of the reptiles Karus had seen over the years, the dragons appeared to be enjoying the warmth of the sun. Cyln'phax flexed a foot, razor-sharp claws digging into one of the paved stone paths that snaked its way through the garden. The dragon flexed a second time, and the paving stone gave an audible crack, snapping in two before the claws dug up large furrows in the dirt underneath.

Karus spared a glance over at Amarra. It had been five days since they'd emerged from the ruins of the High Father's temple with the spear and the Key that Jupiter had given them. She had not left his side for much of those five days.

Karus had never seen anyone like Amarra, with her exotic olive complexion and almond-shaped eyes. Amarra still wore the long white dress she had been wearing when she emerged from the High Father's temple. She had gone in wearing a servant's dress and come out with something that never seemed to wrinkle or become dirty or stained. He wondered how she did it. Was the dress somehow special? She had a natural elegance about her, but in that dress she looked royal. It amazed Karus that she wanted to be with him, a rough old soldier.

Amarra was stunningly beautiful, so much so that standing this close to her got his heart beating a little faster, dragons or not. He had faced enemy in battle who did not unsettle him as much as she did. Karus felt a fierce desire to protect her and keep her safe. The truth was that he knew, with what was headed their way, they were all far from safe.

"What is it?" Karus asked her in Common, for it was clear to him Amarra was troubled.

"It is nothing," Amarra said, twisting a strand of hair.

"I don't think so," Karus said, drumming his fingers on the cold stone of the railing as he turned to her. "Tell me."

"Father." Amarra pointed out into the distance in a vague sort of way. "He is out there, somewhere."

"The High Father?" Karus asked. "Jupiter?"

"No, no," Amarra said, biting her lip, then holding out her arms wide. "High Father is around us, yes?" She touched her heart with her palm. "Inside, too. This is not what I mean."

"I do not understand," Karus said, switching to Latin, considering that he had perhaps misunderstood her. She spoke better Latin than he did Common.

3

"My father." Amarra touched her chest. She held up her right wrist. She touched the damaged skin on her wrist where she had been fettered. The wounds were still fresh and healing. She would be scarred for life, and Karus was certain that went beyond the physical. They had found her chained in a prison cell beneath the palace Karus had claimed for his headquarters.

Her nostrils flared with what seemed like anger.

"My father do this." Amarra tapped the damaged skin, a fierce look in her eyes. "He did this, not High Father. Understand?"

Karus gave a sudden nod. He recalled the ruined temple to the High Father and what Jupiter had said about Amarra alone remaining faithful. The full implication hit him. Amarra's father had been the one to not only imprison her, but also destroy the temple. And if he was understanding correctly, it was all because of her faith.

"Your father ruled this city, didn't he?" Karus asked in Latin.

"Ruled?" She turned to him, a question in her eyes, almost rolling the Latin word around her tongue. "Ruled?"

"A king, perhaps, a leader of the city?" He pointed at the ground beneath them. "He ruled Carthum before leaving. Do I have that right?"

"Yes," Amarra said, the sad look still in her eyes. "He leader."

"Of Carthum?"

Amarra nodded.

In his service to the empire, Karus had seen some fairly awful things. Still, it did not stop him from wondering what kind of a man would lock up his own daughter and leave her to starve or face the mercies of the Horde. Clearly, Amarra's father was a hard and unforgiving man.

"He won't ever hurt you again," Karus said, looking at the woman who had captured his heart. "I won't allow it."

Amarra turned to him, her eyes searching. She leaned in close and reached a hand to caress his stubbled cheek. The sadness gave way to a gentle tenderness, then a trace of a smile.

"Funny man. High Father protects me." Amarra grinned at him. The grin was infectious. "But you can, too. If want."

He pulled her close and kissed her. Her lips were soft and warm, inviting. She pressed in close against him. After a moment, she broke the kiss and leaned her head against his chest as he embraced her. She shuddered slightly.

"Are you sure this is right?" Karus asked.

"What you mean?" Still in his embrace, she looked up into his face, her brow furrowing.

"You are High Priestess now," Karus said, pulling apart from her. His gaze strayed to the crystal staff that lay in the corner. Jupiter had given it to her as a spear. A few hours after she had taken it, somehow the spear had transformed itself into a staff. It throbbed and pulsated slowly with an internal blue light that radiated outward. The staff was imbued with the great god's power. It filled him with a sense of awe just knowing from whom it had come. He turned back to Amarra. "Do you think the High Father will become angry with us? For this? I am just a soldier."

Amarra touched his chest with a hand. "You more than soldier."

"And you are High Priestess."

"Excuse me, sir."

Karus turned to see one of his clerks, Serma, standing in the doorway. He felt himself frown at the untimely interruption.

"Yes?" Karus asked, forcing the irritation away. "What is it?"

"As requested, sir," Serma said. "Centurions Dio and Felix have arrived. They are waiting for you with Centurion Pammon in the great hall."

"Thank you," Karus said with a nod. "I will be along shortly."

"Yes, sir." The clerk gave a salute and left.

Karus watched the clerk leave. A thought occurred to him as he turned back to Amarra.

"Your father ordered the evacuation of the city?" Karus asked.

"Evacuation?" she asked. "What you mean?"

"Leaving the city. Your father made everyone go?"

Amarra nodded. "Big battle with Horde. Far away. We lose. Father say go and people go."

It was Karus's turn to nod.

"Is that why the temple was destroyed?" Karus asked. "Is that why your father pulled down Jupiter's temple?"

"He want High Father to save people," Amarra said. "But people no believe."

"Why not tell me before?"

Amarra chewed her lip a moment. "I no trust yet. Now, I trust and more."

It was as he had thought. He could not fault her for that.

"Are you certain about this—us?" Karus asked, turning back to Amarra. His gaze swept down to the sleeping dragons once again. With the transporting of the legion to this strange world, he wasn't sure about anything anymore. They were a long way from Rome and would never be going back. Worse, there would be no help coming. The legion was on its own and so was he.

Amarra reached up and turned his head to face her.

"High Father love us both," she said, intently. "He want us happy. Trust in that."

"If you say so," Karus said.

"I do." Amarra stamped her foot on the marble for emphasis. "I do. It okay."

She reached up and gripped his face with both hands and pulled him to her. She kissed him again, a brief peck on the lips, then turned back out to the garden and the dragons.

Karus almost let out a sigh.

"Are you certain we must both go to the Fortress of Radiance?" Karus asked after a moment. "I would feel more comfortable taking a cohort or two with me and you remaining here in the safety of the city."

"No safe anywhere. We must both go and get Rarokan," Amarra said. She touched her chest again. "I feel it. We must. You no take soldiers. Too far and Horde in the way."

"But by dragon?" Karus said, his gaze swinging back to the creatures below. "Surely there is another way?"

By us, human, Kordem, the green dragon, said in his mind without untucking his head from under his wing.

Karus almost jumped. He had not realized the dragons had been listening. It still surprised him that they spoke to him in his mind.

"Yes, yes, by dragon," she said, clearly having heard too.

"If the gods had meant us to fly, they would've given us wings," Karus said.

"High Father sent us dragons instead," Amarra countered.

Accept it and leave us to sleep in peace, Kordem said. *The Fortress of Radiance is where we need to go. When you are finally ready to leave, you let us know. We will carry you both. Until then, bring your worries elsewhere. It is too fine a day to ruin it.*

There was a finality in the tone that suggested Karus was testing their patience. He took a deep breath and let it out. He spared the dragons one more look before turning to Amarra.

"I will be back later," Karus said. It was time to see his waiting officers.

She gave him a nod but said nothing further.

Karus left her, bringing his troubled thoughts with him as he stepped off the balcony and back into his office. He made his way through the door out into the adjacent office where his clerks worked. This space was the beating heart of the legion, the administrative headquarters.

The quiet flurry of activity halted as he stepped into the large room. His four clerks, along with two messengers and Tribune Delvaris, stood respectfully. Karus gave the tribune a nod and made his way past them and out into the hallway. The guards at the entrance snapped to attention, along with a messenger who had just been about to enter the headquarters. The messenger stepped aside to allow Karus to pass.

Karus walked at a brisk pace through the palace toward the great hall. He found another pair of guards standing on either side of the double doors, which were open. Both guards assumed a position of attention as Karus approached. He offered them a nod and made his way into the hall.

No matter how many times he visited, Karus could not help but feel impressed. The battle standards and trophies of war that the Kings of Carthum had won over the centuries remained. Only the throne had been removed. In its place on the raised dais was the Ninth's Eagle, along with all of the standards of the legion's cohorts arranged around and below it. This hall had been a seat of power. Now it was the legion's shrine.

Another four guards stood about the Eagle. They guarded not only the legion's honor, but also Rome's. An item had been added to their charge, the Key that Jupiter had given into Karus's care. It lay on the dais next to the Eagle. The Key looked more like a king's scepter rather than anything else. Karus wasn't quite sure what exactly it did, but he knew it was important.

Pammon, Dio, and Felix waited for him farther down the hall around the map inlaid on the floor. They had come dressed in their tunics and without armor. Pammon was Karus's second in command. Dio and Felix were trusted advisors, personal friends, and two of the legion's senior centurions. He had taken to meeting with them here each morning, before his daily duties consumed all available time. Commanding a legion was not easy work.

Their faces were drawn and they appeared troubled. They had been talking softly amongst themselves but broke it off and turned to face Karus as he entered the hall.

"Gentlemen," Karus said as he stepped up to them. He glanced toward the dais. The Eagle's guards were far enough away he was sure they would not overhear their conversation. "You three look grimmer than a funeral procession."

They said nothing at his attempt at levity.

"All right," Karus said, letting out a heavy breath. "Let me have it."

Dio and Felix looked to Pammon to start.

"The sickness, as you are aware, is continuing to spread," Pammon said. "We lost another five men last night. Ampelius still has no idea what it is and, worse, feels there is no way to treat it other than to allow the disease to run its course and quarantine the ill. Those who have managed to recover are left in a weakened state. It may be weeks before they are able to return to full duty."

9

This mystery sickness was perhaps the most worrying thing they had faced to date. There was absolutely nothing Karus could do to combat it other than what was already being done, and that certainly did not seem to be nearly enough.

"The only explanation I can think of is that this must be a plague that is natural to these lands," Felix said, pointing down at the map. "With the rate the sickness is spreading, in another week or two our effective strength will fall below fifty percent. As of now, around thirty-five percent of the legion is ill, and that count does not include the followers."

Two days ago, thirty percent of the legion had been affected. Karus rubbed his jaw. He could face enemy upon the field of battle, cross swords with evil creatures like orcs, and even fight a demon, but this was one battle that could not be handled with steel. His men were dying to this mystery illness, and there was absolutely nothing he could do to save them. Worse, the Horde was coming and Karus knew without a doubt that hard fighting lay in his future. He needed every single sword and shield.

He'd been blessed by a visit from Jupiter, known in these lands as the High Father. Amarra had been given a holy staff imbued with the great god's power. They even had two dragons, which Karus could only describe loosely as allies in the struggle to come. If all of his men sickened, with many dying, Karus could not see how he could be successful in the tasks that Jupiter had set for him. The most important of those tasks was recovering Rarokan and, as incredible as it sounded, escaping this world to another.

"Perhaps Amarra should take a look at those who have fallen ill," Karus said, at a loss for what to do. "She might know what type of disease this is and if there's some way for it to be treated. These are her lands, after all."

Pammon shifted his feet. It was clear he was uncomfortable with the suggestion.

"That is an uncommonly bad idea," Dio said, speaking before Pammon could.

"You are afraid she may catch the plague?" Karus turned his gaze upon his friend. In truth, he had feared that as well when he had suggested it.

"No," Dio said. "Amarra catching this plague might even be better for us."

"How can you say that?" Karus said in a raised voice, feeling his face grow warm with heat. "She is High Priestess to Jupiter. We've been blessed with her presence."

"We may see it that way," Dio said, "but the men do not. No one other than you two witnessed this miraculous visit by Jupiter. Even with the glowing crystal staff, it is one thing to be told something or shown and another to believe and have faith."

"Karus." Felix threw a quick glance at the guards by the Eagle and lowered his voice. "They see her as a witch, with you under her spell and the dragons her creatures. There are those who even think she is responsible for the plague that is afflicting our people."

"That's absurd," Karus said.

"Regardless," Felix said, "it is how many of the men feel, and as the sickness continues to spread, so will that belief. It could soon become dangerous."

"You three don't feel she's a witch, do you?" Karus asked, his gaze traveling from one to the other, meeting their eyes.

"Of course not." Pammon held up both hands. "With all that I've seen in the last few weeks and days, it is hard not to see Jupiter's hand in our deliverance. It is very clear that you and the Ninth as a whole have been gods blessed."

"And you?" Karus asked, looking to Dio.

"I think you are in love," Dio said, with an expression that was almost pained. "It clouds your vision when it comes to the men and Amarra." He paused, glanced down at his feet and the map, then looked back up. "That said, I do not believe she's a witch. As Pammon put it, it's clear Jupiter's hand delivered us."

"Karus," Felix said, "we've been transported to this land, this world, seen creatures beyond belief, nightmarish even, and that includes the dragons. A sickness is tearing its way through the legion. You of all people should know how superstitious the men can be. It will be very hard to convince them otherwise that Amarra's presence amongst us is a blessing and not a curse."

Karus was silent for a long moment. His gaze traveled to the Eagle and then the Key on the dais.

"Do you see any way to do that?" Karus asked them. "Is there any way we can show them she is here by Jupiter's grace?"

Dio glanced over at Felix, and then the two of them looked to Pammon. The senior centurion for the legion gave a slow shake of his head.

"I'm truly sorry, Karus," Pammon said. "I am afraid nothing short of a miracle from Jupiter will do."

"Like being transported from certain death to a new world?" Karus asked indignantly. "Is that the kind of miracle you are talking about?"

Pammon, Dio, and Felix said nothing to that.

"Well," Karus said with more than a little dissatisfaction and frustration as he calmed himself down, "it bears some thinking on. I will keep her out of sight for the time being and as much as possible. However, I will ask Ampelius to spare some time to speak with her concerning the symptoms. Perhaps there is some treatment she is aware of that can cure those who have fallen ill. If there is, however unlikely, maybe that can help change a few minds."

"Let us hope," Pammon said.

"You still intend on leaving?" Dio asked bluntly, changing the subject.

They had spoken on this the day before. None of them were happy with the idea, Karus included.

"I do," Karus said. "There is no avoiding it. Jupiter commanded me to go to the Fortress of Radiance and retrieve the sword. I must get it before we quit Carthum and travel west."

"I don't see how one sword can be so important," Dio said. "I don't much like the idea of you leaving the legion, especially now. The timing is terrible."

"It must be magical, a holy relic," Felix said. "Why else have you go get it? What did Jupiter call the sword?"

"Rarokan, the Soul Breaker," Karus said.

"That sounds exceptionally cheery," Dio said. "A frightening name for a mysterious sword. Where is this fortress?"

"I don't exactly know," Karus said, unhappily. "The dragons do, and that's what matters."

"You will be going with the dragons?" Pammon gave a slight shake of his head, as if he could not believe it.

"Yes," Karus said, thinking that flying seemed so unnatural, unreal. "And I'm none too happy about that. I'd rather take a couple of cohorts there myself if it were possible. Unfortunately, I am told by the dragons the fortress is very distant and to march there would take far too long. Worse, we would need to cross lands already controlled by the enemy. Even if we managed to get there, I am led to believe the Horde would arrive at Carthum before we could return. With any luck, according to Kordem, Amarra and I will be gone just five days, maybe six at the most."

There was a brief silence, the other officers sharing brief looks. None of them were happy with Karus's decision to go. In truth, Karus found little to be cheered about.

Pammon spoke first. "We must conceal your departure from the men. They're already unnerved enough about Amarra and the dragons. It would only make things worse to see you and her flying off, almost as if you were abandoning the legion in favor of her." Pammon hesitated a moment. "I would recommend you depart at night, preferably when the moon is low in the sky and it is difficult to see. We, along with your clerks, can cover for you while you are gone. Though we will need to bring in the other senior officers."

"You are right," Karus said. "They deserve to know."

"Speaking of which," Felix said, "when exactly will you be leaving?"

"In two days' time," Karus said, "after that group of refugees has arrived. They're still heading our way, right?"

"Nothing's changed. As of this morning, a report from the cavalry came in and confirmed they're making a beeline toward the city," Pammon said. "My guess is they're probably hoping to find food and shelter here." Pammon let out a breath that was laced with frustration. "Why delay leaving? Get it over with. I don't understand why you do not wish to leave immediately. We can easily deal with these refugees and turn them away."

"I am certain you could," Karus said. "However, for our first meeting with another people of this world, I would feel more comfortable being present." He paused for a heartbeat. It was time to share his thinking with them, which he had hesitated to do until now. "We may even want to consider taking them in."

"Are you serious?" Dio asked, brows drawing closer together. "We have limited supplies as it is, and you want to take in another five thousand hungry mouths? Karus, whatever for?"

"Jupiter said we may find allies in these lands," Karus said. "There may be some long-term advantage to be gained by accepting them."

"These are civilians," Dio said. "They're not soldiers. By the gods, I don't see how they can help us. We need more shields and swords, not mouths to feed."

"I don't either," Karus admitted. "However, I want to see them with my own eyes and speak with their leaders. Only then, perhaps, will I know if there can be anything gained from taking them in. If there is none, we send them on their way."

They fell into an uneasy silence again at that. Karus felt very strongly on this issue and was not about to back down. He wanted to meet these people. It was more than a gut feeling that he should stay until he had. It was almost as if something inside him were urging and encouraging him to remain. The feeling was incredibly hard to put into words, but delaying his departure just seemed like the right thing to do. He did not feel like explaining it to them, either. They would think him crazy, and Karus understood he didn't need to undermine his position as leader of the legion any further than he had by taking Amarra into his arms.

He had to tread carefully, even around his friends.

"Look, we know we have to quit this city," Karus said, pointing down at the map. "An enemy is coming with such overwhelming numbers we cannot withstand them by ourselves. We need allies. Jupiter even said so. It is as simple as that. Maybe it starts with this group of refugees. Perhaps it doesn't. Worst case, we learn a little more about this world."

"All right, Karus," Pammon said with a glance at the other two. "You have my support in this."

"How are the wagons coming?" Karus asked Felix, intentionally changing the subject.

"They're coming," Felix said. "Unfortunately, the sickness is hampering production. If it comes time to depart prematurely, we will be leaving a good portion of our food and stores behind."

"Do you think you can speed up production?" Karus asked hopefully. He knew it was unlikely but felt the need to ask anyway.

"No," Felix said, "I do not. If anything, due to the sickness production will slow in the coming days."

"Well," Karus said, "keep on it. Do the best you can."

"I will," Felix said.

"Karus," Pammon said, "it might be good for you to be seen more by the men. With the sickness, morale is low and rumors abound concerning the orcs, demons, the dragons, and Amarra. The men love you and would be heartened by seeing you more often."

"And if I fall sick?" Karus asked.

"It's a risk we have to take," Pammon said, "especially if we wish to keep the legion from dissolving."

Karus understood Pammon's meaning, only too well. Things were rapidly coming to a head and the men were scared. Should discipline fail, all would be lost.

"Soon as we're done here, I shall take a tour of the city, our defenses, and wagon production," Karus said. "I will make sure that I am quite visible."

"Good," Pammon said with a satisfied nod.

"Next order of business?" Karus asked.

"We received a second report from Valens this morning. He has located a body of soldiers moving our way from the west." Pammon pulled a dispatch from his tunic pocket.

"This came into headquarters just before our meeting. I told Serma I would handle it and share it with you."

Karus took the dispatch, opened it, and read the contents written by his cavalry wing commander. When he was done, he blew out a long breath.

"Five hundred strong," Karus said, looking up from the report. He tapped the dispatch with a finger. "Another reason to stay, I think."

"I thought you might see it that way," Pammon said with a slightly lopsided smirk.

Karus returned his attention to the dispatch and finished reading it. He handed it off to Felix, who began reading.

"Not human," Felix exclaimed softly as he read.

"As the report states, they wear what appears to be identical armor to what we found stored here in Carthum with the supplies," Pammon said. "I believe we've discovered the people who left us that convenient store of food."

"Incredible," Felix breathed, glancing up from the dispatch. "From what Valens reports, based upon their pace, they should be here around the time the refugees arrive."

Felix turned back to the dispatch, rereading it.

"Care to wager they will be rather surprised to find us occupying Carthum?" Pammon asked.

"No, I would not take that bet," Karus said. "I don't expect them to be pleased, either."

"You know they will want their supplies back," Pammon said. "Five hundred seems a rather small number for the quantity of supply they stockpiled here. I wonder where the rest of them are."

"There is that," Felix said and handed the dispatch to Dio, who began to read.

"Well," Karus said, "they're not getting it back. We need it."

"And if they are the potential allies Jupiter spoke of?" Felix asked.

"We will just have to cross that bridge when we come to it," Karus said, feeling terribly troubled. If he had made the wrong decision, he could turn possible friends to enemies. Still, he could not give up the supply cache they'd discovered. He desperately needed it to feed his people.

"Hopefully," Dio said, "we won't burn the bridge at the same time."

"Oh, one other thing," Pammon said. "One of Valens's patrols checking out a forest road to the west reported spotting those people in the trees again."

"The forest?" Felix said with a quick glance over at Karus. "The forest wraiths."

Karus felt a headache coming on. He well remembered the bodies they had found amongst the trees. He had more worries than seemed right. This was just one more complication he did not need.

CHAPTER TWO

K arus leaned his forearms on the stone of the city wall and clasped his hands together as he looked out beyond the city. Pammon and Amarra stood with him. Below, two hundred yards away from the walls, were the refugees. Valens's scouts had estimated their number to be around five thousand, but studying them, Karus felt there were more than that. The cavalry scouts had shadowed the group from a distance, careful not to be seen, which had likely led to the discrepancy. He estimated there were perhaps fifty-five hundred people spread out before the east gate.

A delegation from the refugees had broken off from the main group and advanced forward. These stopped around fifty yards from the gate, which was closed. The delegation consisted of three men, one elderly and two middle-aged. The old man wore a gray robe. A long white beard flowed down his chest, and he clutched a rough wooden staff. All three gazed up at the legionaries manning the wall and appeared to be simply waiting.

Karus's eyes swept beyond them and once again over the refugees, who had grouped together in a great mass. There was no order or uniformity amongst them. There were hundreds of wagons and carts pulled by teska, the strange six-legged oxen-like creatures native to these lands.

Most of the refugees were afoot, with women and children mixed in. They were a motley bunch. They had herd animals with them, several hundred sheep and cattle, which trailed a hundred yards behind. Under the supervision of a handful of shepherds, the animals were happily grazing on the grass that had grown long outside of the city walls.

"Well," Pammon said, also studying the refugees below, "they are a bit ragged-looking."

Karus had to agree. There was really no telling how far they had come or what they'd been through just to get to Carthum. The thought of the city caused Karus to turn and gaze back upon it. His eyes swept across the jumble of tightly packed buildings, the slums, the wealthier dwellings, the temple district, lingering a moment on the ruin of the High Father's temple before moving on to the palace and the fortress. Though the legion, auxiliary cohorts, and camp followers occupied the city, much of it was abandoned, just as they'd found it. Carthum was, for all practical purposes, a city of ghosts and only a temporary home until they were able to move on. He glanced over at Pammon before returning his gaze back to the refugees.

"They don't have the look of being a nomadic people. I would imagine they've lost their homes," Karus said. "Everything they could manage to take with them is there below us."

"Suffering," Amarra said in Latin, shaking her head slightly. There was a note of sadness to her tone that drew Karus's attention. "Horde make life on many hard. So hard, so much suffering and sadness."

"Undoubtedly," Pammon said, looking back out on the refugees. "Their hardship may be to our advantage, sir. They have wagons, carts, and food on hooves. We have a great need for it all."

Again, Karus had to agree with Pammon.

"You take what little they have?" Amarra asked, aghast, looking between them. She shifted her staff from one hand to the other as she glanced from Pammon to Karus. She tilted her head slightly. "You won't—"

"We are of Rome," Pammon said to her. "Our survival must come first. We take what we want and need from barbarians like these."

Amarra's gaze hardened.

"Perhaps, perhaps not," Karus said quickly, glancing over at her and Pammon before things could worsen between the two of them. He could not afford for Pammon to grow to dislike her. There was too much of that already. "We shall see."

"Karus, you can't let them leave and take those wagons and carts with them," Pammon said. "We don't know if there will be enough time to produce the transport we need before this Horde you two keep speaking about gets here."

Amarra rested a hand on his arm, drawing his attention.

"You will help them," Amarra said, a fiery look in her eyes, "or let them go. Understand me on this?"

Karus was about to reply to that when the sound of thunder drew his attention out beyond the refugees. Several squadrons of Valens's cavalry galloped into the view. They rode in a column of two and emerged from behind a series of small hills to the refugees' rear. Traveling on a dirt road, the horses kicked up a light dust cloud as they advanced. Under the midday sun, the tips of the cavalry's lances glittered brilliantly. Their polished armor flashed as they broke from the column and began forming a line of battle.

Another column of cavalry appeared to the left, riding around the side of the city wall. A moment later, a third column came into view from the other side. These two additional columns of cavalry each formed their own lines and maneuvered until they came together, forming a near box against the city wall, stopping only when they were three hundred yards from the refugees. The maneuvering had been neatly and efficiently handled.

From the refugees there had been a stunned silence at the appearance of the cavalry. Now there arose a great cry of dismay, mixed with panic and general agitation as they realized they were trapped. From the top of the wall, Karus could hear men and women shouting, much screaming and wailing. He could also see swords being drawn. Karus could almost smell the fear on the air. There were no horses in this land, and he understood it was very possible the refugees had never seen mounted soldiers. Valens's troopers must have appeared very impressive.

Karus's eyes went to the delegation. They'd not moved but were speaking intently amongst themselves. The old man held out a hand and pointed his staff up at the wall toward Karus. The other two with him stilled, their eyes on Karus, Pammon, and Amarra.

"Is needed?" Amarra asked, clearly put out. "They fear you."

"It is required," Karus said, turning to her. She needed to understand why he had done what he had. "I'm going to be treating with whoever's in charge below and I intend to do so from a position of strength, not weakness."

"Well, you need to deal with them quickly," Pammon said. "The other group, the soldiers, should arrive within the hour. I am guessing they will not be so easily impressed as this bunch here."

Karus silently agreed with Pammon.

"Let's get this over with, then." Karus gave a nod. "Pammon, send out the cohorts."

Pammon looked over to a legionary who was standing nearby with a horn. The man snapped to attention.

"Sound the call for the gate to be opened and the cohorts to march out," Pammon ordered.

"Yes, sir," the legionary said and brought his horn to his lips. He blew three long blasts that cut over the cries of fear and panic from the refugees. The horn fell silent and so too did the refugees, clearly wondering what would happen next.

Beneath them, Karus could hear the gates being opened, hinges grinding loudly. Karus moved to the back side of the wall. There below, two cohorts, the Second and Fourth, were drawn up in marching formation. The sickness had taken its toll on both cohorts, and men from other units had been called upon to fill out the ranks. It was a worrying sign. Karus's eyes first sought out Dio and then Felix. Both centurions stood to the front of their respective cohorts, just ahead of their standard-bearers.

"Forward, march," Dio shouted. His cohort began moving with the sound of hundreds of sandals crunching in unison. Felix's cohort started after Dio's. Karus moved back to the outer side of the wall and looked out upon the refugees. The delegation had drawn back several yards as the Roman heavy infantry began emerging from the city like an armored snake.

Once outside the gate, both cohorts were called to a halt. Officers shouted orders. The marching columns broke up as the cohorts reformed into a line of battle, two ranks deep. Normally they would have four, six, or eight ranks depending upon need, but Karus and Pammon had wanted to impress. So the line was made longer, thinner. To the refugees, the Romans would appear an overwhelming force.

Though the refugees had, from what Karus could see, numerous men of fighting age mixed in amongst them, they would be no match against the Roman infantry and cavalry. By marching the cohorts out after the cavalry, Karus was sending a message. He was making it abundantly clear that any resistance would be futile and a wasted effort. He was also communicating to them that the Romans were not to be trifled with.

"I do believe you've made your point," Pammon said with a chuckle, looking back over the wall.

Amarra shot him a heated look. Her fierceness made her look more beautiful to Karus. He had to drag his eyes from her face. Like a moth to a flame, her bold spirit and inner strength were part of what drew him to her.

"Shall we go down and introduce ourselves?" Karus cleared his throat and looked from Pammon to Amarra. He turned and made his way into the guardroom at the top of the wall and then quickly down the stairs. Amarra and Pammon followed after him. A few moments later, they emerged out from the wall and back into the sunlight. Karus turned toward the gate. He noted several of the sentries who had been posted to the gate eye Amarra warily as they passed. One of the looks was downright hostile. It pissed Karus off, but now was not the time or place to confront such attitudes.

It bothered him to no end that the men viewed her as a witch and a threat. There had to be something he could do to show them she was no danger and, more importantly, someone not to be feared but loved as the representative of Jupiter. Ahead, they found Dio and Felix were waiting where the lines of the two cohorts met. Putting the looks from his mind, he led the way through the gate and out of the city.

A file of men stood just outside the gate, along with the legion's aquilifer, who carried the Eagle. The gold of the Eagle flashed under the morning sunlight. It was a stirring sight and never failed to lift his heart. Karus gestured to the aquilifer and the men to follow. The file of men and the aquilifer started just after Karus, Pammon, and Amarra had passed them. Karus walked up to Dio and Felix.

To their front, perhaps ten yards away, stood the waiting delegation and, behind them, the frightened refugees. Dio's expression hardened slightly as he took in Amarra. Felix nodded amiably, first to Karus and then respectfully to Amarra.

"Good job," Karus said to both of them.

"It was nothing but a bit of marching and showing off, sir," Felix said and then turned slightly to look at the refugees. "I do believe they're good and ready for you."

"Very well," Karus said and took a moment to look over both cohorts. Drawn up tightly in neatly organized ranks, with shields resting at their feet and javelins held easily, they were a fine sight. He turned his attention back to the refugees. "I will take it from here. Pammon, Amarra, you both are with me. Dio and Felix remain here."

He stepped out toward the delegation. Amarra, Pammon, the file of men, and the Eagle-bearer followed after.

Karus made his pace intentionally slow so that he could study the men of the delegation as he approached. He noted they were armed with long swords, even the old man with the staff. The swords appeared similar to a spatha.

The older man was clearly in his sixties, or perhaps even his seventies. He wore a robe that had been patched in numerous places. He leaned heavily upon the staff he carried, which was a stout piece of carved wood that looked worn from prolonged use. The old man had an unforgiving look about him, like a hardened warrior well past his prime, angered that age was slowly sapping his strength. He took a step forward and moved with a slight limp, perhaps, Karus thought, from an old wound. The man's eyes were fixated on Karus, likely doing the same, assessing the other.

Karus's gaze flicked to the other two. They were in their twenties and wore lightweight, black, studded-leather chest armor. They wore simple brown pants and boots, which had clearly seen better days. Despite Karus's overwhelming show of military force, all three men had a confident air about them that spoke of being accustomed to leadership. They appeared nervous but not overly panicked. This, Karus thought, was a good sign. It showed their mettle, which was something he could respect.

Karus stopped when he was five feet from the delegation. The aquilifer came to a halt one step behind and to the right of Karus. He planted the legion's standard in the ground with a soft thud and at an angle, with the Eagle leaning slightly forward and toward the delegation. The file of men took up positions just behind Karus and the Eagle. They held their shields ready, hands on the hilts of their short swords, clearly ready for trouble and to protect Karus should the need come. Karus saw the old man's eyes flick toward the legionaries before returning to Karus. Amarra stepped up to Karus's left and Pammon to his right.

Karus kept his face hard as granite. Uncertainty flickered in the old man's eyes. Karus figured the man was clearly thinking he had made a mistake by leading his people to Carthum, knowing there was not much he could do about that now. He studied Karus before shifting his gaze to Amarra and Pammon, taking a moment to scrutinize them as well.

No one said anything for several moments.

"Do you recognize these people?" Karus asked Amarra in Latin.

"No," she said, shaking her head. "I do not."

At that, the old man spoke, his eyes falling upon Amarra's crystal staff. In the sunlight, it had lost all of its glow and simply looked to be made of a pale blue crystal, perhaps even glass. Karus looked over at Amarra in question.

She shook her head, and then switched to the common tongue. "Do you speak Common?"

"I do," the old man said in a voice that was hard and firm, but also slightly raspy with age. He pointed at Karus before gesturing at the city with his staff. "You are not of Carthum. Who are you people?"

"We are of Rome," Karus said in Common. "We are Romans."

The old man looked over at the two other men with him, raising an eyebrow in question. Both shook their heads.

"I do not know of Rome," the old man said.

"You would not," Karus said, conscious that his Common was poor, but passable. Karus understood he must sound quite harsh. Though he was getting better every day at speaking Amarra's tongue, he still felt somewhat uncomfortable using it to communicate with these people. It was why he had brought Amarra and risked taking her out before the men. When things got complicated, he expected her to step in and translate on his behalf. Or at the very least make his intention clear, limiting the possibility of miscommunication.

"Your land must be far away," the old man said.

"It is," Karus said. "Who are your people?"

"We are of the Adile," the old man said. "I am Xresex, headman of my people. We flee the Horde."

Karus looked over at Amarra. In Latin, he asked, "Do you know of these Adile?"

"I do," she said. "But only by word. I no meet one. They people from far land. They like ... how you say, war?"

"You mean warlike?" Karus asked, turning his gaze back to Xresex. "They are good at making war?"

"Yes," she said with a firm nod. "They good at war."

Karus looked out upon the refugees and felt himself frown slightly. They certainly did not have the appearance of being very warlike. They looked more like scavengers than anything else. Perhaps it was simply a result of losing their land and being forced to flee that had turned them to such a sad fate. As a people, he understood they had been broken.

"We also have people of the Sersay and Taka'noon with us," the old man said. He turned to the man with the leather armor. "This is Logex of the Sersay and"—he gestured at one of the men—"Ord of the Taka'noon."

Logex had a long, thick scar running down his left cheek. Like Xresex, he had an unforgiving look to him. His arms were quite muscular, with a myriad of scars on his forearms a clear sign of years of weapons training. Ord appeared just as tough, though not as muscular. If anything, he appeared wiry. Ord was going prematurely bald and his pate reflected the sunlight.

"I no know other peoples," Amarra said to Karus in Latin.

"I am Camp Prefect Karus," he said, switching back to Common, though he spoke the Roman ranks in Latin. "This is Centurion Pammon and ..." He turned to Amarra, hesitating. He wasn't sure how to say "priestess" in Common and was certain they would not understand the Latin.

"I am High Priestess of the High Father," Amarra said in Common, clearly picking up on Karus's difficulty.

Xresex shared a glance with the other two before returning his attention to Amarra.

"My people once worshiped the High Father," Xresex said, voice hardening and becoming bitter. "But no more.

28

The High Father turned away from us all. He cast a blind eye upon my people as we suffered and died to the Horde. We owe him nothing, no devotion and certainly no love."

"He never turned away," Amarra said calmly but in a hard tone. She pointed at the refugees with her staff. "You and others like you turned away from him. You spoke falsely of your faith, mouthing the words but never truly believing with your hearts. You never thought to ask for help, but instead demanded it, called upon the great god to save you." She paused and sucked in a breath. "As if he would lift a finger to help the faithless and empty-hearted. Oh yes, I can read you well, Xresex, Logex, and Ord. I can sense your souls, the emptiness, the hole within. You know of what I speak." She tapped the ground with the butt of her staff. "Is it but a wonder the High Father never answered your call? You have but yourselves to blame."

Karus had not expected that from Amarra. It almost made him smile with pride, for she was bold, fearless, and unafraid to confront these men.

Xresex's jaw flexed as he shared another glance with the other men. He looked as if he wanted to argue, and so too did the younger men, but clearly he thought better of it. To Karus's right, Pammon shifted his stance and crossed his arms. The centurion had not been able to follow the conversation in Common, but Karus saw he could sense the tension increasing, particularly from Amarra as she confronted the three men of the delegation.

"Have they said why they have come?" Pammon asked Karus in Latin.

"No," Karus replied and then switched to Common. He pointed at Xresex. "Why do you come here? What do you seek?"

"We seek"—Xresex said a word that Karus did not understand. Karus looked over at Amarra in question.

"He seek safe place," Amarra said in Latin.

"My people and their people," Xresex continued, "fought the Horde. The people of Carthum joined us for the battle. We lost."

"So you come here to seek help from Carthum?" Karus asked.

"We do. The Horde destroyed our"—he said another word that Karus did not understand.

"He means home, right?" Karus said to Amarra in Latin before she could translate. "The Horde destroyed their homelands?"

"Yes," Amarra said. "That is what he meant."

"The people of Carthum have left," Karus said.

"I know," Xresex said. "Finding you Romans here tells me that."

Karus looked beyond the delegation and once again took in the refugees. He wondered how much food they carried with them, beyond their few hundred head of cattle and a large number of sheep. He could see the tiredness and weariness etched upon Xresex's face. It was matched by the other two, almost radiating from their posture and manner. They'd clearly traveled far in a bid to escape the enemy that was even now overrunning this world. As his eyes raked the refugees, an idea hit him. Really, it had already been there all along, but now that he had seen the refugees with his own eyes, it had grown and matured. Karus understood it was time to act.

"You seek…" Karus hesitated and then turned to Amarra, feeling frustration at his inability to communicate adequately. "How do you say 'sanctuary'?"

Amarra's brow furrowed.

"Safe place," Karus said to Amarra.

She translated in Common to Xresex.

"Yes," Xresex said. "We seek safe place."

Karus turned to Amarra and spoke in Latin. "Would you kindly translate for me? I want no mistakes."

"I will," Amarra said.

"Ask him how many men of fighting age he has."

Amarra asked.

Xresex turned and conversed briefly with the two other men in another language and then spoke to Amarra rapidly in Common. Karus did not fully understand the reply. It had been too fast for him. He realized she had been speaking to him slowly as he worked to master the tongue and so had Xresex.

"I know not how to say big number," Amarra said, switching to Latin. Instead, she showed all ten fingers and then flashed them at Karus five times before closing one fist and holding up just five fingers.

"Either she means fifty-five," Pammon said to Karus, "or around five hundred."

Karus thought a moment and then pointed to Dio's cohort, asking in Common, "Do you mean that many men?"

Amarra and Xresex looked at Dio's cohort before turning to the other two. They conversed briefly amongst themselves.

"Yes," Xresex said, turning back. "That many."

Pammon uncrossed his arms and leaned toward Karus. "They can't have much in the way of supply. Whatever they have out there will not last them more than a few months at best. Worse, they will eat up our food stores. Tell me you are not seriously considering taking them in, are you, sir?"

"I am," Karus said to Pammon. "We are facing overwhelming numbers and they have five hundred men of fighting age. We could form them into an auxiliary cohort. It would be an increase to our strength, our combat power."

"We don't even know if they are good fighters," Pammon said. "They may have once been warlike, but by the gods, they look like they've been beaten nearly into submission. Honestly, their wagons, cattle, and sheep are more valuable to us than additional swords. Besides, they owe no allegiance to Rome."

"They may not owe anything to Rome, but they might find common cause with us," Karus said.

"I don't know about that, sir," Pammon said with a glance out at the refugees.

"They are fleeing this Horde," Karus said, becoming irritated with Pammon. It was time his second in command began thinking on a larger scale. "Sooner or later, our enemy will catch up to us, and when they do, I would like greater numbers and more than a few allies, if possible." Karus paused. He let out a heated breath. "Their backs are up against the wall. If their women, children, and loved ones are with ours, perhaps they will fight for that."

"That's debatable," Pammon said with an unhappy look, clearly not wholly convinced by the argument. "What if it doesn't work out? What if we take them in and they prove nothing but trouble?"

"Then we push them out," Karus said. "There is safety and security with us. Without us, they don't have that, now, do they?"

"I agree," Amarra said, speaking up and stepping closer to Karus. "You take risk. It is right to do, yes?"

Xresex said something to Amarra that Karus did not fully understand. From it, Karus got the gist that Xresex was wanting to know what they were discussing.

"Amarra," Karus said, "I want you to continue to translate for me so there can be no misunderstanding between me and them. If I do speak and make a mistake that could be misunderstood, I want you to correct me. Got that?"

"I understand," Amarra said. "I will speak for you."

Karus turned to face Xresex again.

"We will take in your people," Karus said in Latin, "provided you meet certain conditions."

Amarra translated and Karus waited. When she finished, he saw the sudden flaring of hope in their eyes as they looked at each other. Then a look of suspicion crept over Xresex's face as the old man understood there would be a catch.

"What is it you want?" Xresex asked warily.

"Your men of fighting age will join our army," Karus said. "They will be led by Romans. They will be trained and will fight under our rules. While with us, your peoples will live under our laws and customs. Any trouble and we will throw you out."

Karus waited once again for Amarra to translate. When she finished, Xresex gave a nod of understanding.

"We must discuss," Xresex said.

"I expected nothing less." Karus nodded as Xresex turned away to speak with his two companions. They took several steps back, so as not to be overheard. They spoke for some time, and at one point it got quite heated. Karus, Amarra, and Pammon waited as the discussion amongst the three leaders dragged on. Finally, they fell silent, shared nods all around, and returned.

"We agree," Xresex said without any preamble.

"There is more," Karus said. "We have food stores for many months, which we will share with your people. We ultimately intend upon leaving Carthum to find additional allies." He did not wish to discuss the path Jupiter had set him and Amarra on. There would be time for that later.

"For this to be a successful alliance, you will turn over all food supplies, your wagons, carts, and draft animals."

Amarra hesitated. She clearly did not understand every word, but she got most of it and once again translated. Xresex and his two companions did not appear too happy with Karus's terms. Xresex turned back to look at the other two. No words were exchanged this time, but shortly after he turned back.

"We agree," Xresex said.

"One more thing," Karus said. "There's a sickness amongst my people. You should know this before you enter the city. Carthum is large enough that we can put you away from my people who are ill, at least until the sickness is over and past."

Amarra again translated after a slight hesitation.

"What kind of sickness?" Xresex asked.

"Fever, cough, a loosening of the bowels," Karus said.

Amarra translated.

The three men began speaking heatedly with each other again. Xresex and the other two paused in mid-discussion, eyes tracking toward the sky above the city. A distant cry split the air. Xresex's eyes widened and there was astonishment in them.

The red dragon had taken to the air behind them, rising up into the sky from the palace gardens. Its wings beat rapidly at the air. The magnificent creature gained both altitude and speed. The green dragon followed a moment later. Where they were off to, Karus had no idea. Over the last few days, the dragons had come and gone as they willed.

Karus turned back to the delegation.

"They are with us," Karus said in Common to Xresex, jerking a thumb at the massive creatures. "You need not fear them."

Xresex's eyes flicked to Karus and then returned to watch the two dragons. They turned north, banked slightly, and then dove for the ground, picking up speed and disappearing from view behind the city walls.

"We accept your offer," Xresex said simply, a note of what Karus took to be awe in his tone. He bowed respectfully to Amarra. "You have the High Father's dragons. It is clear to me you are a true priestess, blessed by the High Father himself. I apologize for my earlier rudeness, mistress."

"There is nothing to apologize for. You spoke your mind and I mine. I serve my god," Amarra said. "He will welcome your return, and those of your peoples, if you so desire."

Xresex gave another bow. "Please understand. Much has happened. We have suffered terribly. There is much ill will toward the High Father amongst my people. They blame him for our troubles."

"I understand," Amarra said. "I will work to change such feelings."

"Mistress," Xresex said, "I make no promises other than we will listen to your words."

"That is more than fair," Amarra said. "Thank you."

"Excellent," Karus said and held out a hand. "Welcome to Carthum."

Xresex stepped forward. They clasped each other by the arm. Karus repeated it with each man, and with that, it was done. They officially had their first allies in this strange land.

"If we can get five hundred soldiers from a group such as this," Karus said to Pammon, "perhaps there is the opportunity to gain additional allies from other groups of refugees passing near Carthum."

"Maybe." Pammon sounded doubtful.

"I think it's worth a try," Karus said. "Especially with many of our men down with the sickness. When we are done here, send a messenger to Valens. I wish to see him back at the palace tonight. We need to reach out to those other groups of refugees."

"Yes, sir," Pammon said.

"Karus," Amarra said, speaking in Latin. She pointed at Xresex. "They can teach your men Common."

Karus gave a nod of agreement.

"She's right. It's time the officers and men also begin learning this common tongue," Karus said to Pammon. He turned back to Xresex and continued in Latin. "I will detail officers to see your people settled in the city. My people do not speak your language. I would like you to select ten men for language instruction."

Karus glanced over at Amarra, who scowled slightly at him, clearly not understanding all of the words, but then began translating. Xresex listened.

"We will begin teaching your people," Xresex said to Karus in Common.

"Also," Karus continued, "Centurion Pammon will see to the settling of your people in the city. Tomorrow morning your men of fighting age will present themselves for training. They will train under our officers."

Amarra once again translated.

"Yes," Xresex said. "I understand."

"What will we call this new cohort?" Pammon asked, sounding resigned.

Karus gave it a moment's thought and glanced back at the city behind them. They had found large stores of weapons within the city, including light armor, but very little heavy armor, at least suitable for a man. Glancing out at the refugees, there appeared to be a wide range of weapons and armor amongst their fighting men. "The First Light Carthum Cohort. We can arm and equip them uniformly with the weapons and light armor we found in the city."

"That works," Pammon said. "I already have two junior officers in mind to train the cohort. Do you wish them completely detached and replaced?"

"Who are you thinking of?" Karus asked. He wanted to be certain the men Pammon would be selecting were good, solid officers.

"Centurion Bannus and Optio Ipax. Both have proven themselves repeatedly and are not only steady, but patient. I am thinking that training men who do not understand your language will be quite frustrating."

"Very well," Karus said, in agreement with Pammon. "I want them permanently detached. Consult their superiors as to who will replace them amongst their own cohorts."

"What will their ranks be within the First Light Carthum Cohort?" Pammon asked.

"Promote Bannus to Prefect and Ipax to Centurion," Karus said and then looked back over at the delegation. "Let's get this bunch settled. I want them isolated tonight. Make sure you place guards and put out patrols. Trust is earned."

"I agree, sir," Pammon said.

"Can I tell them that?" Amarra asked.

"Yes," Karus said. "Please do."

She began translating.

"Excuse me, sir."

Karus turned to find a legionary, who saluted. The man's face was red and he was out of breath, sweating profusely.

"You are wanted at the west gate, sir," the legionary said and handed over a dispatch.

Karus opened the dispatch. As expected, the formation of strange soldiers had come into view on the west side of the city. They were two miles off. He understood that the dispatch had been written at least half an hour before. The approaching formation would be much closer. He handed the dispatch over to Pammon, who read it.

"It looks like our other friends have arrived," Pammon said. "Do you want to put on a similar show? Should Dio or Felix's cohorts march for the west gate?"

Karus gave it a moment's thought. "No, just cavalry this time. We have one cohort stationed inside the western gate. I am thinking that should be sufficient."

"I hope so, sir," Pammon said.

"Very well," Karus said and turned back Xresex. "I have to go. I will leave you with Centurion Pammon. We will speak later."

"I look forward to that," Xresex said.

Karus turned away and walked toward the gate, with Amarra following. He wondered if his next encounter with another people of this world would go as smoothly.

CHAPTER THREE

K arus and Amarra moved through the ordered ranks of legionaries. The men of Fifth Century stepped aside to let them pass. Once through, Karus spotted their commander, Flaccus. He glanced over as Karus stepped up. The centurion offered a crisp salute, which Karus returned.

The first sun had climbed higher up into the sky. The second sun was lazily following. Karus had still not gotten used to the sight of the two suns. It was yet another daily reminder they were on a different world than their own.

The day was growing warm, relieved only by intermittent gusts of a gentle breeze. He had no idea what season it was. Then again, he did not even know if this world had a change in seasons. It was something else to ask Amarra. He would make sure to do so later.

Karus's gaze shifted from Flaccus to the strange formation of soldiers, around five hundred strong, two hundred yards away. The black-cloaked soldiers had marched to Carthum along the road that led outward from the western gate. Karus knew from Valens's reports that this paved road traveled westward for a few miles before eventually switching over to dirt. To either side of the road was pastureland. With no animals to graze, the grass had grown long. A few farms and barns dotted the rolling landscape.

With a black standard held proudly to their front, the formation of soldiers waited. They were still in a marching column. Without a cloud in the sky, the suns were bright. Karus held his hand above his eyes to better see. They looked like men, in that they walked on two legs, had two arms and a head. But they were something else. Each was short, standing around chest height for an average man, and stocky.

"By Jupiter's beard, Karus," Flaccus said quietly so the men standing just behind them could not overhear. He gestured out to their front with a small jerk of his head, his polished helmet reflecting a flash of sunlight. "What in the gods are they?"

Karus did not immediately respond, for he didn't know, but continued to study them. With their black cloaks, the formation had a sinister look to it. The strangers wore heavy plate armor that seemed to cover as much of their body as possible. For some reason, they reminded him of great big walking turtles, with their heads sticking out of the shell.

Armed with what appeared to be some form of short spear and sword, they carried large rectangular shields that were almost as tall as they were. Being kitted out as they were, Karus could only imagine how difficult it would be to march long distances under such a burden. Still, based on the reports he had received from his cavalry scouts, this group had made good time. Apparently, they could easily bear the weight and were not much slowed by it.

Just to the rear of the formation waited four large wagons pulled by teams of shaggy teska. The teamsters had dismounted and stood in a small cluster. They appeared to be speaking amongst themselves. These four did not wear armor, but instead just black tunics with brown pants and boots.

"Dvergr," Amarra said and pointed with the tip her staff. "They be dvergr."

The tone of disgust in her voice pulled Karus's attention away from the strange-looking formation. He turned to her as a light gust blew around them. It ruffled her snow-white dress and caused the knee-high grass that crowded both sides of the roadway to sway back and forth until the gust of wind subsided.

Under the light of the two suns, there was almost a radiant glow about her. Her long, black hair had been blown slightly askew and a delicate ear was exposed. She idly reached up and moved several strands of hair out of her face. His breath caught as the moment struck him with surprising force. Then what she said registered.

"What did you call them?" Karus asked. "Dverg … what?"

"Dvergr." Amarra said the word slowly and glanced over at him. "They no friends."

"Enemy, then," Flaccus said. It came out almost as an angry growl. Flaccus's hand moved to the hilt of his sword as the centurion looked behind them at his century. Karus followed the centurion's gaze.

Bottoms of their shields resting on the ground before them, Fifth Century waited for orders. Like Dio and Felix's cohort, Flaccus's had been reinforced for this demonstration as well. The sickness that was ravaging the legion was taking a serious toll on unit strength. Flaccus's cohort had also taken heavy casualties in Britannia before the legion had come to this world.

Karus noticed that the men split their gazes from the strangers to their officers and Amarra. There was no warmth there as they gazed upon her. Several glanced away as they saw him looking their way. Karus could only imagine their thoughts.

"No enemy," Amarra said firmly. She let out what sounded like an unhappy breath and tapped her staff upon the ground for emphasis. "They no friends but to themselves. No trust between my people and them." She paused and frowned slightly as she struggled to put her thoughts into Roman words. "They do what want, not what we need."

"They do their own thing?" Karus asked as his eyes fell upon her staff. He sucked in a startled breath. The staff abruptly reminded him of the vision the High Father had shown him. Karus snapped his eyes back to the formation of dvergr.

Was it possible?

He thought it might be. These dvergr looked nearly identical to some of those alien peoples Jupiter had shown him fighting against the Horde on distant worlds.

"Yes, they do own thing," Amarra said, failing to notice Karus's reaction. Her eyes had been on the dvergr. She took a half step forward and set the butt of her staff on the stone paving of the road. "They do their own thing."

"What is it?" Flaccus asked, having noticed Karus's reaction.

Karus did not answer as his thoughts raced. He was certain these were one of the peoples the High Father had shown him. It could not have been a coincidence. The great god had wanted him to see the dvergr. Otherwise, why bother? Had the High Father meant for Karus to ally with them? It was an intriguing thought.

"They fight the Horde," Karus said, looking over at Amarra for confirmation. "Don't they?"

"Yes," Amarra said. "They fight Horde, but not with people like us." She paused, eyeing him warily. "Why you ask?"

Was this the High Father's will? Or was he just reading too much into the great god's intentions? Was he coming to the conclusion he badly desired? Karus had known those who had done the same, failing to consider things objectively. The foremost example that came to mind was the Ninth's late commander, Julionus, who had led the legion unsupported deep into Celtic territory. It had cost the legate his life and a great many others. Karus let out a breath and reminded himself to temper his expectations when it came to allies.

"The enemy of my enemy, then ..." Flaccus said, his voice trailing off as he, too, studied the strange soldiers.

"Indeed," Karus said. "The enemy of my enemy could be my friend."

"You are thinking they could be allies?" Flaccus asked and stroked his freshly shaved chin with his thumb.

"It's possible," Karus said distantly, "but until we speak with them, I won't know for certain whether we can work toward a common purpose."

"My people think like you." Amarra took a step closer to Karus. She caught his arm with her free hand and held it a moment before releasing it. She pointed out at the dvergr formation. "They walk own path. No care for others. No care for us. Understand?"

He nodded and wondered if she was right. It was quite possible that the dvergr did not get along with the peoples of this land. Would they be willing to deal with him, a Roman?

"They sound a little difficult," Flaccus said.

"Perhaps," Karus said, his thoughts moving to the armor that had been found along with the cache of stores left in Carthum. It was identical to what he was seeing just two hundred yards off. He now knew with complete certainty who had left them.

"They walk own path," Amarra repeated.

"And you walk ours," Karus said, looking into her eyes. "You belong with us now, not those who abandoned you when they quit this city."

Amarra held his gaze a long moment, her eyes becoming slightly glossy. She swallowed and cleared her throat before replying. "It is as you say. I belong at your side."

He gave a nod and then returned his attention outward toward the dvergr.

"We are a different animal than those who once lived in Carthum," Karus said. "We are of Rome."

Amarra gave him a scowl as she worked out his meaning. Then she shook her head.

"It make no different to dvergr," Amarra said.

"It makes no difference," Karus automatically corrected. Having spent long hours teaching her his language, it had become something of an unconscious habit that popped up now and then.

One of the dvergr stepped from the formation. Karus guessed he was an officer. He regarded the Romans for a long moment before swinging about to face his formation. He shouted something that sounded very much like an order. The marching formation dissolved and rapidly reformed itself into a line of battle, five ranks deep. The standard-bearer, black banner fluttering in the wind, positioned himself to the front of the formation. Karus did not recognize the symbol displayed on the standard. But that was not what caught his eye. The movement from marching column to line of battle had been smartly done. It had been an impressive display, one that Karus could well appreciate.

"Disciplined, then," Flaccus said.

"It seems that way," Karus said. The dvergr had moved with practiced precision. "If I am any judge, they are likely a professional force."

"I would like to send for additional men, sir," Flaccus said, shifting his stance. "Another cohort would make me feel a bit more comfortable, especially if it comes to a fight."

Karus considered Flaccus's request. After several heart-beats, he shook his head.

"No, I don't believe that will be necessary," Karus said. "We will talk some, threaten each other perhaps, or get along like old retired comrades whiling away the days in a veterans' colony, but it will not come to fighting. They will go on their way without incident."

"How can you be so certain?" Flaccus asked. "You and I have fought against barbarians our entire lives. Great gods, you've seen the treachery those bastard Celts were capable of when roused. We're in a strange land with peoples and creatures we know nothing about. We can't be sure of any-thing, sir."

"You're right," Karus said. "We can't be certain of any-thing. That said, there should be no fight today, especially when they see the surprise waiting for them."

"Surprise?" Flaccus asked as a scowl slipped over his face. "Karus, what are you talking about?"

"I have our entire cavalry wing hidden just out of view," Karus said, gesturing at the dvergr formation. "Valens has his orders. Once the parley begins, he will make his pres-ence known. Should it come to trouble, we will have more than enough on hand to deal with that bunch."

"Yes, sir," Flaccus said quietly, his tone contemplative. After a moment, he gave a soft grunt as he dislodged a loose stone from the roadway and kicked it with his sandal. The stone skittered off the road and into the tall grass. "Bloody cavalry."

A second dvergr officer joined the first. They spoke amongst themselves, clearly inspecting the legionary cohort arrayed just outside of the gate and the sentries along the walls. Under the dual suns, Karus was growing hot in his armor. Sweat began to run down his forehead. He wiped it away.

Just as he was growing impatient, the two officers stepped away from their formation and began moving toward them. They came forward without an escort and with an arrogant boldness that Karus found slightly surprising.

"Come on," Karus said, making a snap decision. He would meet the two dvergr halfway, instead of forcing them to come to him, and he too would do it without an escort. He started forward with Amarra on his right and Flaccus on his left. Both parties stopped five feet apart. They said nothing, studying each other.

Up close, Karus got the impression that under the armor the dvergr were powerfully built. He had examined the armor that had been found amongst the stores in the city and knew it was incredibly heavy. These two before him wore their armor with ease, almost as if it were a second skin. In no way did they seem to be slowed or seriously hindered by the added weight.

Both wore helmets with black crested tops. Since there were no horses in these lands, Karus wondered briefly from what kind of animal they had gotten the long hair for the crests. His gaze traveled back to their armor. As officers, it stood to reason their armor would be of better quality than their subordinates. These two proved no exception to that rule. Their armor appeared to have been made with incredible skill and craftsmanship. Black etchings of strange runes and symbols ran over their chest plates.

Their black cloaks were also quite fine, and richly cut. Karus's critical gaze took in the frayed and torn edges. This was an indicator and sure sign of extended time spent in the field. His own crimson cloak was just as frayed.

Their faces were almost completely obscured by their beards, which were a dark brown. The beards were tightly braided with black ties and reached down over their armor toward their midriffs. The exposed skin on their faces was browned by the sun. One was clearly older than the other, perhaps middle-aged, though Karus understood he had no point of reference to determine that to be certain. He just seemed older. The skin of his face had more lines and his beard was longer, with strands of gray running through it. He had piercing brown eyes and a squint that gave him the appearance of being irritated.

Both of the dvergrs' expressions were cold, perhaps even hostile, but at the same time supremely self-assured. The older one placed his hands upon his hips. Despite his diminutive height, his manner screamed of arrogance. He appeared accustomed to getting his way. Karus did not like that, not one bit, for he would most certainly not get his way here and that would prove a bone of contention.

The silence stretched and grew uncomfortable. It was only broken when the older one cracked his knuckles.

"I am Camp Prefect Karus," he said in Common, deciding to break the ice. He hoped they spoke the tongue Amarra was teaching him.

"I am Torga, of the Rock Breakers Clan." Torga's voice was so deep that it almost seemed to boom forth at them. Torga turned slightly and indicated the dvergr to his right. "My son, and second in command, Ontho."

"Centurion Flaccus and High Priestess Amarra," Karus said, gesturing to each in turn. He was pleased he remembered her title, though still conscious his Common was rough at best. He had to work on that, for there were times he was certain he used the wrong words. Amarra did not always correct him.

Idly stroking his beard with a hand, Torga eyed Amarra speculatively for a heartbeat. Karus noted the silver ring on

Torga's index finger. It was quite large. He also counted six meaty fingers where a man would have five.

Torga's gaze returned to Karus and hardened. The beard twitched a little at the corners of his mouth as he gave a partial frown. The hand fell to his side.

"High Priestess of what god?" Torga asked Karus.

"The High Father," Amarra said firmly, tapping her staff lightly on the stone paving, which made a clacking sound. Under the bright sunlight, her staff looked almost glasslike, with no internal glow whatsoever. Torga paid it no attention, but his eyes narrowed dangerously as his gaze shifted back to Amarra. Karus did not care for his look.

Ontho said something in another language to his father. The tongue sounded quite harsh and guttural. Karus assumed it was their own tongue. Whatever was said caused Torga to scowl deeply. He appeared as if he wanted to say something, then changed his mind and returned his full attention back to Karus.

"Where is Shoega?" Torga asked. It was more a demand than anything else, or perhaps even an accusation.

Karus glanced over at Amarra in question.

"I know not that word," Amarra said in Latin, shifting her staff from one hand to the other. "I think it might be name."

A gentle gust of wind blew by them, causing the grass to rustle. It was a little welcome relief to the heat.

"Amarra speaks better Common than I," Karus said to Torga. He did not trust his Common enough for this discussion. "She will speak my words, so there are no mistakes between us."

"That is acceptable." Torga gave a nod, but kept his attention fixed upon Karus. Both dvergrs' expressions were far from friendly, bordering on outright hostility. That bothered Karus not at all. He was accustomed to dealing with barbarians who did not like him and despised, if not hated, Rome with every fiber of their being.

"Ask him the meaning of this word, or if it is a name?" Karus said.

Amarra asked.

"Shoega of the Ironbound Clan," Torga said and pointed at the city walls behind them. "He was here in this city. We've had no word from him. I demand to know what you did with him and his dvergr."

Amarra translated the reply, mainly for Flaccus's benefit.

"A person, then," Flaccus said, with a glance thrown to Karus.

"Tell him we do not know of Shoega," Karus said. "Make sure he understands this city was empty when we came here. There were none of his kind present, nor did we come across any in the surrounding countryside. This is the first of his kind we've ever seen."

"Seems like he was expecting to find a garrison here," Flaccus said.

"Maybe," Karus said.

"I wonder where they wandered off to?" Flaccus said. "If they were nearby, I'd think our cavalry scouts would have stumbled across them."

Karus gave a nod of agreement as Amarra translated what he had asked her to relay.

A deeply suspicious look stole over Torga's face as she finished. His jaw clenched, the beard flexing a bit. It was immediately apparent to Karus that he was disbelieved. Karus saw no way to prove to Torga the truth other than invite him into the city to poke around, and he was unwilling to do that. If the dvergr proved hostile, Karus would be potentially giving an enemy information on the legion's strength and dispositions. Or worse, the legion's potential weakness due to the sickness that was eating up his effective strength.

"You have never seen dvergr before?" Ontho asked, speaking up. "Come now, how can that be?"

"Who are you people?" Torga asked before Karus could respond, his gaze flicking to Fifth Century. "I do not recognize your armor or your standards. What land do you hail from?"

Karus waited for Amarra to translate before replying. He wanted Flaccus to follow as much of the conversation as possible.

"We are of Rome," Karus said. "It is an empire far from here. I would be surprised if you've heard of us."

Amarra translated.

The dvergr turned to his son and said something in their rough, harsh tongue.

"We fight the Horde," Karus said. "I understand your people do as well."

Amarra once again translated.

Torga looked back on Karus and his face hardened once again, as if it were made from stone. To his side, his son gave a low chuckle and spat on the ground. The message was clear.

"We do not fight alongside your kind," Torga said, pointing at Fifth Century with a whole hand, "and never will. Forget even the thought of doing so."

"Why?" Karus asked. It made no sense to him. A terrible enemy was sweeping across the face of this world. It was incomprehensible that these dvergr would rather go it alone.

Torga did not wait for a translation but had clearly understood the question, even though he did not speak Latin. He pointed squarely at Karus, and his face twisted with disgust and barely concealed rage. "You are weak, all of you. Humans are pathetic creatures. To us you are nothing more than manure to be scraped off our boots. We are the strong ones."

Amarra sucked in a startled breath. She looked quite irked, her dark eyes flashing with her anger. She tightened her grip upon her staff.

Karus had never before been called weak. Torga's attitude rankled him immensely.

"What did the bastard say?" Flaccus asked.

Karus glanced over at Flaccus.

"He just called us weak."

"Did he?" Flaccus asked, barking out a laugh that drew Torga's full attention. "Cheeky bastard, isn't he? What say we give him an education on Roman strength, eh? Let's send them on their way with a new appreciation for their betters."

"It is shared thinking by them," Amarra said, anger trembling her voice. "Dwarves don't like our people. I not sure they like anyone but dwarven people. Every dwarf I knew was same."

"What did you call them?" Karus asked. "I thought you said they were dvergr?"

"They are," Amarra said, with a glance thrown to Torga. "My people call them dwarves, too. He a dwarf."

"A nickname, then?" Flaccus asked.

"What?" Amarra asked, clearly not understanding the word.

"We are dvergr," Torga said. He had gone red in the face, his eyes bulging. He held up a clenched fist, which he shook slightly at Karus and Amarra. Torga spoke rapidly in Common, most of which Karus could not follow.

"He says ..." Amarra hesitated a moment, gathering her words. "We not give insult by calling them dwarves."

"Tell him we meant no offense," Karus said. He had hoped things would go better than this. If anything, both sides were simply insulting each other. Nothing productive was being accomplished. Worse, Karus now had the feeling he was wasting his time.

Amarra spoke, and as she did, Karus saw a look of disdain and pure hostility sweep over Torga. Perhaps it was disgust? Karus wasn't sure, but it was clear his apology had been taken for weakness. Karus had had enough.

"If he does not wish to consider working with us, we have nothing more to discuss here," Karus said to Amarra. "Tell him to be on his way and bother us no more before he tries my patience."

Amarra seemed surprised by his sudden attitude change. She looked over at him and arched an eyebrow in question.

"Are you sure?" Amarra asked. "Dwarves tell others what to do. They get way more than not."

"Not today," Karus said.

"I don't like him either," Flaccus said. "He's too full of himself. The pompous bastard needs to learn some respect."

"Tell him what I said." Karus gave her an encouraging nod. "I am just establishing that we will not tolerate his attitude or disrespect. Nor shall I permit us to be bullied. This will set the stage for future talks as equals, is all. At least, I hope it will."

Amarra hesitated a moment, took a resigned breath, as if she thought it a bad idea, and then translated.

Torga and his son both stiffened as she finished. Ontho's hand dropped to the hilt of his sword.

"That's not a good idea, son," Flaccus said in a low tone, his own hand gripping his sword hilt and looking Ontho meaningfully in the eye. "Draw that and you die."

Thunder rumbled. Torga frowned, for it was a clear day with no hint of any storm on the horizon. The thunder grew louder and turned into a steady rumble. Karus could feel the vibration of it through his sandals and almost smiled—almost. He could not have asked for better timing. The sound came from the direction of the dvergr formation.

Torga and his son turned around and looked. Just behind the dwarven formation, on the rolling hill over which the paved road traveled, the cavalry had finally made their appearance. It was the entirety of the legion's cavalry, all of them, nearly four hundred horses moving in a line of battle four ranks deep.

Valens rode several yards to their front. A standard-bearer kept pace alongside the prefect. The standard flapped in the wind as they galloped forward toward the dwarves. The tips of their lances, held upright, flashed and glittered with reflected sunlight.

A horn call from the cavalry ripped across the air. It was a perfectly clear single note. With it, Valens brought his cavalry to a halt just over the crest of the hill, perhaps one hundred yards from the dwarven formation. The low rumbling of the hooves ceased almost instantaneously. Karus heard Valens shout an order. The cavalry began dressing their ranks, closing up on their spacing and becoming better ordered.

Karus had to admit, Valens had put on a good show, even better than earlier with the refugees. The cavalry looked intimidating. For several moments there was much disruption in the ranks of Torga's formation. Then, part of the dwarven formation turned about to face the cavalry and locked their shields, with spears held at the ready and pointed outward.

Torga said something quietly to his son. Ontho replied with a shake of his head.

"Who are you people?" Torga asked, swinging back, his eyes searching Karus's face. The poor attitude and hostility had gone, vanished as if it had never been. In its place was something else. Karus wasn't sure what that was. Torga pointed a finger at the cavalry. "I've not seen a *hervach* since before we came through the *maktalon*. Where are you from?"

"I do not know *hervach*," Amarra said. "Or *maktalon*."

"I believe he means horse," Karus said to her, before returning his gaze to Torga. "I've already told you where we come from. We are Romans and we're far from weak. Now, I tire of your insolence. I think it is time for you to go"— Karus paused—"unless you have something of interest to us that you wish to discuss?"

Amarra translated.

Torga's jaw flexed, the anger and hostility returning. He ran his gaze over Fifth Century, studying Flaccus's men and then the cavalry, before returning his attention to Karus.

"You will not tell me what's happened to Shoega and his dvergr?" Torga asked.

"I know nothing of him," Karus said in Common. "If I did, I would tell you."

"He was charged with holding this city," Torga said. "You being here tells me you either forced him out or took the city from him."

"He is not here, and was not when we came," Karus said again in Common. "We did nothing to him."

"I make no threats," Torga said, "only promises. Our army is near. We will come in search of Shoega. Nothing will stop us from finding out what happened to him, not even your soldiers or"—Torga pointed back at the cavalry— "them, if you had something to do with it."

"We, too, have an army," Karus said. "Do not test me."

Torga hesitated a moment, as if about to reply. He apparently thought better, for he turned with his son and stomped back toward his soldiers.

"I assume he just made a threat?" Flaccus's expression was sour.

Karus nodded.

"They are missing a force of their own," Karus said. "It was charged with holding this city. He suspects we had something to do with that. Heck, if I were in his shoes, I might think we were responsible as well."

"There's nothing like making new friends, is there?" Flaccus's gaze followed Torga and his son as they stomped back to their own. "Wanna bet the supplies we found belong to those that are missing?"

"That is one wager I will not take," Karus said, his eyes lingering on Torga. "Still, we need allies in the fight to come, and I can't help but think they potentially could be it."

"They don't seem like they're looking for allies, let alone friends, sir," Flaccus said. "Arrogant bastards."

"No more arrogant than us," Karus said.

"But we're Roman, sir," Flaccus said, "we've earned the right to be arrogant. Those short little bastards can't hold a candle to us Romans when it comes to arrogance."

Karus gave a laugh to that and his mood lightened slightly.

"I think Karus be right," Amarra said, turning to face both of them. "If stand chance to fight darkness, we must do together. We must show them we be friends."

"Against what we've seen and already faced," Flaccus said, "we're gonna need all the help we can get."

Karus was surprised by the conviction in Flaccus's tone. Then again, he knew he should not have been. In the prison under the palace and then in the temple district, Flaccus had seen firsthand the face of evil in this city.

Karus watched the dwarves as they formed up for a road march and departed. They moved up the hill, directly toward the cavalry, which parted to allow them through. Karus had given orders for Valens to detail scouts to tail and follow them back to wherever they were going. With luck, it would tell him how far their army was from Carthum and whether or not the threat Torga had made was real. He rather suspected it was. Karus's feelings were deeply troubled as he watched the last of the dwarves march out of sight.

CHAPTER FOUR

Kneeling down upon one knee, Karus finished securing the pack to one of the many spikes that ran from the back of the dragon's head to nearly the tip of her tail. He was at a point on Cyln'phax's back where the spikes were thicker and longer. When Karus stood next to them, most were chest-high. The spikes appeared to be bone covered over in thick skin that was extremely rough to the touch.

The spot Karus had chosen for himself and the packs was just ahead of the dragon's wings. Cyln'phax's wings were folded back along her side, reminding Karus of a bird. However, the dragon was no bird. She was more lizard-like than anything else. A great, big, fearsome lizard at that. Karus was man enough to admit the dragons unsettled him something terrible. They were true-to-life monsters, something out of a nightmare.

Putting such thoughts from his mind, he continued his work. He grabbed another length of rope and looped it around the pack and the spike several times, pulling it as tight as he could before tying the knot. In the darkness, the task of securing the packs had proven more difficult than it should have been. He had had to do it mostly by feel rather than sight.

After tugging on the pack some, Karus decided it could be better secured. This particular pack carried their food. He was loath to have it fall off in flight due to a shoddy job on his part. Grabbing his last length of rope, he tied it to the pack and then to another spike, making certain to tuck the rope under the edge of one of the rock-hard metallic red scales that covered the dragon's back and entire body. He tugged the pack again and was satisfied with his work.

Karus stood up and found the dragon had snaked her head around. She was watching him carefully, head cocked slightly to the side. Cyln'phax's muzzle was so close that when she expelled a hot breath of air, it came out as an explosive hiss that washed over him. Startled, Karus took an involuntary step backward and almost tripped. He grabbed at a spike and just barely managed to keep himself from tumbling off her back and to the ground below.

Eyes intently focused on Karus, the snout of the dragon moved closer until it was just two feet from him. Her nostrils flaring, the dragon sucked in a deep breath. Through his sandals, Karus could feel the beast's lungs fill and expand. The dragon exhaled violently. Intense, hot air reeking of an ash-like stench gusted over him. It lasted but a moment and then passed.

The dragon's jaws parted slightly. A thin, red tongue snaked out, almost as if the massive creature were intent upon tasting him. Karus could see rows of white, serrated teeth, each as thick as his thigh and nearly as tall as a man. Then the tongue retreated and the mouth snapped closed with a clap.

Karus became irritated, for the dragon had likely intended to startle him. The irritation grew to a mounting anger. With all of his headaches and problems, he did not need this.

By my sacred ancestors, Karus thought to himself as he clenched his jaw and stiffened his back, I will not back down from you, beast.

"Cyln'phax," Karus said after a moment, his voice trembling, not from fear, but rage. He met her gaze as best he could, looking into the depths of the dragon's red eyes. The anger helped. He found them incredibly deep, almost mesmerizing. Despite his rage, it took all of his willpower not to look away.

And you are Karus, favored son of the High Father. The dragon's tone sounded somewhat mocking.

"That's right," Karus said, hardening his voice. "What of it?"

Karus heard the dragon in his mind as a menacing hiss. *Were you anything less, I would certainly not defile myself by allowing you to ride upon my back. After this journey is done and we retrieve Rarokan, I will be forced to have my mate cleanse me with his fire, a humiliation for my kind.*

"Humiliation? Cleanse you?" Karus asked. "Whatever for?"

Your kind is known to be infested, the dragon said in a tone that reeked of utter disgust. Cyln'phax shook herself slightly, which Karus felt as a giant tremble. *You will undoubtedly leave me with vermin.*

"Vermin?" Karus asked indignantly, having difficulty believing the dragon was serious. He wondered for a moment if he was being toyed with. "You think I have vermin? I'll have you know I am most certainly not infested. I bathe regularly."

The dragon brought her head closer, coming to within a couple inches of his. She sniffed at him. Karus found his willpower sorely tested as Cyln'phax tilted her head and gazed at him with a single baleful eye.

You could have fooled me, the dragon said. She held his gaze a moment more, then snaked her head away to look at her mate. Amarra was in the process of securing her own packs to Kordem's back a few yards away.

Karus let out a relieved breath. Should the dragon wish it, he knew she could easily tear him limb from limb or burn him with her fire. That said, he seriously doubted she would do it. They were allies of a sort, and yet he still found it troubling to feel so helpless and small in her presence.

Dio and Pammon waited fifteen yards away, a healthy distance to be sure, standing well clear of both dragons. They looked more than a little uncomfortable with their proximity to the two fearsome creatures. He could well understand their feelings.

Shaking his head, Karus began climbing down off of the dragon's back. As he was working his way down, Karus spotted Felix emerging from the palace. Felix paused, gazing at the dragons a moment before starting down the steps and moving toward Dio and Pammon.

High above, the moon was hidden behind a thick layer of clouds. In the darkness, he could just make Amarra out thirty yards off, and only because of her white dress. It was almost pitch black. Occasionally, the moon poked out or managed to shine through a cloud to provide a bit of light.

Karus could not have asked for a better night to make his departure. He judged it would be very difficult for anyone out in the city to see the dragons leave, even as they flew directly overhead. It was so dark that in the unlikely event they were spotted, all that would be seen from below would be the silhouettes of the massive creatures against the sky. No one would see Karus and Amarra on the creatures' backs. At least, he hoped so.

Karus glanced around the darkened gardens. A couple of torches had been staked into the ground by the steps that led up and into the palace forty yards distant. Beyond that, there were no other light sources. That was intentional. They could not risk being seen, even by the palace sentries.

He had also taken the extra precaution of having the palace quietly emptied out, just long enough for him and Amarra to be away. Only a skeleton guard remained, along with Karus's clerks, and they had been ordered to stay well clear of the gardens. Other than the cohort commanders, only Serma, his chief clerk, knew they were leaving.

Flickering shadows from the torches played over the damaged and overgrown gardens, giving the scene a ghostly appearance. Both dragons had made the back side of the palace their home over the last few days. The creatures had all but wrecked what remained of the once beautifully and meticulously cared for gardens, tearing up paving stones, shattering fountains, knocking over the decorative walls, and flattening the plants.

The gardens had been overgrown and neglected when the legion had arrived in Carthum. Still, it had been peaceful and pleasant enough to stroll through with Amarra as he learned her language and she Rome's. The gardens had, in a way, been a sanctuary, well away from prying eyes. The destruction had not been done on purpose. It was just that the dragons were so massive that they could not help it.

The damage to the gardens mattered little to Karus. Carthum was only a temporary base of operations, and certainly not a permanent home. The Horde would eventually come, and from what he had learned, Karus very much doubted they would appreciate the palace gardens or Carthum, for that matter, other than for what they could loot from it. Once Karus had what he needed in transport, the legion would march and not look back. When that happened, it was very much unlikely he would ever see Carthum again. In fact, Karus planned on destroying the city as he gave it up, rather than leave anything useful for the enemy, especially the shelter it could provide.

"Let them have ruin," Karus said to himself as his sandals slapped down on the ground.

Cyln'phax was lying down and it was still a twelve-foot climb up to her back. Karus looked back up the dragon's side. It was a near-vertical wall of armored scales. The beasts were massive. He almost couldn't believe they were real.

He turned to look over to Kordem to see how Amarra was progressing and had to squint to see. Holding the hem of her dress, Amarra was carefully climbing down off of Kordem's back. He had offered to secure the packs for her, but Amarra had flatly refused him. She had insisted, making it abundantly clear to him in no uncertain terms she wanted to do the job herself. From what he could see, she seemed to have everything well in hand. So, Karus walked over to his officers. It was time to finish up his business here so they could depart.

"I think they both like her," Dio said with a nod toward Amarra.

"They do," Pammon said, "don't they?"

Kordem's head hovered over Amarra, but it wasn't in a threatening manner. Amarra could be heard chatting pleasantly with the dragon. To Karus it was a one-sided conversation, as he could not hear Kordem's replies. It seemed the dragons had the ability to silently communicate to whomever they wished, while screening out others when desired.

Kordem appeared much more deferential toward Amarra than Cyln'phax was to him. Now that he thought on it, both dragons showed Amarra great deference and respect. He felt himself frown as his gaze slid back to his own dragon. Cyln'phax had given him nothing but attitude, disdain, and hostility from the moment they'd met.

Like has nothing to do with it, Cyln'phax said, speaking to them all, head swinging around to look down on them balefully. *We help her, human. There is a world of difference.*

Dio gazed up at the dragon. He swallowed before responding. "I suppose you are correct."

Suppose all you want, the dragon said with a condescending air. *We don't like your kind. You are beneath us, no more than dirt to be shaken off our claws at the end of the day.* The dragon's head swung to look at Amarra. *However, we have sworn to assist the child of the High Father, and so we shall, to our dying breaths.*

All four of them turned to look at Amarra and fell into an uneasy silence.

"I'm glad you're going on this little journey, instead of me, that is," Dio said, looking over at Karus with something approaching a grin. He hesitated a moment and the grin grew into a smirk. "I would like to thank you for that."

"I can't tell you how pleased I am to save you from shouldering my burden," Karus said, feeling sour but at the same time somewhat amused. "You're welcome, by the way."

Dio grew serious. "Are you certain you don't want to take a few men with you?"

"No," Karus said with a glance at the dragon. He had thought about it, and brought it up, but the dragons had refused him. "They said they'd take only the two of us, and that we don't need more." Karus paused. "This is something I think Amarra and I must do ourselves, as the High Father charged us with retrieving Rarokan."

Dio gave an unhappy nod, but looked far from convinced.

Karus turned to Felix, who had been out and about in the city until just a short while ago.

"Did Xresex do as I asked him?" Karus asked.

"Once Amarra explained things to him," Felix said, "he was only too eager to help. He sent several of his boys to act as emissaries on our behalf. I was delayed seeing them off. Getting them on the horses was a bit of a challenge.

None of them had ever seen a horse before." Felix paused and chucked. He looked up at Cyln'phax and then back at Karus. "In a way, it's kind of like you and the dragons. I am sure the prospect of riding a dragon is a bit disconcerting for you too."

"There is a lot of truth in that," Karus said.

"Well," Felix continued, "Valens will make sure they get to the bands of refugees he's located. Though we don't yet speak this common tongue, I am sure Xresex's boys will do a good job of passing along the same offer you gave his bunch." He paused and glanced at the dragons. "With luck, you will be back before any additional groups can join us, which I think is good. As our commander, you need to meet their leaders yourself before accepting them into the city. There are bound to be peoples whom we simply cannot live with. They will be either downright hostile or have too much barbarian in them."

"Agreed," Karus said, pleased that offers were going out to the nearest bands of refugees. From the latest report he'd received from Valens, ten such groups had been spotted moving through the region and were close enough to easily contact. How many would come, he did not know. With luck, several of these groups would accept his offer of shelter and food in exchange for their fighting men serving alongside Karus's legionaries. This would ultimately increase his combat power. On the downside, it would also mean he'd have more mouths to feed. One solution created another problem.

"I'm still unhappy with this arrangement," Dio said. "We invited them into the city. I can't help but think we might want to delay with these other groups until we know for certain how well it will go. We take in too many and soon we might find ourselves outnumbered. It creates a security concern. Heck, we don't know if this will work out with Xresex's bunch."

"That's right," Karus said, anger coloring his voice somewhat. "We won't know until we've tried."

Karus sucked in a calming breath and paused before letting it out. He had to remind himself they'd not seen the vision of the enemy that the High Father had shown Karus. Besides, Karus was already unhappy at having to leave, even if it was only for a handful of days. It was unfair to take it out on his friend. Dio was only being honest with his opinion, which was something Karus valued.

"Dio," Karus said, starting again, "it may have escaped your notice, but evil is sweeping across this land. We need allies if we are to stand any chance at all of escaping this world. We need allies sooner rather than later." He paused and looked at his officers. "All of you have laid eyes on the orcs, but you've not seen the Horde. The High Father showed me our enemy. I tell you, what I saw is terrifying. You need to believe me in this. We have to take a chance on these people. It is the only way I see of us having a shot at beating the odds, which are stacked heavily against us."

Dio held up his hands. "Karus, I did not mean to—"

Cyln'phax laughed. It was a dark, almost bitter sound that rang in his head. Karus knew they'd all heard it because their heads turned toward the dragon, gazing upward.

Terrifying does not begin to describe the Horde, Cyln'phax said to them. The dragon's intense gaze bored down upon them. The words boomed in their minds. *This world is a backwater. The Horde on Tannis is but a tiny shadow of what it is on other worlds. Still, that shadow alone should keep you all awake at night. The enemy is coming for us. It will not rest. There is no reasoning, no negotiated peace. There will be no mercy. The Horde will keep coming until we all have fallen.* The dragon fell silent a moment. *The Horde terrifies me more than you can ever hope to comprehend.*

Pammon, Dio, and Felix exchanged glances. Karus knew what they were thinking. Whatever frightened such a fearsome creature as Cyln'phax was something to be taken very seriously. Karus turned back to the others. He needed to use what the dragon said to reinforce his own position.

"I could not have said it better. That is why we need additional allies," Karus said, gesturing toward the dragon. "We will not be able to face what is coming by ourselves."

No, you cannot, the dragon said. *I am pleased one amongst you has some semblance of common sense. I have come to learn it is a rare quality with you humans.*

Karus glanced up at the dragon and shook his head. Cyln'phax shifted almost impatiently, and the ground trembled with the dragon's movement. Karus understood it was time to go. There was no point in delaying. The sooner he was away, the quicker he'd be back.

"Right," Karus said, turning to Pammon. "I should be gone no more than a week at most. Look after the shop for me, will you, Pammon?" Karus paused and felt a shadow of a grin tug at his lips. "Try to keep Dio out of trouble, will you?"

"Me?" Dio asked, suddenly looking hurt. "Cause trouble? Karus, how long have we known each other?"

"Yes, he means you." Felix grinned.

"We'll hold things together for you," Pammon assured him, sharing a look with the other two officers. "Don't you worry. Get that bloody sword and return to us quick as you can."

"We will deal with everything else after that," Felix added, "including finding additional allies."

A sheepish expression crossed over Dio's face. He jabbed a thumb at Felix. "What he said."

Karus gave a nod before turning away and walking over to Amarra. She had climbed up to secure the last pack and was clambering back down off the dragon's back. A look of excitement shone in her eyes as she spotted him coming over. Her hair had been tied back into a single tight braid, that ran down her back.

"I ready," Amarra said. "Are you?"

"I am," Karus said, wondering if he should check her packs to make sure they were properly secured. No, he decided after a moment's reflection. It was important that he show trust in her. "Let's get moving, then, shall we?"

Amarra grinned as she looked up into his eyes. Her enthusiasm was almost infectious—almost. Despite being deeply troubled about leaving, he felt a slight lightening of his mood. Absently, he glanced back at his officers, who were talking amongst themselves. They certainly appeared troubled. It was no more than he felt himself, and his concerns about leaving returned in a rush. He sucked in a deep breath and released it.

As he turned back to Amarra, she leaned forward and gave him a quick peck on the cheek.

"Have faith in High Father," Amarra said and kissed him again. "You no worry so much."

"It's kept me alive this long," Karus said.

"Put worries aside. Now we fly." Amarra shot him a wink and turned back to Kordem. She hiked up her dress, exposing her shapely legs, and began climbing back up onto the dragon's back. As he watched her pull herself up using the dragon's scales for handholds, Karus brought a hand up to his cheek where she had kissed him. He shook his head and chuckled. Amarra had a boundless optimism that he found quite refreshing, almost invigorating and restorative to the spirit. He found he could breathe a little easier when Amarra was around.

Karus walked back to Cyln'phax. The dragon swung her head around to regard him as he approached, but said nothing. With a nod to his officers, Karus gripped at the rough edges of the armored scales that ran along the dragon's side and pulled himself up and onto her back. Climbing in his armor took some effort. Once up, he made for the spot he'd selected for himself. He had left thick leather straps to tie himself onto the dragon's back just ahead of where he had secured the packs.

Glancing at the massive wings, which were still folded back, Karus knew with certainty in moments he would be in the air. He found that thought more than a little disconcerting. The dragon had warned him to tie himself down, and Karus fully intended to do so.

He made himself comfortable, for he understood he would be in that position for some hours to come. Karus began tying the straps around his waist. He tied the other ends of the straps tightly around several of the closest spikes. Once he had finished work on the knots, he checked them again just to be certain they would hold, tugging on each for good measure. It was a makeshift job, but would do. Should traveling by dragonback become a regular occurrence, Karus wondered if some form of a saddle could be fashioned to make it more comfortable for the rider. It was certainly something to think on.

Are you prepared, human? Cyln'phax asked, looking back at him. Karus sensed an eagerness to be off and away.

"My name is Karus."

Your name is "human" until you prove to me you deserve to be called by anything other. With that, Cyln'phax arched her head up into the air. The dragon stood, causing Karus to rock alarmingly on her back. The leather straps tied about his waist held him firmly in place. Despite that, he grabbed onto the nearest spike to his front. Cyln'phax extended her wings. Karus looked over at his officers below and to the right.

Pammon, Dio, and Felix backpedaled rapidly, seeking to gain space as the dragon's massive, leathery wings unfolded. Karus could not believe the creature's wingspan, which he estimated to be at least one hundred thirty feet.

Beneath him, he felt the dragon flex her powerful shoulders. The wings extended farther. A heartbeat later, she gave a mighty flap, leaping forward and up into the air. Then, she gave another powerful flap of her wings. Karus felt pressed into his seat. He looked down and was alarmed to see the ground, shrouded in darkness, rapidly retreating from view. He gripped the spike even tighter as the dragon continued to climb, beating her wings in steady pulses that propelled them upward and at greater speed into the night sky. The cool night air, at first a breeze, began to blow as a strong wind in his face.

Karus glanced backward, wondering how Amarra was faring. Behind them, perhaps one hundred yards distant, he saw Kordem following after Cyln'phax, wings pumping at the air. In the darkness, Karus could barely make out Amarra on Kordem's back. Karus suddenly grinned. Somehow, he suspected she was fully enjoying the experience of flying. He could almost picture her delightedly laughing.

His stomach clenched as he looked downward at the ground far below them. He'd never much liked heights. Flying like a bird, Karus decided, was an experience he could have happily done without.

Cyln'phax began to beat her wings at an increased pace. Judging by the force of the wind, the dragon was continuing to pick up speed, even as she climbed ever higher into the night sky. Karus turned back to face front. The wind blew more strongly in his face, whipping about his ears. It was like standing outside in a storm, without the rain, facing the power of the wind head on, the strength of it trying to batter him backward.

He looked down again and off to the right. Much of the city below was obscured in darkness. There were few lights, as it was very late. He was able to make out the city walls marked by the sentries' watchfires and torches. They twinkled as little, bright sparks in the greater darkness.

The watchfires disappeared beneath the dragon's wings as they left the city behind, even as they climbed higher and higher. The moon abruptly appeared, slipping from behind a cloud in all its brightness. It illuminated the edges of the nearest clouds. They were so close, Karus almost felt he could reach out and touch them. It was an incredible thought and he marveled at it for a moment before looking downward again toward the ground. The moon bathed the land beneath them in a pale white glow. Karus sucked in a breath at the beauty of the view.

Without any warning, and just as he was getting comfortable with flying, Cyln'phax abruptly banked to the right and tucked her wings back. She dove for the ground. Karus's stomach did a backflip as the land below them began rushing up to meet them. He clung tightly to the spike, wondering if something was wrong, even as he floated up off his seat an inch or so before the straps stopped any further movement. The wind buffeted his face and chest, pushing powerfully against his death grip on the spike and the straps. The wind screamed through his helmet. He did his best to keep from crying out in panic as the dragon hurtled toward the ground.

Cyln'phax laughed. Karus sensed a wild joy in that laugh, mixed with amusement at his expense.

Do not worry, human, Cyln'phax said as she leveled off at the last moment before they would have smacked into the ground. They were traveling at an almost unbelievable speed, skimming just over the land. Wings outstretched, the dragon followed the contour of the rolling hills, rising and falling with each. The terrain below flashed by in a dizzyingly dark blur. Cyln'phax flexed her wings, and they climbed just enough to clear a stand of trees. The dragon let out a roar of what he took to be satisfaction.

Enjoy the ride, for very few of your kind have been honored in such a way.

Behind them, Karus heard Kordem let out a matching roar.

CHAPTER FIVE

Karus tossed the pack with the tent, blankets, and spare tunics down to the ground below. It landed next to the other pack with a solid-sounding thump. He climbed carefully off the back of the dragon, working his way down her side. His sandals sank slightly into a carpet of soft, green moss, scattered over with brown and yellow leaves from the previous season. The leaves crunched underfoot.

It felt good to once again have his feet back on solid ground. Karus was stiff, tired, and cold. He stretched out his back. The unrelenting wind as the dragon flew through the sky had chilled to the bone. If he ever took another journey with the dragons, he would make certain to bring along a heavy cloak for warmth. His service cloak just didn't cut it.

Karus rubbed his hands together for warmth before he untied the straps to his helmet. Lifting the heavy thing off his head, he cracked his neck. It was always a relief to take the bloody thing off. Tucking the helmet under an arm, he ran a hand through his short-cropped hair and looked around the forest clearing. The smell of decaying leaves, moss, and moist soil filled the air.

They had been flying over a vast forest when the dragons had decided it was time to land and rest. The forest stretched for as far as the eye could see. Prior to landing, Karus had been unable to spot any settlements or, for that matter, breaks in the forest canopy. The dragons had slowed to a hover and made their own clearing as they landed, knocking down and shattering the hardwoods below them. Once down, they quickly made the clearing larger by swinging their powerful tails around, shattering and snapping tree trunks. Between the two them, the dragons had cleared a space roughly two hundred yards around. They had made an effort to push most of the shattered limbs and trunks aside. It was an impressive bit of work and had been completed in just a matter of minutes.

Karus studied the hardwoods that surrounded the clearing. The trees were old, with thickened trunks. They reached upward around eighty to one hundred feet with a nearly impenetrable green, leafy canopy. As a result, the forest floor was fairly open, with very little brush or undergrowth.

The forest was dark and had an ominous atmosphere to it. It was too quiet, almost silent. Karus had the uncomfortable feeling that they shouldn't be here. Though the trees were smaller, the forest had a similar feel to the one the legion had found itself surrounded by the day they had arrived on this world. Karus found that thought not a comfort but instead a concern.

He looked over at Kordem to see how Amarra was doing. Carrying her staff, she climbed down off the dragon's back one-handed and jumped down the last couple feet. Her packs were already on the ground. Karus saw she was speaking with Kordem. Amarra spotted him looking her way and waved enthusiastically before turning back to the dragon, clearly deep in conversation.

The suns emerged from a cloud and bathed the clearing in brilliant sunlight. Both suns had been up for about three hours. The warmth was a welcome relief. Karus relished the feeling and closed his eyes, breathing in through his mouth. He held the breath a moment before releasing it through his nose. He now understood what a bird felt like. Despite the chilling wind and his fear of heights, after the sky had lightened, Karus had found himself enjoying the experience of flying, somewhat.

He had watched, almost mesmerized, as the first of the two suns had pulled itself up and over the horizon, followed shortly after by the second. It had been a magnificent sight. The ground beneath them went from complete darkness to shadow and then to brilliant color as the sunlight slowly forced the night back. They had passed over a large lake, the surface burning with reflected sunlight. He had found it all quite impressive, awe-inspiring.

Still, Karus had decided flying was not quite for him. Heck, he did not even feel that comfortable on the back of a horse, though he had managed well enough when needed. Over the years, he had marched many miles with just his own two feet. He was a soldier through and through, an infantry officer first and foremost. His place was firmly on the ground, with his men.

Cyln'phax, seeing that he was off her back, huffed out a breath of what Karus took to be impatient relief. The dragon took several steps forward and then to the side, each step landing with a heavy thud, her claws digging deeply into the soft soil of what twenty minutes before had been the forest floor. Her right fore-foot crushed an ancient stump into the ground as she moved. Karus heard it crack and snap under her weight. The dragon's head swung to the left and toward the forest only a few yards away. A moment later, she whipped her tail around. It connected with a tree that had managed to escape the destruction of her landing.

The oak had stood for countless years. It went down with a thunderous crash, falling into the forest and taking a second tree down with it. Silence followed as Cyln'phax raised her head into the air and looked over her work. Karus got the sense she was satisfied, for she shook herself and then lay down. Neck stretched out, the dragon lowered her head to the ground, where it landed with another heavy thud, setting the branches on the nearest trees shaking. She rolled over onto her side and rubbed herself along the ground like a horse might. She looked to be scratching an itch. She rolled back onto her belly and her head swung around to look at Karus.

You may wish to get some sleep, Cyln'phax said in a tone laced with weariness. *We will remain here for no more than four hours.*

"How far have we come?" Karus asked. They had traveled through much of the night. In the darkness, the distance had been difficult to judge. He figured they had gone several hundred miles at least.

Human, I have to tolerate your presence and bear the indignity of having you upon my back, Cyln'phax said. *Do not test my patience. Just know we will reach the fortress sooner than you could have marched on your two tiny and pathetic little feet.*

Karus rubbed his jaw with frustration as he gazed back at the dragon.

We've come a ways, Kordem said, joining the conversation. *As I've just told Amarra, we must make an important stop first before we continue on to the fortress.*

"A stop?" Karus asked, wheeling about to look at Kordem. The other dragon had curled up at the far end of the clearing, thirty yards away. His head was up and he was gazing at Karus. "You did not mention this before. Why and what for?"

You must visit the Elantric Warden first, Kordem said, and ask permission for us to travel to the fortress.

"The Elantric Warden?" Karus felt his temper flare. "Who's that?"

Why had the two dragons concealed this information from them until now? Whatever their reason, it likely did not bode well.

All of these trees around you belong to her. This is the warden's forest and we are trespassing in one of her realms, Cyln'phax said in a tone that smacked of condescension. *The warden's people inhabit forests like this one. Be grateful, human, for had you made this journey on foot, her people would likely have killed you and anyone with you before you made it a half day's hike into the forest.*

"What?" Karus was dismayed, glancing around. Were the people who lived here the same as the phantoms and wraiths his men had reported spotting in the trees when they had first come to this world? The ones who had killed the strange scouts and left their bodies amongst the giant trees? It was a worrying thought.

Fear not, Kordem said, a note of finality in his tone. The dragon lowered his head slowly to the ground. *You will be safe in our company. Now, bother us no more. We must rest. All will become clear in time. On that I promise.*

Karus looked between the two dragons and clenched a fist. He sucked in a breath and let it out slowly. Incredibly frustrated, he picked up one of the packs by its strap and slung it over a shoulder. He did not much enjoy feeling helpless. He was at the dragons' mercy and they had withheld vital information. He could not see what he could do about it now. They certainly could not go back, for he did not know the way and the forest was apparently dangerous, with a hostile people. He and Amarra were, for good or ill, stuck.

There was only one thing to do, and that was to go forward and see this through.

Karus walked to the center of the clearing, where there was some open space without any shattered and broken tree limbs. One thing was certain, he decided as he stopped and looked back at Cyln'phax. He could not trust the dragons to be open with him. Withholding information was the same as misleading. Karus set the pack down on the ground and put his helmet on the shattered stump of a tree.

He glanced around again. He had to concede that the clearing was a good spot to rest for a few hours, especially with the sun beating down on it. He went back for the second pack. As he returned with it, Amarra joined him. She set down her packs and leaned her staff against a stump.

"I cold," Amarra said and shivered. He noticed the tiny puckered goosebumps on her arms, which he found strangely attractive. She sat down on a fallen trunk and started rummaging through her pack. After several moments, she pulled out a wool blanket, which she wrapped about her shoulders, and looked up into the sky. She closed her eyes. "Suns feel good."

"They do," Karus said in agreement. He looked over at Cyln'phax. A feeling of deep concern once again washed over him. What sort of dangerous path were the dragons leading them down?

"You no happy. What wrong?"

He found her looking up at him, brow furrowed. She stood and bent over her pack. Her single braid fell over a shoulder and dangled forward. She pulled a second blanket from the bag and straightened. This one was thicker and made for camping. She laid it upon the ground over a soft bed of moss.

"Why you no happy?" she asked when he failed to respond.

"Friendly bunch," Karus said, and gestured at Cyln'phax and then Kordem, "aren't they?"

"They are," Amarra said, failing to pick up on his sarcasm. "Kordem is wonderful. Once suns come up, he kept me, how you say ... fun, amused?"

"Entertained?" Karus suggested.

"He tell me stories of he and his mate and of different worlds." She shook her head in amazement. "He point out places we fly over. Did Cyln'phax do same?"

"No," Karus said, casting the female dragon an unhappy look. "She was rather reserved."

"Reserved?" Amarra asked, looking up at him. "What mean?"

Karus thought a moment on how to explain it. "Distant, cold, not too friendly. She said little to me."

"Not friendly?" Amarra asked with a surprised look. She turned her gaze briefly on Cyln'phax and her eyes narrowed ever so slightly.

"No, not friendly," Karus said, setting the pack down next to hers. "Do you know of this Elantric Warden they speak of?"

"Kordem said we to talk to her about going to fortress," Amarra said.

"I don't like surprises," Karus said, feeling testy. "It would have been nice if they'd told us in advance."

"They not want tell you or me," Amarra said. "They worried we say no about going to fortress and telling about warden."

"You think?" Karus said.

"This her land, warden land," Amarra said and held out both arms to encompass the entire forest that surrounded the clearing.

"That's what I'm afraid of," Karus said. "Do you know of her, this Elantric Warden? Her people?"

Amarra was silent for a long moment, clearly thinking through what she wanted to say.

"I know not of warden. Kordem say she spiritual leader of her people. But if people I think on"—she gave a slight nod—"then yes, I know them by talk."

She did not appear too happy about that. Karus's concern intensified.

"Are they as dangerous as the dragons say?" Karus asked. "Her people, that is?"

Amarra inclined her head slowly in a shallow nod. "They no like other people."

"Like the dwarves?" Karus asked. It seemed none of the people on this world got along. "They don't like other people as well?"

"No," Amarra said. "Worse, much worse."

"Great." Karus ran his gaze around at the impenetrable forest that surrounded the freshly made clearing. "Just bloody great."

"It be okay," Amarra said. "Kordem say we safe here. They not bother us."

"You said that the warden was the spiritual leader of her people," Karus said. "Do you think she is like you, a priestess of her god?"

Amarra closed her eyes a long moment. When she opened them, she shook her head. There was a steady look in her eyes. When she spoke, it was in a firm tone. "She not like me, nothing like me."

"How can you be so certain?" Karus asked. "Did Kordem tell you?"

Amarra was silent a long moment. "High Father tell me."

"What?" Karus asked, at first wondering if she had mis-spoken. "What do you mean he told you?"

"High Father told me so."

"He speaks to you?" Karus said.

Amarra bit her lip as she studied him, once again hesi-tating before replying. "He no speak words I hear. Is more feeling inside." She touched her chest. "I search, I ask and feel answer, sometimes. Not always get answer I want. It start after we visit by High Father."

Karus must have frowned or appeared doubtful, for her expression hardened.

"You must believe," Amarra said. "Trust in me as I trust in you and High Father."

"I do." Karus gave a slow nod of acceptance. The great god had appeared and set them both tasks. Had he not experienced it himself, he knew he would have had trouble believing her. A few weeks ago, he would have viewed her as a crazed madwoman. Now, she was close to his heart.

Amarra held his gaze a long moment before turning her attention to the blanket she had laid out on the ground.

"We rest," Amarra said and bent down, smoothing out the blanket. "Yes?"

"Not the worst place I've ever stayed," Karus said as he opened his pack and drew out a blanket of his own. He laid it out next to hers.

Amarra straightened and moved her foot over the forest floor. She shifted some of the leaves aside. She touched the ugly scar on her right wrist.

"You found me in prison," Amarra said quietly and looked up at him. Her eyes became moist.

"I did." Karus recalled her dreadful state. She had been covered in dirt and grime and smelled plain awful when his men had pulled her out of the cell.

"I almost lost faith." Amarra touched her chest. "It hurt very bad. I give up everything because I believe. I watch priests I love suffer for faith. Kind, loving Father Lohert, who opened my eyes and showed me the bright within me"—she tapped her chest again—"he die. They all die because of me."

"No," Karus said. "I don't believe that."

"It was because of me," Amarra insisted. "My father so angry at me. He punished them."

"Never believe that. They died because of your father's decisions," Karus said. "It is not your fault. The blame lies with him."

Amarra cleared her throat. "It doesn't feel that way."

"It never does," Karus said. "I've watched plenty of good boys die under my command. It always feels like it's your fault, even when it's not."

Amarra gave an absent nod, averting her gaze toward the trees. She wiped at her eyes. "It still hurts, so much."

"I wish I could tell you it gets easier," Karus said.

"When I alone in prison," Amarra said, her gaze still on the trees, "in the dark for so long, I almost lose faith. I came close to giving up." She paused and then in a near whisper said, "It was so hard."

"But you didn't." Karus could only imagine the nightmare she had gone through. "You held onto your faith. You persevered."

Amarra sucked in a deep breath that shuddered. She turned her eyes back on Karus. "After Father Lohert and others die with their faith, how could I give up? It would dishonor their memory."

"The High Father blessed and made you his High Priestess. You have absolutely nothing to be ashamed of, nothing."

Amarra was silent for a long moment, her eyes searching his face.

"I know," Amarra said, her tone becoming firm, her gaze piercing. "I honor them best way I can. I carry on and spread the High Father's love, his word. I tend his flock, help it grow."

"We will do it together," Karus said, "yes?"

Amarra's eyes narrowed as she regarded him for several heartbeats. He sensed a slight lightening of her mood, a softening in her eyes. "You found me in prison."

"Let's be honest, my men found you," Karus said with a sudden grin. "They only brought you to me, the most beautiful woman I ever laid eyes upon. I was truly blessed that fateful day."

"You think I am beautiful?" Amarra asked him.

"I do," Karus said, "very much so."

"Well, even if you did not find me … my hero." A hint of a smile traced its way onto her face as she gestured around the clearing. "This much better than prison. Much better, I think."

Karus gave a low chuckle that died prematurely as a shadow fell over the both of them. He looked up to find Cyln'phax gazing downward.

You both should rest. Our next flight will take us across lands overrun by the Horde, Cyln'phax said. *It will be risky and dangerous. We should arrive at the warden's palace by dusk.*

"You said nothing of this warden before we left," Karus said, becoming heated. "Why not?"

You did not ask, Kordem said from across the clearing, sounding almost surly. *We risk much for this venture. Show some gratitude, human.*

"You should have told us!" Karus found himself steaming mad. "When were you going to tell us? Going forward, how can I trust you?"

You dare question your betters? Cyln'phax's mouth opened slightly, a stream of smoke escaping.

We promised to get you to the fortress and we will, Kordem said. *But first, we must stop and ask for the warden's blessing. It may reduce the complications of getting into the fortress and out with the sword, or so we hope.*

"Complications? I already didn't like this venture to begin with," Karus said. "Amarra tells me the warden's people are dangerous."

They are very dangerous, Kordem said. *It was one of the reasons we decided to wait to tell you. We suspected you would take it badly and might delay this journey until it was too late, with the Horde on Carthum's doorstep.*

"You should have told us straight away," Karus said with heat. He cracked his neck, for it was stiff from his helmet. A thought occurred to him. "If these people are so dangerous, then we should go right to the fortress. Why go looking for trouble? What complications do you speak of?"

"Yes," Amarra said in agreement with him. "Why not go to fortress?"

The fortress is guarded by the Warriors of Anagradoom, Kordem said. *They are an ancient order. We understand they have pledged their lives to protect Rarokan. As was prophesized, you will seek permission to take the dread sword from its keepers. Without permission and blessing from the warden, we think they may not willingly surrender the sword to you.*

"What? Prophecy?" Karus was dismayed. He glanced over at Amarra, who looked none too happy either about this news. "Did you know of a prophecy?"

Amarra shook her head. "No."

Your coming was foretold, as was Amarra's, Kordem said. *You know this, for we told you. But you've not seen the prophecy of which we speak. The warden knows the prophecy, for the sword was given into the care of her people, who were charged with keeping it in sacred trust for your coming.*

"For me?" Karus shared a glance with Amarra before turning his gaze back to Kordem. "They know I am coming."

Not you particularly, not by name, but the revered son of the High Father. You are to be but the first to wield Rarokan, Kordem said. *The prophecy, though confusing, makes that much clear. Rarokan is an ancient and powerful artifact, a weapon to be feared by all. Yet, it is also a tool that, in the right hands, may be able to save all that we love or, in the wrong ones, may be able to challenge the gods themselves. Though that is not your destiny, but another's. You need not worry about that. However, the path you follow must see you bear the burden of Rarokan, as the High Father intended, and be its first master. That will be no easy thing.*

Karus just shook his head, stunned by what they were telling him.

"And if this warden refuses to give up this powerful weapon?" Karus asked. "What if she does not recognize I am the one to take the sword? What then?"

It seems you are uncommonly perceptive for a human, Cyln'phax said. *The warden is known to be difficult. We will help convince her of the correct path.*

Should the warden prove shortsighted, we shall go anyway, Kordem said. *The sword belongs in your hands. Without it, our chances of withstanding the Horde and escaping Tannis decrease dramatically.*

"These warriors guarding the fortress won't give up the sword without her permission," Karus said. It was a statement, not a question.

We believe they will not, Kordem said. *But who can tell for certain? We think it better to see the warden first, gain her support. Then go.*

If need be, we will kill the Warriors of Anagradoom and take the sword by force, Cyln'phax said as if it were a simple thing. *To do so, you will need to break the enchantment over the fortress, for we cannot go near it.*

"Enchantment? Just great." Karus pinched the bridge of his nose, feeling a headache coming on. "It would've been nice to know this in advance. I would have brought more men along."

Your men would not have made any difference, Kordem said. *They would be useless against the followers of Anagradoom, and there were other considerations.*

"Useless?" Karus asked, incredulous that he was hearing all of this now. "How so?"

The fortress's defenders are imbued and armed with occult powers, Kordem said. *Their will has been enhanced. Your men would not have stood a chance against them.*

"And we will?" Karus asked.

We believe so, for you both have been blessed by the High Father, Kordem said. *Besides, the prophecy only mentions you two and three others picked up along the way. Five of you will enter the fortress. We could not allow you to take more men and threaten the fulfillment of the prophecy. To do so might have ruined everything. Meddling where prophecy is concerned can be dangerous. It is considered most unwise.*

"You should have told us," Amarra said in Common, anger plain in her voice. Karus glanced over at her. Her gaze was fierce as she looked up at Cyln'phax. "You should have told us, especially me, about this prophecy. I am blessed by the High Father, his direct instrument and *will* upon this world. You will conceal nothing from us again. Do you understand me?"

The dragon lowered its head to their level. It leaned in close, muzzle less than a foot from Amarra and Karus. She did not flinch or back down so much as an inch, but stood angry, confident, and proud against the dragon's gaze. Karus found himself admiring her steadfast strength of will, for he knew what it took to face off a dragon.

My apologies, revered daughter, Cyln'phax said and Karus sensed the dragon meant it. *When we return to Carthum, we shall reveal the prophecy in its entirety. I warn you now, reading and translating prophecy can be tricky. It is almost an art form, and when you think you understand it, you discover you were most wrong. The portion that concerns us now says the following...*

> *Five shall climb the hill up into the fortress afflicted beyond recognition, the chosen and three others who shall join this desperate venture along the way. Two shall betray all they hold dear and for good cause. One who is lost shall rediscover himself and a talisman that shall ultimately tie fate to another's. Five shall come out, or not at all, with the sword Rarokan in the hands of he who is the High Father's revered son. So too shall come the Anagradoom. Beware of the Dark Lord, for darkness shall reign should the Rarokan come into his keeping.*

Cyln'phax paused a moment, pulling back from Amarra and Karus. *Whether the Anagradoom come out as allies or enemies we do not know. The prophecy mentions three shall join the chosen, whom we believe to be you both. We feel we will pick up additional companions at Irin'Surall, the warden's home, but we know not who they will be.*

"Who is this Dark Lord?" Karus asked.

Something else we do not know, Kordem said. *We think he is an agent of the enemy. However, it is possible he could also be of the Anagradoom. We do know the enemy has a prophecy of their own.*

Before you ask, Cyln'phax said, *we know not what that prophecy says. Do not judge us too harshly. We have been at this a very long time. Again, our apologies for keeping this from you. Our intentions were only for the best. Now,* the dragon said, suddenly sounding weary, *we must rest, for our journey will continue before long.*

Cyln'phax curled her tail around her and tucked her head under a wing, clearly intent upon sleep. The message was clear: The conversation was over. Kordem did the same.

Amarra's expression softened a little as she looked over at Karus. She shook her head slightly. Karus was rocked by what the dragons had just revealed. He was certain Amarra felt the same way. That there was a prophecy concerned him greatly, and the enemy had one, too. He wondered if the dragons were playing some game of their own. Had they just been completely honest and open? He suspected they had, but only time would tell.

"The warden's people. Who are they?" Karus asked. "Tell me more about them."

"They like us," Amarra said, clearly trying to explain and struggling with it, "but not."

"Like us, but not?" Karus repeated. "Are they anything like the orcs?"

"No," Amarra said. "I never seen one. Not many do. They stay in trees. But, I think they old people. They do not mix with others. I know little of them. No one does." She paused and spared a glance around at the trees that crowded the clearing. "One thing people know is stay out of their trees. To go in them is to find death."

Karus felt himself frown.

"The trees?" Karus asked. "You mean the forest?"

"They no let people into lands," Amarra said with a nod. "They people of legend. How you say, secret? They kill all who enter lands without asking."

Karus thought about that for a few moments. The dragon had said they were trespassing in the warden's lands. Would they try to kill him, Amarra, and the dragons? His thoughts shifted. He wondered how these people could have managed to avoid the war that was even now raging across this world. Were they part of it in some way? Had they made an accommodation with the Horde? What had seemed like a simple journey of retrieval had now become complicated. His eyes fell upon Amarra's staff, which she had leaned against a shattered stump. His thoughts returned to what Kordem had said about the fortress's defenders having occult powers.

"Have you figured out how to use that yet?" Karus asked, gesturing toward the staff.

"No," Amarra said with a sad shake of her head. She touched her chest. "I feel High Father's strength here, but I can no use. I not ready."

"Well," Karus said, "the High Father said not to squander its power. I guess you can't do that unless you know how it works, now, can you?"

"High Father will show me when time or I figure out on own." Amarra glanced at the two dragons, who were showing no sign of being awake or taking an interest in their conversation. Karus suspected they were still paying attention.

"We sleep, yes?" Amarra asked.

"You go ahead," Karus said. "Someone must stand watch."

Even though we rest, Kordem said, speaking up, *we will watch. We will know if anyone comes near. Now cease your talking and get some rest.*

"We sleep, yes?" Amarra asked again.

"We sleep," Karus said, giving in. He unclipped his cloak and laid it aside. He began undoing the straps to his armor, unlacing it. He shrugged out of the armor as Amarra lay down on her blanket. She smoothed out her long white dress, which looked immaculate, with not a speck of dirt on it. Karus set his armor against a nearby stump. It felt good to shed the dead weight.

He took his cloak and laid it over Amarra. She drew it close about her. He then lay down next to her on his own blanket. They lay on their sides, looking at each other, Amarra's eyes searching his face. She reached out a hand and stroked his forearm with a light touch.

"Hold me," Amarra said.

Not needing to be asked twice, Karus pulled her to him. She tucked herself into his body, snuggling close. She felt slight within his arms and shuddered as she placed her head against his chest. He wanted nothing other than to keep this woman safe, to be her protector. But somehow, Karus knew deep down there would be battles that, as High Priestess, she alone would have to fight. That frightened him more than he cared to admit. He wasn't quite sure how he knew this, but he did. Karus understood he would have his own challenges to face.

"Sleep," Amarra whispered to him. "Think no more, worry no more"—she hesitated a bare heartbeat—"my love."

Karus gave her a squeeze and then closed his eyes. He had long mastered the skill of falling asleep when the opportunity presented itself. Service in the legion had taught him how. Karus put his worries from his mind. He had not slept a wink in over a day, and yet, with his arms wrapped around Amarra, it took a little more effort than usual. He sucked in a breath through his nose, inhaling deeply. The air was full of the scent of the forest. Within moments, he surrendered to the oblivion, Amarra tucked comfortably within his arms.

CHAPTER SIX

The last of the two suns was still up, hovering just above the horizon. What little warmth it shed was negated by the wind. They had been flying for hours. Karus was cold and stiff, his fingers almost numb. He stretched as best he could. The straps holding him securely in place were tight, almost to the point of being painful. Karus wasn't taking any chances. The last thing he wanted was to fall off the dragon's back.

He rubbed his hands together for warmth. With the onset of the coming night, it would become colder still. He hoped they would reach their destination soon or at the very least take another break. He leaned over to his right, the wind whistling through his helmet as he shifted to better see. The forest had long since given way to a series of gently rolling hills and small river valleys. In the far distance, he could see a range of mountains. They were craggy and rocky, their tops capped in white snow and devoid of trees. Despite the chill and long hours in the air, Karus found the view majestic, and at times almost breathtaking. It had been like that for much of the day. He was seeing the lay of the land in a way that few humans ever had. Cyln'phax had made a point to tell him as much, and Karus did not doubt the dragon in the least.

They were so high up, any villages or settlements that passed by below them were tiny beyond belief. The buildings had a toy-like quality to them, almost as if they were not quite real. It made Karus feel as if he were some fabled giant, with a god's eye view of the world. Hour after hour, the land spread out before him, for as far as the eye could see. It was much like a map but with all the color, contours, and shapes a cartographer could never hope to capture.

Karus glanced over at Amarra and Kordem flying a few yards to their right. Amarra caught his gaze. She flashed him a broad smile and waved. Karus returned her wave. They had tried shouting to each other, but with the wind, it was incredibly difficult to be heard. So they had long since given up even making the attempt, settling for simple hand gestures.

Karus ran his eyes over Kordem. The dragon's long neck and head were stretched out straight ahead, his wings fully extended, coasting along. The leathery wings shifted and moved ever so slightly with the wind and the air currents. The dragon's legs were pulled up close to his body, claws retracted. Kordem's long, thick spiked tail snaked along behind him, straight as an arrow and when turning curved.

Karus's gaze shifted back to Amarra, who was firmly anchored on Kordem's back, just as he was on Cyln'phax's. Prior to leaving the clearing, Karus had given her his service cloak for the next leg of their journey. He had also insisted she take the blankets, which were thin. They were wrapped about her under his cloak. It was scant protection against the cold, but it was better than nothing. She had secured the cloak tightly about her person. The ends of the cloak flapped and fluttered under the unrelenting wind. It was a splash of red against the green of the dragon and the blue of the sky.

Amarra threw him another wave and then turned away to look at something off to her right. At that moment,

Cyln'phax gave a powerful flap of her wings. It took them higher, with Kordem and Amarra falling below and out of sight. Cyln'phax extended her wings, coasting along on the air. Kordem and Amarra came back into view a moment later as the other dragon beat his wings against the air and climbed ever so slightly, rising higher into the sky. For a time, the two dragons coasted along on a strong draft of air.

They glided high above the land on currents, which Cyln'phax had likened to invisible rivers in the sky. Karus wasn't sure he fully understood. For the dragons, the currents of air apparently allowed them to travel long distances with little effort. The evidence was plain enough for Karus to witness. Most of the time, they flew with their wings extended, gliding along on these invisible rivers of wind, only occasionally giving a flap. He had seen birds do the same, but the dragons flew much higher, with the land below them passing slowly by in an endless parade.

Karus turned his gaze upward. The scattered clouds, puffy and white as the freshest of snows, seemed almost within reach. Though he was still not quite comfortable flying, the more time he spent on the dragon's back, the more he was becoming accustomed to it. He just wished he were a little warmer and wrapped up in something heavy, like furs, for the continued exposure was chilling him to the bone.

Karus returned his attention to the landscape far below. The countryside passed slowly and steadily. The rolling hills and river valleys fell behind them and eventually disappeared altogether. They gave way to vast grasslands that seemed to stretch on and on with no end in sight. Eventually the grasslands made way to pasture and neatly cultivated fields as the last sun worked its way steadily closer toward the horizon.

Karus leaned over to better study the fields passing beneath them, wondering on the peoples that lived below. Gray lines bordered each field, seeming to box them in. It took Karus a moment to realize the gray lines were stone walls. He had seen the like in Britannia, where the fields at times seemed to produce more stone than crops. Farmers used the stones they pulled out of the ground to build the walls that bordered their fields. He had listened to more than one farmer complain that with each passing year there seemed to be more stones, making the job of working the soil and pulling crops from the earth that much more difficult.

Thoughts of working the land reminded Karus of his brother in Sicily. Karus had had an open invitation to come help run the family interests, one of the largest plantations on the island. A sudden pang of sadness washed over him. He had been transported to a different world. Karus and the Ninth were now stuck on Tannis, at least until they could find a way off this world. Even then, there would be no returning to Rome, for the High Father had told him as much. For better or worse, he was on his own, cast adrift in a vast and nearly incomprehensible war not of his making. Well, he consoled himself, he wasn't really alone. He had Amarra and the legion.

Karus's gaze was drawn ahead and to the right. A walled city came into view. With each passing moment, it grew as they flew nearer. The city was spread over a series of small rolling hills. A haze of blue-gray smoke hung above the city. Karus figured the city was almost as large as Carthum and, judging from the smoke, was clearly inhabited. As they drew nearer, he could see smoke trails from tens of thousands of cook fires and hearths lazily drifting upward, joining the haze that clung just above the city like a dirty raincloud.

Cyln'phax gently banked to the right. Kordem began making a turn at the same time. It was clear both dragons were adjusting their course away from the city so they would not have to fly over it, but instead around it. After their leisurely turn, the dragons straightened out, with the city now squarely on their left. Cyln'phax craned her neck slightly to gaze upon the city, then returned her attention to the front.

Karus imagined that those below looking up would have no difficulty spotting the two dragons making their way slowly across the sky. What would they think? Were dragons common in these parts? Or would they gaze up in fear, or perhaps even wonder? Karus thought back to his own feelings at sighting the dragons for the first time. It had been a mixture of wonder, shock, fear, and deep concern.

He continued to study the city as they came nearer and began to pass it by. Neatly cultivated fields crowded in upon the city and spread outward. Single family farms dotted the landscape in a random manner. Karus could not see any indication of large-scale plantations with their telltale housing blocks for slaves or hired workers. Many of the fields were brown with wheat and, by their color, were near ready to harvest. Others were green with some other sort of crop. They were too high up and far away for Karus to tell what was being grown in these fields. It could be anything from beans to cabbage or more than a dozen other crops, some of which there was a good chance he'd never seen before.

A series of dirt roads expanded outward from the city's walls, working their way through the intricate network of fields and traveling off into the distance. Karus saw several wagons crawling along the roads, either toward or away from the city. They seemed to move at a snail's pace, painfully slow.

A blue river glittered with reflected sunlight, at times flashing brilliantly. The river snaked its way around the far side of the city and then away off into the distance. Karus could see a number of large boats navigating its waters, their gray sails a contrast against the blue.

He continued to soak in the city. Next to Carthum, this was only the second city he'd seen on this world and the first he'd ever seen by dragonback in daylight. They were too high up and far off to make out very many details of the individual buildings, but he found it fascinating to see the city from above. He spotted what he thought was a palace and perhaps a handful of temples atop one of the larger hills.

The temples had large white marble columns that reminded him of those he'd seen in Rome. On another hill, there was a solid-looking, square-shaped stone fortress, with walls and a central keep. It appeared as if the stone of the keep had been painted a dark, dull red, giving the fortress an ominous look. Beyond that, the rest of the city had a jumbled appearance to it, as if the other buildings had been built on top of each other by a mad builder.

That is Lyre, Cyln'phax said as she glanced back at him with a single eye. *It is an enemy-held city.*

"Really?" Karus called back, surprised. He could see no damage or breached walls. He would have expected the Horde to destroy all in their path. The High Father had shown him the enemy overrunning cities and entire worlds, spreading destruction wherever they went. Neatly cultivated fields and an intact city were certainly not what he had expected from the masses of savage orcs working their way across the face of this world.

The Horde took these lands nearly a decade ago, Cyln'phax continued, in a tone that seemed filled with regret. *Lyre was once a beacon of learning, with a great library known as the Well of Wisdom, or just the Well for short. It was a beautiful place, devoted to the accumulation and spreading of knowledge. Sadly, the library was destroyed by the enemy.* Karus sensed a heavy mental sigh from the dragon, followed by a touch of bitterness. *The library's guardians saved what they could...*

"But much could not be saved?" Karus finished the thought, sympathizing with the dragon. Karus was one who enjoyed good books, especially those that dealt with history. His own meager collection, which had taken years at great personal expense to accumulate, was lost to him, left behind in Britannia.

Correct. Much that was irreplaceable was lost forever.

Cyln'phax let out a huff of breath, which Karus took to be a sigh. A tongue of flame curled outward from the dragon's nostrils. Karus felt a puff of heated air on his face for a moment, then the cold returned.

It was a tragic day when the library was brought down, Cyln'phax said. *The books and scrolls that could not be moved were burned.*

Karus shook his head at the dragon's words. He found it hard to believe the lands below were held by the enemy, let alone that a great library had once stood within that city. He would have loved to have seen it. The dragon's words reminded Karus of the great library at Alexandria. Though he understood the fabled library was reputedly not what it once had been, he still had long wanted to see the famed store of knowledge. Upon his retirement, Karus had intended to travel to the library. He felt another wash of sadness. He forced it aside, for it was best not to dwell on things that couldn't be changed. Karus returned his attention to the city.

Lyre and the lands around it looked peaceful enough, almost serene. They were too high up to make out much detail, other than groups of animals in the surrounding fields that appeared more antlike than anything else. Karus thought they were perhaps the shaggy teska, but was far from certain. He rubbed his jaw as he considered the dragon's words. Something about them bothered him.

"You read?" Karus shouted back at the dragon as it hit him. Cyln'phax was pining away at the lost knowledge of the library. It meant the creature most probably was capable of reading. It was the only explanation, and one he would never have guessed at in his wildest imaginations. He wondered for a moment how the dragon had learned to read. Or, for that matter, how such a large creature could manage it. The dragon's claws could not possibly hold a scroll or book, let alone opening one without damaging it.

You ignorant savage. Cyln'phax's condescending tone changed to one of hostility. *Of course I read. Don't you?*

Karus was about to reply when movement caught his attention, and he squinted to better see. Just outside of the city walls, his eyes were drawn to what appeared to be insects taking to the air, one after another, six in total. Karus knew that couldn't be right. Bugs would be too small to be seen at this distance. They weren't birds, either. Karus sucked in a startled breath as an icy sensation slithered down his spine.

"Are those dragons?" Karus shouted above the wind that was buffeting his face and rushing through his helmet. He wasn't sure he'd been heard, for there was no immediate reaction from Cyln'phax, so he shouted even louder. "Are those dragons down there off to our left? Do you see them? They appear to have just taken off."

Cyln'phax turned her long neck slightly and tilted her head to the side as she gazed down toward the city. Karus felt the massive creature beneath him stiffen in what he took to be surprise, perhaps even shock. It lasted but a heartbeat. She then began beating at the air with her powerful wings. Kordem was doing the same. The two dragons angled upward toward the clouds above. Beating at the air in an accelerated rhythm, they began picking up speed as they climbed higher into the sky.

Karus understood there was something wrong.

Those aren't dragons, Cyln'phax said after a moment as she gazed back down toward the city. Disgust laced her tone. *They are wyrms.*

Wondering what a wyrm was, Karus decided that whatever the creatures were, they were enough to alarm the dragons and therefore should be considered a deadly threat. The dragons had said that traveling over enemy lands would be dangerous. He looked back toward the wyrms, trying to make out what they were. Was this the danger the dragons had warned about?

"They are with the enemy?" Karus shouted back. "Is that right?"

Yes, Cyln'phax confirmed, a grim hardness to her tone that alarmed Karus even more. *We will try to lose them in the clouds. However, that could prove difficult. Wyrms are known to be tenacious and unrelenting hunters. Should it become impossible to shake them, we will set you down. If we do so, you must get off as quick as you can so that we can fight them. Do you understand me? Kordem has told Amarra the same thing. You have to get off as quickly as possible. Tell me you understand.*

"I do," Karus said, becoming seriously worried. "Do you stand a chance against them? Six against two?"

Not good odds, Cyln'phax agreed and titled her head slightly to keep an eye upon the enemy. *Still, they risk much coming after us.*

Karus looked back down toward the approaching wyrms. They had closed the distance with surprising speed.

The wyrms appeared quite fast. As the enemy grew nearer, Karus was able to make out their features. Squinting, he felt they looked very much to him like dragons.

The wyrms were not brightly colored, like Kordem or Cyln'phax, but black as midnight. Other than skin color, and being perhaps slightly smaller, he did not understand the difference between the creature he was riding and the enemy rapidly approaching from below. He was about to ask when Kordem screamed in his head.

Noctalum!

There came a deafening roar that shattered the air. It seemed filled with an impossible mind-crushing rage and came from above. It was close, too close for comfort. Karus's gaze snapped upward toward the puffy white clouds a handful of yards away that they were headed into. A massive gray shape emerged from the nearest of the clouds, almost on top of them.

Cyln'phax twisted and rolled violently to the right, banking away. Karus was grateful that he was tied down, for he suddenly found himself upside down and looking straight down at the ground as Cyln'phax twisted again and then rolled completely over. A heartbeat later, Karus found himself right side up again, with Cyln'phax pumping madly at the air for all she was worth. He could sense and almost feel the desperation of the dragon as she worked to get away from whatever it was that had emerged out of the cloud.

The gray shape flashed by them, so close that Karus could feel its passage as a momentary disruption in the blast of air against his face. It was gone from view as quickly as it had appeared. He was about to turn to look when another terrible cry of rage cut over the rushing wind whistling through his helmet. A second massive gray shape emerged from the clouds just off to their left, less than thirty yards away. Before Karus could get a good look at what it was, Cyln'phax tucked her wings in, aimed her head downward, and dove for the ground.

They dropped like a hefty rock tossed off a cliff. Karus held on for dear life, a white-knuckled grip on the nearest spike as they plunged downward out of the heavens. His stomach rose up into his chest as the feeling and terror of falling fully grabbed hold. It intensified, for he saw the ground rushing up to greet him, getting closer and closer by the moment. They were traveling so fast, the wind stung his face. It took all of his effort to keep from crying out. Had he not been gritting his teeth, he might have screamed in terror.

Karus thought of Amarra. Was she okay? With some effort, he tore his gaze from the ground that was rushing up with shocking rapidity and looked around. It took him a moment to locate the other dragon, but he finally spotted Kordem just behind them and slightly above. Kordem was diving for the ground as well.

There was a brilliant flash of light, almost like lightning. It was followed instantly by a powerful thunderclap that set his ears ringing. Karus felt a funny tingling run over his body that made his hair stand on end.

Cyln'phax violently twisted again in midair, as if desperately dodging some sort of attack. He turned back to his front. The ground was impossibly close. They were diving straight for one of the neatly cultivated fields. It loomed large before them. They plunged closer and closer.

Just when he thought they would hit, Cyln'phax spread her wings and leveled out. Karus grunted as he was violently pressed down against the dragon's back. For several heartbeats it felt as if he weighed as much as a horse, or perhaps even a supply wagon with a full load. The pressure rapidly eased and then passed.

The ground flashed by in a dizzying blur. They were moving at a frightful speed, skimming along a mere twenty feet above the field. They passed over a stone row fence and then another field full of brown wheat. Ahead was pasture surrounded by a wooden fence, this one full of cow-like creatures that began to run in all directions, madly fleeing the dragon. Then they were over and by the pasture. A farm with an overly large barn flashed by next, the dragon angling her wings and turning almost sideways to avoid hitting it. Once past, she straightened out.

Karus saw humans working a field. They dove for cover as the dragon passed them by. Ahead was a large hill, and Cyln'phax skimmed up and over it, flashing by another cultivated field on the far side. Karus had a fleeting glimpse of people below, frozen in the act of working the field, looking up in shock and amazement.

He turned and looked up behind them, scanning the sky. Shockingly, the wyrms had scattered and appeared to be flying away as fast as they could, fleeing, just as Cyln'phax and Kordem were doing. One of the wyrms was falling out of the sky, limp as could be, and twisting in a spiral as it dropped from the heavens. The two gray shapes turned out to be dragons as well, and massive ones at that. They were easily twice the size of Kordem and Cyln'phax. The wyrms looked puny by comparison.

The two grays were magnificent, fearsome, and dreadful to behold. Karus felt a stab of fear gnaw at him as he took them in. He watched in horrified fascination as one of the massive grays caught a fleeing wyrm. The dragon, just above, reached out and grabbed the smaller wyrm with its claws. At the moment of contact, the wyrm twisted around and the two creatures locked in a death grip, ripping at each other with their claws and teeth. They twisted, seeming to almost wrestle in midair, tumbling and falling toward the ground. The struggle was a terrible thing to behold. The two dragons continued to rip and tear at one another as they fell out of the sky. The wyrm blew a jet of fire upon the gray and then screamed before biting the larger dragon along the neck.

There was a brilliant flash of light that seemed to emanate from the gray dragon. Karus blinked, momentarily blinded. When his vision cleared a heartbeat later, he saw the wyrm was limp in the larger dragon's grip.

The gray released the wyrm, unfurled its wings, and began correcting its uncontrolled tumble for the ground. Once it had righted itself, the dragon began flapping at the air, slowing its descent. A moment later, the limp wyrm slammed into the ground with frightful force, kicking up a shower of dirt and crops. Over the rush of the air, Karus could clearly hear the deep thump of the wyrm's impact.

The dragon hovered over the wyrm's body a few moments, flapping its wings in steady, measured beats. It arched its head and breathed a long jet of reddish fire over the body as if to make sure the wyrm was finished. When the stream ceased, the dragon let loose a roar of what seemed like satisfaction. Then, it began slowly climbing its way back up into the air, moving after another of the wyrms that was now some distance off and closely pursued by the other massive gray dragon.

Karus shook his head in amazement, not quite sure he believed what he had just witnessed. At that moment, another roar of pure animal-like rage sounded from above. He looked up and spotted two more large gray dragons as they emerged from the clouds, diving downward and traveling at great speed. Would they turn and come after Kordem and Cyln'phax? Karus desperately hoped not.

Cyln'phax and Kordem were not taking any chances. They had not slowed their flight. They continued onward and away, flying just as fast as they could. A large tree-topped hill rose up before them. Cyln'phax turned slightly, wings extended, and coasted around the hill. The tops of the trees flashed by bare inches beneath them, leaves and limbs disturbed by their passage.

We are lucky today, for they hunt the wyrms and not us, Kordem said with evident relief.

Very lucky, Cyln'phax agreed and turned her head to look behind, eyes searching the sky.

"The wyrms are of the Horde," Karus shouted over the powerful rush of the wind. "Those dragons were attacking the wyrms. They fight the Horde, like we do, do I have that right?"

The noctalum no longer take sides, Cyln'phax said. *They are best avoided, for they are dread creatures from the age of creation. All with any bit of sanity or sense should fear and avoid them.*

Noctalum are unpredictable at best, Kordem added. *We are most unlucky a few of their kind are trapped upon this world. They make our struggle that much more difficult, for their objectives are unknown to us and sometimes they interfere.*

"But they are dragons, like you," Karus said, not understanding the difference.

We are only distantly related to the noctalum, Cyln'phax said. *You could consider them cousins, but nothing more. They are certainly not to be counted as family, nor in any way trusted.*

We are of the taltalum, Kordem added, as if that explained things. *The noctalum view us as little better than the wyrms, the araltalum. That is likely why they went after the wyrms instead of us. They hate them more.*

Both dragons began climbing back up into the sky once again, gaining altitude. The danger seemed past, and they slowed their speed a hair. Karus could feel Cyln'phax's lungs filling and expelling air beneath him at a rapid, labored pace, like a runner out of breath.

"I don't understand," Karus said.

You don't need to, Cyln'phax said. *I grow weary of making words with you, human.*

Karus felt his anger surge once again, but kept a tight leash on it. He glanced behind them, searching the sky. It was clear. The city was lost from view, now far behind them, as were the wyrms and the noctalum. Below were rolling hills, interspersed with small farms and pastures filled with herd animals. Ahead in the distance was another vast forest, a dark green smudge of a line that appeared to take up the entire horizon. Karus found his heart was racing, hammering away. Their brush with death had seemed a close thing. Had the wyrms not been there, would the noctalum have come after them? Karus suspected they would have.

He took a deep breath and closed his eyes. Karus let the breath out long and slow, working to steady his heart. Then he opened his eyes and looked downward. The farmland below looked idyllic and peaceful. Karus now knew it was deceptive. There was danger about.

These are conquered lands, Kordem said, almost as if the dragon could read his thoughts. Karus glanced over and saw the dragon to their side looking his way. So, too, was Amarra. She was gripping the spike to her front tightly, her eyes wide as she looked back at him. The dragon's tone turned to one of disgust. Karus got the sense Amarra could hear what was being said as well. *The peoples living below gave in to the Horde. They, like the people of Lyre, chose not to resist and are now no better than slaves, feeding and supporting our enemy's war effort.*

Karus gazed downward with fresh eyes. If these were the conquered lands ... where were the enemy's armies?

CHAPTER SEVEN

*R*eady yourself, human.

Karus's eyes snapped open. He had been dozing. Blinking, he glanced around. It was just after sunset. The last of the two suns had slipped beneath the horizon, yet the final rays of the day's sunlight were on the clouds high above them. The dying light gave the clouds a brilliant fiery hue.

Cyln'phax banked to the right, angling slightly downward. *We will be landing shortly at Irin'Surall. This is the seat of the warden's power.* The dragon paused a moment. *Our reception is likely to be far from friendly.*

The land below was already dark and heavily shadowed. When he had dozed off, they had been flying over a large forest. The forest still spread outward in all directions, for as far as the eye could see.

The dragon began descending faster. Karus's stomach tightened with the uncomfortable sensation of falling. The wind buffeting him intensified as the dragon picked up speed. He glanced behind them and saw Kordem was following close on Cyln'phax's tail. Amarra, wrapped in his cloak, was gripping one of the dragon's spikes.

Karus turned back and gazed down at the forest. He made out some lights amongst the trees and what appeared to be a large clearing ahead. Cyln'phax folded her wings back a little more and picked up even greater speed, while dumping altitude at an alarming rate. As they closed on the clearing, the dragon tucked her wings in closer to her body. Karus leaned back as far as the straps holding him in would allow as the dragon dove at a steeper angle for the clearing. There were more lights below them now. The lights winked and flickered through the leafy canopy around the clearing.

There was a city amongst the trees. He was surprised, for it was very deep into the forest, with no cultivated fields anywhere within view. He peered closer and discovered the city was up in the trees themselves, which were giants, like those the legion had been greeted with when first brought to this world.

In a flash, Karus saw lots of buildings. They were slim, graceful, yet alien in appearance. There was what looked like a complex network of bridges suspended between trees. This he caught in a moment, as they hurtled downward and into the clearing.

Cyln'phax flared out her wings, giving powerful slowing flaps as she came in for a landing. Karus was pushed down against the dragon's back as she worked to check her forward momentum. The landing that followed was rapid and rough. Then Karus was thrown forward against the straps holding him in place. Cyln'phax reared backward, throwing her head up. The dragon took a couple of steps before she came to a halt.

Cyln'phax gave forth a deafening roar and blew a jet of flame almost straight up into the air. Karus could feel the intense heat from the blast on his face and exposed skin. Then she came down on her front two feet, claws digging into the ground. The trees around the clearing trembled, branches rustling and creaking. The nearest bridges swayed.

Get off, Cyln'phax said urgently. *I have announced ourselves. Do it quick, before the elves can organize themselves. Get off, now! I need to be free of you should it come to a fight!*

Fingers half numb with cold, he scrambled to untie himself. Kordem landed a few feet away. Karus got the first knot untied and began working on the second. An indistinct shout came from beyond the clearing, out in the darkness of the forest. It was followed by the blast of a horn, which spurred his efforts onward.

Cursing, Karus managed to get the last knot untied. He hurriedly climbed off the dragon's back, jumping the last few feet to the ground, where his hobnailed sandals landed with a loud clap of metal on stone. He took several steps away from Cyln'phax as the dragon unfurled her wings and gave a flap, which generated almost enough wind to bowl him over.

He looked around for Amarra and spotted her climbing down from Kordem's back. Clutched in her hand was the crystal staff, which, in the growing darkness, glowed a brilliant blue. It seemed to throb with power. Once she was off and clear, Kordem reared back and stood straight up, flapping his wings mightily. He gave a roar and then blew a blast of fire into the night sky as Cyln'phax had done a few moments before.

Hear me, elves, Kordem said. *We come here not to fight. Instead, we bring holy representatives of the High Father who have need to make words with Elantric Warden.*

Kordem fell back forward, landing on his front two feet. It caused the ground beneath Karus's sandals to shake.

Your cowering within these trees is detestable to us, Cyln'phax added, her tone dripping with loathing. *By not standing up to the Horde, you do no better than aid our enemy.*

Karus glanced around and his mouth fell open as he realized this was no simple forest clearing. It was instead a city square built on the forest floor. Carved granite paving stones were underfoot. Thin lines of trimmed grass separated each stone. Intricate geometric patterns had been carved onto the surfaces of the paving stones.

You should fight with us, Cyln'phax continued. *There is no honor in standing apart.*

Karus sucked in a breath as he gazed about, gawking at the city that surrounded them. It was amazing, incredible, and that didn't even come close to describing what he saw. He shook his head in utter wonder. Just when he thought this world could surprise him no more, it did.

His eyes were drawn to the giant trees that surrounded the square. Windows had been cut into the massive trunks, from which yellowed light spilled outward. The buildings he had spotted from above had been erected amongst the branches in the canopy. They were wooden structures that had been constructed along the limbs of many of the trees, seeming to have sprung outward from the trunks themselves. It was an impressive engineering achievement.

He squinted up at the buildings, wondering just how the builders had managed to pull it off. Some of the structures were even two or three stories in height from the base level. The structures weren't square or box-like, such as Karus was familiar with. They had rounded edges that gave many of them an oblong or curved look, unnatural, at least to Karus's eyes. Or perhaps it was that the buildings appeared too natural, almost one with the tree. If Karus had not known better, he would have said the buildings had grown out of the trees themselves. But that was not possible. He decided those who had built this city must be master artisans, impressively skilled at their craft.

His eyes went to one of the bridges suspended between trees in the canopy. He saw people lining the railing looking down upon them. They were so high up that, in the gloom, he could only make out their outlines. The bridge had a simple railing, but for the life of him, Karus could not see how it was supported. Lanterns attached to the railings emitted a pale and somewhat dim white light. Karus wondered if they were magical, like the lanterns in Carthum.

Cyln'phax gave another roar. Karus jumped, the moment of awe shattered. A gout of flame arced up into the sky. He glanced back at the dragon, snapping back to the reality of the moment. They were facing the potential for a fight. He scanned about, searching for threats.

There was a large fountain directly in the center of the square. It captured and held Karus's gaze a moment. Two exquisitely carved marble statues, a man and woman holding hands, were standing in the center of the fountain. It had been designed to appear as if they were walking on the surface of the water. The fountain shot streams of water up into the air around the two figures. The streams fell back down into the pool. The statues were not what had seized his attention. It was the water, for it glowed with an unearthly white light.

Cyln'phax flexed one of her claws, cracking and ripping up the stone paving behind him. Karus pulled his gaze from the fountain and continued scanning about them. He noticed for the first time that scattered throughout the square were a dozen or so people. They had fallen back and away from the two dragons, moving closer to the trees.

From amongst the base of the trees, Karus got the sense there were more people there, hidden by the growing darkness. Those he could see pointed and gesticulated amongst themselves at the two dragons. He realized that their arrival had taken these people by surprise, which was what the dragons had likely intended. Karus could see no weapons amongst them. The people in the square appeared to be civilians, yet the dragons were ready for action. Karus wondered what dire danger lay out in the darkness amongst the trees.

He stole a glance over at Amarra, who appeared just as amazed by their surroundings. Clearly, like him, she'd never seen anything like it. Karus's gaze flicked around the square again. He had not noticed before, but a man wearing a long brown robe stood just ten yards away, by the side of the fountain. He was still and as unmoving as the statues themselves.

Karus began moving toward him, making certain to keep his hands in view and away from his sword. The man held his ground as Karus neared. The man stood with his back to the fountain, and in the growing darkness, Karus could not clearly see his face.

Cyln'phax shot another gout of flame high up into the air. In that moment, Karus almost missed a step. He recalled the dragon's word ... *elves.*

This was no man.

He appeared human enough, but wasn't. He was tall, almost whipcord thin. In the light of the flame, Karus could see that his face had an unnatural look and cast to it, almost olive-like. It was somehow wrong to Karus's mind, the shape too symmetrical, too perfect. There were no blemishes, nor the hint of stubble. The eyes were more rounded than they should have been.

The elf appeared very young, though, by his bearing, that somehow did not seem quite right. Karus wasn't sure how, but he sensed tremendous dignity and age within the eyes. The elf's black hair was pulled back into a single long braid. Two delicate ears had been exposed, long and pointed, most definitely not human.

Karus came to a stop some five feet from the other, more from surprise than anything else. The dragons had named the people who lived here elves. They were yet another strange race that inhabited this world, like the orcs and dwarves. How many more races were there? Karus realized that the elves must be the warden's people. The fire from the dragon's blast died out and darkness returned.

Curious, Karus moved toward the fountain, making his way around the elf, being exceptionally careful to keep his distance. A row of metal buttons ran down the front of the elf's robes, which trailed on the ground and concealed his feet. Though the elf carried no visible weapon, Karus understood that did not mean he wasn't dangerous. He was, however, carrying a book, which he held by his right hand to his chest. The elf's eyes glittered as they followed Karus.

The falling streams of water from the fountain tinkled with a sound that was pleasant to the ear. Karus glanced down into the fountain's pool. The bottom of the fountain was lined with sand and rounded river rocks that had been arranged neatly. There was no visible light source. The light seemed to be coming directly from the water. What made it glow? Was the water magic? There was so much to this world he just did not understand, and that made him uncomfortable.

Karus returned his gaze to the elf. Their eyes met. He found the other's gaze downright unfriendly. The elf remained nearly motionless as Karus looked him over. He did not exhibit any fear or concern. He simply stood there, holding his ground and gazing back on Karus.

"I do not seek a fight," Karus said in Latin. "We come only to talk."

He was rewarded with an unhappy scowl. Karus realized what an idiot he had been for speaking Latin.

"I want no fight," Karus said, switching to his accented Common. He tapped his chest armor, deciding to keep it simple. "No fight. Talk only, understand?"

The other continued to stare at him and then shook his head in a slow, somewhat sad manner. Despite that, Karus felt that he had been understood. He suspected the shake of the head was meant to communicate something else. With a sinking feeling, Karus knew that by coming here to this place they had essentially invited a fight. Was this sacred ground? He glanced back at the dragons. Had they known? Surely they had.

He looked for Amarra, hoping she could help, and spotted her making her way across the square toward him. She held her staff in her right hand, the bottom clicking on the paving stones with each and every step. Oddly, her staff no longer emitted any light. It had gone dark and cold, as if the blue fire within had been completely extinguished. She, however, looked bold and unafraid as she approached. Karus turned back to the elf.

"I am Karus." He touched his chest and then pointed at the elf.

"You are not welcome here," the elf said quietly in Common. The tone had a soft singsong quality to it that was alien to Karus's ears. "This is our place, not yours. Go now before you can't."

"We do not want trouble," Karus said.

"You have found it," the elf said. It wasn't a threat, but an assertion of certainty.

There was a loud crack. Where a moment before there had been one now stood a second elf. Karus jumped, startled. Dressed in long midnight-black robes, this elf had appeared out of thin air. He carried a polished wooden staff, black runes running up its length. It was topped by a crystal that throbbed with a pale blue light. A gold necklace with an amulet reached down the newcomer's chest, almost to his midriff. The amulet's center held a small hourglass that emitted a faint glow. The elf's long brown hair, perfectly brushed, cascaded down around his shoulders. He had a hard, unforgiving face, with cold eyes that settled on Karus.

"No fight," Karus said in Common, hand on his sword hilt. It took all of his self-restraint to keep from drawing it, for he felt pure menace from this newcomer. "No fight. We come to talk."

"You come here," the newcomer said as quietly as the other elf, "you invite your own suffering and death."

Karus had had enough. He drew his sword, just as Amarra joined him. She stepped up beside him. Making sure not to take his eyes off the two elves, he held out a protective arm and attempted to push her behind him, for he feared something bad was about to happen. He wanted her out of the way. She forced his arm away and took her place squarely at his side, a reproachful look in her eye as she glanced at him.

The elf with the staff spared her a quick look, then stretched forth a slender hand toward Karus. His fingers flashed with orange light and something akin to liquid fire shot forth in a long, thin stream. It happened so fast and unexpectedly that Karus couldn't help but blink in astonishment.

Amarra's staff flared brilliantly in the darkness, lighting up the entire square. A transparent blue sphere appeared around the two of them. There was a solid *crack* as the liquid fire impacted the sphere. It ricocheted off and away into the darkness.

Both elves took a step backward at that. The transparent sphere slowly faded away. Darkness returned to the square. Karus glanced over at Amarra, who appeared as shocked as the elf who had launched the attack.

"We come to speak with the warden," Amarra said in Common, having rapidly regained her composure. "I am Amarra, High Priestess of the High Father. We do not seek a fight."

The elf's eyes narrowed dangerously as he regarded her.

"Oh, just bloody great," Karus said in Latin to the elf as he realized there would be no avoiding a fight. "You stupid cuss. You're gonna make me kill you, aren't you?"

The elf's eyes moved back to Karus.

"No," Amarra said firmly in Common. "We come not to kill, but for their help."

The ground shook as Cyln'phax moved up closer behind them.

The wizard's eyes travel to the dragon and Karus read uncertainty within them, which he felt was a damn fine sign. There was a chance it would not come to an all-out fight.

Wizard, Cyln'phax said, tone dripping with a surprising level of menace, *you will not again assault the revered daughter and son of the High Father.*

The dragon took another step and the ground shook. From the darkness, Karus heard the telltale twang of a bow. Before he could react, the transparent sphere reappeared just as a brown-fletched arrow impacted it directly to the front of his chest, a foot from him. The arrow hung in mid-air a moment, as if held by an unseen hand. A heartbeat later it exploded into flame, flaring brilliantly as it burned up. The sphere disappeared once again. The ash, all that remained from the arrow shaft, rained downward. The metal arrowhead clinked down on the stone at their feet.

Above him, the dragon's head swung in the direction the arrow had come from. She opened her mouth, jaws parting. A ball of fire shot out into the darkness. Karus ducked as the fireball roared over his head. He saw a figure with a bow a few yards off dodging to the side and rolling away to safety as the dragon fire exploded in a tremendous blast where he had just been.

"Cyln'phax, stop," Amarra snapped.

As you wish, revered daughter.

There was resentment in the dragon's tone at having been checked at meting out what she apparently thought well-deserved punishment. The dragon eyed the elf who had fired the bow with a baleful eye as he picked himself up.

Karus returned his attention to the two elves. Neither had moved, but their eyes were upon the dragon. It was then that he noticed the transparent sphere protecting them had returned. Several more arrows were suspended in midair. They were burning themselves up, one after another. A heartbeat later, the sphere disappeared and the ash cascaded downward, as did the metal arrow tips.

"Did you do that?" Karus asked in Latin to Amarra.

"Yes," Amarra said back to him and then hesitated. "At first, I know not how. It come to me, sudden-like. I think High Father show me. Still, magic from wizard surprised when it come."

Karus sucked in an uneasy breath and glanced over at her. She turned her gaze back upon the elves. The wizard was studying them curiously now. The hostility had gone, vanished as if it had never been.

Karus knew he had to try again. He switched back to Common. "We come to speak, not fight."

Wizard, Cyln'phax said, *you would do well to listen. For if you or your people attempt to harm the revered daughter again,*

I promise you we shall lose our patience. Doubt not, our will *is greater than yours and we've been saving it for quite some time.*

The wizard's gaze slid from Karus and Amarra to the dragon, then back. He turned in a swirling of robes and shouted something out into the darkness. Karus hoped it was an order to stand down. The wizard turned back to them and let out a weary breath that was part sigh.

"The High Father looks not upon these forsaken lands," the wizard said in perfect Latin. Karus blinked in surprise. "He has long since turned from us. No longer do my people honor the gods as they once did. You waste your time here, priestess. The gods do not deserve our worship." The wizard tapped his staff upon the ground and waved his free hand at them in a dismissive manner. "Leave now, while you can. You have no place here, nor are you welcome."

"How do you know Latin?" Karus asked.

"I do not speak your language, human," the wizard said. "You hear my words and your language because of my *will*, what your pathetic kind calls magic."

The day had been harrowing enough with their escape from the noctalum and wyrms, not to mention the long flight just to get here. He had left his legion behind, something he had been loath to do in the first place. Karus was tired and frustrated, with a mounting anger that was fast becoming a full-blown rage. The world he had known was gone. He was in a strange land with fantastic creatures and beasts that just weeks ago he would never have conceived possible. He was done with being spoken down to and disrespected, whether it was from the smug dragons or these elves.

"My name is Lucius Grackus Lisidius Karus. By the gods, I am a Roman citizen. I command the Imperial Ninth Legion, Hispana. You shall accord me respect. You may call me Karus or Camp Prefect. You will not call me human, ever again."

The wizard studied Karus for a long moment in an unblinking gaze. He waved his staff in the air, the crystal on top flashing brightly once before rapidly fading back to a sullen blue.

"You are not of this world," the wizard said, his grip tightening upon his staff. "Both Gates are in the hands of the Horde. Were you of the Horde, I would know it. Tell me, Karus. How is it you came to be here?"

"Jupiter's hand brought my legion to these lands," Karus said, forcing himself to calm down a little. "We have a job to do and part of that is why we have come here."

"Jupiter?" The wizard rolled the name over his tongue and cocked his head to the side in an angle that no human could ever match. His eyes slid over to Amarra and then to her crystal staff, which had resumed its throbbing glow. He appeared to consider it for the first time.

"We call him the High Father," Amarra said in her own language, and Karus understood her perfectly, as if she had spoken fluent Latin her entire life. "He is our god. He delivered Karus and his warriors. Together we are here to save all who desire it. Though your people have turned away from the gods, it is not too late. The gates of salvation are open to all who wish to enter."

"We do not require saving," the other elf said with a nasty sneer. "The Horde dares not come unto our lands. They have tried. Each time they have paid a heavy price. The warden and our rangers are too strong for them."

You elves can cower all you want, Kordem said. *When the Horde finishes with the rest of us, they will come for you and your people. They will root you out of your precious forests, warden ... no warden. Your rangers will fall one by one until you have none left.*

You know this to be true. It has happened before and it will happen again. Do not pretend to act otherwise.

The elves regarded the dragon for a silent moment.

"You come to enlist our aid, is that it?" the wizard said. "Others have tried. We stand apart."

"We come to speak with the Elantric Warden," Amarra said. "Enlisting your aid as an ally is a discussion for another time."

"You want Rarokan," the wizard said, his fingers idly tapping the shaft of his staff where he gripped it. "You want to take the dread sword from our keeping?"

"I do," Karus said.

"Long ago, when the weapon was entrusted into our care, such a coming was foretold," the wizard said, eyes squarely upon Karus. "Many have believed that they were the ones portended. If you are not the one it was meant for, all that awaits you, like so many countless others, is a soulless death."

"The High Father sent me to retrieve the weapon," Karus said, not liking the wizard's words. "We were led to believe it can help our cause."

"If you are lucky, it will decide to help you. If not…" The wizard trailed off, and then abruptly turned to the other elf and said something quietly in his own language. The elf bowed gracefully to the wizard and stepped away, moving off into the darkness.

"We shall see if the Elantric Warden will agree to speak with you," the wizard said. "You will remain here. If you leave the confines of this square, you shall be killed." The wizard's eyes shifted from Karus and Amarra to the two dragons. "All of you, no matter how strong you feel your *will* to be."

It is not wise to threaten us, elf, Cyln'phax growled. A small jet of flame escaped her mouth.

"You would do wise not to test us, taltalum." The wizard tapped his staff upon the stone paving. There was a flash of light, followed by a loud crack, and he was gone, as if he'd never been. Wispy tendrils of smoke rose from where he had been standing.

That went better than I expected, Cyln'phax said, sounding satisfied with herself. *I thought we would have to kill a few of them, just to get their attention. I concede it is possible in the long years since we've dealt with their kind, the elves may have finally developed some common sense.*

Our arrival certainly got their attention, Kordem said with amusement. Karus could almost hear the dragon chuckle in his mind.

The elves have always acted as if they were the superior race, Cyln'phax said. *It's been a long time coming, but they needed to be put in their place.*

Both dragons bubbled over with amusement. Karus looked up at the red dragon, thoroughly disgusted.

"We have to work on your communication skills," Karus said. "It would've been nice to know in advance what you were flying us into."

Now where would the fun be in that? Cyln'phax said, laughing in Karus's mind. A jet of steam escaped from her snout. It came out almost as a snort. *You should have seen your face.*

Kordem joined in the laughter.

Feeling frustrated and helpless, Karus glanced over at Amarra. Her face hardened. She turned to the dragons and spoke rapidly in her own language, her voice trembling. Her speech was so fast he could not understand much of it. Then it hit him. Without the wizard present and his power, he had lost the ability to fully understand her. Amarra smacked the butt of her staff hard on the paving stone.

The staff flashed brilliantly and the stone paving split in two with a solid snapping sound. Both dragons ceased their laughter. The sense of amusement drained away and they turned their gazes upon her. After a moment, they bowed their heads respectfully.

Forgive us, mistress, Kordem said. *It shall not happen again.*

"What did you say to them?" Karus asked.

"I say what you say," Amarra said, eyes flashing with heat as she gazed back at him. "But I angry. Real angry. I tell them this no game."

Both dragons appeared sheepish, looking away. Then Kordem lifted his head and gazed intently out into the darkness. Cyln'phax did the same, a growl-like sound coming from her. Karus turned around, scanning the square. From out of the gloom and darkness came a number of what Karus took to be warriors. They moved with a lithe grace that told Karus they knew what they were doing and were deadly competent. Each held a bow in one hand and a handful of arrows in the other. Karus counted thirty as they spread out around them in a loose ring.

These are the famous elven rangers, Cyln'phax said, no hint of the recent amusement in her tone. *They are respected masters of the forest, unconventional warriors of skill. Should the warden decline to speak with you, we will need to kill them.*

"I guess it's too much to hope that they would just let us leave?" Karus let out a heavy breath. He already knew the answer.

We desire to travel to the Fortress of Radiance and retrieve Rarokan, Cyln'phax said. *Without the warden's permission and blessing, we would have to do it by force, killing the elves who stand guard over the relic. She will know this and seek our deaths to keep us from ever making it to the fortress.*

"The Warriors of Anagradoom are elves?" Karus asked.

They are, Kordem confirmed. *The elves gave over the best of their warriors to the task of guarding Rarokan.*

"Why would the warden keep us from the sword?" Karus asked.

Why indeed? Kordem said. *Elves do not always think like the rest of us. If you believe we are frustrating, try working with an elf.*

Karus glanced around at the elven rangers. He rubbed his jaw as he considered them.

"Just when I thought things couldn't get any worse," Karus said quietly to himself.

Human, it can get a lot worse than this, Cyln'phax said.

Karus let out a long breath. There was no doubt in his mind that Cyln'phax was correct. He turned to Amarra.H

"Let's get the packs down," Karus said. "There's no telling how long we will be here. We should eat, while we have the chance."

She nodded and moved off toward Kordem. He watched her, hoping and praying that things would work out with the warden. Karus turned to Cyln'phax, ready to climb back up for the packs. All they could do now was wait.

CHAPTER EIGHT

Karus figured over an hour had passed. The moon bathed the square in a muted but pale light. The dragons had seemingly gone to sleep, as if the presence of the elven rangers bothered them not in the least. Karus stood there in the darkness with Amarra. They had eaten and were now just simply waiting. The rangers had not moved. However, they had lowered their bows, some even slinging them over their shoulders as they silently watched the intruders.

Karus had long since mastered the skill of waiting. The army was great at teaching a person how to properly wait for someone else to do their job. It had occurred to him more than once that he'd spent more time waiting and cooling his heels over the years than actually doing something. He was accustomed to waiting, usually patient as could be, but now he was becoming aggravated. Perhaps it was this strange elven city that surrounded them? Or maybe it was the threat of the rangers standing watch around them? Karus did not know, but somehow it seemed like things were slipping out of control. No, that wasn't true. He had already lost control. It was as if he were on a runaway cart, charging down a steep hill from which there was no return, the reins having slipped from his grasp.

He glanced over at Amarra. Under the soft moonlight, her snow-white dress made her appear almost as if she were one of the marble statues standing a few yards away in the fountain. She was a rock, with a core inner strength and faith he could well respect.

She knelt down on a paving stone and laid her staff to her side. She bowed her head and began praying, offering up a silent devotion to their god. The staff throbbed dully, as if it, too, were bored and tired of the waiting. Karus watched her for a time, saying nothing. She eventually finished and clambered back to her feet, picking the staff up. Her dress showed no sign of wear. There were no wrinkles and it was free of even the tiniest hint of dirt. Karus wondered again how she had managed that, for his armor badly needed attention. After their stop in the forest clearing, it was due for a good cleaning.

Amarra caught his look and broke the long silence that had grown between them. "The warden will see us." She seemed calm, thoroughly collected, as if her devotion had given her peace. She touched her chest. "The High Father means us to be here. I feel it."

"The elves don't want us to be here." Karus glanced over at the nearest of the rangers. He wondered if they were impatient as well. "That much is apparent."

"Elves need us. High Father sends us to show them need. I feel truth."

Karus regarded her a long moment. He wondered how she could be so sure about the elves. She seemed certain. He supposed it boiled down to faith. Just a few weeks prior, he would have had his doubts. That had been before being personally visited by the great god of Rome and set on a quest.

The High Father had given him his marching orders directly, and Karus intended to follow them as best he could. Amarra was the direct conduit to their god. She seemed to have some sort of a special connection to the High Father, to feel his intentions and wishes. It was something Karus was struggling to understand, but if she said it was so, then he accepted it as truth.

"Will the elves listen?" Karus asked.

Amarra let out an unhappy breath that was part frustrated grunt.

"I pray and hope they do," Amarra said and then looked about them. She pursed her lips. "Something not right here. Something is wrong."

"What do you mean?" Karus asked, looking around, alarmed. Nothing he could see had changed. The rangers were in the same positions they had been in moments before. There was no hint that they were preparing to attack or take any sort of action. The dragons were still seemingly asleep as well. "I don't see what's wrong."

"We are here to help," Amarra said. "Something is not right with elves. We need to fix."

"We came for the sword," Karus said, not quite understanding what she meant and reminding her of their goal. "That is all. We get it and go as quick as we can."

"That too," Amarra said, returning her gaze to him. "But we have, how you say … more to do?"

"What do you mean, more to do? You need to explain."

"Elves are, uh … hard neck?" Amarra asked. "That right words?"

"You mean stiff-necked?" Karus asked, to which she nodded. "They certainly seem more than a little difficult."

"Yes," Amarra said. She ran her hand slowly down the crystal shaft of the staff. The glow brightened around her fingers and trailed after where they had been. "We come for sword, but also I think to help. High Father tell me."

"He told you? You mean he spoke to you again?"

Amarra said nothing as she gazed at the nearest ranger.

"They may not want our help," Karus said. "Have you considered that?"

"I have."

"How can we help them? Getting them to join our cause? By the gods, we need allies, but they don't seem terribly open to that idea."

Amarra gave a slight shrug of her shoulders. "I not yet know how to help, to fix."

Karus rubbed at his jaw, feeling the growing stubble with the palm of his hand. Helping the elves or not, he understood that even with the dragons, they were in a precarious position. He suspected that, should it come to a fight, their chances were questionable at best. The wizard was no charlatan, plying cheap tricks and using sleight of hand for entertainment or coin. He had command of frightening powers Karus could not even hope to begin to comprehend.

Amarra's staff was clearly powerful. She had stopped one attack from the wizard. Karus suspected the wizard was capable of much more than he had shown. There was no telling what he was truly capable of when pressed. Would her staff prove enough to hold him off?

Karus doubted he would be able to adequately protect Amarra should things go balls up. That frightened him more than he cared to admit. He did not know how he could guard her against magic, other than attempting to stick the bastard with his sword.

"What else can your staff do?" Karus asked.

"High Father show me how to stop"—she gave a frustrated scowl—"how you say?"

Amarra made a flying motion with her hand. Using her index finger pointed straight outward, she sailed it through the air in an arc. She made a slight whistling noise for effect.

"Arrow?" Karus said and mimed shooting a small bow.

"Yes," Amarra said. "That it. Arrow. When I come to you by fountain, I feel High Father. He show me what to do to protect us. It more feeling than words. I do. It stay hidden until they shoot arrow." She paused and looked at the staff in her hand. The staff strobed briefly with increased light, almost as if it were following their conversation and was pleased it had helped. "That all I know of staff."

It had grown somewhat cool with the onset of night. Karus breathed in deeply. The air smelled strongly of trees, moss, decaying leaves, but also woodsmoke. He could smell something delicious wafting through the air. Someone out in the city was cooking a nightly meal. He turned his eyes up to the lights in the canopy. They twinkled back at him as a light wind stirred the leaves of the nearest trees. Karus wondered how many elves lived in this city.

"It seems the High Father was looking out for us," Karus said, letting the breath out.

"He is with us, always." Amarra stepped closer. She laid a palm upon his chest armor. "He speaks to me, not with words. I feel him here. Can you?"

Karus thought about that for a moment. He believed in the High Father, knew for certainty that the god was real. But he did not feel any presence, not like he had in the chapel under the ruined temple back in Carthum. He shook his head. "No, I don't think so."

"I feel him. You learn, too," Amarra said, removing her hand. "I show. It come with faith, yes?"

126

"I can try," Karus said, though he very much doubted he would ever have the same type of connection to the High Father that Amarra had.

"No," Amarra said. "You do. You not try."

Karus chuckled at the sudden force of her attitude. It was something that attracted him to her. She was determined, focused, and at times single-minded. Amarra was a woman who knew what she wanted and went for it.

"You no laugh," Amarra said. She slapped his chest armor with the same hand. "No laugh. You understand?"

He pulled her to him and gave her a kiss. At first, she resisted, then she gave in and kissed him back, her soft lips pressing passionately against his. He held her tight against him. Then, still in his arms, she looked up into his face.

"You need to know," Amarra said. "He tell me he not always be there, like he show me with stopping arrow."

"What do you mean?" Karus asked.

"I must learn to use staff on own," Amarra said. "Open secrets, find out what else it do. High Father made me know we must look to us to fix problems, not always to him."

"Why?" Karus asked, concerned. It almost sounded like the High Father was abandoning them, and just when they needed him the most. That alarmed him, for he was here in this elven city because the god had sent him after the sword Rarokan.

"Like children, we grow, yes? We must walk our own path in time. Understand?"

Karus considered her words. "So, we are on our own then? There will be no more help from the High Father? Is that it?"

"No," Amarra said. "High Father always with us, always. He give us what we need." She stepped back out of his embrace and shook the staff slightly. It flickered with each shake. "Is our turn now. We do things, as it meant to be."

"The shield that stopped the arrows," Karus said. He could not think of another word that would adequately describe the blue sphere. "The shield? Is it still up?"

Amarra shook her head. "I no waste High Father's power. He said not to, remember?"

"I do." Karus swung his gaze back to the elven rangers. He considered the closest for a long moment. "We have to help them, you say?"

"Yes."

"But we don't know what they need help doing?" Karus looked over at Amarra.

"No, we not know how help them," she confirmed.

He gave a nod, more to himself. He turned away from Amarra and started walking toward the nearest ranger, who was almost completely shrouded in darkness.

"Where go?" Amarra asked.

He paused and glanced back. "I want to speak with one of these rangers. If we have to fight, I would take their measure. Besides, if I talk to one of them, perhaps I can learn something we can use to help us help them."

Cyln'phax raised her head as Karus continued on and by the dragon. They shared a quick look. The dragon appeared about to stop him, then changed her mind. Karus felt the dragon's eyes upon his back as he continued forward.

As he got closer, the elf's features began to reveal themselves. A rounder face, full lips, a delicate nose. Karus almost missed a step. The ranger was a woman! Serving in Britannia, Karus had seen women fight alongside their men. This had only happened during desperate moments, when the legion had surrounded the enemy or trapped them in a hill fort with no hope of escape. Still, he'd not expected a woman to be a ranger.

The elf appeared far from threatened by his approach. She didn't raise her bow, but instead settled for studying him, almost as intently as he was her. He came to a stop just five feet from her. Karus found her beautiful almost beyond belief, a goddess, like Venus come to life.

It was her eyes that seemed to pull him in. In the darkness, he could not tell their color, but they were captivating, compelling, and deep. Gazing into their depths was a near-hypnotic experience. He felt he could lose himself in eyes like hers.

With some effort, Karus pulled his gaze away and continued his examination. Her hair was blonde. She had it pulled back into a single tightly weaved braid, which exposed her pointed ears. Under the moonlight, her skin shown like freshly ground flour.

She wore no armor to speak of, just soft brown leather pants and a tunic that was cinched about her thin waist with a black leather belt threaded with silver. The clothing was loose, but not baggy. Karus got the impression it was designed for easy movement and comfort rather than style. Her light brown boots were made of soft, flexible leather.

She carried a short bow along with a half dozen arrows in one hand. She was also armed with a pair of large bone-handled daggers, sheathed along her upper thighs. These daggers were about half the length of a legionary gladius. One was straight and the other held a slight curve to it.

Her beauty was overwhelming, overpowering, and set his heart racing at an unnatural gait. He felt a desperate desire to want her to love him, to protect her and grant her every desire. It was irrational.

Their eyes locked again. Karus found himself trapped, like a fly caught in amber or, perhaps more appropriately, a spider's web. He struggled to draw a breath. It was as if she had captured his soul with her gaze and held it in a fist-like grip. Her lips quirked in a hint of a knowing, somewhat mocking smile. It broke the spell that had fallen over him.

Blinking and unsure exactly what had just occurred, he sucked in a deep breath and glanced back at Amarra. He found her starkly plain in comparison to the elven ranger. Yet, it was almost as if the sight of Amarra was a breath of fresh air in a stale room. Karus took another deep breath and shuddered slightly as he let it out. The gods and fate had seen fit to throw them together. His heart was with her. He steeled himself and turned back. The elf seemed slightly less beautiful than she had a moment before. He wondered what strange power had been at work.

He cleared his throat.

"I am Karus," he said in Common.

Her smile vanished.

"Si'Cara," she said.

Karus hesitated a moment and held out his hand. It was an intentional act, by which he intended to convey he meant no threat to her. She scowled slightly at the proffered hand. It was as if he were offering her a poisonous snake, angry at having been pulled from its snug hole.

Karus kept his hand extended and open, waiting. She looked up at him, her gaze once again locking with his. This time her eyes did not have the same effect that they had just moments before. Though she appeared youthful, a mere child just out of her teens, he sensed an unexpected maturity as she regarded the proffered hand.

After a moment's more hesitation, Si'Cara gave a half shrug of her shoulders. She moved her bow and arrows to her left hand, then reached out. She took his hand. He found her grip firm and unexpectedly warm to the touch, almost fevered hot. The skin was not soft, as he had expected, but rough, hard, and calloused. She quickly shook and then released, as if personal contact with him had been extremely distasteful. Karus got the feeling she desired very badly to wipe her hand clean, but common courtesy kept her from doing so.

"Do you speak Common?" Karus asked.

"I do," Si'Cara said. Her tone had the same singsong quality he'd heard from the other elves, but it was also as rock-solid as her grip had been. "It was not wise to come here."

She was wholly confident in herself, Karus realized, not intimidated in the slightest by him or the dragons. That much was plain. He also found that disconcerting.

"I had little choice," Karus said, conscious of his poor Common. He knew his accent was rough and his words poorly formed, some perhaps even incorrect. That said, he was resolved to have this conversation without Amarra acting as translator or go-between. He needed to master Common, and the sooner the better.

"We all have free will." Si'Cara tilted her head forward slightly. "You should have known better than to come, even with dragons."

"We should be allies," Karus said, "certainly not enemies."

"If that were meant to be, it would be," Si'Cara said.

"The Horde threatens all. It is unwise to stand alone."

"And you think to have my people stand with yours?" She said this with an amused grin that vanished as soon as she'd posed her question.

"Such would be good, but that is not why we are here," Karus said.

"Oh, really?" Her tone was almost mocking.

"Really," Karus said. "We did not come for that."

"You should know, the dwarves sought to enlist our aid as well."

"They did?" Karus asked, interested.

"The last surviving member of their delegation rots within the warden's prison," Si'Cara said. "That is how much regard the warden holds for the dwarven people. The warden has even less for yours."

Karus did not like the sound of that. She had implied the rest had been killed. If the warden proved obstinate, they would have a problem. This news, he thought, did not bode well for their chances.

"If I were in your place ..." Si'Cara said, glancing at the nearest ranger, who was looking their way curiously. Karus thought he read sympathy in her eyes, as they softened slightly and returned to him. She lowered her voice a tad. "I'd go now and flee whilst you still can."

"The warden has what we need," Karus said, putting the words as best he could into Common and hoping they were right. "I can't go until we have it. The High Father sent us."

Si'Cara was silent for several heartbeats.

"You are a"—she said a word he did not know—"then?" Si'Cara asked.

"I don't know that word," Karus said.

Si'Cara scowled at him.

"Believer," Si'Cara said, choosing a different word. "We still have a few believers amongst us. They imagine the gods guide their path and journey through life. Many consider their"—she said another word he did not know—"of faith nothing but hot air on a"—again another unknown word—"wind."

"Yes," Karus said, getting the gist of what she was going for. "I am a believer."

"Few there are who speak truth these dark days," Si'Cara said. "Are your words nothing but hot air on a"—again a word he did not know—"wind?"

"The High Father brought my legion to this world," Karus said. He spoke slowly, working to form the words properly, for he wanted to be understood. "We fought evil. The High Father blessed us himself. He gave us a holy task and named Amarra his High Priestess. It was he who gave her the staff."

Si'Cara's eyes traveled to Amarra and the staff, clearly considering.

"A relic of some kind, no doubt from an age long past," Si'Cara said. "It may even be holy. Perhaps she found it?"

"It was given to her," Karus insisted.

"What is it you seek from the warden?" Si'Cara's gaze returned to his and hardened.

"A sword," Karus said. "It too is a relic from an age past."

Si'Cara sucked in a startled breath. Her gaze pierced him seemingly to the core. "You do not come here today to seek our alliance?"

"It would be nice, but no," Karus said. "We are here for the sword. That is all."

"You come for Rarokan," Si'Cara said and it came out almost as a hiss of air.

"I do," Karus said.

"She is, as you say, High Priestess?" Si'Cara asked. Her eyes once again traveled to Amarra, a suspicious look harbored within them. "Did she give herself that title, or other humans like you?"

"Jupiter gave it to her," Karus said, thinking his words out and speaking slowly. "I mean the High Father. He named her High Priestess and gave her the staff by his own hand. I was there. I saw it happen."

"Jupiter?" Si'Cara turned her gaze back to him. The intensity of it had sharpened considerably. "The High Father is known by many names. Yet as far as I understand it, he is called Jupiter on only a handful of worlds." Her eyes narrowed. "You come from one of those worlds."

The last was not a question. It was a statement of fact.

"I do," Karus said. "On my world, he is known only as Jupiter. The name High Father is new to us."

"Where do you come from, Karus?"

"Rome," Karus said. "I am a Roman."

Si'Cara's gaze darted to the ranger she had looked to before. This one was clearly a male. He had started walking slowly over to them, almost strolling. Karus noted that he held his bow at the ready, an arrow nocked.

"It is time you return," Si'Cara said and nodded toward Amarra.

"Thank you for speaking with me," Karus said.

"If fortune permits, we shall talk again, Karus of Rome. Now go, before there is trouble."

Karus turned and walked back to Amarra. She raised an eyebrow as he approached.

"That's a woman," Karus said and jerked a thumb back at Si'Cara. "Can you believe that?"

Amarra gave a nod but said nothing.

He glanced back at Si'Cara. The other ranger had come up to her. They were speaking quietly together and looking his way.

There was a loud crack from behind. Karus and Amarra turned, startled. The wizard was back and he looked none too happy. His face was a thundercloud of barely suppressed anger and rage, cheeks flushed and hot. The crystal on his staff throbbed and pulsed brightly, as if reacting to his emotional state.

"The warden will see you both," the wizard said, almost biting the words as they came out. "The dragons stay. Those are the warden's conditions and terms."

Wizard, Kordem said without raising his head or stirring, *when these talks are concluded, you will return Karus and Amarra unharmed. If you fail to do so, we will burn your sacred city to the ground. You shall be left with nothing but ash. Are our terms understood?*

The wizard's eyes snapped to the dragon. The anger and rage passed over rapidly to a mask of schooled inscrutability and equanimity.

The wizard hesitated. "No harm shall come to them. When they have spoken their piece, we shall return them ... unharmed. All of you will be free to go. You have my word."

"Did you make the same promise to the dwarven delegation?" Karus asked the wizard.

The wizard glanced sharply over at Karus. "No promises were made to them. Like you, they should have known better than to trespass within our domain. Still, I have given my word. You shall not be harmed."

The empty words of elves mean nothing to us, Cyln'phax said. *However, we make a promise in return. Should the warden or any of your kin harm Karus or Amarra, the elven nations shall pay a steep price, you included. We are not the only taltalum on this world. Betray us, and our brothers and sisters will know. You may succeed in defeating us, but I assure you they will come to extract blood debt. Their vengeance will be a terrible thing to behold.*

Karus saw the wizard actually swallow. He had paled considerably.

"I understand." The wizard turned to Amarra and Karus. "If you will both follow me, I will take you to the warden."

The wizard turned, robes whirling, and set off in the direction of Si'Cara and the other ranger. Karus shared a glance with Amarra, then looked back on Cyln'phax.

"There are others of your kind?" Karus asked quietly.

Of course, Kordem said. *When we found Amarra, we sent out word. All of our kin upon this world are coming. Soon there shall be a gathering of taltalum like Tannis has never seen nor will likely ever again.*

Now go, Cyln'phax said. *You are wasting time. Obtain permission to enter the Fortress of Radiance and return to us.*

Karus glanced over at Amarra. She shot him a wink. He felt heartened at the news that more dragons were on their way. It made him feel more confident about what they were heading into.

The wizard had stopped by the two rangers. He was looking back at them, clearly wondering why they were not following. With a glance to Amarra, they started forward, joining the wizard and the two rangers. The wizard turned and led them onward. Si'Cara and the other ranger fell in, walking a few paces behind them.

CHAPTER NINE

The wizard led them across the square and onto a winding path that carried them into the forest. They moved past the giant trees that bordered the square. Every few yards, a magical lantern lit the way with just enough light to see the path. After a ten-minute walk, the stone path began steering them toward a tree so large that it almost defied belief.

Karus figured the tree must have been at least fifty feet thick, perhaps greater than one hundred to one hundred fifty feet around. In the darkness, he realized that his estimate may have been conservative, as it was getting more difficult to see. The tree was more of a great shadow than anything else.

He glanced upward toward its towering canopy hundreds of feet above them. Light came from the branches and trunk of the tree higher up. He could just make out the dim outline of buildings that had been constructed in the tree, on the branches, or along the side of the trunk. He marveled not only at the sheer feat of engineering and determination that had made it possible, but also that something so huge could be a living thing.

The stone pathway seemed to meander for no good reason as it brought them closer to the tree. All the while, it led them through what Karus thought to be some sort of rock-and-sand garden. The sand appeared to have been raked, sculpted into geometric designs. But it was hard to tell for sure, as the farther along they moved under the great canopy of leaves and the shadow of the giant tree, the darker it became. The light from the occasional lantern did not spread too far off the path. The darkness of the forest, as if a hungry monster, swallowed up the light.

The pathway eventually led them to the far side of the tree, where a file of twenty guards waited before a pair of double doors that had been set into the bark of the trunk. The guards had been arranged on either side of the pathway.

Additional lanterns, these giving off more light, had been set into the ground along the path leading up to the tree. Two lanterns hung just above the doors, shining their light downward upon the guards.

Unlike the rangers, these elves wore chest and helmet armor that appeared to have been masterfully crafted, with intricate patterns and runes etched into the surface of their chest plates. Karus suspected the armor was more ceremonial than anything else, for it was very pretty, flashy, and clearly meant to impress. The armor looked like works of fancy rather than practical coverings to protect the body.

The chest plates and helms appeared to be made out of burnished silver, but Karus knew that couldn't be. Not only would it have been unsuitable to battle, as silver was nowhere near as strong as steel, but it would also have been cost prohibitive. He instead chalked the shine up to the armor having been polished to a nearly impossible luster that reflected the lantern light in brilliant flashes.

The guards, Karus decided, looked too pretty, too perfect to be real warriors. Still, he reminded himself that looks could be deceiving. Even an untrained boy, given the opportunity, could still manage to stick a veteran with a sword. He studied them carefully as they came nearer. The guards wore no armor on their legs, instead wearing simple black pants and boots. Like Roman heavy infantry, there was not much protection from the waist down.

Each of the guards was armed with a sword and spear. Long and straight, the sword reminded Karus of the Celtic spatha. These were sheathed and carried in ornate scabbards that hung from the left side.

The spear was about six feet from butt to point. It looked heavier and thicker than a javelin. It was clearly not meant for throwing, but for jabbing and swinging. The guards also carried a medium oval shield, which they held to the front in their left hands and the spear in their right. They kept their gazes fixed to the front, faces impassive, unmoving as rock.

The pathway led straight up to the double doors, which were so masterfully made they appeared as if they had always been part of the tree. Each door curved with the shape of the tree and matched the outer bark perfectly. The seams could hardly be seen. Had the path, guards, and magical lanterns not been there, Karus was certain he would not have spotted the double doors without closer study. He suspected he would have to know what to look for, just to find it.

As they began passing through the line of guards, the last two standing next to the doors, who were the only ones without spears, stepped forward. Each pulled open a door. As they opened, bright light spilled out from the interior. The two guards returned to their original positions and stiffened their backs like the rest, once again becoming immobile as statues.

The wizard never slowed, walking right inside. Karus and Amarra followed after him. The lamplight was so brilliant, it almost hurt. It was as if they had stepped from a dark cave into the light of day. Karus held up his hand to shield his eyes and blinked a few times until they'd adjusted.

He glanced around. Hung from the ceiling above were dozens of the exquisitely crafted lanterns. Some were made of gold, others silver and bronze. They were delicate and ornate, almost fragile. These shed their eternal and steady magical light downward.

Karus had not known exactly what to expect from a tree that had been carved out. This certainly wasn't it. He found it was as if he had stepped into the foyer of some strange building where instead of stone or plaster, the walls had been paneled over with what appeared to be cherrywood. He found it both appealing and alien.

Oddly, the foyer was oval. There was no furniture. Directly opposite the doors, a staircase, perhaps fifteen feet wide, climbed upward a dozen or so steps to a small landing. At that point, the staircase pulled apart, splitting in two and ascending in opposite directions. The steps traveled out of sight.

"Come," the wizard said simply. He started up the steps, his staff tapping steadily in solid-sounding thunks on the wood of each step. Karus and Amarra followed.

Karus glanced around and found Si'Cara and the other ranger were still trailing after them. His eyes met Si'Cara's. He found a grimness within her gaze that troubled him deeply. Behind them, the double doors closed with a deep thunk.

The wizard reached the landing and took the left staircase. Karus and Amarra followed after him, climbing in silence at a slow yet steady pace, winding higher and higher into the tree. Lanterns mounted into mirrored wall recesses every five steps provided plenty of light. They passed no doors, just one monotonous step after another.

Finally, after what seemed like hundreds of steps, when Karus's legs had begun to burn from the exertion, they came to a landing with no more steps going upward. Another file of guards, identically armed and equipped as those they had left below, greeted them. These stood arranged strategically around the antechamber, their backs to the curved walls. Looking them over, Karus wondered if they were some sort of royal guard, their charge protecting the warden, just as the praetorians would the emperor.

The landing was really a small antechamber. A second set of double doors waited a few feet ahead. These were opened by two of the guards. Beyond, Karus saw what appeared to be some sort of receiving hall.

The wizard moved toward the entrance to the hall and was about to enter. He hesitated, stopped, and turned around. The schooled expression of equanimity was back. The wizard took a shallow breath as he regarded Karus and Amarra.

"You are both about to meet the Elantric Warden," the wizard said in a low tone. "You may speak in your own languages. I shall see to it she will understand you. It will be as if you spoke fluent Elven."

Karus gave a nod.

"That is good," Amarra said. "Thank you."

The wizard spared her a quick look and then continued.

"The warden's word is law. She rules my people, and has for over two thousand years. I give you fair warning, she has not set eyes on a human for hundreds of those years. My people do not—"

"Two thousand years?" Karus exclaimed. He was not sure he had heard correctly. "Are you serious?"

"My people are long-lived compared to yours," the wizard said. "She has lived for more years than she's ruled."

"How old are you?" Karus asked, finding it hard to believe what the wizard had just confirmed. It seemed impossible.

"I was born over four thousand years past."

Karus and Amarra shared a look. Karus wondered what it would be like to live that long.

"As I was saying, my people do not think favorably on yours," the wizard said. "In point of fact, we hold serious animus toward you humans. We have our reasons, for there was a time when elves were persecuted by your kind and hunted almost to extinction. We are an old people, and there are those alive still who remember those dark and dreadful days, including the warden and several of her advisors. For us, it was the Time of Tears."

Karus sucked in a breath and shared another glance with Amarra.

"I am sorry that my people hurt yours," Amarra said with feeling.

The wizard looked sharply at Amarra. His expression was hard to read.

"We are not the people who hurt yours," Karus said.

"That matters little," the wizard said. "As do words of apology."

"Still," Amarra said. "I offer them nonetheless."

"The warden is also the spiritual leader of our people," the wizard continued. "She is ancient and has been around since nearly the birth of our race. She commands powers far different than my own. I would recommend you take care when you speak with her. You may refer to her as simply 'the warden.'" The wizard paused, hesitating a heartbeat. "No matter what I promised the dragons, this could end badly, very badly, for you. Do you understand?"

"We come to seek your people's aid," Amarra said. "It is not our intention to offend or cause trouble."

"Offend?" the wizard said and his tone became hard. He used his staff to gesture around them. "This forest speaks to our people. We have bonded with it in a way you could never hope to comprehend. It listens to us and grows to our need, shaping not only the land, but our lives. In return, we care for the forest, and keep the Great Mother safe. Irin'Surall is sacred, hallowed ground. No human has ever been permitted to set foot in this tree, nor any other race. You two are the very first. Offend? By just coming here you have insulted us to our very core."

"Would your people have let us come and meet with your warden," Karus asked, "had we done so another way?"

"Doubtful," the wizard said, somewhat grudgingly.

"Then it is good that we came the way we did," Karus said, "even if we unintentionally offended."

"We shall see." The wizard glanced into the receiving hall. He looked back and spared both Amarra and Karus a look. "I warn you, tread carefully, especially if you desire to see the coming sunrise."

The wizard turned and started into the hall. Karus and Amarra followed, with the two rangers several steps behind. The hall was surprisingly large. The ceiling, with six wooden support columns, rose to a dizzying height that Karus estimated to be at least one hundred feet. Rounded, shaped, and smoothed, the columns were each easily the width of a hundred-year oak. They looked very much like the marble columns he had seen holding the temples up in Carthum, the only difference being these had been shaped out of wood. He suspected they had been left in place when the hall had been carved from the tree.

Karus's gaze swept around, taking in the details. The receiving hall was even grander than the throne room back in Carthum. Four large flameless chandeliers hung, suspended from the ceiling by thick chain ropes. These blazed with a brilliant white light that was too intense to keep your eyes upon for more than a heartbeat. The chandeliers drove back the darkness.

The receiving hall stretched out for at least a hundred yards, which seemed impossible when Karus considered the width of the tree. Then he realized that the hall had been built out from the tree, most likely along one of the massive branches. And yet to Karus's practiced eye, the construction method seemed somehow off, odd. There were no straight angles or seams. It was as if the hall had somehow been grown or shaped magically, instead of having the wood cut into boards and then nailed together.

Oval-glassed windows, each twenty feet high and ten wide, ran the length of the hall on both sides. During daytime, Karus imagined that these would provide the hall with plenty of natural light. There was no furniture or any decorations anywhere in the hall.

"Come," the wizard said, turning back to them. "The warden waits."

Karus had not realized that he'd come to a stop. Amarra had also stopped. She, too, had been gazing around them with no little amount of amazement. He wanted to study his surroundings more, but the wizard's words drew his attention to the far end of the hall, where four elves waited for them. One stood squarely apart. The other three stood to her right.

Karus started forward again, Amarra walking at his side. He assumed that the woman standing apart from the others was the warden. She wore a long, delicate, almost

lace-like dress. It was black as midnight and flowed gracefully down around her. The dress clashed with her pale skin
and blonde hair, which was perfectly brushed and cascaded
down over her shoulders. She wore a slender silver crown
made into the shapes of tiny oak leaves.

The warden appeared no older than a young woman in
her twenties, but there was something about her grave and
dignified manner that told him her age was far older and
helped to reinforce the wizard's assertion of her longevity.
She looked remarkably similar to Si'Cara. Karus resisted
the urge to turn and glance at the ranger following a few
steps behind. The two could almost have been twin sisters.
Were they? How old was Si'Cara?

The wizard stopped some ten feet from the warden. He
offered a respectful bow and then took two steps to the left
and turned slightly so that he was still facing the warden,
but also Karus and Amarra. The two rangers remained just
behind them.

"Camp Prefect Lucius Grackus Lisidius Karus, High
Priestess Amarra of the High Father," the wizard said, "may
I present the most glorious ruler of the elven nations, spiri-
tual leader to her people, divine light in the darkness, the
Elantric Warden."

"It is an honor to meet you," Karus said, as respectfully
as he could.

The wizard shot Karus a deeply unhappy scowl.

"It is customary to offer a bow to show your respect to
the warden," the wizard said.

"Romans bow to no one," Karus said, his eyes upon the
warden. He well remembered the time that now seemed like
an age past, when, as a fresh centurion, he and the legate
of his legion had met with a foreign prince. The legate had
refused to bow. In fact, Karus had been surprised it had

been the prince who had paid homage to the legate. That had always stuck with Karus. The message had been clear. Romans were superior to everyone else. It was that simple.

"I am afraid that will be seen as another insult," the wizard said. "I strongly suggest you reconsider your stance."

"It is customary amongst my people to bow to no one," Karus said clearly, continuing to gaze steadfastly at the warden. "We are a free people. We don't even bow to our emperor."

"We shall excuse you," the warden said. Her voice held that same singsong lilt, but it was also cold as ice in the dead of winter. Devoid of any warmth, the sound of it almost sent shivers down his spine.

"Thank you," Karus said.

"Your thanks are not needed, nor required," the warden said. "Since Irin'Surall's founding, this city has been a refuge and safe harbor for my people. We do occasionally allow outsiders in, but not very often. Entire centuries go by without visitors." The warden paused several heartbeats before continuing. "I am certain the Master of Obsidian explained your coming here without permission or invitation is a serious transgression, a violation of our law and against the natural order of things."

"It was necessary," Amarra said. "Had there been time, we would have sought the permission you require."

The warden's eyes went from Karus to Amarra. They lingered momentarily on her staff.

"I know why you have come," the warden said. "You, like many others before you, seek Rarokan. You believe the sword can solve all of your problems, defeat your enemies...and you must have it immediately, or everything you hold dear will be lost. I have heard it all before, listened to desperate pleas, begging, and tortured explanations.

Surely your excuse for violating our peace and tranquility will be nothing new to my ears. Rarokan is why you came, why you have brought the taltalum, an enemy, into my domain. Deny it not. Say what you must and be done with words that I doubt will persuade me to aid you in the slightest."

"We have come for the sword," Karus said, with a glance to Amarra. "But I must confess we never thought the weapon could solve all of our problems. We were commanded to retrieve it."

"Commanded?" The warden's tone was slightly mocking in its disbelief. "The Fortress of Radiance is sacrosanct to my people. A great sacrifice was asked and made...just to guard the sword."

Karus made to reply, but Amarra touched him on the forearm and shook her head.

"Nevertheless, we must go there," Amarra said. "As Karus said, we were commanded to go and retrieve the sword."

"Tell me why I should grant my permission for you to travel to the Fortress of Radiance," the warden said. "Why are you worthy? High Priestess or no, who are you to ask such a favor of my people?"

"I have given up all that I had, everything, who I once was, for the love of my god," Amarra said. "I was rewarded for my faith and service. It is why—"

"Of what god are you High Priestess?" the warden interrupted, her tone becoming sharp, colder, if that was possible.

"The High Father," Amarra said, tilting her head back slightly.

"The Master of Obsidian"—the warden gestured over at the wizard with a delicate hand—"said as much, but I wanted to hear it from your own lips."

"Does that make it any more true to your ears?" Amarra asked. "Perhaps believable?"

"No, it does not," the warden said. "The High Father has turned a blind eye to these lands, and my people. He has left this world to darkness, to wither on the vine, as have the other gods we once honored."

"He has not," Amarra said. "He has always been here. It is the people who turned away."

"You lie," the warden said. "They have abandoned us to our fate. It is why we now make our own."

"No," Amarra said. "I bring truth, whether you desire to hear it or not."

"I wish to know how you came by that staff," the warden said. "We have not seen its like in a very long time. Tell me, child, where did you find it? Or perhaps you took it from some ancient and forgotten ruin?"

Karus felt Amarra stiffen at the words. He was growing angry himself.

"Jupiter, whom you call the High Father, gave it to her," Karus said. "I was there. It was he who commanded us to go to the Fortress of Radiance and retrieve Rarokan. The sword is meant for my keeping and mine alone."

The warden's eyes shifted over to Karus. He found her gaze a truly cold one, filled with time beyond reckoning. Karus almost shuddered.

"Your people," the warden said, "I believe you call them Romans. Is that not correct?"

"It is," Karus said.

"I know of all peoples that live or have lived upon this world," the warden said. "I have never heard of you Romans."

"That is because I am not of this world," Karus said.

148

"So says the Master of Obsidian," the warden said. "Again, I desired to hear it from your own lips. Thank you for confirming that."

"It was your people who came through the portal and into our lands," one of the elves at the warden's side hissed angrily. He looked directly at the warden. "I knew it. It took them an age, but they finally figured out how to operate the portal. They have followed us through, just as I said would happen. Not destroying the portal was a mistake. We should kill them both, immediately, and deal with the dragons, no matter the cost."

"I don't know where you got that idea," Karus said, his anger boiling to the surface. "We didn't ask to come here and certainly did not follow you through any portal."

"He speaks lies," the elf said, "like all other humans. Warden, they are not to be trusted, especially these. They must be of our age-old enemy, the Masseey."

The warden held up a hand, forestalling any further speech by her advisor. Her gaze shifted to Amarra, and a slight, almost cruel smile formed thinly upon her lips.

"Master of Obsidian," the warden said, "fetch me her staff. I would add its *will* to my own."

Karus blinked in surprise. Amarra took a step back.

"I would hesitate to make such an attempt," the wizard said. "Warden, I sense tremendous *will* bound within the staff. I have not felt its like for some time. It may even be from the Time of Wonders. The High Priestess has the ability to use and wield this artifact. Some caution may be in order."

"You will not take this staff," Amarra said firmly, setting her jaw and tightening her grip.

The warden looked from Amarra to the wizard and back again.

"You came here with taltalum," the warden said. "You may have formed the mistaken impression that they somehow protect you. They cannot. You are at my mercy. Now, girl, hand it over."

"You will not take this staff," Amarra said again. Her words were as firm as tempered steel. Karus's hand itched to draw his sword. Amarra apparently sensed that, for she shot him a look that said, *No*.

"I will allow you to leave here with your lives," the warden said and held out an expectant hand, "if you give me the staff. I shall not ask again, girl."

Amarra drew herself up. Her fingers gripping the staff flexed, the crystal flaring with light. "The High Father gave this blessing into my care. I cannot...I *will* not give it away. To do so would be a betrayal of my faith and my lord, to whom I have sworn everlasting service."

The smile on the warden's face grew.

"Si'Cara and Tal'Thor are two of our best rangers," the warden said and gestured behind them. "Their skill amongst the trees is unequaled. They speak to the forest as if they'd been born to it, which I suppose they have."

The warden took several steps to the right, walking slowly around behind them, her dress whispering as she made her way toward the two rangers. She paused and regarded the two for a prolonged moment, then reached up a hand and caressed first Tal'Thor's cheek, then Si'Cara's. Both bowed their heads. It was as if they were favored children. The warden regarded them both for several more heartbeats, then continued around and back to her original position.

"Elven lives are precious in a way you humans could never understand," the warden continued. "Your lives are so fleeting, a mere blink of an eye to my people. One moment you are here and the next gone, while we remain. If you humans are lucky, you are remembered. If not, you are forgotten and lost to the ravages of time, just another faceless human amongst a multitude."

"Why are you telling us this?" Karus asked.

"Why?" The warden arched an eyebrow at him.

"Yes, why?" Karus asked again.

"So you better understand your position," the warden said, and the thin smile slipped from her face. "Humans, orcs, the rest of the lesser races...you all are like a plague of insects ravaging a farmer's field. No matter how hard the farmer works, you consume everything, destroying the harvest, making a mockery of his toil and labor. You multiply and spread without thought of the consequences. You ruin the land, corrupt and contaminate it. There is no harmony with your kind, no balance, no thought to consequence."

"Okay, I get you don't like us," Karus said. "There is no need to insult us."

"No there is not," the warden agreed and fell silent a moment. "This is simply how we view your people."

"You see only what you wish," Amarra said, "what you want."

"Perhaps." The warden's gaze moved beyond them. "It is time I show you truth, my dear." The warden gestured at the two rangers. "All elves are, in a manner of speaking, my children. These two are amongst my most dear, my most precious. They have sworn unquestioning obedience and loyalty to me. Is that not right?"

"It is, warden," Tal'Thor said.

"As you say, warden," Si'Cara said.

"See?" the warden asked of Karus and Amarra.

"Not quite." Karus spared a glance over at Amarra, who was frowning slightly, clearly troubled.

"Then let me show you," the warden said. "Tal'Thor?"

"Command me, my warden," the ranger said.

"Give Si'Cara a mortal wound. I do not want her to die too quickly."

Karus turned in shock. Tal'Thor glanced to Si'Cara, then to the warden and back again. His eyes narrowed. Before Karus could react, he moved with lightning quickness. Si'Cara stood, as if frozen in place. She stared in disbelief at the warden, even as the other ranger pulled out a dagger and drove it deeply into her side. Her eyes widened with shock as her breath whooshed out in an agonized grunt, the dagger driven violently to its hilt. Si'Cara staggered as Tal'Thor pulled the dagger out and stepped back and away from her, blood dripping from his blade.

Crimson blood fountained and bubbled up from the wound to her side and splashed onto the floor. Si'Cara reached for the wound with both hands, struggling in a vain attempt to staunch the blood flow as it spilled out down her side. Her eyes went to Tal'Thor. Karus thought he read a deep, terrible hurt within them, a clear accusation of betrayal. Tal'Thor returned her gaze with a stony expression of his own.

Si'Cara turned her gaze to the warden, the shock and hurt plain for all to see. She looked as if she intended to speak, then gritted her teeth as a terrible spasm of pain ran through her.

"Why did you do that?" Amarra screamed, stepping back from the warden. "You'd kill your own to make a point?"

"Warden..." Si'Cara fell to a knee, the strength clearly fleeing her body as fast as the blood, which was pooling around her feet. With the amount of blood loss, Karus knew she could not last much longer. "Help me."

The warden ignored Si'Cara's plea, as if it were beneath her.

"Yes, I did this to make a point, but not the one you think," the warden said to Amarra and Karus. Her tone turned mocking. "High Priestess, you are not the only believer in this hall. Si'Cara is a true follower of your god."

Amarra turned her horrified gaze upon Si'Cara. The horror softened to one of deep sadness.

"After the gods turned their backs upon us," the warden continued, "leaving us bereft of their protection, she and a few others yet kept their faith. Despite everything, the suffering, all the gods had done to us, the fools continued to believe." Disgust crept into the warden's voice. Her lip curled. "Look at her. Even now, with death beckoning, she retains her faith." The warden paused to suck in a breath, and her voice became raised. "Look upon her, High Priestess. She prays to a god who will do nothing to save her. Why should we worship the gods? They only use us as no better than a child's plaything to be discarded when a new toy comes along. Tell me why, give me a good reason why we should honor the gods!"

"You're a monster," Amarra said.

"No," the warden replied. "I am a realist."

Karus swung his gaze from the warden back to the stricken ranger. Si'Cara had closed her eyes and, despite being in tremendous pain, was silently mouthing words he took to be prayer. A moment later, she gasped in a convulsion of agony and fell forward, landing on her side, then rolled onto her back and stared up at the ceiling, blinking rapidly. She reached up an imploring hand toward the warden. It was covered in her blood.

Karus had seen plenty of good boys die in his time. Many suffered lingering deaths, from slow loss of blood, terrible stomach wounds, infection, blood poisoning, and more. Sadly, he'd seen it all. He was personally disgusted by the warden. Watching the ranger slowly bleed out tugged at his heart. He felt saddened that she would die such a senseless death. She wasn't an enemy. She'd done nothing to him. She'd served her people, her leader, the warden, faithfully. Karus understood service. For years, service, duty, and honor had been watchwords for him.

Si'Cara cried out as another spasm of pain took her. Karus shook his head slightly. An untimely death was the reward for her service. It was unkind, unjust, and terribly unfair. She deserved better. He knelt by her side and took her hand, which shook slightly. Her blood pooling out around her made his knees wet.

"No one should have to die alone," Karus said to her. "I will remain at your side as you cross over. I will pay the coin to the ferryman."

"Thank you," Si'Cara breathed, looking up at him. A solitary tear ran from her left eye down the side of her cheek. "I would have liked to have talked with you some more."

"As would I," Karus said. Her hand began to tremble violently within his. He could feel the warmth leaving her body. He tightened his grip. "I regret we won't be able to talk more."

"It hurts," Si'Cara said and arched her back until the spasm passed.

Karus could hear the guards entering the hall at a run.

The warden laughed and it drew Karus's attention. It was mirthless, driven by cruelty. He had known others like the warden. They looked upon those who served them, not as people, with thoughts and feelings of their own, but as tools to be used and discarded. He felt sickened.

"See! See, the gods will not lift a finger to save her," the warden said, voice almost a screech, and pointed at the failing ranger. "Si'Cara will die a death that will serve as a lesson to other fools of the faith. Those few of my people who still worship the gods will learn from this. They would do better to worship me. By rights, they should worship at my altar!"

Si'Cara choked, blood frothing to her lips. Karus returned his attention to her. Her eyes met his. In them he read fear at her rapidly approaching death. Her entire body had begun to tremble violently. She turned her head to gaze upon Amarra.

"Priestess, bless me," Si'Cara whispered, struggling to get the words out. "Before I go—" Si'Cara struggled to suck in a breath. It was a pathetic rasping sound. Karus could hear the fluid in her lungs. She coughed up more bloody spittle. "Long has it been since I received a blessing." Si'Cara coughed again. "I have sinned, doubted, questioned and struggled with my faith. Forgive me and bless me. I desire it, very much ... before it is too late."

Karus saw the warden's lip twitch almost into a smile, as if amused by the drama playing out before her.

"High Father, lend me your strength!" Amarra slammed the butt of her staff onto the floor. The staff flashed with an intense blue light, for a moment drowning out the magical light from the chandeliers hanging above.

There was a sound much like a bell tolling. The hall shook mightily, the tree along with it. One of the great windows shattered, glass cascading both inside and outside the hall. Everyone but Amarra struggled to remain standing.

Amarra slammed the butt of her staff down again. The bell tolled once more and the tree shook violently. There was a deep cracking sound from above as the wood in the ceiling split, a great rent opening. Splinters, dust, and chunks of wood showered down around them. A large piece of wood hit and felled one of the guards who had stopped just feet from them. An anchor holding a chandelier snapped with a loud crack. The chandelier crashed to the floor and shattered, its magical light extinguishing itself.

The shaking ceased, and all became silent.

Karus looked up at Amarra and his eyes widened. She was encased in white fire. At first Karus was alarmed at the sight of her burning, but then he realized that she was unhurt by the flames. This was Jupiter's power and she was wielding it. She was using the staff!

Amarra took a step forward toward the warden. The wood smoked behind her where her feet had been. The warden, wizard, and the other elves took several steps back and away from her.

"Warden, you play a petty and cheap game," Amarra said, and somehow her voice seemed louder, magnified, ominous. "The Horde ravages this world. Tannis is being overrun by evil. You challenge and test a god you should honor and love. With devotion and faith comes reward. You believe having command over life and death a great power? You are badly mistaken. I shall show you true power this day. You had best pay close attention, for despite your long years, you may yet learn something."

Amarra whirled around and stepped over to Karus. Si'Cara's grip in his hand slackened. He turned back to her to find the light of life in her eyes fading fast. Amarra knelt down next to her on the opposite side.

Still encased in white fire, Amarra reached forward and gently removed Karus's hand from Si'Cara's. The flame did not burn him, but instead felt soothing to the touch. Amarra took Si'Cara's hand in her own. The mortally wounded elf's eyes closed, a ragged final breath escaping. Amarra, too, closed her eyes. As she did, her staff flared once again with a brilliant, blinding light. The flames around her roared as if they'd been fed fresh oil.

Karus closed his eyes and shielded his gaze from the light with his hand. It wasn't enough. He could still see the brilliant light behind his closed eyelids. Warmth washed over him. It was a measure of what he had felt when visited by Jupiter. It was pure ecstasy. The touch lasted but a moment and then was cruelly snatched away. Karus wanted it back, but the light was rapidly fading, the touch of the god gone.

Karus opened his eyes, blinking away spots of light. Amarra had leaned back. She was no longer encased in fire. The staff had returned to a sullen, throbbing blue. After a moment, he looked down at Si'Cara. The blood no longer flowed from her wound, though she lay in a puddle of it. She'd gone very still, but where he expected to see the pallor of death, he instead saw life. He leaned forward, checking for breath by holding a hand out to her nose. He felt her exhale. Her chest rose and fell. He reached over and checked the wound. There was no longer a hole where Tal'Thor's dagger had punched deeply into her side. Through the hole in her tunic, he felt unbroken skin.

Karus looked up at Amarra, astonished, shocked. She flashed him a tired smile.

Si'Cara stirred, eyes fluttering open. Her gaze went first to Karus and then Amarra.

"The High Father has blessed you this day," Amarra said softly to the ranger. "The great god judged you worthy. You are healed of your grievous wound."

"Thank you for proving my faith true," Si'Cara said, her voice barely a whisper. "Thank you, mistress."

There was an angry hiss from warden.

Karus glanced over at the other elves and read surprise and shock, even with the wizard. Karus turned back to

Si'Cara. She had fallen into what appeared to be a deep sleep. Her chest rose and fell in a steady rhythm.

Amarra stood slowly, almost painfully, as if her joints ached. Karus had never seen her look more bold, strong, and beautiful. She then turned to face the warden, her look stormy.

"Do you require more proof?" Amarra asked.

A look of rage made its way briefly across the warden's face. It rapidly passed over to one that betrayed not a hint of emotion.

"High Priestess of the High Father," the warden said, her tone sounding suddenly respectful, "we welcome you to our land. How may we be of service to you?"

"You know our purpose," Amarra said. "We wish permission to travel to the Fortress of Radiance and retrieve that which we were commanded."

"What is hidden away within the fortress should remain there," the warden said, seeming to regain a measure of herself. "Rarokan is a threat to everything that all peoples hold dear. Some may think it a holy weapon, but it is far more and incredibly dangerous. You should leave it be."

"If it is so dangerous…" Karus said, standing also. The old wound on his leg ached. He resisted massaging it. He shot Tal'Thor a disgusted look. The ranger appeared badly shaken. His dagger had fallen from his hand and lay discarded on the floor a few feet away. Karus turned his gaze to the warden. "Then why would the High Father send us to retrieve it?"

"As I've told you, we are only pawns in the Last War," the warden said. "The gods care nothing for us and so we no longer partake in their eternal struggle. Yet long ago, while we still worshiped them, we were asked to take into trust that which should never have been created." The warden paused. "I know why the High Father sent you. I knew the moment you arrived. I dreaded this day. Yet, it is not my place to interfere in your quest."

"You wanted her staff, demanded it even," Karus spat. "It almost cost Si'Cara her life. I'd call that interfering."

"That was a test," the warden said quietly. "I had to be sure. I had to be certain you are who you say you are. True healing has long been absent from this world. By restoring Si'Cara, you proved you are a disciple of the High Father."

Karus looked between the warden and Amarra. He was still rocked by the healing, but what the warden had just said hit him with as much force. He had known the great god had given her power, named Amarra his High Priestess, but to hear her named "disciple" struck home.

"Then you will grant us access to the Fortress of Radiance?" Amarra asked.

"No," the warden said. "No, I will not."

"What game are you playing at?" Karus demanded, becoming irritated again. He was beginning to dislike elves in general.

"I play only one game and that is of life for my people," the warden said. She shifted her gaze to Amarra. "Though the fortress is in our lands, it is not mine to command. The gods saw to that."

"What do you mean?" Amarra asked.

"Perhaps I can explain," the wizard said, speaking up. "Long ago, the High Master, the leader of my order, cast upon the Fortress of Radiance powerful enchantments. The High Master enlisted several of the most dedicated of our warriors and wove their beings into the enchantments."

"The Warriors of Anagradoom?" Karus asked.

"Yes," the wizard said. "They made the ultimate sacrifice to guard the dread weapon until the time comes to remove it.

You came here under a mistaken assumption. It is not within the warden's ability to grant you access to the fortress, for we ourselves cannot enter. We do not have the power. You carry with you everything that you need." He gestured with a hand toward Amarra's staff. "That and your faith will get you in."

"My staff?"

"We have wasted our time here, then," Karus said, thoroughly disgusted. He looked over at Amarra. "They can't help us. We must help ourselves."

"It was not a waste of time," Amarra said quietly, glancing down at the unconscious Si'Cara.

"It is admirable that you came to ask our permission," the warden said. The superior, almost mocking attitude had returned. "It shows a modicum of respect. I shall show you some in kind, by giving you fair warning."

"What kind of warning?" Karus asked, suddenly wary.

"The sword has a mind of its own," the warden said. "Take care, for it is not a blessing but a curse the High Father will bestow upon you, should you take it. Carrying Rarokan is not the honor you might think it to be. Bearing the weapon will be a burden to the end of your days."

Karus did not like the sound of that. He shared a look with Amarra.

"I can't talk you out of going?" the warden asked. "Leaving the dread relic where it belongs? For once it is removed from the fortress, others will covet the sword and come to take it from you."

"I feel called to go," Amarra said simply.

"As you felt called to be here?" the warden asked.

Amarra's gaze shifted from Karus to the warden and then over to Si'Cara before returning to the warden.

"Yes," Amarra said. "The High Father desired us to come here to fix something that was wrong amongst your people."

"Wrong amongst my people?" the warden asked. "What could be wrong?"

"A failing of faith," Amarra said.

The warden's expression hardened at that, but she said nothing in reply.

"High Priestess," Tal'Thor said, his tone full of self-loathing and what sounded almost like despair. He dropped to his knees before Amarra, bowing his head. "Can you forgive me for harming Si'Cara?"

Amarra stepped closer to him. She regarded him a long moment, then reached down and drew his face up to look into hers.

"I can forgive you and so can the High Father," Amarra said. "I wonder. Can you find it within you to forgive yourself?" She paused and glanced down at the sleeping Si'Cara. "I fear, to do that, you must first receive forgiveness from Si'Cara."

"I shall seek it," Tal'Thor whispered. "Upon my soul, I promise to do just that. I will do what I can to make amends for my actions."

Amarra gave a nod and stepped back from him. Tal'Thor stood.

"I understand you have a dwarf imprisoned," Karus said, looking to the warden. "We will take him off your hands and bring him with us."

"You dare dictate to me?" The warden seemed aghast.

"I need allies, and he came here seeking one," Karus said. "You clearly don't want any. So why not send him with us?"

The warden glanced over to her advisors. The one who had spoken earlier gave a curt nod.

"He shall be delivered to the square," the warden said. "Tell him never to return. The same goes for you as well."

"If you will have me, I would like to come with you."

Karus saw that Si'Cara was awake. She sat up with some effort and then stood. Tal'Thor rushed forward and helped her up to her feet, but she pushed him roughly, almost angrily, away once she was up. She weaved unsteadily for a moment until she found her balance. Her eyes almost rolled back into her head and she appeared ready to pass out.

"I owe you a debt I can never adequately repay," Si'Cara said to Amarra.

"You owe me nothing," Amarra said. "The High Father judged you worthy. Should you feel the need to repay anyone, your continued faith in our lord will be enough."

"I would be honored if you let me accompany you," Si'Cara said. "I have been to the fortress and I feel I can be of help."

"You would leave your duties here?" the warden asked quietly. "You would abandon your post? Leave your people undefended?"

"One less bow will matter little," Si'Cara said, "and I fear my people left me long ago … as did their warden."

There was a moment of frosty silence between warden and ranger.

"What of your oath?" the warden snapped. "Does it mean nothing to you?"

"What of yours to your people?" Si'Cara demanded with heat, balling a fist. She shook it at the warden. "You broke yours when you ordered Tal'Thor to kill me. For that, the bond is severed. I no longer serve you."

"So be it, daughter," the warden said and the coldness returned. "You have turned your back upon your home, your people. Make certain you also never return, outcast."

A stricken look came over Si'Cara's face. She set her jaw and gave a curt nod of acceptance before turning back to Amarra.

"Will you have me, mistress?" Si'Cara asked. "I will pledge myself to your service and be your protector."

"I already have a protector," Amarra said with a little smile and glanced over at Karus. "But you are more than welcome to accompany us as a companion."

"Might I ... might I join you as well?" Tal'Thor asked. "It would be an honor."

Si'Cara shot Tal'Thor an unhappy scowl.

Amarra, however, gave a nod of acceptance.

"So be it, Tal'Thor," the warden said and then turned to Amarra. "You go to liberate what I know is a threat to everything that our people hold dear. I will not lift a finger to help you beyond what I have already done. Now, leave us." The warden turned her gaze back to Amarra. "Priestess, begone from our city and take my former daughter and son with you."

"It is not too late to lead your people to salvation. When we leave this world, there will be room to come with us," Amarra said to the warden. "Should you stay, you will shepherd them to their doom."

"That is far from determined," the warden said. "Our forests are not so easy to conquer. Now leave me while you still can. When we next meet, I may not be so generous."

Amarra held the warden's gaze a moment. She stepped over to Si'Cara, who was clearly having difficulty remaining upright. Amarra took the ranger's arm. Si'Cara looked ready to protest, as if she would go it alone.

"Pride is a sin the High Father frowns upon," Amarra said. "Kindly allow me to help you."

Amarra turned and, walking slowly, helped Si'Cara in the direction they had come. Karus spared another glance at the warden. He saw an unwholesome fury residing within her eyes.

Would she prove trouble down the road?

The warden did not seem the kind to accept defeat easily, for she had clearly not won the game played here this day. Karus let out a slow, unhappy breath, then started after them. Tal'Thor fell in at his side. The guards who had entered the hall had stopped a few feet from them. One guard was tending to the one who had been injured when a piece of wood had hit him from the ceiling. They drew respectfully aside to allow them to pass, bowing deeply to Amarra.

CHAPTER TEN

Karus glanced up at the sky, which had begun to lighten just a tad. He halted his pacing a moment as he rubbed at his tired eyes. Gods, he needed sleep. The birds had begun to wake up. He could hear a number beginning to sing their morning songs high up in the branches. He swung his gaze around the square. The dragons were lying down. Ever since Karus and Amarra's return, and their explanation of what had happened, both appeared watchful, wary, perhaps even uneasy. It added to his impatience.

"I think you wear out sandals," Amarra said, amusement in her weary tone.

He stopped his pacing and looked over. Amarra was sitting on the ground a couple of feet away. She offered him a half smile and then stifled a yawn with the back of her hand. He sat down next to her on the hard and cold paving stone. He gazed upon her for a long moment. Amarra continued to surprise him with her inner strength. She'd faced down the warden without fear and healed Si'Cara. Yet, at this moment, looking into her eyes, she seemed somehow vulnerable and in need of support. He reached an arm around her shoulder and pulled her close. Amarra sighed contentedly, closing her eyes, snuggling and leaning her head against his shoulder armor. She breathed slowly in and out. After a bit she seemed to drift off into sleep. He held her as she breathed rhythmically. Karus enjoyed the moment, her close proximity, the warmth of her skin against his, simply holding her. It was something just a handful of weeks ago he had not known was missing from his life.

Another hour had passed when an owl hooted loudly from somewhere out from the darkness. Amarra stirred awake, blinking and looking around. She straightened, yawning. Their eyes met. She gave him a peck of a kiss upon his cheek and then leaned her head back upon his shoulder.

"What you did, it was …" Karus trailed off.

"Healing Si'Cara?" Amarra asked, picking her head up off his shoulder and looking at him.

"Yes," Karus said. "It was remarkable. You were surrounded by fire that burned white. I thought it would harm you, but then realized it was holy fire."

"Fire?" Amarra asked. She seemed surprised by that. "I had not noticed."

"It was something to see." Karus felt that was an understatement.

"I was so angry," Amarra said softly. She averted her eyes, turning them toward the glowing fountain. Her gaze became distant, almost unfocused. She was silent for a number of heartbeats. When she spoke, it came out as a whisper. "I feel sad."

"Sad?" It was Karus's turn to be surprised. "Really?"

"Yes, I sad."

"Why?"

"For what warden did to Si'Cara," Amarra said, "after I healed her."

"You are upset because the warden banished Si'Cara and Tal'Thor?"

"That," Amarra said. "I sad, unhappy for them. They can never come home."

Karus reached a hand to her chin and turned her face toward his.

"You don't need to be sorry," Karus said. "The warden is not worthy of devotion. Si'Cara will be better off away from that woman. She has a black heart. You did the right thing by healing her."

A breeze blew through the canopy high above them, rustling leaves and causing limbs to creak. Amarra said nothing for several heartbeats, then looked as if she were going to reply but instead gave a shallow nod. She turned her gaze from him back to the fountain. He thought, by the reflection of the light, her eyes had watered.

"You saved Si'Cara's life. There was no coming back from that wound," Karus said. "Did he, the High Father, show you how to heal her?"

"No," Amarra said and sucked in a shuddering breath. "No. High Father not show."

"How did you manage it, then?"

"Warden made me so angry. She hurt Si'Cara because of faith. No one there to help me, until you came. I there. I ask High Father help," Amarra said and gave a slight shrug of her shoulders. "It seemed right thing to do, to beg help. High Father answer." She paused and touched her chest. "I healed Si'Cara with his..." She gave a slight frown. "His power? That right word?"

"I think so," Karus said and then grew silent as he considered what she'd just told him. There was so much he did not understand about this world. One thing was very apparent. The High Father had graced Amarra with tremendous power and ability, a reward for her faith. By comparison, she made Roman priests seem like cheap impostors. Karus wondered about that for a moment. Why did the priests back in Rome not use their powers to heal? To help fight

167

Rome's enemies? Did they lack true faith? It was an interesting line of thought. He was about to ask another question when Amarra spoke.

"Si'Cara and Tal'Thor said they would be back soon."

"That was over two hours ago," Karus said, picking up her cue and changing the subject. He felt an intense desire to depart from this place. The impatience to get this entire venture over with and get back to his legion returned with a terrible vengeance. "I would have thought they'd be back by now."

"We wait. They come," Amarra said and leaned her head back against his shoulder once again. Karus gave a soft chuckle. She had clearly taken his measure, and of course she was right.

"That business with the warden convinced me we'd be best moving along, and the sooner the better," Karus admitted and glanced around. His eyes roved over the cordon of rangers ringing the square. He pursed his lips as he considered them. Facing enemy warriors on the line Karus could easily manage. Magic, gods, the warden, elves, dragons, evil creatures like the orcs, and Amarra's strange power... it was new. He found it all incredibly unsettling. Still, it was the world he now lived in, and it was that simple. "I will feel better once we are far away from here."

That makes two of us, human, Cyln'phax said. The dragon slid her long, thick tail across the paving stones. Its armored scales sounded like sand being ground on a millstone. *These elves live under the delusion they are sheltered from what is coming. I assure you, once the Horde overruns this world, and when there are no more enemies for them to fight, they will turn on forests like this one. They will root out the elves that cower within. There will be no quarter, no mercy, no rest. Our enemy will do it, yes... at tremendous cost, even if they have to chop each and every tree down.*

No power, no will *can save the elves from what is coming.* The dragon gave a loud snort. *Sadly, elves never learn. They are too thickheaded and deluded by their perceived greatness to realize what they are facing. It is a failing of their race.* Cyln'phax lapsed into a brief silence. *This place is doomed. I can feel it. You can taste it on the wind. These are the last days of Irin'Surall.*

Was this city really doomed?

That the elves were willing to turn a blind eye to what was coming was disturbing. At the same time, Karus felt a tinge of sadness. There was no telling how long this city had stood, lasting century after century, most likely even thousands of years. Though he had only seen it at night, Irin'Surall was beautiful, almost beyond imagining.

What would it look like by daylight? What wonders, like the glowing fountain, lay hidden by the shade of night? Despite his desire to be away, Karus would have very much liked to see it all.

The elves, like their city, were a pretty people, and yet he'd also witnessed their dark side. That's where the beauty ended, with their cruelty. Perhaps it was all just a façade to conceal the darkness within? It wasn't that he'd never seen such callous brutality before; he had just not expected it to be directed at their own, here, just to make a point.

He suspected that the dragon was right. These were this city's last days. Perhaps by banishing Si'Cara and Tal'Thor, the warden had inadvertently saved their lives? Only time would tell.

The Horde was coming for them all in the end. For the elves, it was just a matter of time. Before it became too late, Karus understood only too keenly he had to find a way off this world. Arm still wrapped protectively around Amarra's shoulders, Karus looked at the dragon. A thought occurred to him. He sat up straighter. Stifling a yawn, Amarra looked over, clearly wondering what was wrong.

Karus wanted to kick himself. Why had he not thought to ask before now? It was such a simple thing, and he was certain they knew the answer.

"How long until the Horde reaches Carthum?" Karus asked Cyln'phax and then looked over at Kordem when there was no answer. "How much time do we have? Tell me."

Both dragons had heard him. They always seemed to be listening. Neither at first answered, clearly hesitating. That worried Karus, for he knew it would be bad news.

The nearest enemy army is two weeks' hard march from the city, Kordem said. *At least, they were when we saw them last. The wyrms obviously can reach Carthum much quicker should they desire.*

"And when was that?" Karus asked, pressing them. "When did you last see that army?"

Four days before we saved you from Castor's minion, Cyln'phax said.

"That close?" Karus said, dismayed. He would never have agreed to come had he known the enemy was so near. It was likely why the dragons had withheld that information. "I had hoped they were farther away."

"It is why my people left," Amarra said, as if it surprised her not at all. "Horde was getting close. It was leave or risk being trapped."

"What are their numbers?" Karus asked. "Are they marching to the city?"

They were pursuing the remains of a dwarven army, Cyln'phax said. *The dwarves are falling back on Carthum. So, in answer to your question, yes, the Horde is moving toward the city.*

Karus rubbed his jaw, feeling a headache coming on. Whether it was from lack of sleep or the news he had just received, he wasn't quite sure. He had pulled in much of Valens's cavalry to impress and awe the refugees with the legion's might. Valens was to have pushed his scouts back out, but Karus was now wondering how close the enemy had come in that span when most of his eyes had been pulled in. Had he made a mistake? Perhaps. He suspected he had run out of time, or was about to, at any rate. They needed to get this magical sword and return as rapidly as possible. The legion had to move west, and fast, lest they become closely pursued or caught. Such thoughts reminded him of the Greek general Xenophon, who had arrived late to a war and discovered his allies had already lost and the enemy was after him.

Tactically speaking, the wyrms were also a problem. He suspected that the dragons would be a good counter, if there were enough of them. It all depended on how many wyrms the enemy had and how they used them. There were more dragons on the way, but right now there were no dragons to protect his legion from the enemy's wyrms. Karus rubbed his jaw. There had to be a way to deal with the wyrms when the dragons weren't around. Perhaps the bolt throwers might be the answer, he considered. They would need reconfiguring. It bore some thinking on. He would also need to speak with his engineers to get their thoughts.

"You did not fully answer my question," Karus asked. "What is the size of this enemy army?"

Cyln'phax swung her head toward Karus and flexed a claw, digging up some of the stone paving of the square.

Around twenty thousand, Cyln'phax said. *Maybe a little more or less. I was very high when I spotted them and the fleeing dwarven army.*

That didn't sound as bad as he had feared. He had been concerned the numbers would be overwhelming, like he had seen in the vision the High Father had shown him.

Yet, it still wasn't good. The enemy army outnumbered his legion.

"And the dwarves?" Karus asked. "How many do you suppose there are?"

At the time, Cyln'phax said, *maybe eight thousand. There may be fewer now, if they had a battle. Though vile creatures, dwarves are tenacious fighters. There is no telling how they have fared since I saw them last.*

Karus considered that. The enemy army needed to be dealt with before they left Carthum. If the dwarven army was destroyed, the enemy might easily turn their attention his way. With a large train of civilians, Karus did not relish the idea of being the pursued. If, perhaps, he could somehow convince the dwarves to work with him, between the legion and the dwarven army they'd have near parity with the approaching enemy army. Perhaps they might even have an edge, considering Karus had a large cavalry wing at his disposal. Since this world seemed to lack horses, it gave him a tremendous advantage. Then his thoughts darkened. There was a sickness tearing its way through the legion. He had no idea what his effective strength was currently or what it might be in the coming days.

The column is only an advance force, Kordem added. *A month's march from Carthum waits a larger army, numbering in the hundreds of thousands. They are likely gathering sufficient supplies before the next major push.*

"Wonderful," Karus said. "Just wonderful news."

"I no understand," Amarra said. "Why good?"

"It's not," Karus said. "We have to quit Carthum sooner than I'd hoped."

"I see," Amarra said. "No good then?"

"Definitely not good," Karus said, shook his head, and then breathed to himself. "One problem at a time, old boy."

Your problems are only just beginning, Cyln'phax said.

"Thanks for cheering me up," Karus said, though he quite agreed with the dragon. His greatest challenges lay ahead.

Pleased I could help, Cyln'phax said.

Karus blew out a long stream of air. When he returned, he would have to find ways to accelerate the construction of the wagons, if that was even possible. He understood, whatever efforts could be made, it wouldn't be enough. He would be forced to quit Carthum before they were fully ready. Large quantities of valuable supply would have to be left behind. The fact that he would have to cut his losses and move early was yet another thing that worried at him. He had a lot on his plate.

"I don't like running," Karus said and then turned to the dragons. "Will you help us if it comes to a fight with the Horde?"

We are here to help Amarra, Kordem said. *As our lord has commanded.*

"That does not answer my question," Karus said, "now, does it? Will you fight with us?"

The Horde is our enemy, Cyln'phax said.

"You will fight, then?" Karus asked. "Do I have that right?"

If the High Priestess desires us to do so, Kordem said, *then we shall.*

Karus turned to Amarra, looking for her input.

"I so desire," Amarra said. "We all fight together. Yes?"

Kordem lowered his head, as if bowing to Amarra's will. *It is as we expected, mistress. We will fight along with your legion, Karus.*

"I am grateful for that," Karus said to the dragons. The question was how to use the dragons to best effect, especially now that he knew the enemy had dragons as well, wyrms.

You are a favored son of the High Father, Cyln'phax said and sounded somewhat grudging. *I would not let you face the might of the Horde alone. I could not.* The dragon looked at her mate. *It would shame us.*

Karus gave a nod as he eyed the dragons. Abruptly, both swung their heads to Karus's left. He followed their gazes. He saw Si'Cara, along with Tal'Thor, emerging from the darkness. Both were carrying large packs. There was another elf with them, a male. He wore a robe. They stopped a few paces away and turned to face one another.

Amarra separated herself from Karus. She stood. Karus pulled himself to his feet. His old wound in his thigh ached. He massaged it with the palm of his hand as he looked at the elves. Si'Cara said something in a low tone. The other elf nodded and spoke in reply, and Karus could not quite make out what was said. But that did not matter. He supposed they were speaking in their own language. Si'Cara bowed her head respectfully, then started to make her way over to them. Tal'Thor remained behind, speaking with the other elf.

Pack slung over her shoulder, Si'Cara held her short bow loosely in one hand and a tightly tied bundle of arrows in the other. She appeared weary, weak even, as if run down and exhausted from a debilitating illness. She moved slowly, stiffly. Even though it was still dark, Karus thought she appeared extremely pale. It was clear the ordeal of having been stabbed and then healed had taken a lot out of her.

"I am ready." Her voice trembled with exhaustion as she spoke Common. "The dwarf should be here soon, not long."

Si'Cara can fly with me and Amarra, Kordem said. *The male ranger and dwarf will go with Cyln'phax.*

I shudder just thinking of allowing them upon my back, Cyln'phax said, sounding thoroughly disgusted.

"Fair enough." Karus glanced over at the dragons and considered the traveling arrangements. He did not see a problem with it. He was just pleased they'd not outright refused to take along the additional passengers.

How can you say that? There is nothing fair about this, Cyln'phax said. *A dwarf and an elf! It seems just wrong.*

Nevertheless, that's how it shall be, Kordem said.

Si'Cara glanced warily over at the dragons, then turned back to Karus and Amarra.

"I brought extra straps and ropes." Si'Cara dropped her pack to the ground. She began pulling them out, then looked up at Karus. "As you asked, I also brought warm blankets for you both and one for the dwarf."

Si'Cara removed three neatly folded gray blankets. They were made of wool and appeared thick enough to keep them warm. She set them on the ground next to her pack.

"Will they be good?" she asked.

"Thank you," Karus said. "It will make the journey more comfortable."

Si'Cara straightened and glanced over at Cyln'phax. Karus sensed her mood went from one of weariness to near excitement. She abruptly grinned and looked for a moment like a little girl about to get sweetmeats at the local fair. "Never thought I would ever go flying. I must admit I am quite eager."

"Neither did we," Karus said. "Can't say, from what I've seen of it already, I am terribly fond of flying."

She looked over at him dubiously. "Seriously? To soar like the birds must be glorious."

"We were almost killed by wyrms and noctalum on our way here," Karus said. "I found it somewhat less than glorious."

She glanced back at the dragons and chewed her lip, perhaps a little less excited than a moment ago. "What's life without a little risk?"

"Ah …" Amarra said, smiling at the elf. "Perhaps a little safer?"

"No," Si'Cara said. "It's boring."

"I've had enough excitement to last me a lifetime," Karus said.

A few feet away, Tal'Thor gripped the other elf's forearm. He gave a slow but firm nod, almost as if he had just agreed to something. He stepped away and joined them. Tal'Thor had his short bow slung over a shoulder, as well as a tightly bound quiver of arrows. He set his own pack down next to Si'Cara's. Her grin slipped from her face. She shot him a deeply unhappy look, but said nothing.

"Let me help you with your pack." Amarra moved between them and bent down to pick it up.

"I can manage," Si'Cara said quickly, stopping her with a hand. She hoisted it up before Amarra could get to it. Karus noticed the ranger's arms shook slightly from the effort. He realized she was ready to drop. Pride was the only thing keeping her going.

"How about I help you get the pack secured on Kordem's back?" Amarra suggested and offered a reassuring smile. "It's quite a climb up. I think you will like him. He's fearsome, to be sure, but a softie at heart."

Cyln'phax gave an unhappy snort, which shot tongues of flame from her nostrils.

"Okay," Si'Cara said, and together the two of them moved off toward Kordem.

Tal'Thor watched Si'Cara and Amarra walk off, his expression inscrutable. Cyln'phax was watching as well. Karus sensed a sourness from her.

"That's our ride," Karus said to the ranger. After what he'd done to Si'Cara, Karus would be damned if he'd lift a finger to help him. He could manage his own kit. "Better go and secure your pack."

The ranger eyed the dragon. He sucked in a deep breath and started over to Cyln'phax. He did not seem to share Si'Cara's excitement.

If there is any race I despise more than humans, it's elves, Cyln'phax said, her head swinging to fix Tal'Thor in a baleful gaze. *I like gnomes more than elves.*

Tal'Thor came to an abrupt, uncertain stop a few feet from the dragon.

Karus wondered what a gnome was. He hoped they weren't another enemy that he'd yet to meet.

You're almost as slow and dimwitted as Karus, Cyln'phax said, *which is saying something. Now stop dawdling, you fool, and get that bag of yours tied down.*

Karus almost grinned as Tal'Thor glanced back at him in question. Despite his dislike for the elf, Karus offered a shrug. At least, Karus thought, he would no longer be the exclusive butt of Cyln'phax's abuse. There was now another to share that burden, and for that tender mercy, he was grateful.

Karus glanced over at the elf who had accompanied Si'Cara and Tal'Thor and found him standing just two feet away. Karus almost jumped. It was the warden's advisor, the one who had counseled killing them. He'd approached unheard and unseen. Where before he'd sensed menace in the other's manner, now there was something else there. It was hard to read the elf in the near darkness, but Karus thought he detected a semblance of concern and perhaps a touch of worry.

"Yes?" Karus asked. "What is it?"

"I am Di'Cara," the elf said and offered a slight bow.

Karus said nothing in reply. This elf was in the warden's camp and was not to be considered anything close to a friend. So, he just waited for the elf to say more.

Di'Cara's gaze shifted to Si'Cara briefly, lingering almost regretfully for a moment before returning to Karus.

"The fortress is no longer what it was intended to be, a secure place to hold treasures of wonder and items of dread," Di'Cara said. He reached out a hand and gripped Karus's arm, as if to show the importance of his words. He held it but a moment, then raised a finger and shook it in Karus's face. "The fortress has been corrupted, twisted. The warden has kept this from our people."

"What do you mean, corrupted?" Karus asked.

Di'Cara cast his gaze behind him, back into the dark forest.

"I have said too much. Be on your guard, Karus. The Warriors of Anagradoom will not welcome you as they once might have. Listen to my daughter in the days, months, and years to come. Be guided by her. She has seen much of this world and can help. You can trust Si'Cara with your life. She will not betray you, unless you betray her."

"Your daughter?" Karus asked. Di'Cara looked no older than Si'Cara. In fact, they could have been brother and sister. Heck, he thought, elves looked too much alike.

Sadness swept over Di'Cara. His gaze abruptly became piercing and his voice trembled with anger. "I had hoped for so much from her. Now, she has no future. She is without house and family. My daughter has been cast out for taking your side."

"If you are looking to place blame," Karus said, "I would look to your warden. Besides, what kind of a father are you?

I didn't see you lift a finger to help her or, for that matter, try to stop the warden."

The elf stiffened, his face becoming flushed in the darkness. He turned away and began striding off across the square in the direction he had come, robes rustling across the stone.

"I will do what I can to look after her," Karus called. He wasn't sure why he said that. The words seemed to slip out.

Di'Cara stopped and partially turned back. He held Karus's gaze a moment, then continued on his way off into the night, leaving Karus feeling frustrated at not knowing what dangers lay ahead.

Elves, Cyln'phax said. *Always lots to say and less than helpful.*

Karus glanced over at the dragon. He could not agree more. Troubled, he looked back toward Si'Cara's father and blinked in surprise. Di'Cara had vanished, as if he had never been. Under the moonlight, there had not been enough time for him to make it across the square and into the trees. Karus looked around, carefully scanning the darkness. He could see the rangers still where they had been moments before. They'd not moved.

Scowling, Karus turned his gaze to Kordem. Amarra was climbing up onto the dragon's back, wearing Si'Cara's pack as she made her way up. Si'Cara waited just below, looking upward.

Where had Di'Cara gone?

Karus scanned the square once more. Instead of spotting Di'Cara, he spied the dwarf emerging from the darkness, escorted by six of the warden's pretty-looking guards. The dwarf wore only a tunic and carried no sword, nor any weapon. He paused at seeing the dragons, almost missing a step. One of the guards, clearly impatient, roughly shoved him from behind with his spear. The dwarf stumbled forward several paces, barely managing to keep his feet. He turned, fists balling, and said something harsh. Another guard hit him in the chest with the butt of his spear, knocking him to the ground. Two of the guards began kicking the dwarf, who was on the ground and helpless.

Karus became enraged at the sight.

"That's enough," Karus shouted in his best parade-ground voice and stormed over. "I said, that's enough!"

Two of the nearest lowered their spear points toward Karus, menace and malice written across their expressions. One, whom Karus took to be the leader, called something back to him in Elven. This one's armor was more ornate, more splendid than the others'. Whatever it was that was said, it did not sound terribly pleasant to Karus's ears. He assumed he had just been insulted. Ignoring the words, Karus moved into their midst and roughly pushed one of the spears away as the guard attempted to block him.

He stared daggers at the elf, daring him to do something. When the elf did not move, Karus bent down and helped the dwarf up, grasping him by his arm and hauling him to his feet. Karus almost groaned with the effort, for the dwarf was surprisingly heavy for his size.

The leader spoke again to Karus. It sounded quite nasty. The expression only confirmed it.

"Care to say that to me in Common?" Karus turned to the elf. "Want to back up those words, you fancy prick?"

The leader took a step forward, but stopped. The hate was almost physical. Karus itched to draw his sword.

"He said some unkind words about your parentage," the dwarf said in a voice that was deep, gravelly, and coarse. His Common, like Karus's, was heavily accented. He coughed, spitting up blood onto his hand.

"He did, did he?" Karus said.

The dwarf nodded wearily. "Something about your mother breeding with a teska. My elf speak isn't that great."

From the old bruises on his face, along with fresh ones, it was apparent he had been beaten, perhaps even tortured. Compared to the other dwarves Karus had seen, he also appeared half-starved, as his cheeks were quite thin and hollow. His beard and hair were unkempt. However, Karus saw in his eyes and in the way he held himself a sort of grim determination, a spirit that refused to yield. Here was someone who would keep doggedly going in the face of adversity. Karus liked him already.

"I am Karus."

"Dennig," the dwarf said and spat bloody spittle on the ground toward the feet of one of the elves. The leader hissed in reply. Dennig ignored him. "I take it I have you to thank for my freedom?"

"You do," Karus said and then addressed himself to the leader, waving his hand. "You can go. No need to stay."

"What if we don't want to?" the elf asked.

"Then we're gonna have a problem, friend," Karus said and rested his hand upon the hilt of his sword. "And it's not going to end well for you or your mates. On that, I promise."

The ground shook as Cyln'phax stood, growling. It was an ugly sound, like a rabid dog might make, but much more intimidating and threatening. All eyes turned to the dragon. Having yet to secure himself, Tal'Thor was clinging to a spike on the dragon's back. The dragon's head whipped their way, and she took several steps toward them.

Should I kill them for you? Cyln'phax asked. Her voice boomed in Karus's mind. *It has been many years since I tasted elf flesh.*

The guards backpedaled as the dragon came closer still. The ground shuddered with each step, her claws digging deeply into the stone paving, cracking and tearing the stone up. When they departed, serious work would need to be done to repair all of the damage. Karus noticed the rangers had remained where they were and had not moved or raised a bow. He thought that curious. The guards, on the other hand, had taken several steps backward, away from the enraged dragon, Karus, and Dennig.

"In all honesty, I don't think they are worth the effort," Karus said.

You may be right. They appear rather scrawny and are likely too bony for my tastes... Still, perhaps I'll take just one.

The dragon's jaws parted, revealing rows of serrated teeth. Her red tongue licked at the air, before the jaws snapped twice with a loud popping sound. Cyln'phax took another step closer.

May I have one of them, Karus? You brought food with you. I haven't eaten since before we left Carthum. I am quite hungry. A snack before the next leg of our journey might just hit the spot.

Karus wondered if the dragon was serious. He decided she wasn't—at least, he hoped so.

"Were I you, I'd get going," Karus told the leader, who shot him a quick look before returning his attention to the dragon.

Cyln'phax let loose a small jet of flame. The light from it lit up the square around them. Karus could feel the intense heat upon his skin. The guards did not need any more convincing. They turned and rapidly made tracks across the square. Their flight made Karus grin. It served them right. He hated bullies and always had.

"Well, Dennig," Karus said, turning back to the dwarf, who appeared just as amused, "we need to leave. Let's get you up and secured on Cyln'phax's back."

"What?" Dennig asked, eyes going wide as he glanced toward the dragon. "You must be joking."

Sadly, he's not, dwarf, Cyln'phax said. *Trust me, this wasn't my idea. It was all him.*

"I will not," Dennig said firmly, looking back on Karus. "You can't ask this of me. My kind and theirs are not what you might say…generally on the best of terms. Hateful enemies would be more like it."

Karus felt himself frown at the dwarf and shot a look at Cyln'phax.

You dwarves hunt our kind, too, the dragon said, as if that made things right between them. *Let's just agree not to like one another and get it over with. Once we're away from elven lands, I can set you down. You can be on your way and we on ours.*

"I am not going," Dennig said forcefully. "No way, no how."

"This is the only way," Karus said, becoming frustrated and wondering on the bad blood between dragon and dwarf.

This is good, Cyln'phax said, suddenly sounding pleased. *I did not want to sully myself by carrying a dwarf anyway. The shame is almost more than I can bear. Karus, you can now leave him, and with no regrets, too.*

"Look," Karus said to the dwarf, "I really don't want to leave you behind. Just climb onto the beast so we can go. It is as simple as that."

Who are you calling a beast? Cyln'phax asked indignantly.

Karus ignored the dragon and did his best with Common, making sure he spoke slowly so as not to make a mistake. "I've gotten you out of the warden's prison. I will do my best to get you back to your people. The dragons are the only way out of here. I can't force you, but I'd suggest you come with us. Unless you'd like to remain a guest of the warden?"

The dwarf sucked in a breath, regarding Karus. He looked back into the trees, suddenly less than certain.

"No thank you. The warden's accommodations are not the nicest, nor friendliest," Dennig said. "Why did you free me?"

"I'd heard you came seeking allies," Karus said.

"We do not ally with humans," Dennig said matter-of-factly. His eyes narrowed. "Still want to take me with you?"

"I don't care if our people ally or not. I wouldn't leave you here with the warden," Karus said. "She's too much of a nasty bitch, with whom I'd not even entrust my enemies."

"That I can appreciate." Dennig barked out a laugh and then sobered, turning to look at the dragons. He shook his head slightly. "We must ride them, you say?"

Karus gave a nod.

"All right," Dennig said and puffed up his chest. "No one will call me weak-kneed." He bellowed out a laugh. "I will gain much legend from this."

And I shame, Cyln'phax said sullenly.

Karus motioned for Dennig to follow and walked over to where Si'Cara had left the wool blankets. Amarra had already taken a blanket for herself. He handed one to Dennig, who looked back on him curiously.

"It's cold up there." Karus pointed toward the sky. "This will help to keep you warm."

They moved over to Cyln'phax, who lay back down so that they could climb up onto her back. Karus allowed Dennig to go first. The dwarf quickly clambered up. Karus started after him.

Karus looked in the direction the guards had gone as he pulled himself up. So fast was their flight from the square, there was no longer any sign of them.

Tal'Thor had already secured himself. Their eyes met. The elf puffed out his cheeks.

"Would you really have eaten them?" Karus asked.

No, Cyln'phax said. *As I said, elves are too bony. Not enough meat. Besides, they actually taste terrible.* The dragon swung her gaze around to look upon Dennig, jaws opening to reveal her long teeth. *Now dwarves ... that's an entirely different matter. Plenty of meat on their bones.*

Dennig looked to Karus, alarmed.

"She's not serious," Karus said, even though he was concerned the dragon might be.

Of course I am, Cyln'phax said with a slight trace of amusement. *Now, get yourselves tied down. I want to be out of this den of the senselessness.*

Karus shook his head, moving over to where he had left his straps and ties. Tal'Thor tossed Dennig a few. The dwarf, without needing to question their necessity, began to tie himself down a few feet away.

It was time to go. He began securing himself, making sure the straps were tied tightly. He did not ever wish to return to Irin'Surall.

CHAPTER ELEVEN

Cyln'phax blew a narrow stream of fire onto the stacked pile of wood Karus and Dennig had built. Having been scavenged from the forest a few yards away, the wood was damp from a recent rain that Karus was thankful they had not flown through. The wind was bad enough by itself. There was no need to add rain.

The wood hissed against the jet of fire, steaming and hissing loudly. The dragon paused for several heartbeats to regard her work, then shot out a second longer stream of fire. Karus had made sure to stand back, well clear of the fire. He resisted the urge to take another step backward as the heat intensified. After a dozen heartbeats, the stream of fire ceased. Cyln'phax's jaw closed with an audible snap.

"That's a good fire," Karus said. The blaze cracked and popped loudly, almost pleasantly. Starting a fire from wet wood was always a pain in the ass. The dragon's effort had saved him considerable time. "Thank you."

The dragon tilted her head, fixing Karus with one baleful eye.

Don't mention it ... ever.

Karus and Dennig were alone with the two dragons. Si'Cara, Amarra, and Tal'Thor had gone for water. Karus was none too happy about that, but Amarra had left him little say in the matter.

186

Cyln'phax eyed him a moment longer, then drew her head back and away from him. The dragon moved a little closer toward the forest. The ground trembled at her movement. She lay down, tail curling protectively around her body. On the other side of the fire, Kordem had already lowered himself to the ground and was watching Karus. The end of the dragon's tail was swishing about in the grass, like a cat toying with a mouse. The dragon's scrutiny seemed rather intense and made Karus slightly uncomfortable.

Since they had landed at the base of the hill upon which sat the Fortress of Radiance, both dragons had almost seemed ill at ease. If Karus had not known better, he would have thought something was bothering them, for they were fidgety, constantly shifting about.

"That was great." Dennig was standing next to Karus. He held his hands out toward the fire, warming them. "I can now see the advantage of having a pet dragon."

Watch your mouth, dwarf—Cyln'phax swung her head toward them, jaws parting to display her vicious-looking teeth—*or you will end up in mine.*

Dennig glanced sharply at Cyln'phax, then to Karus and back again to the dragon. He blinked several times, but he said nothing further. After what Karus was sure were several uncomfortable moments for the dwarf, Cyln'phax turned away, as if she had lost interest in him. Dennig let out an almost imperceptible breath he had been holding.

Karus found himself somewhat amused. He was beginning to suspect Cyln'phax was mostly bluster, with little if no bite, when it came to those she thought were friends. Karus certainly wasn't about to test that himself. She was a dragon after all—a dread creature.

The blankets Si'Cara had provided had made the trip much more comfortable. Yet, it still had been a long flight, and the inability to stretch his legs had made it rather uncomfortable. His old thigh wound ached abominably, and in fact his entire body was sore. This was partly due to the lack of sleep. Karus understood that years spent marching under the emperor's Eagle had also taken their toll. He was feeling his age. With each passing year, the aches and pains were growing. Karus stretched out his stiff back and then cracked his neck.

It was well past noon. Both suns were high up in the sky. The air was just warm enough not to be uncomfortable. It seemed almost like an early fall day. However, he understood this was deceiving. They were only a few yards from the edge of the forest and the shade of the massive trees. The cool air from the dark forest flowed outward, washing over and around them.

The dragons had landed them at the base of a large hill, upon which was perched the Fortress of Radiance. From his vantage, Karus could only see one side of the fortress's outer walls. He suspected the hill was not a natural feature, as it had a mound-like shape to it. It was as if a child had formed it out of sand at the beach, which led Karus to the conclusion the hill had been made. It was the only elevated ground for miles and miles around, completely surrounded by a veritable sea of trees, which reinforced his feeling. It reminded him very much of the hill the legion had found itself upon when they'd been transported to this world. Like that one, this hill was also bare of trees, covered only in long grass and scrub brush.

"Are you hungry?" Karus asked Dennig, who was still staring warily at the dragon.

Karus bent down and opened the pack that contained their food. He rummaged around inside as Dennig tore his gaze away from the dragon.

"I am so hungry I could eat a teska by myself," Dennig said.

While they had been gathering wood in the forest, Karus had noticed that Dennig moved like an old man. He observed how the dwarf's legs seemed unsteady and his arms trembled with the effort of picking up and carrying the wood they'd scavenged. Still, the dwarf had not complained while they worked. Karus felt certain that while in the custody of the warden, Dennig had missed more than a few meals. He was clearly too proud to show or admit any hint of weakness, especially to a human. He had not even asked for food. Karus knew the dwarf's type well. Dennig would keep going 'til he collapsed.

Karus pulled out a small bundle of bread and a wedge of cheese. Both had been wrapped in gray cloth. Dennig's eyes lit up at the sight of the food and he held his hands out. Karus tossed them one after the other to him. The dwarf caught both and moved away a few paces, settling down in the knee-high grass near the warmth of the fire.

Earlier, Karus had made sure to uproot the grass all around where he had placed the wood for the fire. A second pile of wood, mostly broken and snapped branches, sat off to the side, ready to be tossed in when the blaze began to die down.

A gentle breeze caused the nearby trees to rustle and creak. The flames shifted with the breeze, the smoke abruptly swirling and blowing in Karus's direction. He held his breath until the wind passed and the smoke shifted once again.

Unwrapping the food, Dennig began to greedily eat, first choosing to tear into the cheese with serious relish. He closed his eyes as he chewed rapidly and swallowed the first bite, nearly wolfing it down.

Karus left the dwarf to eat and walked over to where Kordem lay. Still intently following his every move, the dragon watched him with what seemed to Karus more like curiosity than anything else. Karus approached but said nothing. He felt like a mouse trapped in a cat's mesmerizing gaze, the hunter coiled and ready to spring for the kill, or perhaps catch and just play with him for a time. Despite his earlier feelings about Cyln'phax being all bluster, he wasn't sure if he would ever become comfortable with the two monstrous creatures.

Putting that thought from his mind, he grabbed both Amarra's and Si'Cara's packs where they had left them and brought them over to the fire, setting them down next to the others. The blaze had fully taken hold and the fire was shedding quite a lot of heat. So much so that Dennig had scooted several feet back from the blaze. The fire pushed back at the chill air emanating from the forest.

Karus turned toward the tree line, sweeping it with his gaze, eyeing the spaces in between the giant trunks warily. Dark and heavily shaded, the forest felt more than foreboding, especially now that he knew elves lived out there amongst the trees. He still found he had some difficulty believing such massive trees could be real, even when he could walk over and touch them himself. It was like the dragons, orcs, elves, gods, and magic … hard to credit such things were possible. At times he felt as if he were in a dream come to life. Or was it all just a terrible nightmare?

Before landing, they had spotted a large river winding its way through the forest. Amarra, Si'Cara, and Tal'Thor had decided to go to this river to fetch fresh water. Karus figured it was about a quarter mile from where the dragons had put down. The forest was so thick and impenetrable-looking, he voiced concerns that they might lose their way.

"We know this forest," Tal'Thor had said. "No need to worry. We shall not become lost or turned around."

Amarra had been surprisingly eager to go with the elves, to explore the trees. It had left him torn. Though Si'Cara and Tal'Thor seemed sincere enough about helping, Karus had long since learned trust was something that needed to be built and developed over time. However, it was very difficult to do that when distrust already existed. A few hours before, both would have willingly killed him and Amarra without a moment's hesitation.

That aside, Karus had had no choice in the matter. Amarra was determined to go into the forest with the elves, and go she did. Every fiber in Karus's body had screamed, *No, don't go.* Amarra, for her part, had not seemed concerned in the slightest. Karus felt she was being entirely too trusting and had almost voiced this opinion in front of the elves. She had shot him a final look dissuading him from the idea of any additional protest. She was going and that was final. In a way it had been their first disagreement, and a minor one at that.

The entire time she'd been gone had left Karus anxious about her safety. He found himself periodically glancing toward the trees, searching the forest's murky depths for a sign of her. He discovered it was not a good feeling.

"Why are we here?" Dennig asked through a mouth that was half full of cheese, which made his heavily accented Common more difficult to understand. The dwarf gestured with the wedge of cheese toward the fortress. "What's so important that you would come all the way out here to that miserable-looking ruin? What's up there?"

Karus considered Dennig for a long moment. He badly needed allies, and Dennig perhaps was the key, or at least the first step, to gaining more. If Karus could manage to build a bridge with him, it might also be done with the other dwarves. So, he settled for honesty and openness. Besides, he reasoned, the dwarf would find out soon enough why they had come.

"There's something important up in that fortress," Karus said. "We believe it can help us with our struggle against the Horde."

Dennig raised his bushy eyebrows at that. He took another bite and chewed thoughtfully, tilting his head slightly. "What exactly is it that you are looking for?"

Karus was silent a moment as he considered how to best answer. He needed not only allies, but information, particularly about the struggle between the dwarves and the Horde. The dwarf might be able to provide both. At the very least, Karus might be able to gain some valuable intelligence concerning the enemy.

"How about you answer a question of mine and in turn I will answer one of yours?" Karus suggested and paused to let it sink in. "Does that sound agreeable?"

Dwarves are not to be trusted, Cyln'phax said.

"The same could be said for thieving dragons," Dennig retorted acidly, his cheeks coloring.

The only sneak thief here is you, dwarf.

"Stop it," Karus ordered, raising his voice and holding up his hands to Dennig while shooting the dragon a meaningful look. He very much desired to keep this cordial and didn't need Cyln'phax and the dwarf going at it.

The dragon seemed to sense Karus's intention, for she made a loud snorting sound and lowered her head to the ground, where it landed with a solid thud that he felt through his sandals.

"We're going up there to retrieve a sword." Karus jerked a thumb at the fortress. "It's apparently special."

"Special? A sword?" Dennig's brows drew together. "What kind of sword? How is it special?"

"It's your turn to answer a question," Karus said.

"All right," Dennig said, "we'll play your game. Ask away."

"The elves tell me you came seeking allies," Karus said. "Is that correct?"

Dennig took another bite of his cheese, this one smaller than his last. He chewed and swallowed before answering, a sour look overcoming him.

"In the past we have sought to enlist the elves as allies. This time, we came seeking assistance, or really permission." Dennig dug up a tuft of grass with the heel of his boot. "I was sent with a delegation to see if the elves would allow my chieftain's war band to move through elven lands, to take a shortcut, if you will." He stopped talking as he moved the dislodged tuft of grass around with his foot. "I did not expect my mission to be successful, but we had to try." Dennig paused and looked back up at Karus. "So, now it is my turn. What's so special about this sword you are looking for?"

"I don't know," Karus admitted. "We were told to retrieve it before we leave this world, that it would somehow help. From what I understand, it is magical, but I have no idea what it does or can do."

"Magic, ha!"

Dennig snorted as he ran a hand through his long beard, which was unbrushed and almost completely covered his belly. Combined with his long hair, which was blown back from the wind, the dwarf had a wild, almost outlandish look. Dennig's fingers caught in a tangle. He forced them slowly through as he looked upon Karus.

"Some fools put a lot of faith in such things," Dennig said. "Me, I think tinkering with magic is just trouble, pure and simple. That includes special items as well, like this sword you seek. Mark my words, it's all trouble in the end."

Karus thought about that a moment. What Dennig said was possibly true, but he had no choice. The High Father had told him to retrieve the sword and that was what he would do, for good or ill.

"All right," Karus said. "My turn. If you did not think you would be successful, why go to see the elves? Why even bother making the attempt?"

"I am a soldier," Dennig said and hesitated slightly. "I was ordered to go. In truth, I would have volunteered. To save my brothers, I would not hesitate to give my own life."

"You almost did," Karus said.

"Aye." Dennig's gaze became unfocused. He took a deep breath and let it out slowly. "My war band was sent to Carthum to consolidate supplies and forage more from the surrounding countryside, which had just been abandoned by its people. Shortly after we arrived, we learned of some of our fellows who had become trapped behind enemy lines and were besieged in a small castle. My chieftain, ah … our general made the decision to march to their aid. We were successful in breaking the siege, freeing our boys, and killing many of the enemy. However, on the march back, as we were moving out of hostile lands, the enemy managed to surprise us." Dennig paused. "Our pioneers discovered two enemy columns moving to trap us. Outnumbered, we were in a difficult position, nearly boxed in."

Dennig ran his fingers through his beard again, as if attempting to comb it.

"As my chieftain saw it, there were two options. We could fight one of the armies before both could combine against us, break it, and escape, marching like the wind back to Carthum. The other option was to seek permission to cross into elven lands and avoid another costly fight. Long story told short, that's how I came to be in the hands of the elves." The dwarf paused, becoming bitter. "I went to them to talk. They, as you likely know, had different ideas. They killed my escort and threw me into a prison cell and left me to rot."

"I see," Karus said, sympathizing with Dennig's position. Had Karus been in his place, he would have done the same and risked it all with the elves in the hopes he could save his men. Only the elves had proven treacherous, specifically the warden. Had Karus not come, Dennig would still be rotting in the warden's prison.

"Who sent you to get the sword?" Dennig asked.

"The High Father," Karus said.

Dennig burst out a guffaw that turned into a belly laugh. He fell silent when he saw that Karus was thoroughly serious. His eyes narrowed.

"Truly?" Dennig asked suspiciously. "You are not having one over on me?"

Karus shook his head.

"You and the woman with the funny staff are believers?" Dennig genuinely seemed surprised by Karus's admission.

"We are and do believe," Karus said. "Amarra and I both."

"My father kept the faith," Dennig said, a sad note creeping into his voice. A fraction of a moment later, that note turned rock hard. "He honored our gods. In the end, it did not save him or my mum from an orc's sword. They were butchered like sheep when our village was overrun." He shook what was left of the cheese at Karus. "Faith only gets you so far in this world. These days, very few, if any, of my people bother to make serious devotions towards the gods, beyond simply mouthing the words." Dennig ran his fingers through his beard again as he gazed up at Karus. "I thought most humans had given up on the gods as well. You really keep the faith?"

We are all believers, Kordem said, shifting his bulk, his massive tail swishing loudly through the grass. *It is why we have come to this forsaken place.*

Dennig glanced Kordem's way. He sat up straighter, nostrils flaring as he sucked in a deep breath. The dwarf's eyes flicked from the dragon to Karus.

"Your general," Karus said, deciding to move things along, "he wouldn't be named Shoega, would he?"

Dennig froze in mid-chew, gaze locked upon Karus. He recovered a moment later and swallowed.

"The elves told you about me and my mission," Dennig said and took another smaller bite of his bread, chewing thoughtfully. "Why play this game of pretending not to know? You are toying with me."

"I met another of your kind," Karus said.

"You did?" Dennig seemed surprised by this revelation.

"Torga. He was looking for your general, your chieftain," Karus said. "Thought my legion might have had something to do with him going missing."

"Did he, now?" Dennig's eyes lit up. "My, that is encouraging, very encouraging."

"He threatened me," Karus said.

"Now, that sounds like Torga," Dennig said and grinned. "It pleases me greatly to know we have not been completely forgotten. Okay, my turn again. You said you were leaving. How do you intend to manage that? With the Horde controlling both World Gates, how do you plan on getting off this shithole of a world? That I'd very much like to know."

Until this moment, Karus had not known there were two World Gates. He recalled the High Father telling them there was more than one, but not how many. Karus had no idea where the Gates were, but it was good to know that the dwarves knew. Dennig had also revealed something else of value to him. The dwarves wanted off this world as well and, if Karus was any judge, they desired it desperately.

Karus had a Key to one of the Gates, which supposedly would allow him to operate it. He suddenly wondered if the enemy knew of the Key and were searching for it as well, like he had come in search for Rarokan. Would the enemy come for the Key? Had that been why they'd entered the city? Or had it been to free the druids and cause mayhem?

Perhaps, he considered, the dwarves were looking too, for the Key potentially represented a possible escape from this world that was being overrun by the enemy. Beyond the strength of his legion, Karus was now keenly aware he had something of incredible value to offer for a potential alliance. Would the dwarves be interested in working with him? Or would they try to take the Key by force once they learned he had it?

Another question came to mind, a troubling one at that. His Key...which World Gate did it go to?

"Well?" Dennig asked, having become impatient at not receiving an immediate reply. The dwarf gave a cynical laugh. "Tell me, Karus, how will you get off this world? How do you plan to get through enemy lines to a Gate?"

Karus glanced over at the dragons, hoping they would remain silent. Kordem was still watching him, and quite intently, too. The dragon dipped his head slightly, as if indicating Karus should continue. Both dragons knew about the Key, for he and Amarra had emerged from the ruins of the High Father's temple with it.

"I still have to figure that one out," Karus admitted. He was not yet ready to tell Dennig about the Key, at least until he knew more about the dwarves and felt they could be trusted. "I think it starts by making allies, though. I don't believe we can manage it alone, especially if the Horde holds both Gates."

"I told you already," Dennig said, "my people don't ally with humans."

"We'll see," Karus said. "Tell me more of your army, your general."

"I am tired of playing this game, Karus," Dennig said, becoming surly. "I will tell you nothing more on that other than what I've already said. You don't need to know more. At this point, I just want to return to my people."

"I understand," Karus said, and he did.

"Are you a man of your word, Karus?"

"I try to be," Karus said.

"Good. I will hold you to it."

The dwarf took a bite of bread and turned away from him. In the silence that followed, the fire snapped and crackled loudly. Karus rubbed his jaw, feeling the growing stubble and thinking on what he'd just learned. Movement to his left drew his attention.

Amarra, Si'Cara, and Tal'Thor emerged from the trees. Amarra gave him a wave. Karus let out a relieved breath at seeing her safe and sound. Carrying more than a dozen full canteens between them, the trio walked up to the fire and set them down next to the packs.

Everyone appeared tired and more than weary. They'd all spent most of the night with little, if any, sleep, then the morning and early afternoon getting here on dragonback. Karus was bone-tired. He glanced up at the fortress that capped the hill and studied it for several heartbeats, then turned back to the others.

"I think we should spend the night here," Karus said. He had become resigned to that little fact of necessity, though he'd have liked nothing more than to immediately march up the hill and get it all over with so he could return to the legion. "We need rest. In the morning, we can hike up to the fortress and get the sword."

"I think that's a good idea," Amarra said with evident relief and a concerned glance thrown over to Si'Cara, who appeared about ready to collapse. Si'Cara gave a tired nod and woodenly sat down in the grass by the fire.

We agree, Kordem stood, unfurling his wings and stretching out his tail. The dragon shook himself like a dog might.

Cyln'phax stood as well.

It has been a few days since we have eaten, Kordem said. *We will hunt and return in the morning, by midday at the latest.*

When you decide to go up into the fortress, Cyln'phax said, *do not wait on us.*

"You won't be going with us?" Amarra asked, voicing the alarm Karus felt.

No, mistress. Kordem's tone was full of great respect, but it was also firm. *This is as far as we can go. The web of will that has been spun over the fortress was cast by a wizard of nearly unsurpassed power, a High Master of the Order of Obsidian. We are repelled by it, repulsed by its strength. Not even the noctalum, with all of their considerable will, could go up there, if they so desired. The web needs to be brought down, or broken for us to join you. This is something you will have to do without us.*

Karus certainly did not like the sound of that, especially the part about them going it alone. He turned his gaze to the fortress. The top of the wall facing them was visible and illuminated under the bright light from the two suns. Much of it was covered over in green, which Karus assumed was ivy. From the air, the fortress had seemed a formidable position. Constructed of stone, the walls were box-like, with what appeared to be a good-sized central multistory, crenulated keep. He had seen all of that from a distance. It now made sense to him why the dragons had not landed them atop the hill. He had assumed it was not to unduly alarm the defenders. But it now seemed there was more to it than that.

"This web you speak of, what is it?" Karus asked, for it certainly sounded like magic.

An enchantment designed to keep all out but those who were foretold and belong, Kordem said, while stretching and craning his neck outward. *Even this far removed, we can feel it pushing us away. It is quite an uncomfortable sensation, almost painful.*

We are forced to expend our own will *to remain here with you,* Cyln'phax added. *We can go no closer and should really depart, for the strain wears unduly upon us both.*

"And what of us?" Amarra asked, gesturing around. "It's safe for us to go up there?"

I did not say that, mistress, Kordem said. *It may prove to be quite unsafe. We simply do not know what is up in the fortress, other than the sword. However, as foretold, you are able to go where we cannot.*

Karus wondered who had done the foretelling. Was there an oracle on this world? It was an interesting line of thought. There had always been loads of priests and holy men from barbarian religions who claimed to know of future events or to be able to divine the answers to difficult questions. Scrying and sacrifices had always been popular but incredibly unreliable. Even Roman priests practiced sacrificial rites to determine omens and the intentions of the gods. However, an oracle was different, at least in Karus's mind. He had read about the Oracle at Delphi. Oracles were known to give reliable answers to difficult questions, provide guidance, and predict the future with uncanny success. If there was a true oracle on this world, a visit might be in order. The oracle might be able to tell him more on what he needed to know in how to save his legion and escape this world.

We don't know what is waiting for you, Cyln'phax said, *or what dangers you will face. But go you must, and without us.*

We regret we cannot go with you, Kordem said.

Karus and Amarra shared a concerned look.

"My brother Kol is up there," Si'Cara said, pointing toward the top of the hill from where she sat in the grass. "He is the leader of the Anagradoom. They are honorable, noble warriors, the best amongst us. I tell you it will be all right. You will see. The warriors will not hurt, nor seek to harm us. If anything, they will give over what you seek."

I pray it is as you say, Kordem said. *Truly.*

Karus's thoughts went to what Di'Cara had told him about the fortress. From the hooded look Tal'Thor cast Si'Cara, Karus suspected the ranger had been told something similar. Karus wondered why Si'Cara's father had said nothing to her. Had he attempted to shield her from the truth? Or had she not listened to his concerns?

"I don't feel comfortable with you leaving us," Karus said to the dragons. It wasn't just that they could not go with them up to the fortress. The warden had shown she could not be trusted. Were there any other elves out in the forest, hidden from view? Were they even now being watched? The warden was a great distance removed from them, but that did not make Karus feel any better.

We won't be far, Kordem said and swung his head toward the two elves, almost as if he could read Karus's thoughts. *And I doubt very much that there are any elves nearby. Your people do not come near this place, do they?*

"You have the right of it. By order of the warden, we avoid the fortress," Tal'Thor said. "The only elves within fifty miles are the Warriors of Anagradoom, and they are unable to leave."

Good. Then rest, eat. Kordem's tone held a note of finality to it. *We shall return.*

With that, the dragon flapped his powerful wings, sending a tremendous gust of wind over them. It was almost strong enough to extinguish the fire and knock Karus over. He was forced to brace himself and shield his eyes from the dirt, fallen leaves, and debris kicked up. Kordem continued to beat at the air with his leathery wings. Cyln'phax took off a moment later, leaping up from the ground.

The dragons climbed, circling above them higher and higher as they clawed their way skyward, toward the clouds. Yet, even though they were leaving, Karus felt a small measure of relief he was not going with them. His two feet belonged planted firmly on the solid ground.

Silently, they watched the dragons. Silhouetted against the sky, Kordem and Cyln'phax were magnificent, beautiful even, despite their fearsomeness. He couldn't help but look as both creatures climbed ever skyward, for he was being treated to something few had the pleasure to see.

Then the dragons ceased their beating. Wings outstretched, they seemed to hang on the air, suspended by an unseen hand, before abruptly banking. Together, they dove toward the ground, picking up tremendous speed. Then they were gone, disappearing from view as they crossed behind the tree cover. Karus heard one of the dragons distantly cry out. Then nothing more. Silence returned. Not even the birds dared yet call to one another. They seemed scared stiff.

"If only we could get rid of the elves so easily." Dennig spat on the ground, breaking the silence after a long moment. "Then I'd be a happy dvergr."

Tal'Thor turned a cold gaze upon the dwarf. Karus could sense the intense dislike between the two as it flared white hot.

"Perhaps I should finish the work the warden started," Tal'Thor said, hand slipping toward one of his daggers. "The world won't miss one less dwarf."

"You can try, pretty boy," Dennig said, standing and balling his fists. "You can try."

Karus had had enough.

"Cease this!" Karus shouted and both were startled enough to look over at him. He needed to set the expectation that they were required to get along with one another. "I don't care what has transpired or who wronged whom. As long as we travel together, there will be no violence between us, nor harsh words. We keep the peace here, amongst ourselves. I will tolerate nothing less." He pointed off toward the trees. "Otherwise you can go on your way now." Karus paused, looking between the elves and Dennig. "Is that understood?"

The silence returned as the elves and dwarf stared back at him. Amarra had turned her gaze upon him as well. He resisted the temptation to glance her way.

"I asked," Karus said, becoming seriously irritated and taking a step toward them, "is that understood?"

"It is," Dennig said, deflating. He sat back down in the grass. "All I ask is you return me to my people."

Karus looked to Tal'Thor.

"We will not harm the dwarf," Si'Cara said, speaking for them both with a disapproving glare thrown to Tal'Thor. The other ranger, meeting Karus's gaze, gave a curt nod of acceptance.

"Dennig," Karus said and turned to the dwarf, "once we retrieve the sword, I will do my best to return you to your people. Just as I promised."

"And I will appreciate that … if it happens. That's right, Karus … you are a man of your word."

Karus sucked in an irritated breath and was about to say more when Dennig spoke again, holding up a hand, almost in apology.

"I am being unkind. Forgive me." Dennig glanced down at the ground and then looked back up as if a thought had hit him. "Instead of simply returning me to my people, do you think it possible you can get me back to my army? That is, if they managed to escape. I know not where you are going after this, but your dragons cover a lot of ground easily. Perhaps they can find my boys?"

It was a reasonable enough request and at the same time served Karus's interests. If they could find Shoega's army, then he would have some idea how close the Horde had gotten to Carthum. He would know how much time he had before he was forced to quit the city. The more Karus thought on the idea, the more he warmed to it.

"I will need to speak with the dragons about that," Karus said. "I can tell you they saw what I think is your army a few days ago. It was being pursued by the enemy. If we can, we will get you back to them."

Dennig fell silent at that, but gave a satisfied nod of his head.

A little frustrated at his traveling companions, Karus sucked in a breath and looked over at Amarra. She offered him a weary smile as she stepped nearer. Her proximity filled him with a warm glow that cheered against the weariness and exhaustion.

"Hungry?" he asked her.

"And tired," Amarra said to him in Latin, stifling a yawn with the back of her hand. "I very tired."

"We eat first, then make camp," Karus said to everyone. He bent down and retrieved another bundle of cheese and bread from the pack. He handed these over to Amarra and then grabbed some bread for himself.

"Thanks," Amarra said. "We eat together, yes?"

"Together," Karus said and retrieved a wedge of cheese for himself.

Amarra led him over to where Cyln'phax's bulk had flattened the grass. She sat down and patted the ground next to her. Karus found the ground still warm from the dragon's body heat. She leaned against him as she unwrapped her cheese. She sniffed at the wedge before taking a small nibble.

Karus sucked in a deep breath through his nose. He could smell the strong scent of the forest a few yards off. With Amarra by his side, and his daily responsibilities with the legion miles away, Karus suddenly and absurdly felt as if everything was as near perfect as could be. And this despite his disagreeable and cantankerous traveling companions.

Amarra was here, with him. That seemed to make everything just a little bit better, more bearable. Then, his eye snagged on the fortress upon the crest of the hill, and a sense of foreboding washed over him. His gaze moved from the hill toward his traveling companions, who were doing their best not to look at one another. He let out an unhappy breath.

"They act like spoiled children," Karus said.

"My children," Amarra said, following his gaze. "They mine."

Karus looked over at her in question.

"I High Priestess," Amarra said. "They mine flock, spoiled or not. I teach them to grow and love our god."

Karus felt himself scowl a little at that. None of the other three were sitting together. It was as if they did not want to associate, except Tal'Thor, who had eyes only for Si'Cara. He glanced her way whenever he thought she was not looking. And when she looked his way, he averted his gaze.

"You enjoy," Amarra said, patting his thigh and drawing his attention back to her. "Like moment, you and I. We together ... enjoy. Worry later, yes?"

"As you wish, mistress," Karus said, mimicking the dragons. "Your desire is my command."

She sat up and slapped him lightly on the arm before pointing a finger at him. "I am love of your life, not mistress. Understand?"

"I think you might be," Karus said to her.

Amarra giggled and smacked him again. "Think? You think? I find shocking."

Grinning, he pulled her to him and kissed her.

CHAPTER TWELVE

Karus wrapped the small brush up in the oil-stained towel he used for cleaning and returned both to his pack, stowing them away. He looked over his armor once again with a critical eye and was thoroughly satisfied with his work. It had needed some serious attention and was now free of dirt, debris, and grit, just how he preferred it. There was not even a hint of rust—a legionary's worst enemy.

Amarra, Si'Cara, Tal'Thor, and Dennig sat around the fire. They were finishing up their breakfast, which consisted of bread, cheese, and some sort of sweet tea the elves had made from a flower. Si'Cara said it came from a plant that grew up in the trees, which sounded remarkable to Karus. How could a plant grow without roots and soil? Though Karus preferred heated wine, the tea had been a warm and welcome surprise.

The night had been chilly, bordering on frigid. In the shadow of both the fortress and the forest, Karus was feeling somewhat unsettled. He had long since learned to trust his gut, and it told him danger was near. The elves, on the other hand, were quite certain they were safe, that nothing would trouble them in their camp. Karus had decided that, regardless, a watch would be set. He could feel it in his bones. Something just wasn't right. Whether it was out in the forest or up on the hill, he did not know.

Once his decision had been made, no one argued, which had been a relief. Dennig must have felt as he did, for the dwarf heartily embraced the idea of posting a sentry. So, Karus had set the example and taken first watch, while the others turned in. He had remained awake, listening to the sounds of the forest and occasionally taking a walk just beyond the firelight.

The night had worn on. Several hours later, Tal'Thor had relieved him for the second watch. They had not exchanged any words, just a soundless nod. Dennig had volunteered to stand the last watch, which would see the coming of dawn. Karus had moved back to the fire, past the softly snoring dwarf, and over to Amarra, careful not to make any undue noise as he settled down next to her.

Sleeping on the ground was always an uncomfortable prospect. However, Karus had long since become accustomed to it. They shared their blankets and his cloak. Between the fire and Amarra snuggling close against him, he had been warm enough. The warmth of her body pressing against his had been quite pleasant, enough so that he'd slept pretty soundly.

Karus rubbed his jaw. Looking up at the fortress, he felt the weight of his duty press upon him. He had never expected to command the legion, to effectively step into the legate's sandals when Julionus had died and Saturninus had cowardly fled.

Duty had been thrust upon him and there it would stay. He was unwilling to pass on the responsibility that was his and his alone. To do so would have been wrong, a betrayal of the trust placed in him as camp prefect. The trust came not from the late Julionus, but directly from the emperor and the measure of imperium that had been placed in his hands. Jupiter had blessed him as well, which meant Karus would soldier on no matter what difficulties he encountered. So, there could be no thought of passing along the burden of command. Upon his shoulders rested the world, and Karus could feel every pound.

Karus swept his gaze around their camp. Si'Cara was sitting across the fire, talking quietly with Amarra. The two women were deep in conversation and were speaking low enough that Karus could not overhear what was said. He suspected they were discussing scripture and faith. Sleep seemed to have been a curative for Si'Cara. She appeared much improved from her ordeal. Her eyes were brighter and her posture straighter.

Tal'Thor, on the other hand, if Karus was any judge, may have been damaged by the experience of what had happened with the warden, perhaps scarred even. He was sitting off to Karus's left, eating listlessly, and had not said a word since they had risen. Had he been human, Karus would have described the elf as downright depressed. Karus noticed the ranger's gaze occasionally flick toward Si'Cara before quickly shifting away when she glanced or turned her head in his direction.

Dennig was sitting off by himself, eating his second helping of cheese for breakfast. A half loaf of bread rested upon his thigh. He also seemed much improved. He was entirely wrapped up in his breakfast and fastidiously ignoring everyone else. At least, he was pretending. Karus had caught the dwarf covertly studying his traveling companions. Despite his gruff and cantankerous manner, Karus sensed a shrewdness concealed behind the wild beard. Dennig was beginning to grow on Karus. The dwarf was blunt and to the point. He most always said what was on his mind. Karus found that refreshing. Perhaps it was also that the dwarf was an old soldier like himself?

It was time to move things along. The fortress waited just up the hill and Karus desired to get moving. He began putting his armor on. With expert skill honed over a lifetime of service, he rapidly laced it up and then tied the ends off, making sure the knots were secure. He shrugged his shoulders about until the armor was where he was accustomed to having it and the fit was good, comfortable.

He picked up his sword, slipped the strap on over his shoulder, and settled it into position at his side. He carefully unfolded his cloak and shook it out. He had spent time cleaning and brushing it, at least as best he could while in the field. The ends of the cloak were frayed and ragged. There were also a number of rips where the cloak had caught on something and torn. Then there were about a dozen small holes and tears, as if moths had feasted on the cloak.

He had no idea where the holes had come from but figured it was entirely possible that they had been caused in battle. Perhaps he had gotten them during the legion's fighting retreat as they pulled back from the Celts in Britannia and fatefully went up that hill. It had gotten frisky and Karus had been in the thick of it. An enemy's weapon could have easily caused the damage. Sadly, it would soon need replacing. He swung the cloak around and clipped it securely in place.

Picking up on his cue, Si'Cara began packing away her food and the few personal items she had removed from her pack. This included the small pot with which she had made the tea. Tal'Thor followed her lead, gathering up his things as well. Dennig continued eating, loudly smacking his lips with gusto after finishing off his cheese.

Sucking in a deep breath of the cool morning air through his nose, Karus looked skyward, searching. There was no sign of the dragons. He had not really expected to see them, but still he found himself looking. The first rays of the day's light had reached the fortress, lighting up the outer defensive wall with a fiery hue of orange that was a harsh contrast to the darkened terrain of the hill just below it.

Though the fortress was an impressive fortification, it was on the smaller side and was certainly not the strongest Karus had ever seen. From this distance, he could see nothing radiant about it, other than the sunlight striking the ivy-covered wall. Not for the first time did he wonder how it had gotten its name.

"Is time to go, I think," Amarra said to Karus in Latin from across the fire. She patted Si'Cara's thigh and stood. Si'Cara had finished tying her pack closed and came to her feet as well.

"Si'Cara," Karus said. The troubling thought on his mind needed to be voiced. "Before we left, your father told me that the fortress is no longer what it once was. He said it had been corrupted."

She looked over at him, brows knitting together, before she glanced up the hill uncertainly. Her reaction seemed natural enough. It told him what he needed to know. She was ignorant of any danger or whatever Di'Cara had meant by "corruption." Her father had kept this knowledge from her.

"That cannot be," Si'Cara said. "My brother is up there."

"Di'Cara said that the warriors would not welcome us," Karus said.

"That cannot be," Si'Cara repeated, then chewed her lip. She appeared frightened by the possibility something had happened to her brother. "Long have I dreamed of this day, when I would be reunited with Kol. You must have misunderstood him."

"He did not misunderstand," Tal'Thor said. "I too have heard such rumors and reports supporting your father's suspicions. There is something wrong in the fortress. We just don't know what."

Si'Cara's look became frosty. "And you said nothing?"

"I said nothing"—Tal'Thor cleared his throat—"for you. I could not bear—"

"For me?" Si'Cara's face darkened like a thunderstorm. "You withheld this from me?"

"Kol'Cara is your only brother. I did it to spare you—"

Si'Cara cut him off, speaking heatedly in Elven, clearly incensed, and pointing an accusing finger at him. Tal'Thor snapped something back when she stopped long enough to catch a breath. Her cheeks flushed with anger and her eyes flashed at his retort. She replied, her voice shaking with rage. Tal'Thor paled and glanced away, clearly shaken.

"If I did not know better..." Dennig said, pulling himself to his feet. He tossed the last of his bread into the fire. "They fight like a married couple."

"You have the right of it, dwarf," Si'Cara snapped, her voice shaking with anger. "This sorry excuse for a"—she said an Elven word—"is my husband."

"See, I called it!" Dennig slapped his thigh in pleased amusement, looking over at Karus. "From personal experience, only love can bring someone to such a hot rage."

Karus shared a brief glance with Amarra before turning his attention back to Si'Cara. This certainly was not welcome news. That the two were married only complicated things further and made the warden's order to Tal'Thor just that much baser and crueler. He had no idea how Tal'Thor could have ever carried out the warden's order. It seemed to speak of a fanatical devotion and for a moment reminded him of the cruelties he'd seen the hated druids inflict upon their own people back in Britannia.

"We need to be on our guard," Tal'Thor said. "I do not know what we will find up there, or even if the Warriors of Anagradoom still live. But something has clearly happened, and not for the better."

Si'Cara turned her gaze toward the fortress. She brought a hand to her mouth, a profound look of sorrow on her lovely face.

"Well, there is no sense in delaying things anymore. Daylight's burning," Karus said. The first of the suns was now visible, poking above the trees.

Amarra retrieved her staff from where she had laid it on the ground. Tal'Thor grabbed his bow. He pulled the bowstring from a pocket and quickly strung it, tested the pull, and then, seemingly satisfied, slung it over a shoulder. He bent down and picked up his bundle of arrows.

Si'Cara hesitated a moment more, scrutinizing the fortress, then picked up her bow and a bundle of tied arrows. Karus noted that several of her arrows, which poked out of the bundle, had brightly colored fletching—blue, red, green, and black.

Dennig leaned toward the fire, which was beginning to die down. He held his hands out and rubbed them together for warmth. Then he began kicking dirt on it, rapidly extinguishing the blaze.

"Where do you think you are going?" Karus asked him, surprised. He had expected the dwarf to stay behind.

"Why, with you, of course," Dennig said, as if it were obvious, and kicked more dirt on the fire. The fire hissed loudly as it met with moisture in the freshly dug soil.

"You may not have been listening," Karus said. "It could be dangerous up there."

"I was," Dennig said, snuffing out the last of the flames with dirt. "And I am coming."

"There is no need for you to go," Karus said. "You can remain here if you wish."

"And if the dragons return?" Dennig asked, bushy eyebrows raised. "Who's to stop them from making a snack out of me? No thank you. I am coming along for the hike up that there hill."

Karus almost laughed, at first thinking the dwarf had made a joke. But he seemed wholly serious.

"I don't think they're going to eat you," Amarra said.

"I'm not prepared to take that chance," Dennig said firmly. "I'm going with you and that's my last word on it."

"Fine. You can come along." Karus decided it was not worth arguing. If Dennig desired to brave whatever dangers were up there...well, that was his business. Karus turned and pointed up the hill for everyone to see. "There appears to be some sort of a path or track. See it there? I suggest we take it as opposed to fighting our way through the grass and brush."

"That was a paved road, once," Si'Cara said. "I remember it well. It should still be the best way up."

Karus figured it had been a good long while since anyone cared for the road, because what he saw now seemed no better than a goat trail, and that was being generous.

"Right...everyone ready?" Karus glanced around. No one objected. "Let's go then."

He started out leading, with Amarra keeping pace with him. They worked their way through the long grass toward the path. Some of the low-lying scrub bushes were thick with thorns and had to be avoided or carefully traversed.

As he reached the path, Karus could see a handful of worn stones poking up at odd angles or partially sunk into the ground. These had likely been the paving stones. He followed the path with his eyes up to the fortress. Switching back and forth, it led a meandering route up the steep hill. He looked toward the forest. The path seemed to have once gone into the trees, but now it ended at the tree line. A giant of a tree grew where the road should have continued. Time, it seemed, had been a hard mistress.

Karus began climbing. Following the path up the hill was not as easy as it had appeared from their camp. The path had seriously deteriorated, at points proving to be nearly impassable without some scrambling. Karus figured a mountain goat would have had difficulty negotiating parts of the trail.

The path was washed away in places from runoff or was badly rutted with an abundance of loose stones. They moved slowly, carefully working their way up the path. Karus found himself focusing intently on where he placed his feet, for fear of turning an ankle.

Si'Cara and Tal'Thor soon moved by him, taking the lead. The elves set a fast pace. Karus consoled himself with the fact that he was wearing armor and they were not. The way up would undoubtedly be easier for the rangers.

They climbed in silence for a time, Si'Cara ranging ten yards ahead with Tal'Thor a few paces behind her. Only occasionally did anyone pause or stop to point something out or caution where loose rocks or large stones were a particular hazard.

Despite the exertion of climbing the hill, Karus found the air was growing colder. It seemed the higher they went the cooler it got, which didn't seem right, as the hill was really not tall enough to be considered a mountain and any such altitude change measured in the hundreds of feet, not thousands.

Halfway up the hill, the air turned so cold it felt like a brisk winter day. The two suns did nothing to provide any warmth. Karus's exposed toes began to ache a little, as did his fingers, which he began rubbing together for warmth. He was about to say something when Si'Cara, just ahead, came to an abrupt halt and knelt down. Tal'Thor did the same.

"Someone's ahead," Si'Cara said quietly, pointing with her bow as Karus and Amarra came up to her.

Sure enough, fifty yards up the slope, Karus spotted a figure. He was standing there in the middle of the trail, motionless, like a deer spotting the hunter a heartbeat before the arrow is loosed.

Karus squinted to see better. Something wasn't right... He couldn't put his finger on exactly what was off about the figure. They studied him in silence, staring up the hill. The person up there didn't move, not a muscle or an inch. Tal'Thor and Si'Cara each brought their bows up, nocking an arrow.

Tal'Thor looked back at Karus in question.

"Stay back," Karus said to Amarra, who gave a nod. Then he turned back to the elf. "Let's go."

They continued up the hill, moving cautiously toward the figure. Tal'Thor made a series of hand motions that Karus recognized as some sort of sign language to Si'Cara. She began working her way off the trail to the right, as Tal'Thor went left. Karus continued up the trail with the rangers on either side, flanking the person. As they neared, both rangers lowered their bows and came to an uncertain stop a few yards from the figure.

Karus ground to a stop as well.

It was no person, but the remains of one. Karus was both fascinated and horrified. He found himself looking upon a complete skeleton, bones bleached white by the sun.

It was stopped in mid-motion, frozen, as if whoever it had been had died in the act of running downhill, fleeing some unknown threat.

The skeleton had ragged bits of clothing clinging to it, wrapped around the waist below a badly rusted breastplate. A rusted sword was held in the right hand, and what looked like a small shield had once been held in the left. Much of the laminated shield had disintegrated, leaving behind only the metal handle, still gripped by the skeletal warrior. The rusted shield boss lay on the ground at the skeleton's feet, where the boots had also mostly disintegrated as well. All that remained were the soles and some of the sides of the boots.

Karus could not see what was holding the bones together and in place. It was as if someone had intentionally glued the bones to one another. He looked closer, but could see no glue or any sign of the telltale marks on the bones that would have come from carrion eaters. That was damn odd all by itself.

He glanced around them as he realized there were no birds about. His eyes scanned the brush on either side of the trail, searching, and then the sky. There was a complete absence of birds. He couldn't even hear any down in the forest below. With the exception of the occasional gust of wind, it was completely, eerily quiet. Karus found that unnerving.

"I am thinking you noticed the birds," Tal'Thor said in a hushed voice, coming nearer.

"Yeah," Karus said. "Last night I'd thought the dragons had scared them quiet, but now…"

"There aren't any bees buzzing around either," Tal'Thor said. "No bugs in the air. Something has chased them all away."

Karus did not want to think about that something. If the animals had fled, there was something dire to be feared. It was likely whatever this poor soul-turned-skeleton had been fleeing.

Karus heard the scuff of approaching footsteps. Dennig and Amarra came up. They too stared in horror on the skeletal warrior.

"This is not a good omen." Dennig absently ran his fingers through his beard. "Perhaps, in hindsight, I should have remained back at camp."

"It's not too late. You can still go back," Karus said.

There was a long moment of silence as the dwarf considered his words.

"I am a dvergr, a devout follower of the Way," Dennig said. "Should I go now, I will lose legend. No, you will not see me running back down the hill like some fool coward."

"He was human," Si'Cara said, walking completely around skeleton.

"How can you tell?" Karus asked. "Could he not be an elf? These are your forests, after all."

"Our skulls are shaped differently than a human's," Tal'Thor answered when Si'Cara did not reply.

"Have you ever seen anything like this?" Karus asked the ranger.

"No," Tal'Thor admitted, his eyes upon the skeletal warrior. "In all of my long years, this is a first."

Dennig stepped forward and reached out a hand toward the rusted sword.

"I wouldn't touch him," Amarra said in a voice that was part whisper. It caused Dennig to freeze in mid-motion, bare inches from the skeletal warrior's rusted sword. The dwarf looked back at Amarra in question.

"I sense something not quite right here," Amarra said. "Which is obvious, but I feel…" She paused and shuddered slightly, almost in revulsion. "It would be wise to touch nothing."

"Do so at your own risk, dwarf," Tal'Thor said.

"What do you mean you 'feel'?" Dennig asked, ignoring the elf. He stepped back and away from the skeleton.

"She is a revered daughter to the High Father, his chosen priestess," Si'Cara said, as if that was answer enough for the dwarf.

"You would do well to listen," Karus added.

"I believe I might do just that." Dennig looked from Si'Cara to Amarra, eyes appraising her. His gaze settled briefly upon the staff, which was emitting a sullen blue glow. Dennig scratched under his beard at an itch, eyes narrowing.

"I think we should push on," Karus said. He wanted to get the sword and be done, returning forthwith to his legion. "Anyone have a problem with that?"

No one voiced any objections.

They started forward, once again following the winding path up the hill. The grade increased steeply the nearer they got to the summit. Despite the air becoming quite chill, Karus found that he was starting to perspire from the effort, for the quality of the trail worsened the higher they got.

They passed another frozen skeletal warrior, this one a dwarf. He also appeared to be in the act of fleeing down the hill, running for all he was worth. Dennig said nothing as they moved by, but his face tightened and his fingers began to repeatedly comb through his beard. It seemed like a nervous habit.

The nearer they got to the summit of the hill and the fortress, the more skeletal warriors they encountered—dwarves, humans, and what looked like an orc. The tusks were a dead giveaway. There were no elves, though. All were frozen. One was half-turned and staring back up the hill in what Karus assumed might have been horror.

"What were they fleeing?" Dennig asked.

"I think the real question is, what evil magic did this?" Karus pointed with his sword at the nearest skeleton. He suddenly felt foolish for still having it out and sheathed the weapon. Then he noticed the elves. Each had an arrow nocked and ready.

"I do not want to find out," Dennig said.

"I could not agree more," Karus said.

The walls of the fortress loomed above them now, only thirty yards distant. They were almost completely covered over in thick ivy, with only spots of sun-bleached stone peeking through. Parts of the wall at the top had collapsed, giving the battlements a sort of sawtooth look. The closer they came, the more the fortress gave off the appearance of serious neglect, almost a complete ruin.

The path ran up around the side of the hill, ultimately leading them to a wooden double-door gate that looked solid, well-preserved, and surprisingly intact, given how the walls showed their age. A number of frozen skeletal warriors were clustered about the gate. Karus counted them. There were twenty in total. Most were human. Two were dwarves.

"What could have done this?" Karus asked, more to himself than anyone else.

No one answered, almost as if they dared not.

Karus glanced over at Amarra. She was studying several of the frozen skeletal warriors. Then her gaze went to the gate. After a moment, she closed her eyes, breathing slowly in and then out, as if steeling herself to make the effort just to continue to move forward. She opened her eyes and there was determination in them.

"I think we should try the gate." Amarra's voice was a whisper, as if for fear of waking the skeletal warriors. She blew on her hands for warmth, then rubbed them together. "Be sure not to touch them. Don't even brush up against them if you can help it."

When no one moved, Karus took the lead and started forward. He glanced back and saw the others following a few yards behind him. Karus carefully worked his way between the skeletal warriors. As he weaved a path through their midst, the temperature continued to drop. With each and every step nearer the gate, the air became more bitter, seeming to leach the warmth from his body.

His breath began to steam. Karus gritted his teeth to keep them from chattering as his fingers and toes began to ache terribly from the cold. He shuddered in the biting air. It felt almost as if death were reaching out from the great beyond to claim him, as if the warmth of the living world around him were fading. Was this what it was like when the ferryman carried you across the great river?

He glanced back at Amarra to make sure she was okay, wondering if she was experiencing the same thing. He saw her breath steam in the air. Karus continued on, one careful step after another.

As he came to within five feet of the gate, he suddenly found he had some difficulty moving forward. It was as if he were walking through waist-high water. It took effort to keep his legs going. He stopped, wondering what was wrong, and glanced down at his feet. Nothing appeared wrong with them, but the simple movement of looking seemed to take an eternity. Time had slowed down for him. Or was it that he was moving faster than time? Had the world slowed?

Turning took even more effort, as if the bitingly cold air was actively resisting him, fighting against his movement.

He looked back at the others and saw expressions of alarm. Whatever was hampering him was also affecting them. With every passing breath, it was becoming incredibly difficult to move. In a shorter time than it took to count to ten, Karus could no longer turn his body to face back front. He was frozen in place, just like the skeletal warriors.

Then, in a heartbeat, he could no longer move all, not even a finger. He strained for all he was worth. Nothing. He was completely frozen, like an insect caught in amber. The chill of the air stinging his fingers and hands had gone from a painfully aching sensation to one of growing numbness.

With alarming clarity, Karus understood that the strength was rapidly being leached out of his body as the biting cold grew more intense. Once, many years before, while ice fishing in the dead of winter, the ice beneath his feet had unexpectedly given way and he had plunged into the frigid waters of the lake. This was nearly the same feeling. Like then, his body rapidly numbed after the initial shock. Karus knew he had just mere moments before the cold completely took him. Yet, he did not know what to do. Nor could he see how to break the magic that was doing its best to kill him.

Death was close at hand.

His eyes sought out Amarra and saw her in a similar state. He wanted to call out to her, to protect her as he ought to be able to ... but there was absolutely nothing he could do. He was thoroughly stuck.

His chest felt compressed and he began having difficulty breathing.

High Father, Karus begged with desperation as his vision began to tunnel and then dim. He felt himself on the verge of passing out. *Please don't let it end this way.*

The intensity of the cold slackened slightly and a smidgen of warmth returned to his chest. Had he imagined it? Karus's fingers began to sting. A moment ago they'd been completely numb from the cold. He struggled to move, hoping against hope he could break free. His pinky finger twitched, then the rest of his fingers!

Karus swallowed and was able to open his mouth. He sucked in a gasping breath of air as a drowning man might. His vision began to return.

"High Father," Karus gasped, with all his heart. "Help us fight this evil magic."

Karus felt the force holding him in place slacken even more. A moment later, he saw Amarra begin to move as well. Her lips were moving silently in what he took to be prayer.

Help had been granted, the spell broken by faith.

Karus was able to move his legs. He staggered a step. The cold retreated even more. He could feel the warmth of the suns against his face. It felt wonderful. He gulped in another deep breath. The fresh air was bliss.

"Thank you, High Father," Karus said. As if an ice dam had broken under the strain of the meltwaters, he was suddenly and completely free from the magic.

The cold was gone, like it had never been. His breath no longer steamed. He took a shuddering breath as he gazed upon the nearest skeleton. Karus now understood. These poor souls had died, frozen in place, all from a lack of faith. It had been a simple trap. Those who had faith in the High Father could advance. Those who did not would become frozen and die. It was a terrible way to go, but Karus had long since learned there was really no good way to die. When your time was up, that was it. If you were lucky, your death would occur with friends or family at your side.

He looked over at Amarra and their eyes met. She was free, too, and for that tender mercy Karus felt a wave of relief wash over him. She flashed him a huge smile, full of white teeth, clearly relieved to have escaped the trap. Karus's eyes moved to his companions. In alarm, he realized Si'Cara, Tal'Thor, and Dennig were still frozen in place. He rushed over to the nearest, Si'Cara.

"The answer is faith," Karus shouted at them, hoping they could still hear him. "Pray to the High Father. Ask him for help, beg him."

"Faith will free you," Amarra said desperately and reached out a hand to Si'Cara's arm. She almost immediately snatched it back, as if she'd been burned by fire. Amarra shook her hand. "Faith will free you!"

Nothing happened.

"Come on, Si'Cara," Karus urged. "Pray to your god. Ask for his help."

Si'Cara took a great shuddering breath, gasping for air. She moved her head, looking over at Amarra, tears filling her eyes. Si'Cara's fingers twitched, then an arm. In mere heartbeats, she began to move with greater freedom. Then she was completely free of the spell. Si'Cara rested her hands upon her thighs, sucking in gulps of air. She straightened and turned to Tal'Thor.

"Pray," she ordered, moving to her husband's side. "Pray as the priestess instructed. Return to the High Father and he will free you as he did me."

There was gasp from Dennig. Karus glanced over and saw the dwarf beginning to move freely.

"Do it," Si'Cara said urgently.

"I didn't think that would work," Dennig gasped, "not one bit, but I figured, as it was the end, I might as well give it my all. Though I prayed to my family's patron, Thulla, and not your god."

"Thulla stands with the High Father," Amarra said, her eyes on Tal'Thor, who had yet to move. He remained frozen stiff, locked in the magic.

"Pray, accept the High Father," Amarra said, stepping nearer. She tapped her staff on the ground. It flashed with light. "I can't do it for you. The spell is countered by faith. Only those who believe may pass."

"Do it!" Si'Cara screamed at him, desperation creeping into her voice.

Tal'Thor was turning blue in the face. His eyes moved from Amarra to Si'Cara. Karus read in them panic. They heard a rattle of breath escape from his lungs. Si'Cara said something rapidly to him in Elven, anguish plain for all to witness. Nothing seemed to happen and Karus began to get a sinking feeling. Tal'Thor's eyelids closed.

The ranger was going to die.

Si'Cara gave a cry of grief.

Tal'Thor gasped, sucking in air. His eyes snapped open. The bluish hue to his cheeks began to rapidly fade. His color returned in a rush as he began to stiffly move. He turned toward Si'Cara, a trace of a grin on his face. She shouted something in Elven and lunged forward, throwing her arms around him and knocking him to the ground. She shook him roughly as if angry, then hugged him tightly. She began kissing him on the face and then lips. He kissed her back, then said something in Elven.

"Well," Dennig said, bouncing on his heels and glancing uncomfortably away, "I guess perhaps there is hope for them as a couple after all."

"Yesterday, on the warden's orders, he tried to kill her," Karus said to the dwarf.

"Is that so?" The dwarf turned his gaze back upon the happy couple. "It's a complicated relationship, then. What's love without a little thing like attempted murder, eh?" Dennig flashed Karus a smirk, then gave a heaving sigh. "It looks like all is forgiven."

"No." Si'Cara stood, leaving Tal'Thor on the ground, lying upon his back and gazing up at the sky. "Nothing is forgiven. My husband still needs to earn that."

Tal'Thor groaned and slowly pulled himself to his feet. He glanced at the frozen skeletal warriors and flashed a relieved grin, full of needle-sharp teeth. Karus had seen such grins before. They were driven by the elation at having cheated death and survived.

"That was unexpected." Tal'Thor's grin faded and he sobered. He turned to Amarra. "I never thought to regain my faith, ever. Thank you."

"The High Father welcomes you back," Amarra said. "He is not only forgiving but loving. He is also the one who deserves your thanks."

"He has it," Tal'Thor said as he bent down and picked up his bow and arrows, which he had dropped.

Si'Cara fell to her knees before Amarra.

"Would you bless me, mistress?"

Amarra blinked, shifting the grip upon her staff.

"You have already been blessed," Amarra said, puzzlement plain as she gazed down on Si'Cara.

"I know. Still," Si'Cara said, "it has been many years since I've been properly blessed by one of the cloth. Before we continue on into the fortress, bless me, mistress. I beg you, please."

Amarra hesitated a long moment before reaching out a hand toward the top of the elf's head. She paused, appearing uncertain. Karus saw her hand tremble ever so slightly.

Then she placed her palm upon Si'Cara's head and closed her eyes.

"Bless this splendid soul, for her faith is strong and true," Amarra said. Her staff pulsed brilliantly once and then returned to the dull, sullen glow. Amarra removed her hand.

Si'Cara looked up, blinking rapidly.

"Rise, daughter of the faith." Amarra helped Si'Cara to her feet.

"Thank you, mistress," Si'Cara said reverently. "If it is acceptable, I shall honor the High Father and his many blessings with my service to you."

"I only ask that you do what you feel is right," Amarra said.

"It is right to serve," Si'Cara said.

Amarra said nothing for several heartbeats. Karus knew something extraordinary and significant was happening. The grin had slipped from Tal'Thor's face, which only confirmed his suspicion. The ranger gave a slight scowl. It vanished in an instant.

Karus glanced over at Dennig, who appeared thoroughly fascinated by what was occurring. The dwarf caught his look and shot him a wink.

"When it no longer does," Amarra said finally, "or you feel called to do something else, you are free to go, released from my service."

"As you wish, mistress," Si'Cara said.

"An elven ranger swearing service to a human," Dennig said quietly so that only Karus could hear. "That is something I never thought to see. Your lady is very fortunate."

Karus spared the dwarf a look as Amarra stepped over to him.

"Shall we go on?" Amarra asked calmly, as if nothing out of the ordinary had just happened.

Karus gave a nod and turned toward the gate. Moving closer, he no longer felt the chill on the air. It was warm, almost hot. Whatever curse had lain upon the ground leading up to the gate had thoroughly and completely gone. The others followed after him, carefully moving around and between the skeletal warriors forever locked in place and death.

Karus stood before the gate and reached out a tentative hand, hesitant to touch it. Then, gathering his determination, he put his hand upon the rough wood of the gate. Nothing happened. Relieved, he pushed and felt a slight movement. The gate was not locked, but the hinges seemed fixed in place, most likely by rust. He had been concerned they would have to climb the crumbling walls.

"Help me," Karus said to Tal'Thor and Dennig.

Both moved forward and together they pushed on the left gate, throwing their shoulders into it. With the hinges screaming and groaning in protest, the gate surprisingly swung slowly inward. They were able to move the gate halfway open before it locked in place, giving no more. Something in the hinge mechanism had frozen out any further movement.

Karus stood back. Before them lay an overgrown courtyard or, as some would call it, a bailey. It seemed as if a small forest had grown up within the fortress. Ivy climbed the inside walls and some of the smaller stone buildings, too. Karus wondered what horrors and dangers lay within, just waiting to be discovered.

CHAPTER THIRTEEN

"Gods, what a mess." Dennig spat on the ground. "No one's been in here for years."

A hand still on the rough-worn wood of the gate, Karus had to agree. The fortress appeared to be no more than an ancient, crumbling ruin. His eyes swept the overgrown interior, scanning, searching, committing it all to memory.

The fortress's courtyard was choked with vegetation. Long grass, ivy, brush, and even trees had sprung up within the walls. Oddly, the trees were nothing like the giants at the base of the hill. They were a different variety altogether, some sort of a pine. The needles were long and thin and had a greenish blue color that Karus had never seen before on a tree. Combined with the ruins, it was all otherworldly. Karus hadn't known exactly what to expect, but this wasn't it.

His eyes went to the nearest of the crumbling buildings. It was a good-sized rectangular structure, thirty yards in length and twenty deep. The ivy was so thick, it almost completely obscured the walls of the building. It was as if the Terra Mater, the earth mother, had reached forth her green tentacles to drag the building down into the depths for the sin of its construction.

There was no telling how long the fortress had been abandoned, but it certainly seemed like it had been a very long time. Nature was slowly working to reclaim what had been taken from it. Ivy seemed everywhere. It climbed up all of the buildings and walls, snaking through and over the brush. The only place it wasn't visible was on the pine trees. For some reason the ivy seemed to avoid them. Karus idly wondered why.

"The fortress was in better condition when I was here last," Si'Cara said.

"Long ago, then," Dennig said, irony lacing his tone. "Though well-constructed, this place is falling apart. Another fifty years and none of these buildings will be standing—well, maybe some of the outer walls and parts of the keep, but you know what I mean. I'd almost say this fortress was made by my people."

Taking in the ruin of the fortress, Karus rubbed the back of his neck. Nothing, it seemed, was ever easy. Then again, he knew from experience nothing done right was ever easy. He had expected more difficulty, but nothing like what was laid out before him. He looked over at Amarra and let go a breath he had been holding.

"It might take longer to find the sword than I antici-pated," Karus said, putting his thoughts to voice. Gazing upon the wild overgrowth and the near-ruin of the fortress, he wondered how long it would take to locate the sword. That was, if they could find it, and the *if* was a becoming a serious question in his mind.

All of the buildings he could see had lost their roofs, and several of the smaller outbuildings had collapsed in upon themselves. Was the sword buried under piles of decaying debris? Would he need to dig it out? If so, he thought it slightly ironic that he had not thought to bring a shovel. There was really no telling how long it would take to find Rarokan.

"The High Father said the sword is here," Amarra said in a tone that spoke of surety, "and it will be. Trust in our god. We need to find it, no matter how long that takes."

"Right." Karus looked over at Si'Cara. "You've been here before. Tell me what I'm looking at."

"That central building is obviously the keep," Si'Cara said. She pointed off to the left. "That two-story rectangular building is the guardhouse and armory. On the second floor is a place for the guards to sleep. That is where the Anagradoom had planned to live, or so I was led to understand from my brother." Si'Cara swung her hand, pointing out an overgrown mound. "The collapsed building just next to it was the fortress's storehouse. If I recall, it has a large cellar that doubles as a cold house for storage." She pointed at another collapsed building, no more than a mound of stones covered with plants and ivy. "That smaller structure beyond it was a root cellar. The keep also has an underground space, though I have never seen it."

"And that large building off to the right?" Karus gestured at the two-story structure that was also rectangular, but twice the size of the guardhouse and with large barn-like doors. One door, half rotted away, barely remained attached to some of its hinges and hung at an odd angle. The other had long since fallen off and was nearly hidden from view by the wild vegetation.

The building Karus indicated appeared to be some sort of a stable. Since he'd seen no horses on this world, he figured it might have at one time been meant to house animals should the fortress come under siege. The roof of the building had fallen in as well.

"That big one there," Karus said, "what is it?"

"That was the prison," Si'Cara said.

"A prison?" Amarra asked, looking at the building more closely. Her lips formed a line. She cleared her throat. "Here? This place was once a prison?"

"Yes," Tal'Thor said, "the Fortress of Radiance for centuries was a prison. It was both a place of despair and rebirth."

"As you know, our people are long-lived," Si'Cara said. "Imprisonment within walls of stone is the worst imaginable punishment for an elf. Even death is not feared as much. Stone is so unfeeling, cold, and lifeless. It drains from their beings the passions and impulses that caused them to violate our laws, customs, and teachings. The criminals held within these walls were locked away for a very long time. The loss of one's freedom and ability to wander and explore the mysteries of life is a cruel thing, almost enough to drive one mad." She paused. "It was in this isolated place where the guilty were meant and expected to rediscover the radiance of their soul and reform their ways. The isolation and confinement was but one part of that process."

"Are you serious?" Dennig scoffed. "I've seen the inside of your prisons, and let me tell you, I don't know how one could rediscover themselves, let alone feel good about it at the end. All I got out of the experience was bitterness. Like me, I suspect all they found in this place was despair. No one truly reforms, no matter how long they are locked away. Prison only changes a person, and not always for the good."

"The prisons for our people," Si'Cara said, "are very different than those intended for outsiders. They are more comfortable."

Dennig gave a disbelieving grunt.

"Regardless of how you feel, dwarf, our prisons are meant to reform, correct undesirable or abnormal behaviors, and educate," Tal'Thor said. "Such a process begins with isolation. The Fortress of Radiance gave those confined within an opportunity to meditate, to contemplate their life, their choices, and to learn from their mistakes." Tal'Thor paused and swept his gaze around the interior of the fortress. "At least, our prisons used to be meant for reform. Things have changed."

"What do you mean, used to be?" Karus asked. "How are they different?"

"Around the time this fortress was set aside for the sword, the warden altered how we punished our criminals," Tal'Thor said with a slight scowl, his eyes darting briefly toward Si'Cara before returning to the prison. "We lost something when we gave up such places. Now, our punishments are intolerant, harsh, and absolute, with no thought to reform."

It wasn't hard to guess what the main punishment had become. The warden certainly did not seem like a kind and forgiving person.

"How did the fortress become the place to guard the sword?" Amarra asked. "Did the warden choose it?"

"No," Si'Cara said. "The High Master of Obsidian is a law unto himself. He made that decision. He stands above the warden, who was far from happy with his choice. There was something about the Fortress of Radiance he felt made it ideal."

"Wizards!" Dennig said. "They are without legend and nothing but trouble."

"You met the Master of Obsidian, En'Sis'Lith," Si'Cara said. "The High Master is the leader of En'Sis'Lith's order. We do not know much about him, other than he travels the worlds at will and is actively engaged in the war of the gods, the Last War."

"I am aware of him visiting Tannis only once, and when he did, he brought Rarokan with him," Tal'Thor said. "He was the one who placed it within the fortress, selected the Anagradoom as its guardians, and then left. He has not returned, at least that we know."

"How long ago was that?" Karus asked, noticing Dennig paying close attention to all that was said.

"At least a thousand years," Tal'Thor said, "give or take a hundred. At the time, I paid little attention to the event. I had no idea my destiny would be linked to that fateful visit."

Dennig whistled. "That's even a long time for my people."

"For us also," Si'Cara said, turning her gaze back to the interior of the fortress. "Long years indeed."

"Do you know where the sword would've been kept?" Karus turned his gaze back to the fortress.

"In the keep," Si'Cara said without hesitation. "That would be the most secure place within the fortress. It will have been placed there, if anywhere."

"Are you certain?" Karus asked hopefully, for the keep looked like the most intact building of the lot. He might not have to dig through the rubble of ages after all.

"I was not here when the sword was brought to the fortress," Si'Cara said. "Before my brother led the Anagradoom here, he told me that is where it would go."

Karus turned his gaze upon the keep. It was at least four stories high. Ivy ran from the base right up to the top. There were few windows, and those that he could make out were partially hidden behind the ivy. Through the trees, brush, and ivy, he spotted what appeared to be a stout wooden door. From what he could see of it, the door was intact. Karus wondered if it would open as easily as the main gate.

"Maybe you can help me understand something." Karus ran his hand over the rough wood of the gate, lightly feeling its age-worn texture. "This place looks long-deserted. If the sword was placed here over a thousand years ago, how is it that this wood"—he rapped on the wood with his knuckles—"still survives? A legionary has to work daily to keep the rust off of his armor. A few days of inattention and you've got rust, and loads of it too. Why did this gate not just rot away, the hinges rusting to nothing?"

There was a moment of silence at that. Tal'Thor and Si'Cara exchanged a look. Some silent communication seemed to pass between them.

"This place is special," Si'Cara said. "Long before we came and settled these lands, there was magic at the fortress. It is possible some of the enchantments or protections long ago placed upon the gates and these walls linger yet."

Karus removed his hand from the gate, as if it might bite him. He had felt nothing out of the ordinary, other than coarse weather-aged and worn wood.

"We know the High Master left his own enchantments," Tal'Thor added. "There is really no way to tell what was done and why."

"If we knew more," Si'Cara said, "we would tell you."

"I would expect so," Karus said.

"After what happened with the warden, there are few secrets we feel compelled to keep," Tal'Thor added.

"These warriors of yours," Dennig said, "they were expected to maintain the fortress?"

"Yes," Tal'Thor said. "Part of their responsibility would surely be to perform repairs and keep it in a fit state."

"Then it is also possible," Dennig said thoughtfully, "they could have been doing that up until recently. Maybe at some point in the near past, something caused them to stop their work."

"That is also a possibility," Tal'Thor said.

Karus felt Dennig had made a very good point. There was simply no telling what had happened here.

"Before we go in," Dennig said, with a meaningful look thrown to Amarra, "maybe the High Priestess could tell us if she senses evil about, particularly in there."

All eyes turned to Amarra. She gave the tiniest of nods, then closed her eyes. She breathed slowly in and then out for what seemed like a long time. They waited. Karus found himself holding his breath. Feeling foolish, he released it. Instead, Karus began to count. When he reached thirty-two, Amarra opened her eyes, blinking.

"What I feel out there"—Amarra gestured with her staff toward the courtyard—"is not welcoming."

"I had hoped for a little more than that," Dennig said grumpily.

"There is something pushing back," Amarra said. "I don't know what it is, but the push seems to slacken when I think of the High Father. I don't feel anything waiting, no evil at hand, if that is what you mean. What I sense is hard to describe. I think it is meant to keep others out, or perhaps it is a warning to stay away. But it is also fading, becoming less strong, even as we stand here and speak."

"Might as well get this over with." Karus, intent upon setting the example, started forward, but felt a restraining hand upon his shoulder. He looked over at Tal'Thor in question.

"If you do not mind, we shall lead," Tal'Thor said. "This has long been a place for elves. It is fitting we should go first. Should the Warriors of Anagradoom be inside, waiting on intruders, they may hesitate should they see elves leading and perhaps seek answers before attacking."

"Fine," Karus said, thinking that Tal'Thor was making a lot of sense. He stepped aside.

"I think it wise to check each building before venturing into the keep," Tal'Thor said. "I want to make sure we clear them first. Are you agreeable?"

"That works." Karus thought this suggestion also made sense, but he seriously doubted anyone living remained within the fortress. It was abandoned as could be. He wondered if the same fate that befell the skeletal warriors had also affected the Anagradoom.

Tal'Thor and Si'Cara started forward into the courtyard. They moved slowly, carefully working their way through the thick brush and undergrowth with a practiced ease Karus could only envy. The two rangers seemed almost to glide through the greenery, barely disturbing it with their passage and making hardly a sound.

"Stay behind me," Karus said to Amarra, for if they were attacked, she was not trained to fight, and he wanted no harm to come to her.

"I will be right behind you, fearless leader." Dennig smirked at him.

Ignoring Dennig, Karus stepped through the gate, entering the fortress. He felt as if he were crossing some unknown line in the sand—a line from which there was no return. Karus forced such thoughts away.

Unlike the elves, Karus, Dennig, and Amarra made plenty of noise as they moved farther into the courtyard. Each footfall sounded like an army trooping wildly through a forest. The rangers moved steadily deeper into the courtyard, pausing every few steps to listen and look. They began angling their way toward the guardhouse, which was the nearest building. No one said anything, not a single word. It was as if they were concerned that they might be overheard and give themselves away. Karus was certain there were dangers about. He just didn't know what they were yet. Until he did, caution would be the rule of the day.

They reached the main door to the guardhouse. The building had been constructed using granite blocks stacked neatly together. There were still isolated patches of plaster clinging to the walls. These perhaps had been shielded by the thick ivy growing over nearly everything and densely across the ground, threatening to trip with every step.

Karus realized the guardhouse was itself a mini fortress, the walls quite thick and solid. Behind the ivy, there were small slit windows on the first floor, with larger ones on the second floor that could permit someone with a bow to shoot out and downward.

Studying the larger windows, Karus decided that there was not enough room for a person to climb in or out. One such window was slightly larger than the others and positioned right over the door into the building. Karus figured that, should it come to an assault, the window would have been used to toss hot oil, boiling water, and baked sand on those below attempting to break down the door and force their way inside.

Karus's eyes slid upward. The roof had been constructed out of wood. A handful of rotted support timbers entwined with ivy were all that remained, and these were a fragile shell of what they had once held up.

The door, which was heavily reinforced with rusted iron, was partially ajar, about four inches. Si'Cara peered briefly inside, careful not to disturb the door. She turned to Tal'Thor. They exchanged a series of hand signals. Tal'Thor turned to Karus, Amarra, and Dennig. He held a finger up to his lips and then made a waiting motion with his hand, holding it out palm up. Karus gave a nod of understanding.

The two rangers split up, moving around opposite ends of the guardhouse, clearly intent upon scouting the other side. While he waited, Karus looked around. The fortress was deathly quiet. All that could be heard was the occasional gentle gust of wind, which stirred some of the vegetation within the fortress. When the wind blew stronger, it whistled through the upper reaches of the keep. Karus found the sound eerie, almost disconcerting. It was as if a long-lost soul were trapped up there, suffering and moaning.

There were no bugs buzzing around their heads or amongst the brush. No birds flew or flitted here and there. Karus could see no animals of any kind.

A short while later, the rangers were back. They moved up to the door. Karus went with them. Tal'Thor pushed on it, at first gentle and then with more force. The door did not move. Si'Cara joined him and still it didn't budge.

"Let me lend a hand." Karus stepped forward, and between the three of them they were able to shove the door inward several more inches. The door groaned as it shifted, scraping heavily along the stone floor as it moved ever so slightly. The more they pushed, it seemed the more resistant the door became. They strained and forced it open another inch, then it would go no farther, no matter how hard they shoved. Something was right behind the door, preventing it from further movement.

The gap they had created was wide enough to admit Si'Cara. With a bit of squeezing, she managed to slip through and disappeared inside.

She could be heard moving something aside. It sounded very much like she was tossing large rocks. Karus could hear the heavy thud from each toss as it landed. Then she reappeared, gripping the edges of the door. Working from their side, Karus and Tal'Thor pushed, shoving the door with their shoulders. The door opened a little more, enough for the rest of them to slip inside.

The interior was only dimly lit by the partially open door and the slit windows. The air inside the guardhouse was stale and musty, smelling strongly of decay. The ceiling just above and behind the door had partially collapsed. The debris from that collapse was what had blocked the door.

It was a large rectangular room that occupied much of the ground floor. There appeared to be a small storage room and what might have been an office to Karus's left. The doors to both of these rooms had long since pulled free from their hinges and crashed to the floor, where both still lay, covered in dust. To the right was a staircase.

There was so much debris behind the door that Karus figured some of it was likely from the roof as well as the ceiling. The hole above where the collapse had occurred had been thoroughly filled in from the remains of the roof. This had sealed the ground floor off neatly from the elements. Glancing up at the ceiling and the thick wooden support beams that ran across, Karus wondered on its stability. He hoped it did not come down on their heads.

For the most part, somewhat surprisingly, the interior of the guardhouse seemed to be intact. Everything was covered over in a thick layer of dust. There was a large stout table in the center of the room. On either side of the table, racks had been mounted to the walls. In these, an assortment of weapons rested where they had been placed so very long ago. Beyond that, the only other furnishings in the room were a handful of stools, several trunks, and two barrels, both of which had been placed in the corner by the staircase. A single unstrung bow rested on the tabletop. It looked very similar to the kind of bows Si'Cara and Tal'Thor carried, which meant it was most likely of elven make.

Amarra joined them in the room, and a moment later Dennig. The dwarf was so wide that he had to struggle a bit to fit through the door. Once in, he peered around as Karus poked his head into the storage room. There was only an old bucket and broom inside. The office next to it had a stool and a small camp table. One of the legs had long since given way and the table lay tilted over. A dust-covered stylus lay on the floor.

"Good old dvergr work," Dennig said. He patted the interior side of the stone wall, setting off a small puff of dust. "I thought so, but now that I see the construction of this building up close, I am certain. It really holds up against the long years. It's why we take such care when we build. We want to leave something of ourselves behind, a lasting moment to our life's work."

"I thought the elves built this," Karus said.

"Them fairies? Don't make me laugh." Dennig barked and drew the ire of Tal'Thor in the form of a withering glare. If looks could cut, Dennig would be bleeding. The dwarf grinned back at the elf. "Elves prefer to work mostly with wood," Dennig said to Karus, becoming serious. "They have strange notions about cutting and shaping stone into buildings. They think it's cold and an insult to life or some-thing like that." Dennig patted the wall again, sending more dust into the air. A moment later he sneezed loudly, then wiped his nose with the back of his forearm. "This is most certainly dvergr work. Some of my people must have been here long before the elves moved in and claimed these lands. I wonder who they were and what clan they belonged to. Maybe there will be a sign somewhere."

Dennig moved deeper into the room. Each footfall kicked up a small puff of dust. He stepped over to the racks of weapons and leaned forward, studying them. The dwarf walked slowly along, looking carefully over the rusty old weapons. Like everything else, they were covered in dust.

With his sandal, Karus moved aside the dust on the floor. Unsurprisingly, he found the foundation was some form of concrete. When possible, Romans preferred to build using concrete. It made construction easier and quicker than working exclusively with stone.

Now that they were moving about the room, more dust found its way up into the air. It tickled at Karus's nose as he followed after the dwarf. Dennig sneezed again. It sounded like a blast in the room.

"You could wake the dead with that sneeze," Tal'Thor said, looking around.

"I don't think we want to do that," Amarra said quietly. "With luck, the dead will rest until we leave this place."

Dennig glanced over at her. His eyes narrowed as he clearly wondered if Amarra had been jesting. A moment later he appeared about to sneeze again. The dwarf made a monumental effort to suppress it, holding his nose tightly and scrunching up his face. He relaxed several heartbeats later, the sneeze fully suppressed.

"So," Dennig said, glancing back at Karus, "what does this sword of yours look like?"

"That is a good question," Karus said, for he was not sure.

"You don't know, do you?" Dennig asked with some surprise. Then he stopped and looked around the dimly lit room. "There have to be at least three dozen swords here. How will you know the sword when you find it?"

Dennig had a point. Karus had absolutely no idea what Rarokan looked like. For all Karus knew, the sword was in this very room and not in the keep like Si'Cara had said it would be. He gazed about, eyes raking the weapons.

"The sword will make itself known," Amarra said, sounding very sure of herself. "Karus will recognize it."

He wondered for a moment how she could be so certain but then chalked it up to her connection with the High Father. If Amarra said the sword would make itself known, he had faith that it would. He would not leave this ruin of a fortress without Rarokan. It was as simple as that.

Karus began looking at the various swords resting in the racks. They were covered over in the dust of ages. Cobwebs traced their way in an intricate lattice between the weapons, the racks, and the table. Karus brushed a web he'd just walked through off his arm. It was very apparent no one had entered the guardhouse in years.

There were a wide range of weapons on the racks—battle hammers, axes, spears, bows, and even a mace. However, the vast majority of the weapons in the room were swords. These ranged in size and scope from the two-handed kind to a single badly rusted and corroded short sword that looked very much like a gladius. There was something about it that drew his curiosity. Had other Romans come to this world before the Ninth?

Karus reached out a hand. He considered picking it up, then changed his mind and moved on. It might once have been a fine weapon, but now it was nothing but junk.

"Would you look at this beauty," Dennig said, moving closer to one of the racks on the other side of the room. Karus turned. The dwarf was studying a very large two-headed battle axe that was thick with dust. Under the dust the blade had a dull appearance to it, but without rust like all of the other weapons. Dennig looked over at Amarra, eyebrows raised. "This axe is dvergr make. I would like very much to examine it. Do you think it safe?"

Amarra joined Dennig and visually examined the axe. She held out her hand toward it, but did not quite contact the weapon. She closed her eyes, once again searching within herself. Everyone waited. Her staff pulsed, momentarily lighting up the room. Then it faded back to a dull, somber blue glow. She opened her eyes and reached out to touch the axe with a finger. It was a momentary touch, then she pulled her hand away, shaking the gray dust off her fingers.

"Unlike the sword belonging to the skeletal warrior, I sense nothing wrong with this weapon," Amarra said. "That was different."

"How so?" Dennig asked, both eager and concerned at the same time.

"It was almost as if touching the warrior's sword might awaken the soul trapped within," Amarra said. "But this is different. I believe it should be safe for you to examine it."

Karus did not want to see the dead come to life or have to deal with the shades of those deceased, killed by the magic of the fortress. Dennig, however, seemed wholly unconcerned. He did not need any further prompting. He reached forth a hand and gripped the thick wooden handle of the axe and pulled it off the rack. Dust flew in the air as he swung around, admiring the axe in his hands.

"This is a weapon fit for a thane," Dennig exclaimed excitedly. "I would very much like to keep it. Does anyone have a problem with that? Speak now if you do."

Karus looked to the elves. "This is your fortress. What do you think?"

"I don't have a problem with him taking the axe," Tal'Thor said. "Elves do not use such weapons. Si'Cara, what about you? Do you care if the dwarf claims what was once his people's?"

Si'Cara shook her head, indicating that she did not have an issue with him taking the axe.

Karus turned to Amarra. "Well?"

"He is the only one of us without a weapon," Amarra said with a shrug of her shoulders. She gazed a moment more at the axe in the dwarf's hands. "I would feel better were he armed."

"It's yours," Karus said, turning back to the dwarf.

"Hah!" Dennig did a little dance. "I am very happy I elected to come along with you. I shall do the master smith who crafted this beautiful piece of art proper justice. It shall sing in the face of my enemies. Together we shall gain great legend ... great legend indeed." Dennig paused, looking down at the axe in his hands. "But first, my new friend, I must name you. A weapon such as this deserves a name."

"Maybe it already has one," Karus said, not a stranger to named weapons. It was not uncommon for legionaries to give their swords a name. The Celts did the same. The finer the sword, the more likely it was named.

Dennig looked over at him, a strange expression crossing his face. "You think so?"

"I don't know," Karus admitted, somewhat amused. "If it is as fine as you say, what do you think?"

"Hmmm ... that is something to think on. Some say once named, it's unlucky to rename a weapon." Dennig gazed down on the axe, his enthusiasm waning slightly. "But it's been here a while." The dwarf ran his fingers through his beard. "I suppose even if it were named, it would be impossible to know, as the previous owner is surely dead and gone, feasting in the Hall of Ancestors." He looked up at Karus. "I don't think his shade would mind. No, there should not be any harm in giving it a new name. What shall I call it?"

"Something else for you to think on, I guess," Karus said.

"Wise advice," Dennig said seriously and gave a nod. "Such decisions should never be rushed. I will think long and hard on this and give it the thought it deserves."

Si'Cara picked up one of the unstrung bows that had been lying on a rack. She shook the dust off and then turned the weapon over gingerly in her hands. Under the dust of ages, there was a slight gleam to the smooth wood, almost as if it were lacquered. She blew more dust off the bow and ran her hand along the smooth edge, feeling the grain of the wood with her thumb.

"Do you recognize this?" Si'Cara asked, handing the bow over to her husband.

Tal'Thor examined the bow closely in the dim light and then shook his head. "I do not see any marks which might tell me of ownership." He looked up at Si'Cara briefly. "It was a very long time ago. Without a mark, it could belong to any of them or none. It may have simply been here before they came, a replacement or spare should one of the prison guards have need."

A frustrated look came over Si'Cara as Tal'Thor set the unstrung bow back down, returning it where it had been on the rack. He was about to turn away to explore further, then hesitated, looking down at the floor by the table's edge. He squatted down, peering underneath.

"What do we have here?" the ranger breathed.

A moment later, Tal'Thor emerged with a large leather-wrapped bundle, very much like the sealed quivers that the rangers carried around. The leather, coated in dust, was cracked and in poor condition. It had turned black with age. He set it gently on the table and began unfastening the knots, which, at his touch, disintegrated into bits, coming apart in his hands.

"What is it?" Karus asked, stepping nearer to the two rangers. Both were looking down at the bundle. Karus could sense their excitement as Tal'Thor opened it, slowly pulling back the leather sleeve.

"Arrows?" Karus said.

Tal'Thor drew out a blue-fletched arrow and held it up for Karus to see. The end of the arrow did not have a sharp point, but was more snub-nosed, almost flat.

"Not just any arrows," the ranger said, with barely concealed excitement. "These are special, very special. My people once made missiles like this one, and in abundance. Sadly, we have lost that art. Only a handful of these remain. They are incredibly valuable, treasures to be conserved until a time of great need. Those few that remain are hoarded by the great families."

Si'Cara took the missile from Tal'Thor, holding it as if it were a precious gem. She ran her finger along the smooth shaft. "They are made with magic."

"Magic," Karus said. He felt uncomfortable at the thought of such things. Magic was something he did not understand and could not control. Certain items like the lanterns were practical enough, but there was so much he did not know, and that worried him.

"I've heard about those." Dennig edged closer. "Never thought that they were real, just tall tales."

"Oh, they are very real," Tal'Thor said as he began to carefully remove the remaining arrows from the bundle, one at a time. He laid them out upon the table, lining them up. There were ten arrows all told, with a variety of different colorations and patterns on their fletching. Both he and Si'Cara gazed down on them with something akin to wonder and amazement.

"Are they dangerous?" Karus asked.

"Only to those who wish us ill." Si'Cara flashed him a ferocious look before turning her attention back to the arrows. She took five. "These are mine. You can have the rest, Tal."

"Can I have that one? You took two of the same." Tal'Thor pointed at one of the arrows in her hand. It was the blue-fletched arrow with the snub nose. "I've always wanted to see what that type could do."

"I don't think so," Si'Cara said. "It's mine. Besides, husband, you owe me for what you did to me."

Tal'Thor shot her an almost pained grimace. Instead of further protest, he withdrew his hand and gathered up the remainder of the arrows, adding them to his own bundle. He carefully tied the bundle closed. He glanced once more under the table, checking to make sure there was nothing else down there.

"If they are so valuable," Karus said, "why just leave them lying about?"

"They were intentionally placed there," Tal'Thor said. "Of that I am sure. One of the Warriors of Anagradoom left them for a reason. Then again, now that I think on it... perhaps they were meant to be retrieved later and just were not, forgotten until we came."

Karus glanced briefly around the room, unhappy with the ranger's explanation.

"The Warriors of Anagradoom were the only ones able to enter the fortress," Karus said as Tal'Thor lifted the top off of one of the trunks, which had broken off its hinges. "Is that right?"

"To our knowledge." Tal'Thor replaced the trunk top after glancing briefly inside and finding nothing of interest. "You are correct."

"Then where are they?" Karus asked. "All of this has been here for years, untouched. Dennig says his axe is incredibly valuable, and the arrows you found are apparently priceless. Where did they go? What happened to them?"

"Nothing good," Tal'Thor said, checking another trunk.

"That's my thinking as well." Karus glanced around once more.

Tal'Thor shot Si'Cara a sorrowful look. "The Anagradoom should have been here to greet us, for you, Karus, are the one for whom the sword was intended. That was how it was meant to be. Whatever happened…"

Si'Cara gave a slow nod. "Tal is correct. Though my heart desires otherwise, I fear the worst now."

Karus gave out a breath as he considered Rarokan. He glanced around at the full racks along the wall. He had no need for any of the weapons here. There was only one that he was interested in.

Karus moved past the elves toward the stairs at the far end the room. Like the floor, they were made out of poured concrete. They were also covered over in an age of dust and littered with debris from above. He placed his foot on the bottom step, testing it before putting his weight upon it. It seemed solid and stable enough. He glanced up the stairs. Part of the ceiling above remained, though it looked lower than it should have been. In the dim light, he realized it had partially collapsed and lay a few feet above the top of the stairs.

There was a lot of debris on the stairs the higher he went. He could see some light from above and it was enough to light his way. He started up toward the second floor, where the quarters had been. Once up, he found there was not much to see. Roots from plants on the other side poked through the wreckage that had been the ceiling and roof. His view of whatever had once been up there was blocked, buried and lost for all time. He started back down the stairs and met Tal'Thor, who had been intending to come up.

"The roof came down and it's impassable," Karus told the elf, who looked somewhat crestfallen at the news. "Let's move on, shall we?"

They emerged back into the sunlight, which now seemed overly bright. Tal'Thor and Si'Cara once again took the lead. Following the elves, they worked their way through the tangle of plants, ivy, and trees toward the remains of the prison. The walls of the building loomed high above them. Karus thought it might once have had a steep-pitched roof, but that was all gone now.

The elves led them up to the two large barn-like doors. One of the doors had long ago fallen off and mostly rotted away, though a few boards could be seen poking up from the vegetation and soil at their feet. The elves looked in, Karus peering over their shoulders. The roof of the building had thoroughly collapsed, along with much of the second floor, so that the building was mainly a shell with a few interior walls and large piles of debris filling the inside, with open sky above. Plants and brush grew over the mounds of debris. One of the back walls had also partially collapsed, falling inward.

"Si'Cara and I will explore the building," Tal'Thor said. "There is no sense in anyone else going in. The walls could be unstable."

"We will wait," Karus said. "Make it quick but also be sure you do it safely. It is a mess in there. I don't want to have to dig you out and pick up the pieces."

Tal'Thor shot him a grin. Then the two elves entered the prison, moving carefully as they worked their way deeper into the building. Karus stepped back out into the light. He gazed around them. His eyes settled on the keep. What would they find there? Was the sword just waiting to be taken? He certainly hoped so. He did not want to spend any more time in this cursed ruin than he had to, for he had a bad feeling about the place. The suns were almost midway across the sky. The last thing Karus wanted was to spend the night in the fortress. If need be, they would return to their camp and come back in the morning, something he hoped they would not have to do.

"This is as fine an axe as I've ever seen." Dennig was still marveling at the weapon he had claimed for his own. The sides of the axe gleamed under the light from the two suns. It had surprised Karus that there was not even the hint of rust anywhere on the metal surface. In fact, the edges even appeared sharp, which he would've expected to have dulled and rusted with the passage of time.

"Why is there no rust?" Karus asked. "Most of the other blades were plenty rusted and useless."

"Now you begin to see why this axe is so valuable." Dennig tapped the side of the axe head. "This is made of a metal alloy, the composition of which is known only to my people." Dennig's tone reeked of pride. "Like those magical elven arrows, it is very, very rare. Mogan steel is difficult to forge. The ores required do not even exist upon this world. Such blades crafted with Mogan never need to be sharpened or polished, for they will not rust."

"Is it magic?" Karus asked.

"It's so good it should be." Dennig shook the axe. "This weapon, and I feel confident when I tell you, was not crafted upon this world."

Karus shook his head slightly. Such things weren't that hard to believe, at least anymore. He himself was from a different world, his own weapons, too. Karus felt a pang of regret. It was a place he would never see again. Rome was forever out of reach. There was no going back.

"I am happy for you," Karus said, amused by the dwarf's enthusiasm. He nodded toward the axe. "Be sure you use it well."

"I intend to," Dennig said, taking a test swing now that he was out in the relative open. He sliced a sapling neatly in two, the blade passing through with ease. "Oh, I intend to."

Karus turned to Amarra. She was silent, staring toward the keep, a distant look in her eyes.

"What is it?" he asked, moving over to her. "What's wrong?"

Amarra did not immediately answer.

"I feel something," Amarra said, switching from Common to Latin and touching her chest. Her gaze flicked toward Dennig, who, like a child, was wholly absorbed with his new toy. It was clear she did not want the dwarf to overhear what was said. "It makes me feel not good inside. It is"—she seemed to struggle with the word—"how you say again, dark and ugly? I forget."

"Evil?" Karus asked, glancing toward the keep with alarm.

"Yes," Amarra said. "I think that is right word, evil."

"There is something evil in the keep then, isn't there?" Karus jerked a thumb toward the keep.

"That is just it," Amarra said and chewed at her lip. She turned in the direction they had come and gazed toward the gate. He got the sense she wasn't really seeing the gate. "I feel it out there. Not here with fortress."

"You do?" Karus asked, surprised.

She nodded, gaze still focused toward the gate. "I feel its power."

"And you don't know what it is?" Karus asked.

"No," Amarra said, turning back to him. She shuddered slightly, as if suddenly chilled. Her eyes searched his face. "It knows we are here. It is coming."

"I don't like the sound of that," Karus said. "Is it near?"

Amarra closed her eyes. A moment later she opened them, her gaze piercing and clear. "Not close, but coming.

We have broken something, a protection, I think, that kept others out. A spell, maybe? Soon... it will be here, and it comes for the sword."

"Is the High Father telling you this?" Karus asked.

Amarra shook her head and then touched her chest. "When we see High Father, he opened up something in me. It unlocked power. I feel things now. I just need to listen inside. I learn to listen better each day. That is how I know, understand?"

Karus rubbed his jaw with his thumb.

"And you don't know how much time we have?" Karus asked. "Before whatever it is gets here?"

"No," Amarra said. "But we need to hurry."

Tal'Thor and Si'Cara emerged from the remains of the prison.

"There's no one in there, nothing," Si'Cara said. "Just empty cells and ruin, no sign that anyone has been in there for some time. It is strange. There are not even any animal tracks or burrows."

"What's wrong?" Tal'Thor asked, eyes narrowing. He had clearly sensed something was not quite right between Karus and Amarra.

"It seems we may not have much time here," Karus said. "Amarra feels something is coming to the fortress—for the sword."

"I don't know what it is," Amarra said, switching back to Common. "But it knows we are here, that we have entered the fortress. It is coming to stop us, to claim the sword."

"Then we must hurry," Si'Cara said. "We have to find the sword and leave this place before whatever it is gets here."

"Wait, wait!" Dennig said in a dramatic fashion, drawing everyone's attention. He held his hand to his temple. "I'm beginning the sense something myself." The dwarf closed his eyes briefly, then opened them, looking straight at Karus. "I sense you attract trouble, son."

Dennig burst out laughing. No one joined in. Amarra looked quite annoyed. The dwarf stopped laughing.

"Poor timing?" Dennig asked and grinned. "I thought I would lighten things up a bit."

"Very funny," Karus said and turned toward the keep. "Let's go."

They worked their way through the brush toward the entrance to the keep. When they were halfway there, they came across a well that was completely covered over in ivy. Karus only found it because he literally stumbled into it. It was now little more than a pile of old stones about waist high. Most of the stone blocks had shifted and tumbled into the well, blocking off the hole where water would have once been drawn. Karus moved around it and continued on.

In the time it took him to work his way around the old well, the elves had passed beyond his vision, the foliage concealing them both. Karus continued in the same direction and pushed through a large bush, shoving the ivy out of the way. He found himself before the door to the keep. It was another heavily reinforced door, the metal bracings rusted and corroded. Tal'Thor and Si'Cara were already trying to force it open. It wouldn't budge. The hinges on the inside were apparently stuck. That or the door was simply locked. Karus tried himself and decided that it was more than simply frozen hinges.

"It's definitely locked," Karus said, "bolted from the inside."

"Stand aside," Dennig ordered, hefting his axe. They stepped back and away. The dwarf raised the axe above his head and then, with a powerful motion, swung it downward at the center of the door.

There was a loud crack and the axe bounced backward, almost smacking Dennig with the reverse side of the blade. The dwarf stumbled back a couple of steps. He set the axe, head down, upon the ground between his legs and groaned in agony. He opened and closed his hands, ringing them out, for the blow had clearly stung. Karus saw the door was untouched, undamaged, the wood not even nicked.

Dennig looked up at the door to the keep. His jaw flexed and his face turned beet red.

"All right, you bastard of a door." Dennig picked the axe back up, hefting it above his head for another go.

"Wait," Si'Cara said.

Ignoring her, the dwarf grunted loudly, yelled something out in his own language, and struck at the door again. So powerful was the blow and unyielding the door that the axe flew backward out of Dennig's hand, landing several feet away in the brush. The dwarf bent over, clutching his hands. Clearly the blow had hurt much more than the previous strike.

After a moment, he straightened up, eyeing the door as if it were a hated adversary.

"Doorknocker," Karus said, inspiration hitting him.

"What?" Dennig asked, looking over and blinking in confusion.

"I think you should name the axe Doorknocker," Karus said.

"Ah!" Dennig shook a finger at Karus and then grinned. "Ha, ha, ha. You have a sense of humor. You are so serious, I had feared you hadn't one."

"I'm in the army," Karus said. "A sense of humor is required."

"Truer words were never said." Dennig went back and picked up his axe. He checked it for damage as he returned to them. There was not a nick or a dent on it. Both the door to the keep and the axe seemed wholly unaffected by Dennig's abuse. "I am starting to like you, Karus."

"Before you try again, you should know something," Si'Cara said to the dwarf.

"And what is that?" Dennig asked, eyeing his new nemesis, the door.

"I am almost certain the door has magic," Si'Cara said. "It is shielded, to preserve it. It is why the fortress gates, the guardhouse door, and this one still stand and have not rotted away like the prison's doors. Your attack upon it only proves it true."

"It might be," Tal'Thor conceded, "but that doesn't explain why the gate to the fortress was unlocked."

"Maybe it was never locked in the first place," Si'Cara countered.

"Then why is this one locked?" Amarra asked.

They fell silent at that.

"We still don't know what happened to the Warriors of Anagradoom," Karus said. "Is it possible that they left the fortress?"

"No," Tal'Thor said with a little shake of his head. "I don't think so. They are still here somewhere, either alive"—he glanced over at Si'Cara—"or dead."

Si'Cara took a deep breath. "Hopefully alive."

"They understood from the beginning when they volunteered," Tal'Thor said, "that the High Master was going to use his magic to ensure they could not leave, at least until the sword was claimed. Besides, someone had to lock this door from the inside, now, didn't they?"

"So," Dennig said, "they could still be in there, waiting for us?"

"Yes," Si'Cara said, with a strained, hopeful expression that did little to hide her true thoughts. "They could be. I am thinking getting past this door could be another test."

Tal'Thor looked upward and stepped back, studying the keep's wall. He held his hand up to shield his eyes from the suns. "If it is another test, ah ... I really don't want to, but I guess we could try climbing. There is a window up there we could get through."

Karus studied the wall as well, which was badly weathered and nearly covered over in ivy. The vines were almost as thick as ropes, the green leaves broad and full. He thought climbing might be doable. The years of weathering had created plenty of handholds amongst the stones, but at the same time, it would still be quite hazardous. There was no telling if any of the stones were loose or would crumble as they took weight.

"I have an idea," Si'Cara said suddenly and stepped back several feet. She set her bundle of arrows on the ground and then untied it, opening it up. She pulled out one of the arrows she had taken from the guardhouse armory. It was the snub-nosed arrow with blue fletching.

"Are you certain that is wise?" Tal'Thor asked. "Those don't grow on trees, you know."

She shot him a feral grin in reply.

"What do you intend?" Karus asked, recognizing the arrow Tal'Thor had shown interest in.

"This was left for some purpose," Si'Cara said. "Only a ranger would know what it was and its true use." She turned to Karus and Amarra. "In our language, it is called a *prinque*. It roughly translates to 'penetrator' in Common."

"Such arrows are designed to break magical shielding," Tal'Thor said, looking on his wife with a wry expression.

"They are quite powerful tools and should not be squandered. But I think she's right. These arrows were left for a purpose."

"How can you be sure?" Karus asked.

"Because they are incredibly valuable and rare," Tal'Thor said. "They would not have been left where they were unless they were meant to be found and used. At least, we will know for sure in a moment. This all depends upon how strong the shielding on the door is. With luck, the *prinque* will take the shield down."

"And if it doesn't?" Dennig asked. "What then?"

"We find another way in, dwarf," Si'Cara said. "Now, stand well back from the door. I've always wanted to see what one of these could do."

They did as instructed.

Si'Cara took up her bow and nocked the arrow. She took a moment to aim and then loosed. There was a brilliant flash of light, followed by a booming sound that shook the ground beneath their feet. The door disintegrated, coming apart and exploding inward. It was as if a ballista ball had smashed straight through the wood. The ground beneath Karus's feet trembled. Had there been anyone standing on the other side of the door, they would have died instantly.

Wisps of smoke swirled about from where the door had been a moment before. There was an acrid, burnt stench on the air. The smoke and smell on the outside of the door to the keep dissipated rapidly as a gust of wind carried it away, revealing a darkened interior beyond. It was like peering into a murky cave.

"Wasn't that just handy," Dennig said with true admiration, looking from Si'Cara to the keep and then back again. "There was a time or two when I could have used such a tool. Would you be interested in selling the last one? I would pay handsomely."

"Forget it, dwarf," Tal'Thor laughed. "You can't have them and we have no need for your money."

"I know," Dennig said with a heavy sigh. "It was worth a try, though."

Drawing his sword, Karus stepped up to the door. He put his hand on the frame, which was warm to the touch. He looked inward. Smoke and dust were heavy on the air within, but from what he could see, it was clear. There was no one inside and had not been for a good number of years.

CHAPTER FOURTEEN

Karus stepped through the shattered door and was greeted by a small dark foyer, crammed with crates, small boxes, casks, amphorae, and sacks. Cobwebs crisscrossed their way from one side of the foyer to the other. He wrinkled his nose as he stepped inside. The air was stale and musty. The acrid stench of smoke from the blast was strong. A lot of dust was on the air. It tickled at his nose and he resisted a sneeze.

Pieces of the door lay scattered haphazardly across the floor. Karus paused a moment, surveying his surroundings before going any farther. The daylight from behind him lit up the interior with sufficient light to see. Beyond the foyer, a small hallway stretched out before him with a staircase at the end leading upward. There were four doors, two on either side of the hallway.

Karus turned his gaze and attention back to the foyer. He had the impression the entrance had been used to store supplies, possibly for the Warriors of Anagradoom. He went over to a small barrel coated in a carpet of dust and cobwebs. The top sat askew. He lifted it with his sword tip and peered inside. The barrel was empty, but he thought it might have once contained flour, as the bottom was coated in white. Though that could have been dust and old, dried mold.

The others filed inside behind him. No one said a word. It was as if they were afraid to speak. Tal'Thor brushed by Karus and tried one of the four doors along the corridor. At first, it refused to open. He threw a shoulder into it, and the door opened with a painful screech, ancient hinges protesting. One of the hinges gave off a tortured cracking sound, then gave way, breaking. The heavy wooden door came loose at the top and hung crazily at an angle. Tal'Thor stepped around it and into the room beyond. Karus moved over and, careful not to disturb the door further lest it completely come off the last hinge, he glanced inside. The room was good-sized and at one time had likely been used as a storeroom for weapons. Along the left wall there was an empty wooden rack. Stacked crates and boxes of various sizes had been placed before it and along the other walls, filling up much of the room.

"Stores, I believe," Tal'Thor said, glancing back at him.

"That was my thinking, too," Karus said, moving into the room.

"For your people?" Dennig peered into the room from behind.

"Yes," Tal'Thor said. He stepped up to a box and lifted the top off. It was filled with what looked like small gray rocks. He picked one up and turned it over in a hand. "Bread."

The elf tossed the small loaf to Karus. The bread had long since hardened and was more solid than hardtack. It was as if it had been made of cement. He dropped the hardened loaf to the floor, where it landed amidst the dust with a solid thud.

Out in the hallway, the hinges of another door squealed and screamed in outraged protest. Karus turned and stepped past Dennig. He found Amarra and Si'Cara opening a door. Karus moved over and saw that this room was similarly stacked with crates and casks. A check of the other rooms revealed the same. One was even filled with large amphorae.

"Think those are spirits of some kind?" Dennig asked, having taken a look at the amphorae. "Perhaps wine? The elves are known to make the finest of wines. Sadly, since they don't take to others and play nice, elven wine is quite rare and expensive."

"Whatever's in there," Karus said, "the contents have long since gone bad."

"A pity," Dennig said. "I hate to see good stuff going to waste. A wee little taste would help take the edge off, if you know what I mean."

Karus could not help but agree with the dwarf. He sheathed his sword. This entire fortress was empty of people, or so it seemed. It was downright unnerving. He had no idea what had happened here and might never know. Whatever had occurred, it clearly wasn't good. More concerning, he now knew there was some sort of enemy on its way. Perhaps it was the Dark Lord mentioned in the prophecy. Karus hoped not, but felt the strong urge to move things along. They were running out of time to find Rarokan.

He turned toward the stairs at the end of the hallway. He was surprised to discover that not only did they go up, but also down. An alcove had hidden the stairs that led downward into absolute darkness. This must have been the underground space Si'Cara had spoken about. Small slit windows lit the way up with a very dim light, but the stairs downward were dark and forbidding.

"Amarra," Karus called, "can you bring your staff over?"

Amarra moved over to him and held her staff out. Together they peered down the stairs, the light of her staff growing, almost as if it sensed her need. The stairs leading downward were not only covered in dust, but also crisscrossed with webs, some nearly as thick as Karus's index finger.

"I really don't want to go down there," Dennig said, peering down the stairs from between them. "Spiders and I... well, let's just say we don't get along."

"Curious," Tal'Thor said.

"What do you find curious?" Amarra asked, glancing over at the elf.

"We've not seen animals, or insects either, on the hill or in the fortress," Tal'Thor said. "There were no tracks, nothing. Now, inside the keep we find evidence of spiders, and big ones too, judging by those webs."

"If I had to make a guess, cave spiders made those." Dennig shuddered. "I've killed more than my fair share of the nasty critters. They are ill-tempered, very venomous, and one of the things I truly detest about this world."

"On that cheery note, let's explore up before we go looking for more trouble than we already have," Karus said, not wanting to meet the spiders that had spun those webs. "Perhaps what we seek will be found on the floors above."

Tal'Thor looked as if he wanted to lead. Karus placed a restraining hand upon Tal'Thor's chest and shook his head in the negative. It was time he shared some of the risks too. Karus started up the stairs, taking one slow and careful step at a time. The stone was covered over in dust and, with his hobnailed sandals, was somewhat slippery. The plaster on the walls had begun to crack and fragment, with large chunks having fallen off. The steps were littered with plaster. It crunched under his sandals. He wondered how long it had been since someone had made their way up the stairs. How many years had passed since the keep had known the tread of a foot?

A dozen steps brought him to a second floor. Another hallway, this one darkened and longer, greeted him. It was lit only by a dim bar of light that came from a slit window behind him on the landing. Like below, there were doors to either side. Karus counted eight in total, four on each side. At the far end of the hallway, there was another staircase that led upward.

The nearest door had come free of its hinges and landed on its side, leaning against the far wall. It partially blocked the hallway. Tal'Thor joined him. Amarra was next up the stairs. Her staff continued to glow brightly, driving back the darkness and illuminating the dust-filled hallway. Thankfully there was no sign of the thick spider webs, which hopefully meant no spiders. Some of the ceiling had come down and lay in chunks on the wooden floor.

Karus took a step forward, tentatively testing his weight upon the ancient wood. It creaked loudly, but held and seemed solid. He continued forward, mostly confident it would hold. Amarra moved past him to the first door, which lay on its side, and entered. Karus followed after her, looking into the room. It appeared to be someone's quarters.

There was a rope bed with the remains of a blanket atop a thin mattress. The supports for the bed had collapsed, leaving the mattress, which appeared to have been stuffed with some sort of hair and was decaying and rotting away. In the corner were a chest and a pack of some sort. The fabric of the pack had mostly disintegrated, revealing the dust-covered contents that had once been carefully packed. These appeared to have been a camp blanket, a brush with a bone handle, a mirror, and some other things Karus could not identify at first glance. There was also a desk that looked surprisingly intact. Si'Cara stepped by them and into the room to examine the contents of the pack more closely.

Karus went to the next room over and slowly, carefully opened the door. The hinges screeched as if in terrible agony. If anyone was hiding in the keep, Si'Cara knocking the front door down had likely announced their presence. Karus saw no point in being quiet now.

He found a similar setting—a bed, a desk, and a decayed pack. All of the rooms along the hallway turned out to be living quarters. He found the empty and abandoned fortress somewhat depressing.

"Tal'Thor," Si'Cara called, "come and see."

Karus left the room he was in and went back to the first one that Amarra had entered. He found Tal'Thor and Si'Cara bent over and gazing down into a small trunk that had been concealed by the desk. She said something in Elven to him as she pulled forth a pair of daggers. They seemed very similar to the ones that she wore.

"These appear to have once belonged to one of the warriors," Tal'Thor told Karus. "Though we both expected them to stay in the guardhouse, this perhaps is where they had intended to live. Who can say for sure?"

With a deep reverence, Si'Cara returned the daggers to the trunk and closed it. She stood and remained for a moment, bowing her head as if in silent prayer.

"Well, we know they were here," Karus said, rubbing his jaw. "What happened to them?"

"I don't know." Tal'Thor pursed his lips.

Karus turned around and walked down the hallway to the next flight of stairs. Tal'Thor and Si'Cara followed. Dennig was busy poking around in one of the rooms as they passed. Amarra emerged from one at the end of the hallway, her staff immediately driving the darkness back as if chasing evil spirits away.

Karus started up the steps, once again leading the way. He emerged into a large open room, with columns supporting what appeared to be an arched stone ceiling above. The room, which could be described as a small hall, stretched out before him toward what appeared to be an altar at the far end. The ceiling was plastered over and covered in its entirety with a fresco. Amarra lifted her staff up to reveal the fresco. Karus could now see it was filled with dwarves—fighting, praying, seeming to honor their gods, while at the same time appearing to tell of some story.

"Ha," Dennig said, coming up the stairs and gazing up at the ceiling. "The tale of Amegdala. This tells the tale of creation. See, I told you dvergr built this fortress."

Karus glanced over at the dwarf, who beamed with pride up at the fresco. Tal'Thor, Si'Cara, and Amarra also stood silently, gazing up at the ceiling. Then Karus turned his attention to the rest of the room. There was a large fireplace, cold and dark, along the left side of the hall. There were no other furnishings. The small hall reminded Karus very much of a large chapel, which seemed somehow out of place. He would have expected some sort of a shrine instead, but nothing like what spread out before him. He reminded himself that the dwarves were an alien culture. They were not human and likely did things very differently.

Unlike the other two floors, the windows were larger and let in in more light. There was another staircase along the right side. It was choked with debris, a sure sign the roof had come down and buried the upper floor. There would be no going up for exploration. That much was apparent.

Karus figured the only reason this floor had escaped destruction was the arched ceiling overhead. It had most likely proved sufficient to withstand not only the ages, but the collapse of the roof and floor above. He wondered how long it would remain that way. He could see large cracks running along the plastered ceiling. Sections of the fresco had fallen away, revealing the stone and brick block behind.

Karus took a step into the room. His attention was drawn to what was on the altar at the far end, where a glint of reflected sunlight caught his eye. His eyes focused in the dim light and he saw what looked like a metal blade. His heart began to race. Was this what they'd come for? He heard Amarra suck in a startled breath.

They shared an excited look. He moved forward, she at his side. He stopped five feet from the altar, eyes upon the sword. Rarokan, for that was only what it could be, rested on a red velvet blanket. It was a magnificent sword, blade highly polished, edge looking razor-sharp. Both the sword and blanket were completely free of dust. A beam of light from a window at the back of the hall shone right down upon the sword, brilliantly illuminating the weapon.

He shared another glance with Amarra, his excitement mixing with hers.

"That's what we've come so far to get," Karus breathed to her, almost in a whisper. The sword they had been sent to fetch was before them, just waiting to be taken, and yet Karus found himself hesitating. Dennig, Tal'Thor, and Si'Cara joined them before the altar. All gazed upon the weapon in wonder.

"That sword is dvergran-made," Dennig said, breaking the silence. "The quality is too fine to be anything else." The dwarf paused, looking over at Karus. "Well, what are you waiting for? You came here to get that. Made me climb a bloody hill, too."

"Made you?" Karus asked and shot a look at the dwarf. "I think you made out quite well with that axe."

"Claim it," Dennig said in a tone that reeked of exasperation.

"It is meant for you." Amarra gave Karus an encouraging nod. "Take the sword as the High Father desires."

Karus stepped closer to the altar, nearer to the sword, still hesitating for a reason he could not quite put his finger on. He leaned toward the magnificent weapon. The sword was longer than the gladius he was accustomed to using. He understood that once he took it, it would be his primary weapon. Others would want to claim it as their own, perhaps even that Dark Lord. He could never let it leave his side, so he would have to become proficient with its use. The good thing about having served in the legions was that over the years he had learned to use a wide variety of weapons, including the longer swords the Celts preferred. Still, he was more comfortable with the weapon now sheathed on his side, the legionary short sword.

He continued to delay. Something just did not seem right. It was more a gut feeling than anything else. Over the years, Karus had learned to trust such feelings. It could not be this easy. Could it?

Taking a deep breath, Karus reached out toward the hilt of the beautiful weapon, feeling the excitement of the moment crash home. He had found what they were seeking, what the High Father had sent them to retrieve. But at the same time, he felt a wrongness. He gripped the hilt. His fingers closed on air, passing right through the sword. He tried to grab it again and—nothing, the same result as before. The sword shimmered like a mirage as his hand passed right through. It both was and wasn't there. It looked as real as could be, but when his fingers passed through it, the sword took on a ghostly image.

"What magic is this?" Karus asked, looking over at Amarra, thoroughly mystified.

She shook her head. "I know not."

"By my grandfather's beard," Dennig said, reaching forward and running his hand through the illusion. "It's truly not real."

"This has to be another test," Karus said, scanning the room and thinking hard. There had to be something he was missing, a puzzle piece that needed to be put in its place. And yet, the feeling of wrongness twisted harder in his gut. He felt a slight tremor beneath his feet. Dennig's bushy brows drew together as he looked downward. Karus swung back around to the altar. The sword and blanket had vanished, gone as if they had never existed. The beam of light that had illuminated the sword was gone too. It its place, all that remained was stone covered in untold years of dust.

The keep shook as the tremor intensified. The stone walls began to vibrate and rumble. They had been tricked, Karus realized. This was not another test, but a trap.

"We need to get out of here," Karus said urgently and grabbed Amarra's arm, pulling her along. "Run!"

They ran for the stairs, racing down the first flight. The vibration of the building became more intense, making it difficult to keep their feet. Dust and debris started to fall, cascading down from the ceiling in a steady rain. Karus knew without a doubt that the building was tearing itself apart. They had mere moments to escape before it collapsed on top of them.

As they reached the second floor, large chunks of the ceiling, pieces of wood and stone, began to crash down around them. Something heavy smashed down onto Karus's shoulder armor and almost knocked him from his feet. Karus careened into the wall painfully but managed to keep himself upright. Amarra tripped on a large chuck of debris, falling roughly to her knees. He hauled her to her feet and shoved her before him.

"Go!" he shouted, for the keep had begun to grumble like a cranky old man.

They tore down the second flight of stairs and reached the ground floor. Karus had once been through an earthquake. This seemed just like one, but more intense. He shoved Amarra out the door and then turned back.

"Come on," Karus shouted. Si'Cara made it down the stairs and sprinted for the door, Tal'Thor not far behind. Dennig was bringing up the rear, his stumpy legs pumping for all they were worth. He made it down the stairs and started for the exit, chasing after Tal'Thor. A section of the ceiling crashed down. For a moment, Tal'Thor and Dennig were lost from view. Then Karus saw Tal'Thor was down, his legs partially buried in debris.

"No," Si'Cara shouted from outside and started back in. Amarra grabbed at her arm, restraining the elf.

"I've got him," Karus shouted at Si'Cara. He ran back to Tal'Thor, who wasn't moving.

Karus dragged him out of the pile of rubble. He hoped the elf still lived. The building shifted. More debris cascaded down around them. Karus knew that in a few heartbeats the entire building was coming down. He strained for all he was worth, dragging Tal'Thor across the floor toward the door. Then Dennig was there. The dwarf hooked an arm under the ranger's shoulder and together they dragged him. A large slab of ceiling collapsed behind them with a great rending crash. A massive cloud of dust rolled over them. Karus could barely see. He just kept moving forward and they emerged into the sunlight.

Large chunks of stone and masonry were coming free from the building and falling to the ground, landing with heavy thuds.

"Get back," Karus shouted at Amarra and Si'Cara, who began to run.

Karus and Dennig dragged the injured elf several yards away from the entrance, well clear, and into the brush. Behind them there was a deep, angry final rumble that was quite deafening as the keep collapsed in upon itself. The trees and brush around them shook and swayed. Then, the tremors became so violent that both Karus and Dennig were thrown from their feet as the ground beneath them seemed to shift and jump. A cloud of dust washed over them and then, a moment later, everything was still and quiet.

Karus rolled over onto his back and sat up. Everything around him was white, as if it had just snowed. The brush, leaves, everything. A gust of wind carried away the dust that was airborne. He, like everything else, was thoroughly coated in white dust. Where the keep had been, there was nothing now but a massive pile of rubble from which a dust cloud swirled.

Karus coughed and spat the dust out of his mouth.

"That was close," Dennig said, coughing and hacking out the dust.

"Too close," Karus agreed and then remembered Tal'Thor.

Covered in white, the elf was lying limply between the two of them, face down. Karus rolled him over. The dust made Tal'Thor look dead. The elf had been hit on the head and was bleeding badly. The blood flowed out from a wound on his scalp and over the sides of his forehead, some of it down his right cheek. It was a shocking contrast set against the white of the dust.

Karus quickly found the wound and examined it. Tal'Thor had a thin laceration about an inch in length on the very top of his head. Karus felt the skull, pressing his fingers over the wound, and was pleased that he didn't feel any breaks, softness, or sharp bone fragments. Just to be safe, he also checked for gray matter or white bits around the wound, which might indicate the skull had broken in some way. He did not see any of that. Lastly, he checked Tal'Thor's pupils to make sure they were equal sized. If they weren't, it meant a serious injury had occurred and death was a distinct possibility. He breathed a sigh of relief that they weren't too big either, for that was a sure indicator that life was leaving the body.

Karus knew from experience that head wounds bled profusely. They could also be tricky. Though the skull might not be broken, he might have been hurt on the inside, his brains mucked up enough to eventually see him die. Karus had known men to take a blow on the head and simply not wake up. He hoped that elves, like humans, presented the same injury signs and he wasn't misreading things.

"Tal!" Si'Cara rushed over and knelt down next to her husband.

"He lives," Karus said. "I don't think his skull is broken, either."

Tal'Thor's eyes fluttered open, which Karus took to be a good sign. Si'Cara gave a shuddering sob at the sight of him awake. Tal'Thor asked her something groggily in Elven. She replied and caressed his face with the palm of her hand. A moment later, his eyes rolled back and he passed out. Si'Cara checked for a pulse. After several long moments, her shoulders relaxed slightly. Si'Cara examined the wound herself, then leaned back.

"It is as you say," Si'Cara said. "He is lucky."

Karus looked up to find Amarra gazing down on the injured elf with concern. Then her eyes flicked to Karus and they widened in alarm.

"It's all his," Karus said, realizing that his hands and chest were covered in the elf's blood. He checked himself over to make certain he did not have an injury, then stood and dusted off his hands. "I am whole."

Amarra let out a breath of relief, then looked back to Tal'Thor. "How is he?"

"He's got a bad knock on the head," Karus said. "That's for sure. I don't think anything's broken, just had the sense knocked out of him is all."

"Can you heal my husband, mistress?" Si'Cara asked Amarra. "Like you healed me?"

"I believe that will be possible," Amarra said and started to kneel next to Tal'Thor. She abruptly froze halfway down as something caught her attention. She stiffened, her gaze fixed toward the gate. Karus looked and blinked in astonishment. He stood there, just as frozen, staring in disbelief. His brain was having difficulty believing what he was seeing.

"By my grandmother's beard!" Dennig exclaimed in barely a whisper. "That just cannot be."

With those words, Karus's momentary paralysis broke. He was rapidly learning that what a few weeks before would have been impossible was now very much probable. Karus knew that nothing should surprise him, and yet there was a lot that still did. He scrambled to his feet and dragged out his sword.

"You ... have ... got ... to be kidding me." Dennig pulled himself to his feet, hefting his axe. He looked over at Karus. "I knew I should have listened to my mother and gone into the family business." Dennig faced back toward the gate.

"Instead, no, I thought I knew better and became a soldier. This just proves the gods hate me."

Karus shook his head slowly from side to side. It hardly seemed possible. Shuffling and shambling through the gate and working their way through the brush were the skeletal warriors they had passed on their way up the hill. The dead had unbelievably come to life. Karus could hear their bones grinding as they advanced. It was a sickening grating sound that made Karus's hair stand on end.

Si'Cara unslung her bundle of arrows, opened it, rapidly picked out a handful of the missiles inside, and dropped the rest. She chose one with red fletching and nocked it, holding the rest against the bow. In a smooth, rapid motion, she pulled back, aimed, and loosed at the nearest of the skeletal warriors. The arrow impacted the warrior's chest plate with a loud crack, followed by a deep *whumpf* sound and then a flash of flame.

Fire exploded over the skeletal warrior, within a heartbeat completely engulfing it. As if in physical pain, the warrior began to dance about as the intense fire burned and ate away at it. Another warrior brushed too close, bumping the one on fire. It, too, burst into flames. This one began to dance, like it was a real person suffering terribly as it burned. So hot were the flames that the rusted breastplates of the warriors turned red, then white, before completely melting. The liquid metal ran like water to the ground. The fire continued to eat hungrily at the bones, until, several heartbeats later, the skeletons ceased to be, turning to nothing more than ash carried away on the wind.

Si'Cara fired a second arrow, with the same result. The arrow impacted the warrior, a dwarf, and he also exploded into flames. The deadly fire did its work, rapidly eating away at the bones. Like the other two, in mere moments the skeleton was nothing but ash, another gust of wind carrying most of it away, the rest falling to the ground. The fire had spread to some of the brush, sending dark, greasy smoke skyward.

"Got enough for all of them?" Dennig asked, sounding hopeful as more shuffled closer.

"I just loosed the last one of that kind," Si'Cara said as she released another arrow, this one with blue fletching. It passed clean through her target's chest cavity, missing the spine by an inch and only taking a bit of rib bone with it. The skeletal warrior barely missed a step. Si'Cara gave a frown. "I don't believe any of my remaining arrows will affect the undead. They are meant for the living."

Just fifteen feet away now, the warriors continued to shamble closer, working their way through the overgrown brush. Their feet and legs caught on the low-lying vines, slowing them down ever so slightly as they fought their way through.

"You wanna play, do you?" Dennig placed himself between the undead and the injured Tal'Thor. He tapped the shaft of his axe into an open palm. "It's time to make my friend here sing."

Karus had fought the living, but never the dead. He studied them carefully as they worked their way closer. He watched as one became tangled in the undergrowth. It stopped struggling against the vine that had caught its foot. Then, it bent down and slowly extricated the foot from the vine. That told Karus the skeletons were not simply mindless, but capable of thought.

"How do we stop them?" Karus almost said, "How do we kill them?" but as they were already dead, he figured they couldn't be killed twice.

"We must hack them apart, sever the spine, break them," Si'Cara said, dropping her bow and arrows to the ground.

She drew her long-bladed daggers, a determined glint in her eyes and a grimness to not only her voice but her manner. "I have seen and fought the undead. Do not, under any circumstances, let them touch you."

"What will happen if they do?" Dennig asked, glancing over at her.

"Their touch," Si'Cara said, "can be enough to kill, if contact is prolonged."

"That just warms my heart," Dennig said and took a couple of steps toward the nearest skeletal warrior that had reached them, coming within five feet. It was carrying a badly rusted sword and its attention was focused on the dwarf. The jaw opened and closed several times, as if speaking.

"Come on, you beauty," Dennig said. "Let me introduce you to my new friend."

Dennig swung his axe in an arc and neatly took off the warrior's head, which sailed off into the air several feet, as if he'd batted it away. The dwarf jumped hastily back, for the headless warrior did not go down, but instead remained upright and swung its sword in return, nearly skewering Dennig. It had not been slowed in the slightest.

After barely managing to block the strike, Dennig recovered quickly. Shoving the rusted sword away, he chopped, aiming for the warrior's chest. It was a powerful blow. The dwarf's weapon cracked loudly as it impacted the rusted chest plate. The axe cleaved straight through with a crunching sound as it shattered, smashed, and sliced apart the bones underneath. The skeletal warrior collapsed, the magic that seemed to have driven it shattered as the bones all fell apart.

"Get behind me… get behind me," Karus shouted at Amarra as another warrior reached them. It swung a sword at Karus. He met it with his own blade, and the ring of steel upon steel sounded in the air. The warrior's sword was badly corroded and rusted. Upon the impact, bits, flakes and pieces of rusted metal sprayed into the air. With a shocking rapidity, the skeletal warrior struck again, stabbing out toward Karus. He met its blade with his own, and there was another loud clang. He felt the blow communicated solidly to his hand as the attack was powerfully driven. Karus gritted his teeth. Despite his opponent being dead, he knew this dance only too well.

Karus fended off a series of strikes. Then the skeletal warrior lunged. Karus had been waiting for it and knocked the blade aside, then kicked out with his foot, using the bottom of his sandal, specifically the hobnails, as a weapon. The blow connected solidly with the knee of the skeletal warrior, which shattered under the impact with a loud snap. The warrior tottered on one leg a moment and then fell backward into the brush. It started to sit up. Before it could, Karus stepped forward and chopped downward at the creature's arm that held the sword, aiming for the elbow joint. The bones crunched as the sword sliced right through and the arm snapped off.

Separated from the rest, the arm fell to pieces, the bones losing whatever cohesive force had held them together. Karus kicked the sword away. Then he hammered downward at the breastplate with his foot, stomping on it as hard as he could. There was a sickening crunch of bones. Like the arm, the skeleton fell apart, moving no more.

To his right, another warrior reached them. Si'Cara attacked, moving in a near blur and too quick for the warrior to strike her. The spear it held punched out and only found air as she easily ducked under the intended blow. Karus had never seen anyone move so fast. She spun around behind it, striking out with her daggers. Karus heard the crunch and snap as her daggers tore into the undead creature. A moment later, the skeletal warrior crashed to the ground, just a heap of bones, its spine severed in multiple places.

Then the mass of warriors were on them, perhaps twenty in number. Dennig waded forward amidst the warriors, swinging his axe this way and that. He cried out dwarven oaths as he attacked. With each powerful swing, there was a crunch of bones as the axe landed.

Then Karus had no more time to think. He was in the thick of it, confronted by another warrior. This one carried a rusted one-headed axe. It chopped at him, swinging a vicious cut at his side. Karus blocked it, his sword catching the axe along its shaft and slicing the weapon in two. The head of the axe glanced off of Karus's side armor but thankfully caused no injury.

With his sword, he shoved the shaft of the axe back, then hammered his sword forward, striking the skeleton in the chest plate. He had been hoping to knock it off balance, but the metal was so rusted that his sword punched clean through. The warrior smacked him on the side of his head with the shaft of the axe, connecting with his helmet. The helmet saved him from being incapacitated or killed. Still, the blow hurt.

Karus pulled to draw the sword backward and out. To his horror, he found the blade was stuck fast in the rusted breastplate. He only succeeded in jerking and pulling the skeletal warrior closer toward him. Its jaw opened wide, as if silently screaming an oath or curse at him.

Karus jerked the sword again with no luck. No matter how hard he tried, he could not free it. The warrior hit him again on the helmet, then dropped the axe handle and grabbed Karus's sword arm in its skeletal grip.

Karus screamed as pain lanced up his arm. It was agony unlike any he had ever felt, burning red hot and frigidly cold at the same time. He struggled to pull free of the grip, but it was too strong, too solid, too unshakable. Death had a hold upon him and did not want to let go. He was unable to free himself. The pain of it was incredible and growing by the moment. He was beginning to lose feeling in his hand.

Desperate, he punched out with his other fist, striking the skeleton a hard blow to the side of the head. Then he grabbed at the rusted chest armor, yanking the warrior closer to him. Karus delivered a head butt from his helmet. The skull crunched as part of it caved inward.

The warrior stumbled back, almost as if the blow had hurt. Karus was suddenly free. He took two steps back, gripping his arm, which stung terribly. A thin sheen of ice had formed along his hand and forearm.

"Ah," Karus groaned, flexing his fingers. The ice shattered and fell to the ground, leaving his arm steaming in the air. The feeling slowly and painfully began returning to his hand.

The warrior lurched forward again. Karus gave up on the sword, which was still stuck fast in the chest plate. He scrambled backward and pulled out his dagger as the warrior and another two joined it, advancing upon him.

Karus quickly glanced around as he retreated several more steps, attempting to give himself room. He found he was cut off from Dennig and Si'Cara. There would be no help from that quarter. Dennig was engaged with several warriors. Si'Cara was fighting three and shielding Amarra at the same time. Karus could see nothing of Tal'Thor, as the brush concealed the unconscious ranger from view.

The three skeletal warriors continued their advance upon him, one beginning to circle around to his right and another to his left in an attempt to surround him. He could hear the painful grinding of their bones as they moved closer and prepared to attack. Karus continued stepping backward, increasing his pace, his eyes on the warriors, hoping he didn't trip over the ivy he was moving through.

He needed a weapon beyond his dagger, and fast. His peripheral vision caught a glimpse of the guardhouse and he recalled the armory of rusted weapons. It was fewer than a dozen paces away. He turned and made a dash for the guardhouse. He could hear the skeletal warriors chasing after him, crashing through the brush. There was a clatter from behind. He glanced back. The warrior that had attacked him with the axe had tripped and fallen.

Then, Karus was at the door to the guardhouse and through. He contemplated attempting to shut the door, but discarded the idea. It might not even close, let alone hold. He needed a weapon and to get back into the fight. He recalled the short sword he'd seen—rusted or not, a weapon he was intimately familiar with. Karus passed the first few swords, a spear, and then spotted the weapon he sought. A warrior entered the guardhouse behind him, bones scraping across the cement floor as it moved toward him.

He considered going for the mace farther down the rack, but decided he might not have time to make it, as the warrior was close on his heels. So he grabbed the short sword's cord-grip handle. It was old and decaying, the blade hopelessly rusted. He ripped the weapon away from the rack and turned in one motion.

At that moment, Karus felt a strange butterfly sensation in his stomach. Time slowed to a crawl, if not having stopped altogether. It was a very odd feeling. Dust upon the air seemed to hang there, frozen for what seemed like an eternity. Then there was what he could only describe as a concussion, or really an explosion without sound. Dust, which had been lying in a thick carpet all around, was kicked violently up into the air. Karus was effectively blinded. Yet he felt like something had been awoken within him. He was not quite sure what. He hacked, choking and coughing as he attempted to draw in a breath.

Karus could hear the skeletal warrior's boney feet scraping along the floor. He took a couple of steps backward, seeking to gain room. Then the dust cloud thinned a little as it began to settle. The warrior was silhouetted by the light from the door. Sword raised to strike, it advanced, then hesitated and took what Karus thought was an uncertain step back from him, as if it were suddenly afraid. It took another step backward, rusted sword now held defensively.

Karus was not about to pass up an opportunity when presented with one. That was one thing service in the legions taught. He advanced to meet it.

The second warrior entered the guardhouse and it too hesitated, stopping in its tracks. Karus paid it no mind as he struck at the first one. Careful not to jab the breastplate, he instead slashed toward the chest, an unforgivable sin amongst the legions, where one was trained to stab. Karus wanted to batter it back, perhaps knock it off balance and then off its feet.

The warrior brought its sword up to block the strike. There was a loud crack and its rusted sword snapped into fragments, flying through the air. Karus was astonished when his sword slashed deep into the rusted armor and beyond, as if he were cutting through butter with a hot knife. There was a flaring of blue light from the warrior's empty eye sockets, and then the skeleton collapsed, bones noisily clattering to the cement floor along with the metal breastplate, which made a solid clunking noise.

Karus's hand gripping the sword felt funny. It tingled, and not in the way it would from a blow. The hilt grew warm in his hand. It was an odd sensation, in that both the tingling and warmth traveled rapidly up his arm and seemed to infuse his body. It happened so quickly that he wondered if he'd just imagined it. The dimness in the guardhouse seemed to lighten ever so slightly.

And so, it begins.

Karus glanced around, wondering who had spoken. It almost seemed like it had been in his mind, much like with the dragons when they spoke. For a heartbeat, he wondered if the skeletal warrior had spoken to him. Then decided it hadn't. The warrior was hastily backing out of the guardhouse, its sightless eye sockets fixed upon the sword in Karus's hands. Outside, Karus could hear the desperate sound of the fighting, the ring of steel. Dennig called out an oath in his own language. It spurred Karus to action.

He lunged forward, attacking before the undead creature could slip out of the guardhouse. The warrior, it seemed, wanted nothing more than to get away from him. It didn't even block Karus's strike as it attempted to turn and flee. Karus's sword slipped underneath the breastplate and connected with the spine. The moment it touched, the bones lost their cohesiveness and clattered to the ground, metal breastplate clunking down at his feet. Karus felt the tingle again in his hand and the warmth intensify, almost to the point of being uncomfortable.

You have awakened me, the disembodied voice spoke again. This time, he knew it was in his mind. *The soul-bond has been forged. Feed me and together we become stronger, our wills become one. Forged for a purpose, forged for a reason, forged for a will. Your will is my will and mine is yours. Together we are one. WIELD ME.*

Karus glanced down at the sword in his hand and realized that it was the sword that was speaking to him. The shock of it stunned him to his core. It also wasn't the rusted thing he'd picked up. The blade was finely crafted, with runes etched up and down the sides. The balance was as perfect as one could ask. He marveled at the blade he held, wondering if in his haste he had grabbed the wrong weapon. No, that wasn't right. How could he have not seen this piece of perfection when he had explored the guardhouse earlier? Surely, Dennig would have said something and pointed it out. No, this was the sword he had picked up, the only short sword that had been on the racks...it had transformed from rusted junk to a piece of infinite beauty.

Then he heard Amarra cry out. Karus's head snapped up, all thoughts and questions on the sword's transformation gone. He rushed to the doorway. The fight had spread out. Amarra had become separated from Si'Cara, who was fighting desperately against four of the skeletal warriors. Dennig was fighting an entire group. They were clustered tightly about him. All Karus could see of the dwarf was the axe as it swung. Wherever it landed, a shower of bones flew up into the air.

Amarra was facing two warriors, her staff held in her hands defensively as they advanced upon her. She was no fighter and Karus saw the staff was poorly held. If they survived this, he would have to take steps to correct that.

He stepped from the guardhouse, intent upon going to her aid. The warrior that had fallen was still on the ground, working to free itself from the vines. In a flash it was free and had pulled itself to its feet. It stared briefly at Karus with empty sockets and then turned in Amarra's direction, clearly seeking easier prey. He was on it before it could take more than two steps. Karus jabbed out, taking the skeleton in the side. The bones again lost their cohesiveness and the warmth in the grip of his hand grew, almost white-hot.

More.

They were almost on Amarra. He ignored the pain and started to run as Amarra struck at one of the warriors with her staff. There was a blinding flash, and when it subsided, both warriors before her had collapsed to the ground. Smoke rose from their bones. Karus stumbled to a stop, astonished. Amarra appeared stunned by what she had done.

Si'Cara screamed. A warrior had gripped her shoulder from behind. With Amarra safe, Karus ran to Si'Cara as she fell to a knee. The warrior put a second hand on her. She screamed again in clear agony and shuddered violently. Karus's sword hammered into the back of the skeleton. The bones rained downward and Si'Cara was suddenly free. She blocked a strike from another warrior that was intended for her neck, then swept her legs around, knocking the warrior from its feet. Karus struck at yet another warrior. Its bones fell to the ground the moment his sword connected. The hilt of the sword burned fiery hot, but Karus dared not let the weapon go.

"High Father, take this unfortunate soul into your keeping." There was another flash of light. Amarra appeared at his side and struck down an undead warrior that had been about to skewer Si'Cara in the back as she was finishing the warrior on the ground. Then there were no more within reach.

Karus turned to Dennig, intent upon helping him. To his shock, only one skeletal warrior remained facing the dwarf. Incredibly, he'd brought them all down. Dennig jabbed the warrior with the end of his axe, knocking it down and onto its back. Concealed partially by the brush, he sliced downward once and then again and again and again until he finally stood back up, axe upon his shoulder, chest heaving. He surveyed the courtyard around him, searching for more foes to slay. All of the skeletal warriors were down, finished. They had won. Their eyes met and Karus saw Dennig's widened slightly.

"Your sword," the dwarf gasped between breaths and pointed with his axe. "It's on fire."

Karus glance downward and almost dropped the sword. He had not noticed that the blade was sheathed in blue flame, which licked the air soundlessly. No wonder it felt heated. It was incredible, amazing, and clearly magical. The hilt was still burning hot, but somehow, he knew it would not harm him. He looked back up at the dwarf and saw that both Si'Cara and Amarra were staring at him, gazes transfixed upon his sword.

"How are you doing that?" Dennig asked, stepping through the brush and approaching him.

"I don't know," Karus said. "I think it is the sword. When I lost mine, I grabbed this one in the guardhouse."

"There wasn't one in there like that," Dennig said. "All of the swords were rusted beyond use. Where did you find it exactly?"

"I grabbed it from the rack," Karus said. "It was rusted like all of the others."

"You found that which we have sought." Amarra sounded both relieved and pleased. "As the High Father commanded, you have taken Rarokan."

Karus looked down at the sword in his hands. The fire coursing along the blade had begun to dim and then in a matter of heartbeats extinguished itself altogether. The hilt had cooled as well. He switched hands and saw that his palm was not burned. His gaze returned to the sword. It appeared like a normal blade now, although the weapon was exceptionally well-made and the balance was as perfect as one could ever want. The steel of the blade glinted brilliantly under the light from the two suns. Karus had never held a finer short sword. It was as if it had been made for him, and for a moment he considered that it might've been.

The High Father had arranged for it to come into his hands, had intended it all long. It was incredible and Karus felt deeply honored that he been entrusted with such a powerful weapon. He offered up a silent prayer of thanks to the High Father.

He looked back up at Amarra as she came nearer. She flashed him a pleased but weary smile and placed a hand upon his shoulder. He wiped some of the dust that coated them all from her cheek.

"We found it," Karus said, feeling intense relief. He could finally return to his legion.

"Yes," Amarra said, "yes, you did."

"May I hold it?" Dennig asked. The dwarf held out an expectant hand.

Karus considered it a moment and saw no harm in the request. He handed the blade over, offering the hilt to the dwarf. As Dennig took the sword, his hand closing upon the hilt, he let loose a bellow of pain and dropped it, along with his axe. He held his hand close to his chest and blew on it.

"It burned me," Dennig said, shaking his hand. "Darned thing burned me. Not too bad, but it damn well hurt, as if I'd touched a hot pan cooking bacon."

"It is meant only for you," Amarra said. "I think Rarokan recognizes its master, is all. While you live, you will be the only one to wield it. Anyone else who tries will suffer."

Karus eyed the weapon, which was lying amongst the vines at their feet, partially concealed by the green leaves.

He had not expected that. What was he dealing with here? It was almost certainly magic. Though he was honored to have been entrusted with Rarokan, magic made him terribly uncomfortable. And yet, he felt inexplicably drawn to the sword. It had nothing to do with the perfection of the weapon. There was something more to it. The sword had mentioned a bond. Was that it?

A little hesitantly, Karus bent down and picked the sword up. It didn't burn, as it had the dwarf. He felt a tingle in his palm that rapidly raced up his arm. It was almost as if the sword was pleased to see him and this was its way of showing it. He decided Amarra was correct. Rarokan was meant for him alone and apparently would tolerate no other touch. He held the sword up, looking at its rune-etched blade. The sword was his and his alone.

"Tal'Thor," Si'Cara said suddenly. She rushed back to where they'd left him.

They found the ranger sitting up and holding his head with both hands. He looked up at them a little blearily, blinking rapidly.

"What happened?" Tal'Thor asked, groaning a little. "I have a terrible headache."

"We had a wee little scrap with the undead." Dennig sauntered up. He thumped his chest with the hand he had tried to hold the sword with. The palm was slightly red, as the sword had given him a mild burn as a warning. The dwarf had retrieved his axe and leaned it upon his shoulder. "You missed out and I gained all the legend. That's what happens when you snooze."

"The undead?" Tal'Thor asked, feeling the wound on the top of his head. "What are you talking about?"

"It seems we triggered something that woke them when we tried to take the"—Karus could not think of a better word—"ghostly sword in the keep. It woke up the skeletal warriors that we passed on the way up to the fortress. They attacked us. We only just put them all down."

Tal'Thor held out a hand to Si'Cara. She pulled him to his feet. He swayed unsteadily for a moment. She held on to him until he was able to manage on his own, though he still looked a little unsteady, his legs wobbly.

Si'Cara leaned forward, grabbed his face in her hands, and kissed him hard. He appeared startled by the sudden move, then gave into it, fully kissing her back. When they broke apart, she slapped him hard, knocking him back on his ass. Si'Cara shook a finger in his face as he looked back up at her, confusion plain. Then she stepped away toward Amarra.

"Karus also found the sword we've been looking for," Dennig said as Tal'Thor got to his feet again. "If he were dvergr, I'd say he earned great legend this day."

Tal'Thor glanced over at Karus, who held the sword up for the elf to see.

"I would advise against touching it," Dennig said and showed his red palm. "It seems he is the only one able to hold it without injury."

Tal'Thor gave a nod, like he had expected as much. He blinked several times and shook his head, as if trying to clear out the cobwebs from a deep sleep.

"I will keep my good old Bone Cleaver here, thank you very much," Dennig said.

"You named it Bone Cleaver?" Karus asked.

"That's what it did, and quite well, too," Dennig said. "Can you think of a better name?"

"I suppose Doorknocker is out?"

Dennig grinned at him.

"What of the Warriors of Anagradoom?" Amarra asked, gazing around the overgrown courtyard. The brush still burned, though it did not appear to be spreading. "Where are they?"

Tal'Thor and Si'Cara exchanged a look.

"I do not know," Si'Cara said. "They don't seem to be here." Her voice caught in her throat. She took a moment to clear it. "Perhaps they died long ago. We never did get to explore the keep's underground."

Karus glanced down once more at Rarokan and then sheathed it in his scabbard. It fit, perfectly. His old sword was still stuck in the breastplate of the skeletal warrior. He considered retrieving it, for the sword had served him well over the years. In the end, he decided against it. He had a new sword now, and it was infinitely better. His old one would remain here with the dead. Though it was a waste, somehow it seemed fitting, a sword for a sword.

"Where is my bow?" Tal'Thor looked around abruptly. "I don't see it or my arrows."

"Back there," Karus said, pointing toward the rubble that shortly before had been the fortress's keep. It was now a large pile of stone blocks, a serious ruin, matching the rest of the fortress. "I am afraid it is buried under all that."

A sorrowful expression passed across Tal'Thor's face as he regarded what was left of the keep. It was as if he had lost an old friend. In a way, Karus sympathized with him. He had mixed emotions about leaving his old sword behind.

"I made that bow myself," Tal'Thor said.

"There was no time to go back for it," Karus said.

"It was either you or the bow," Dennig added. "Honestly, it was a tough choice. I could have sold the bow for some coin. You, I can't. Elves make terrible slaves, or so I've been told."

"You saved me?" Tal'Thor looked sharply at the dwarf.

"We both had a hand in it," Dennig said with a shrug and gestured at Karus with his axe.

Tal'Thor grew silent, glancing down at the ground before looking up.

"Thank you," he said to Dennig and Karus. "Thank you for saving my life."

"What was that?" Dennig asked and held a hand to his ear. "I could not quite hear you. Can you say that again?"

Tal'Thor flushed, going scarlet in the face.

"That's enough," Karus said to the dwarf before hard words could be exchanged. "There is no need to rub it in."

"The gods are the only ones who know the last time an elf properly thanked a dvergr," Dennig said, looking over at Karus. "It never happens. I just wanted to hear it again, is all. There is no telling how many years may pass before such a noteworthy event occurs again."

"I said that's enough," Karus snapped. "It may have been Tal'Thor saving your sorry ass instead of the other way around. You might be the one thanking him. Have you considered that?"

"Aye," Dennig said, sobering. "You might be right at that." He turned to the elf and grinned. "You are welcome, son."

"There was a bow in the guardhouse," Karus said to Tal'Thor. "It's old, but..."

"It may still be good. We make bows to last." Tal'Thor looked toward the guardhouse. He was still bleeding, though the flow had slackened considerably. He touched the wound gingerly and then looked at the blood on his hand, moving it across his fingers. "I think I will take a look at it before we depart."

"I could heal you," Amarra offered, stepping nearer.

"No," Tal'Thor said. "It's just a minor cut and a good bump. I would not have you waste the High Father's attention on it. This wound should heal soon enough."

"When we get back to camp," Karus said, "I have some bandages. We will fix it right up."

The elf gave a nod and then headed off toward the guardhouse. Si'Cara went with him. Karus saw her reach a hand out to his as they stepped through the entrance and disappeared inside.

Dennig made a show of glancing around at the piles of bones that moments before had been intent upon killing them.

"What is it?" Karus asked, for he sensed the dwarf was troubled, perhaps even morose.

"We gained much legend today." Dennig heaved a great breath, becoming downcast. "My kin will never believe this fight with the undead. No, they will not believe it ever happened. They will think I tell tall tales. So, I think I will not be telling of it... a sad waste of hard-earned legend."

The dwarf genuinely seemed upset.

"You do have the axe," Karus said. "If it's as rare as you say, well then ..."

"Ah, I see where you are going," Dennig said, hefting the axe. He shook it slightly. "I could claim I rescued this from a cursed fortress and fought off the undead doing it. For only a weapon as precious as this would be found in such a place. Ha! I like it! I really do approve of your thinking, my friend. You are cunning for a human."

Karus laughed, and it felt good to do so. Only a few minutes before, he had been fighting for his life, with death a very real prospect. The sky was brilliantly blue and the weather incredibly fair. He had once again beaten the odds. It felt great be alive.

He glanced toward Amarra, intent on sharing the moment. She was staring off in the direction of the gate, a scowl upon her beautiful face. Her posture was rigid. Something was wrong.

"We need to get out of here and off this hill," Amarra said in a low tone, as if she were speaking to herself. She looked over at Karus and Dennig, and her eyes appeared haunted. "It knows the fortress's defenses are breached. I can feel the enemy coming, and they are close." Her tone became urgent. "We need to go, and now!"

He did not need to be told twice. Neither did Dennig. They began moving toward the gate, working their way around the fire that still burned amongst the low-lying brush.

"Tal'Thor, Si'Cara ..." Karus shouted, cupping his hands about his mouth. "It's time to go!"

CHAPTER FIFTEEN

The rock shifted underfoot. Karus stumbled, almost falling forward. Dennig caught his arm in a vice grip, so hard it was close to being painful, but it kept him from tumbling down the steep face of the hill.

"Better watch your step there, son," Dennig said, wiping sweat from his brow. "It's rather steep and a long way down."

"Thank you," Karus said, glancing back at the large rock, which had shifted onto its side. Had they been taking their time, he would never have trusted it with his weight. But time was a commodity he did not wish to waste.

"Looks like I'm getting all the thanks today." Dennig grinned.

"Don't worry," Karus said with some amusement. "I am sure it will all come full circle. Just give it some time. I'm certain you'll be thanking Tal'Thor, or maybe even the dragons, before the day is through."

Dennig grunted at that and released his arm. "Is it just you or all humans? You seem really good at souring one's mood."

"They're getting ahead of us," Karus said, clapping the dwarf on the shoulder. "Let's keep moving."

They continued on, hastily following the path on its winding and weaving way down the hill. There were a few spots where they had to do a little scrambling or go slowly, watching every footstep. In patches, the path had deteriorated to scree, which slid and shifted underfoot.

Maddeningly, the scree repeatedly got into Karus's sandals. It proved a serious irritation. Both he and Dennig were forced to stop a couple of times and remove the tiny stones before continuing on.

The two rangers were out front with Amarra. Karus and Dennig were bringing up the rear. The day had turned warm and humid. The heat, combined with their pace, had Karus perspiring heavily.

Wiping sweat away from his face, he scanned the sky again. It had clouded up within the last hour and become heavily overcast. With the humidity on the air, Karus considered it was quite possible that they were in store for some rain. He hoped not, for, should Fortuna smile upon them, they would be on dragonback shortly, heading back to Carthum. The wind was bad enough. Karus did not want to add rain and make the journey any more miserable. Still, if they managed to escape before whatever-it-was arrived, Karus knew he would count himself lucky.

Unfortunately, there had been no sign of the dragons. He wondered why they had yet to return and hoped that something hadn't happened to them. Karus worried that whatever was on the way would arrive before the dragons got back. He tried to push his worries aside but found they kept returning. He felt as if he were missing something. It nagged at him. Karus did not like that feeling, for he had long since learned to trust his gut.

His knees had begun to ache with the descent down the hill. He did not like that either. The pace they had set was punishing, and his knees cried out in protest. Karus wasn't as young as he used to be. Climbing a hill never seemed to be a problem, but going down any type of incline caused his knees to ache terribly after just a few minutes. Bad knees were a common complaint for long-service veterans and usually signaled the beginning of the end, a sign retirement was right around the corner. Years of marching miles upon untold miles while carrying a full kit had taken its inevitable toll. Karus felt it with every step down the hill.

He consoled himself with the knowledge that the pain was transitory, as the hill wasn't large and they'd be to the bottom of it soon enough. He put the discomfort from his mind and soldiered along.

Within fifteen minutes the camp came into sight. The extinguished fire and the packs were lying where they'd been left. He was relieved that no one else was there, waiting. Si'Cara led the way off the path, making a beeline for the camp. Tal'Thor and Amarra were right behind her.

Karus started off the path, following, with Dennig bringing up the rear. Their pace slowed, as they had to work their way through the low-lying brush, careful to avoid the prickly bushes. Still, they moved quickly, and before Karus knew it, he was stumbling into the camp.

Breathing heavily and parched, he grabbed one of the canteens, unstopped it, tipped it back, and drank greedily. Having been left sitting out in the suns with the packs, the water was warm, but incredibly refreshing. Amarra, to his right, was bent over, one hand on a knee, holding her staff loosely. She was working to catch her breath. He handed the canteen over to her as she straightened, holding her hand to her side as if she had a stitch of discomfort. She drank just as deeply. He grabbed a spare canteen and splashed some water on his face, washing away the dust. He did the same to his arms, then drank the canteen dry.

"Do you still feel it coming?" Karus asked when his breathing was better under control.

"I do." Amarra gripped her staff tightly. "Danger is about."

He did not like the sound of that.

"It makes my skin crawl." Amarra pulled her braid over her shoulder and ran her hand along it.

"Karus, do you have that bandage?" Si'Cara asked, drawing his attention. Both elves were barely winded.

"I do," Karus said and went to his pack. He rummaged around in it briefly before pulling out a fresh bandage long enough to be wrapped around Tal'Thor's head. He tossed it to Si'Cara.

"Sit," Si'Cara said to Tal'Thor.

"We should move into the trees," Tal'Thor said.

"Sit," Si'Cara ordered. She tapped her foot impatiently when Tal'Thor failed to move.

"We can tend to my wound in the forest," Tal'Thor said.

"It will only take but a moment. The sooner it is tended to the better," Si'Cara said. "Do not make me ask again, for I will not."

Tal'Thor scowled at his wife. Then, like an obedient child, he sat down and bent his head toward her. Si'Cara carefully examined the wound, probing with her fingers. Tal'Thor winced but beyond that displayed no discomfort.

"I have some vinegar." Karus pulled the small jar out of the pack and held it up for her to see. "Do you want it?"

"Thank you."

Si'Cara took it, unstopped the jar, sniffed at the contents. She nodded with approval. Turning back to her husband, she first rinsed the wound out with water from a canteen. She used two entire canteens, which saw Tal'Thor thoroughly drenched. Next, she poured a little bit of vinegar directly onto the wound. Tal'Thor grimaced. Karus sympathized, for wounds and vinegar did not mix well.

"Hurts," Tal'Thor said as Si'Cara added a little more vinegar.

"Don't be such a baby," Si'Cara said. "It's only a small cut. The bump makes it feel worse than it is. The vinegar will keep it from festering."

Si'Cara studied the wound and poured on more vinegar. She handed the bottle back to Karus. Apparently satisfied she had cleaned the wound out sufficiently, she wrapped his head in the bandage and tied off the end in knots so it would hold. She looked over her work with a pleased expression and then stepped back.

"Don't scratch at it," Si'Cara said reproachfully as Tal'Thor came to his feet. He shot her another scowl.

"We should get into the trees," Tal'Thor said to Karus. "At least until the dragons arrive. I believe it may be safer if we are under cover. Whatever the High Priestess feels is coming will likely look for us in the fortress first. I think it is only logical, for it is what I would do."

"I agree with Tal," Si'Cara said. "The trees are the safe bet."

Dennig was leaning heavily upon the head of his axe, the handle on the ground. The dwarf was still sucking in great gulps of air between draining a canteen dry.

"That sounds like a fine idea," Dennig said, looking at the tree line. His gaze returned to the two rangers. "Are you certain there are none of your brothers and sisters around?"

"There is no elven settlement for miles," Tal'Thor said. "Long ago, the warden declared the trees around this hill forbidden. None would dare trespass without first receiving her permission."

"The warden." Dennig spat upon the ground. "Bloody witch."

"Right. Time to get cracking." Karus moved toward the pack he had drawn the bandages from and returned the bottle of vinegar, making sure the top was securely stopped. He tied the pack closed and hoisted it onto his shoulder. "Let's get these into the trees and out of sight. Dennig, since you are so fond of the food we brought, grab that pack, will you?"

"What of the spent fire?" Dennig asked, not taking the bait but looking sourly upon the ash and half-burnt logs, which still smoldered. They gave an occasional pop but issued no flame. "Don't you think this will stand out a bit?"

"I don't see that we have a choice," Karus said. "There's no way to conceal it quickly, especially since we uprooted the grass around the fire. Hopefully whoever's after us will not pass this way. With a bit of fortune, they won't see the remains of our camp until we're long gone, or at least until the dragons arrive. They're so big, it'd be pretty hard to miss them."

"Speaking of being long gone," Dennig said, sounding exasperated, "where are our rides? Seems to me they would be more useful if they'd been waiting or had come back."

"They'll be along," Amarra said, hoisting up a pack. She sounded certain. "Kordem and Cyln'phax would not leave us stranded. There must be a very good reason they are delayed."

"Can you call them?" Dennig asked after her. "Like dogs?"

"No," Amarra said as she started for the trees a few yards away. "I cannot."

Si'Cara grabbed her pack and one of Amarra's and began making her way toward the forest. Tal'Thor shouldered a couple of packs and started off after her.

"Well, that's downright disappointing," Dennig grumbled. "To be off hunting, when they should be here."

Amarra stopped and looked back at the dwarf. "I would not think of them as pets or hounds for hunting. They are people like us, just different."

"People, you say?" Dennig sounded as if he seriously doubted such a thing were possible. "Bloody dragons as people?"

"Yes," Amarra affirmed, fixing the dwarf with her piercing gaze. "People, and don't forget it."

Dennig gave her an unhappy frown as he picked up the pack containing their food supplies. The dwarf mumbled something under his breath and then started for the forest.

Karus thought Amarra looked troubled as she turned away and continued on, picking up her pace the closer she got to the trees. Whatever the danger was, it was very near and too close for his comfort. At least they'd be safer hidden in the trees. He glanced around their camp once more and then started after her.

As he passed into the trees, with the shade of the canopy settling over them like a shroud, Karus could not help but feel a sense of relief. It was an old forest, full of the giant trees. The air was cooler and the forest smelled strongly of decay, the previous season's leaves lying over a thick carpet of moss crunching underfoot. At least they were now out of view.

Amarra stopped a few yards in and looked back, waiting for the rest of the party to catch up.

"Should we go farther?" Amarra asked, dropping her pack to the soft forest floor.

Tal'Thor looked briefly around and said something in Elven to Si'Cara, who replied.

Karus was concerned that if they went too deep into the forest, the dragons might have difficulty finding them, let alone getting down to them. The tree canopy high above was quite thick. He turned to look back the way they had come. The light under the shade of the massive giants was dim, almost like it was dusk and not the middle of the day. Beyond the tree line, despite it being overcast, the land was bathed in a far brighter light. It was an interesting contrast, almost as if they had gone from the world of light into a one of perpetual shade and darkness, which, in a way, they had. Very little sunlight ever reached the floor of this forest, as evidenced by the thick carpets of moss.

Thunder rumbled off in the distance. It sounded like a cavalry charge.

"No dragons to take us away, and with some nameless threat on the way," Dennig grumbled. "Now rain is coming. Things just keep getting better and better."

"Perhaps you would have liked it better," Karus said, "if I'd left you all nice and cozy in the warden's cell?"

"Hah…hah…hah," Dennig said, shaking his axe at Karus for emphasis. "I was wrong about you. You really do have a way of brightening a lad's mood, now, don't you?"

"We think this should be fine," Tal'Thor said, setting the packs down next to Si'Cara's and also looking back the way they had come. "If need be, we can easily move deeper into the forest."

Karus wasn't so sure about that. Despite his concern about the dragons being able to find them, he knew he would feel more comfortable going a little farther away from the tree line, making it that much more difficult for them to be spotted.

"I—" Whatever Amarra had been about to say was abruptly and savagely cut off. She gave a soft grunt that came with a meaty-sounding thump. Karus spun around in time to see her fall to the ground, where she landed in a heap.

She didn't move.

Karus blinked. His heart stopped cold. He wanted to run to her, but then his mind kicked into gear as the elves brought up their bows.

They were under attack.

He dropped his own pack and drew his sword. The moment he touched the handle, he felt once again the odd tingle run from his palm up his arm. There was something strangely comforting about it. The shade under the trees lightened just a tad. Karus's aches and pains faded, particularly those in his knees, which had been badly used running down the hill. It was a peculiar feeling, and for a heartbeat or two, Karus wondered on it. But then he pushed the strange feeling aside and chalked it all up to the prospect of an impending fight.

He scanned around, peering into the dimness between the massive trunks. Shadowy figures were emerging from the trees all around them. Something flashed out from the dimness, and before he could react, it struck him hard in his chest.

Karus found himself on his back, staring up at the leafy canopy high above. There was an intense pain in his chest. His entire body tingled, his fingers and toes having gone numb. He struggled to draw breath, for whatever had hit him had also stolen his wind. There was a thud nearby as a heavy body hit the ground. Without looking, he was certain it was Dennig.

A shout rang out. It sounded like Elven to his ears. Struggling to breathe, Karus rolled over onto his side. The shadowy figures he had spotted were rushing forward toward them. He dragged himself onto all fours, the feeling coming back to his fingers and toes.

When he had been hit, he'd lost his sword. It lay a few feet away. The pain in his chest was terribly intense, but he could feel it begin to fade away. Karus put a hand to his armor where he'd been struck. It felt warm to the touch, hot even.

That had to have been bloody magic, Karus thought. After several heartbeats, he was finally able to draw a ragged breath. Sweet air filled his lungs. It felt wonderful as he sucked in another gulp.

There were more shouts. Karus glanced around again and saw that their attackers were elves. He made a dive for the sword. A booted foot stomped down painfully upon his hand. A blade appeared before his eyes.

"I don't think so," a voice said in Common.

Karus froze, then looked up the blade of the sword and saw one of the warden's guards standing over him. Karus felt the chill touch of the metal blade press against his throat, the razor-sharp edge scratch against the stubble under his chin. The elf removed his foot from Karus's hand, then switched the blade to the flat side and pushed a little. Karus got the meaning of what the elf wanted and sat up, kneeling. The elf withdrew the sword and moved around behind him, standing right over Karus.

The message was clear. He was a prisoner.

Karus counted two dozen elves, with several more emerging from amongst the trees. Not only were the warden's guards present, but there were also rangers. Tal'Thor and Si'Cara had been surrounded. Two rangers aimed nocked arrows at them. Karus watched as a fellow ranger stepped forward and took Si'Cara's bow, handing it off to another. He removed her daggers, then disarmed Tal'Thor as well. Both held their hands up in the air and were thoroughly patted down. Neither Si'Cara nor Tal'Thor looked pleased at their current predicament.

Karus's eyes went to Amarra. She lay where she had fallen, unmoving. Karus felt a stab of fear that she had been grievously wounded or perhaps even killed. Whatever she'd been hit with, they had wanted to bring her down. He hoped she was just incapacitated, perhaps knocked cold ... anything but dead. He wanted to go to her, but couldn't.

To his right, Dennig was also forced to sit up. The guard roughly gripped Dennig's hair and pulled him into a sitting position.

"You bloody ... High Born bastard," Dennig growled, balling his fists helplessly. "You better kill me, because if I get free, I'm gonna smash that pretty boy smirk off your face."

The elf hit Dennig in the back of the head with the pommel of the sword. The dwarf went down and rolled on the ground, grabbing the back of his head with both hands. Karus saw blood seep through the fingers.

"Keep talking, dwarf," the elf said, "and I promise I will kill you. One less dwarf will make this world a better place. Now get up, filthy ground dweller, before I lose my patience."

Groaning, Dennig sat back up, glaring daggers at the elf, but he said nothing further. He shot a look that spoke of longing at his axe, lying a handful of feet away. He tore his gaze away from his beloved axe and shared a frustrated look with Karus that was saturated with bitterness and anger.

Off to his left, Karus saw movement. The warden and the wizard were walking towards them. Karus briefly closed his eyes. He realized his mistake. Amarra had sensed the warden's coming. He should've expected it, anticipated it, considered it even. They had been safer on the hill but had unwittingly entered the trees, her domain. Karus let out an aggravated breath.

There was a commotion to the right. Si'Cara and Tal'Thor had been brought closer and made to kneel down. Two rangers stood behind both of them. Si'Cara exchanged heated words with one of the rangers. Tal'Thor said something as well. The ranger behind Si'Cara roughly grabbed her by the throat and pulled out a dagger. The other ranger placed his long-bladed dagger against Tal'Thor's throat. Both became very still.

Karus returned his attention to the warden. She had stopped by Amarra, gazing down. She said something to the wizard, who shook his head slightly. The warden replied before stepping around Amarra toward the staff, which lay discarded a few feet beyond. She remained for a number of heartbeats, staring at it, before her gaze shifted to Karus.

The warden's eyes flicked toward the sword lying upon the forest floor, half buried by dried and desiccated leaves. A sense of triumph made itself known upon her face. Karus could see it in her eyes, which fairly shone with exultation. A moment later, her gaze tracked back to Karus, and a cruel and heartless smile formed upon her perfect face.

The warden advanced, coming within a couple paces of him. There she stopped. Karus knew they were all in serious trouble.

"You have brought me what I have long desired," the warden said. "For that, I should thank you. But alas, I will not."

"It was meant for me," Karus said, "not you."

"I know." The warden clasped her hands before her. "Intentions have nothing to do with anything. I want it, and that is all that matters."

The warden brought a finger to her lip and moved around Karus in a slow circle, examining him. Karus felt as if he were a slave at the market, being appraised. The warden returned to her original position, facing him, and then clasped her hands together once again.

"Why?" Karus asked. "Why do this?"

The cruel smile grew. "Since you asked...I shall grace you with an answer." She paused, as if gathering her thoughts. The wizard at her side remained perfectly still. "Karus, you must understand, I have worked toward our meeting under these circumstances for a very long time. It all began with the fortress's defenses, which at one time were quite formidable. It took centuries of study and work just to understand what the High Master had done. In time, I came to comprehend his work as if it were my own. That allowed me to disarm all of the defenses, but for a handful. Those few vexed me terribly. They prevented me from going up into the fortress myself. They kept me from retrieving and claiming Rarokan as my own." She paused, sucking in a breath.

"The High Master had seen to that," the warden continued. "His last webs, which in truth are a masterpiece of magical construction, were what held me at bay." She paused again, the smile slipping from her face. "The web he wove was so skillful, one cannot but help to admire his work. It was tightly bound to the fortress, feeding greedily upon the latent power of the defunct portal that once resided up there. I ultimately came to the conclusion I could not completely break what he had done." Her eyes found his again, and Karus read a deep madness within. "So instead, I set about corrupting the fortress's remaining defenses, altering one ward and web at a time, bending them to my will. The webs were changed and shaped beyond recognition." The warden paused once again. "Then...there was the Anagradoom. I made it so they could no longer fulfill their purpose, guarding the sword, keeping it safe for the one for whom it was intended. You see, they would never have allowed me to take it. So, I dealt with them also."

"No!" Si'Cara screamed. "You killed them?"

"Keep quiet, you silly little girl," the warden snapped, irritation flaring in her tone. "I will deal with you and your husband in a moment."

"I will never be silenced," Si'Cara said, "never again. You are no longer fit to be warden of our people. You have betrayed all that we hold dear ..." Si'Cara slipped into Elven, loosing a diatribe at the warden as she might arrows.

The guard standing over Karus hissed with displeasure. The rangers behind Si'Cara and Tal'Thor shifted uncomfortably, as if they recognized the truth when they heard it but could not act. They shared a glance but did nothing more. Karus wondered if there was dissention in the ranks of the warden's followers.

The warden held forth a long-fingered hand toward Si'Cara.

Suddenly Si'Cara's mouth in mid-speech snapped shut with a clap. Her hands went to her face. She gagged and seemed to be struggling to breathe, as if choking. Tal'Thor looked over at his struggling wife, his alarm plain. He moved with the intention to help her. The ranger behind him forced him back down.

"Stop it," Tal'Thor shouted.

The warden ignored him.

Tal'Thor yelled something in Elven at the warden.

Whatever he had said got the warden's attention. She glanced over at him, before her gaze tracked to the rangers standing over Tal'Thor and Si'Cara. Both looked seriously concerned, grave even. The warden then let her hand drop, and with it, whatever power she had exerted over Si'Cara was withdrawn. Si'Cara fell forward to the leaf and moss-covered ground, gasping for breath. Tal'Thor moved, and this time the ranger did nothing to restrain him. He took Si'Cara into his arms and held her close to him, cradling her like one would a baby. He began whispering into her ear.

"So," the warden said, turning back to him, "where was I? Oh, yes … the Anagradoom. They shall not be troubling us." The warden made a show of glancing around. "Had I failed, I think they would be here … now."

"You're mad," Karus said.

"Maybe." The warden laughed at him. "Maybe not. Karus … I had to wait, to bide my time. You see, ultimately, I learned I had to wait for you. For only you and your High Priestess"—she said the last with a tinge of derision and glanced over at Amarra, who lay still and unmoving—"with the High Father's touch and spark could breach the final defenses and bring me what I have long craved, Rarokan."

"You are responsible for the skeletal warriors then?" Karus asked, figuring only one as evil as the warden was would design such a terrible death. "The trap that freezes?"

"Not quite," the warden said. "That web's original intent was far different. I altered it to my will, to fit my own purposes. With the defenses weakened, another might have managed to sneak in, someone I had not anticipated or desired. I used that web to make certain such a breach did not happen. It was creative, really. Only those of true faith could overcome and continue on."

The warden fell silent, as if she wanted him to digest what she'd said.

"You've still not told me why," Karus said. "Why do this? We need the sword, and badly."

"You need it?" the warden hissed. "Your petty need is nothing compared to mine. You have no idea what Rarokan is capable of doing, the power it contains, the latent ability and the *will* residing within. Fool of a human. You would use it as a simple weapon. I shall utilize it for so much more. With it, I will challenge the gods themselves. I shall become a god. I will end this destructive war and save my people." Her gaze swept the elves around her. "As was written, my people shall worship at my altar. All shall bow before my greatness."

Karus looked from the warden to the wizard, who was standing quietly next to her.

"She's mad," Karus said to En'Sis'Lith in Latin, knowing the wizard would understand. "You have to know this, and yet you willingly serve her?"

"Once the warden becomes a goddess," the wizard said in Common. There was a tinge of madness in the wizard's eyes also, "I shall be first among her disciples, first amongst all others. She shall end this eternal war the gods started. Mad? Oh, I think not. No." His gaze slid over to the warden, and Karus thought he saw what looked like adoration or love shine forth. "She is very sane." The wizard's gaze shifted back to Karus. "It is the gods who have gone mad. Long ago they lost the right to claim our devotion. They deserve what is coming."

Karus could not believe what he was hearing. The warden wanted to become a god. He did not even know if it was possible, but the warden sure believed. She already commanded a strange and mystical power Karus knew he could never hope to comprehend. He was certain there was absolutely no way that, if the warden fulfilled her ambition and became a god, she would be a compassionate one. Her nature was cruel. She was a heartless creature who knew not of love and compassion. She pursued power at the expense of others. The claim she would stop the war of the gods was absurd. He was certain she was not doing this for a benevolent reason or for some high-minded purpose. Karus understood the warden would be an evil deity, one to be feared and dreaded. Darkness would fall in her shadow. She had to be stopped ... but how?

The smile upon the warden's face grew wider, almost as if she could read Karus's thoughts. Very slowly, very deliberately, with her eyes upon him, she bent down toward Rarokan. Karus made a lunge for the sword, but was restrained by the guard behind him, who grabbed him roughly by the armor harness and dragged him backward. The warden laughed.

"Now," she said, "I shall take what should always have been mine. I will make the gods pay for what they have done. This is but the first step."

Her hand closed upon the sword's hilt. There was a brilliant flash and a snapping sound. The warden cried out, both in pain and shock, jumping backward. She wrung her hand, staring incredulously at the sword lying half-concealed by leaves. After a moment, she turned her gaze back upon him, fury plain. It almost made him want to smile.

"You have bonded with the sword," the warden hissed at him. "That should not have been possible. I made sure there was nothing up on that hill, no life, no insect, no animal ... no soul to take other than those that went with you. And they all came down with you. How? How did you manage this? I must know."

Karus did not know what she was talking about or how to answer her question. The warden seemed to think he was intentionally withholding an answer. Unbridled fury clouded her youthful and attractive face, making it seem ugly.

"Release him," the warden snapped to the guard. Suddenly, Karus was free but still on his knees. She stepped nearer. "Answer me or I shall make you suffer. I want to know how you managed to bond with the sword."

"Rarokan is mine," Karus said, "as it was always meant to be. You cannot have it."

Rage mottled her face. The warden let out a hissing breath. She calmed herself after a moment. The look of fury passed.

"Yes, the sword belongs to you," the warden said in a quiet tone, "but once I kill you, the sword will be freed to bond with another. I will ultimately take it. But first, I think I shall make you suffer for your insolence." The warden glanced over at Amarra's body. "Tell me what I wish to know or you shall see your beloved High Priestess die this day, slowly."

Despite their predicament, Karus felt joy at hearing Amarra still lived.

"Then," the warden continued, "I shall take your life. I will send you both on to the High Father. You can tell him that, for his many sins, I am coming for him. The question for you, Karus...will it be slow? Will you both suffer? Or shall it be quick and painless?" The warden paused as if to let it sink in. "Decide now, before I change my mind and give you no choice in your manner of death."

"You evil bitch," Karus growled and made to stand. He was forced back down by the guard.

"That is a matter of perspective." The warden took a step back and turned to the wizard. "Kill her for me"—she paused, and the heartless smile returned—"slowly. I want to see her suffer. Then bring me that staff."

The wizard gave a nod and was about to move off toward Amarra when there was a deep thwacking sound. An arrow, as if by magic, had sprouted from the center of the wizard's chest. The wizard rocked unsteadily upon his feet and gazed down at the arrow, dumbfounded at first and then in growing shock as blood began to leak from the wound, staining his robe dark. The warden seemed just as startled, for she took a hasty step backward and glanced around. The wizard opened his mouth to say something. Blood came fountaining out instead. He began to choke on it, a horrible sound.

There was a crack from directly behind Karus. The guard toppled over, knocking Karus to the ground and falling atop him. The wizard collapsed to his knees. He held out an imploring hand toward the warden, who was looking off behind Karus. She spared no attention to her servant. The wizard fell over onto his side and expired. His sightless eyes stared at Karus.

Shouts of alarm and cries of rage sounded all around. Karus pushed the body off him. The elf did not weigh as much as he had expected. He noticed a black-fletched arrow had pierced the armor. It snapped off as the body rolled over.

The warden, still looking past Karus, shouted something he could not understand and held the back of her arm up before her chest, almost as if she were gripping a shield. A green sphere shimmered into existence around her. An arrow cracked into the sphere and shattered into pieces.

Karus dove to his right for the sword. His hand closed over the grip. He felt the tingle once again, but it was more. Karus was energized, feeling as if he had gotten a full night's sleep. He rolled up into a crouch, facing the warden. She was ignoring him, shouting orders to her elves. An arrow whizzed past Karus's head, bare inches away, and impacted the sphere. He ducked, wondering if they were shooting at him or the warden, or perhaps both.

He glanced around and was astonished to see elves fighting elves. Si'Cara and Tal'Thor were free, up, and struggling for their lives against the warden's guards. Si'Cara had retrieved one of her daggers and was trading strokes against

311

a guard who held a sword. Tal'Thor was locked in a death grip, wrestling around on the ground with another guard.

A few feet away, Dennig was on top of the elf who had hit him. The dwarf was pounding his fist into the elf's face again and again and again. Karus could hear the sickening crunch of bone with each and every punch.

Another arrow zipped by, snapping Karus's head up. Elves wearing black leather armor had entered the clearing. Several were locked in combat with the warden's guards and rangers. Others had bows and were raining death into the clearing.

Karus saw a guard drop as he was hit with two arrows almost simultaneously. One of the warden's rangers dropped dead a few feet away, an arrow having gone straight through the side of his head. Karus could not understand who these newcomers clad in black were, but he did recognize that they were killing the warden's people, which made them potential friends. At least, he hoped they might be. He had learned elves were a complicated race.

He thought of Amarra, and his head whipped around, looking for her. Just then, someone knocked him to the ground from behind. Karus felt the other's weight pressing upon his back and legs. Before he could fight free, there was a flash of green light, then a sickening sizzling above him. It was as if all of his hair stood on end. The person on his back fell over next to him. He saw that it was one of the elves clad in black. Eyes open, he was dead as a doornail. Karus looked up and saw the warden, five feet away, face contorted with fury and hate. Her hand had been outstretched toward Karus. He realized that she had just tried to kill him. The black-clad elf had saved his life.

Karus stood and faced the warden. She was still encased in a sphere of green light. He found her eyes terrible to behold as she gazed upon him. Karus sensed his imminent death. Behind her, more of the guards were emerging from the trees and joining the fight. They badly outnumbered the warriors in black.

She raised her hand toward Karus's heart, and he saw a light begin to glow at the tips of her fingers.

Use me as a shield. Hold me forth.

Karus held Rarokan up before him, and as he did, a green flash of light arced out, shooting toward him. The green light was attracted to the sword, for it impacted directly upon the blade. The force of it was tremendous. Karus braced his feet. He felt himself being shoved backward by the power of the assault. The blade crackled and hissed as it took the brunt of the attack.

The hilt grew warm in his hands, then began to burn white hot. Karus cried out in agony. It seemed to not only sear his skin but tear at his soul. He attempted to release the blade but found that his hand was stuck to the grip. Then, as quickly as it had begun, it was over. The warden stood there, her eyes narrowed as she gazed upon him and the sword. The green sphere that had enclosed her was gone.

Her ward is down. Quickly, before she can restore it. Kill her, take her soul, feed me.

Karus did not need any more encouragement. He felt rage burn within his breast. He had had enough. He wanted blood. It was time to end this madness. He advanced on the warden, with murder in his heart.

Before he could take more than two steps, one of the warden's guards charged him and attacked. Karus turned to receive the attack. Their two swords clanged on the air. The elven guard struck at him again, with lightning quickness. Karus rapidly found himself on the defensive, warding off blow after blow that came in rapid succession. Sweat beaded his brow as he was forced backward to keep from being skewered. The elf was skilled and well-trained, a near-master with his blade. It was all Karus could do just to keep the guard's blade out of reach.

There was an explosion of flame to his right, followed by a scream of animal-like rage. Karus almost grinned, for he knew who had finally arrived. The elf attacking him hesitated, gaze traveling upward. Karus took advantage of the distraction. He lunged forward, aiming for his opponent's neck. The elf saw the strike coming at the last moment and dodged away, but not fast enough. Karus's blade nicked his throat. The elf collapsed like a puppet, as if the strings of life had suddenly been severed. It was like the skeletons in the fortress. Karus felt the blade in his hand grow warm again.

He did not have time to think on this further, for a second guard approached, closing in with deadly intent. There was caution in the other's eyes, which flicked briefly to the body of the guard lying at Karus's feet. The elf's expression hardened. Sword held ready, he coolly assessed Karus. There was another explosion of fire, this one uncomfortably close by. A wave of heat rolled over the two of them, nearly enough to singe. This was followed by a second scream of rage from a dragon. Like the first, the elf's eyes traveled upward toward the canopy.

Karus took the opportunity to lunge. This elf was quicker, for he reacted rapidly and blocked the attack, pushing Karus's blade aside. There was a loud crack. The elf reeled backward, as a black-fletched arrow had punched through his shoulder armor. The force of the missile had almost been enough to spin him completely around. Distracted, and in pain, he never even saw the attack coming as Karus's sword plunged into the back of his leg. The elf screamed in agony and stumbled to a knee. With effort, he turned back around.

Karus wondered why the elf had not died outright, but did not let that stop him. He attacked again. The elf, hobbling and badly wounded, blocked his first strike, but not the second. Karus's sword punched into and through the other's throat. Hot blood sprayed out, coating his arm as the sword grated against the elf's spine. The guard's eyes rolled back in his head. He fell backward to the forest floor, quite dead.

Karus looked around for another threat. He saw more of the warden's guards and rangers emerging from the trees and joining the fight. The warden, however, was nowhere to be seen. Karus felt immense frustration. She had slipped away.

There was another blast of flame, followed by screams of agony. He glanced upward toward where he expected the dragons to be, for he could hear the flapping of their great wings as they beat on the air. Karus stopped, his jaw falling open. These weren't his dragons. They were wyrms, and there were four of them, hovering just above the treetops.

Arrows arced up at the wyrms from the rangers and black-clad elves down below, even as they fought amongst one another. A wyrm breathed fire back, fully engulfing several of the warden's rangers. They screamed horribly as they died, one running off into the forest on fire, leaving a trail of burning leaves in his wake.

Knotted ropes began dropping from the backs of two of the wyrms. The ends of the ropes fell almost to the forest floor, and as they did, orcs began to shimmy downward. He considered that perhaps it had not been the warden Amarra had sensed. He felt a sudden dread as he watched the wyrms unloading dozens of orc warriors, who were rapidly shimmying down the ropes toward the raging battle below.

The Horde had come.

Karus tightened his grip upon Rarokan. There was no doubt in his mind what they wanted. At first, Karus wasn't quite sure what to do. Then he spotted the warden, thirty yards away, by the massive trunk of a tree. She was ringed by guards.

Frustrated yet again that she was for the moment out of reach, his thoughts went to Amarra. He looked around. She was still lying where she had dropped. Putting the warden from his mind, he rushed over to her and found her stirring slightly. He rolled her onto her back. There was an ugly welt upon her right temple. It bled a little. Her eyes fluttered open. She looked up at him and blinked, thoroughly confused. Relief flooded Karus at seeing she was not seriously injured. He quickly checked her for any additional wounds. He did not find any.

The noise of the fight increased. He glanced around, quickly scanning the area about them. He saw the first wave of orcs had reached the ground. They had joined the growing battle, which was now a three-way fight. It was loud, violent, brutal, and ugly, just what Karus had come to expect from war.

"We need to get out of here," Karus said, turning his attention back to Amarra and helping her to sit up. "You need to get up. We need to move, okay? Do you understand me?"

"What?" Amarra's eyes rolled back into her head. Karus gave her a little shake. When that did not have the desired effect, he shook her harder. She blinked and refocused on him. "What? Karus, what's going on?"

An arrow zipped by above his head and struck an orc just three feet away and to his right, felling the creature instantly. The arrow had punched clean through the armored helmet. Karus straightened as a second orc approached.

The orc was at least seven feet tall, with bulging arm muscles. The creature's skin was a dark green. Its armor included a solid-looking chest plate and helmet. The chest plate was plain, without any ornamentation, and, in Karus's estimation, poorly made, but that did not make it any less effective.

The helmet was of the same poor quality. It covered much of the face and head almost in its entirety, with only little holes for the ears and a thin slit for the eyes. Karus could hear the creature's ragged breathing through the helmet as it closed the last few feet.

Beyond the chest plate and helmet, the orc wore no other armor, just black leather pants and old boots that had long since seen their prime. The boots had numerous holes. Karus could even see several hairy toes poking through.

More concerning to Karus was the orc's sword. It was a long, curved blade that, combined with the creature's size, meant it had the advantage on him in reach. The orc carried the sword in its left hand. It had an oval wooden shield that was almost the size of a legionary's in the other. The shield, like the orc's boots, had seen better days. It was dented and chipped. Several nails were exposed where a repair had been made.

He absorbed all this in a flash. Judging by the orc's appearance, Karus came to the conclusion it had poor discipline, for a soldier should care for his equipment above all else. The question in his mind was now on skill. Was the orc a skilled fighter? In Karus's experience, discipline did not always count toward skill. Karus thought the creature had a mean look to it.

Gritting his teeth in determination, he stepped around Amarra to meet the orc, who rushed the last five feet to him. It bashed out with its shield. Karus dodged to the right, barely avoiding the shield and the stroke from the sword that followed. He jabbed at the orc, who danced away, his sword point only managing to scrape against his opponent's side armor.

The orc swung out again with the shield in an attempt to knock him senseless. Karus was forced to dodge. The orc followed up with a slashing attack that almost decapitated him. Karus took two steps back to gain some space. The orc followed as Karus stepped back several more steps.

The creature laughed at him. It said something in a guttural language and then thumped its chest armor with its sword arm. Karus lunged forward, jabbing at a spot just underneath the orc's armor. The move caught the creature by surprise. He felt the sword plunge into the orc's belly and strike bone beyond. Karus heard a sizzling sound. The orc stiffened, exhaled a last breath, and then dropped. As the orc fell, the sword came free. The blade was coated in green blood. The blood blackened before his eyes, smoking and hissing loudly as it boiled off the steel, which burned in blue, soundless fire.

It was such a remarkable sight that Karus actually stopped to watch the last of the blood boil away. Another arrow zipped past, and he abruptly remembered he was in the middle of a fight. He turned back to Amarra. She was still sitting up and looking about, dazed. She reached for her staff. The move seemed more habit than anything else. At her touch, the staff flashed brilliantly with light, and her eyes, which a moment before had been somewhat clouded and uncertain, cleared instantly. She sucked in a startled breath that was part gasp and scrambled to her feet.

There was another blast of dragon fire and more elves burned a few yards off to Karus's right. It caused him to duck. He moved back to Amarra and glanced quickly around. Elves and orcs were engaged in a confused fight that had spread out about them. Karus estimated that at least sixty orcs were on the ground, with a smaller number of elves. More orcs were joining the fight as they climbed down the ropes from the hovering wyrms above. Karus looked up toward the wyrms. Orcs swarmed over their backs as they waited their turn to go down the ropes.

Seeing the sheer number of orcs clustered onto the wyrms' backs, Karus knew they were in serious trouble. It was time to think about fleeing, for he knew he could trust neither the elves nor the orcs. Karus searched for the warden. He had unfinished business with her and she with him. The warden was nowhere to be seen.

He spotted several of the black-clad elven warriors back toward the tree line. They had bows and were raining death into the battle, striking both the orcs and the warden's guards. There were a few of the black-clad warriors mixed in the fight. One of them waved for him and then shouted something that Karus could not understand due to the din of the fight.

There was a sudden brilliant flash of green light that arced up into the air from the forest floor. The fighting seemed to pause as the light struck one of the dragons hovering above. All heads turned upward. The wyrm screamed in agony. A heartbeat later, it ceased its flapping and fell, crashing through the canopy of branches. Karus had a fleeting glimpse of dozens of orcs clinging to its back as the wyrm plummeted ground-ward. It slammed into the forest floor, crushing half a dozen elves and orcs underneath it. Those orcs clinging to the creature's back were thrown violently clear. The ground trembled with the impact.

A stunned moment of silence followed, then an orc roared a battle cry and the fight was back on. The three remaining wyrms began frantically beating at the air, pulling away. One trailed several orcs dangling from ropes and holding on for dear life. An orc hanging from one rope was dragged into a thick branch. He lost his grip and fell, screaming all the way down to the forest floor, where he impacted the ground with a sickening thump.

Karus spotted the warden. It was from her that the green light had emanated. She had been responsible for the blast that had brought the wyrm down. He blinked. She was alone and striding his way, walking calmly through the battle as if she were out for a pleasant stroll on a spring day.

The green sphere was back up and her gaze was focused solely on Karus. An orc turned to face her. Without pausing, a green jet of light shot out from her hand toward the creature. The orc arched its back, crying out, and then collapsed, falling dead. The warden had not broken stride, but kept coming. Karus went to move Amarra behind him, but she resisted.

"Despite evil men … and women, let us hold to the hope, for she who promised is faithful," Amarra said quite calmly, clearly quoting scripture. "We must face her. She is possessed of an evil heart. I think we do this together."

"That witch must die," Karus said, pointing his sword toward the warden. He felt the rage burn within him. The blade matched it with a roaring blue fire that licked and snapped silently at the air.

"We have to kill her," Amarra said and tightened her grip upon the staff. "We cannot allow her to live, for she will not rest until she has the sword."

The warden came within ten feet, then abruptly ground to a halt as Tal'Thor appeared out of nowhere and stepped before her, barring her path. Weaponless, he held a hand up, palm faced toward the warden.

The warden regarded him a moment and said something in the Elven tongue that sounded very much like a command. Karus supposed the warden had ordered him to stand aside. Tal'Thor replied and shook his head. The warden raised a hand and pointed a finger at the ranger.

It was as if a great hand had picked Tal'Thor up into the air. He remained there suspended about three feet above the forest floor, his feet kicking in free space. The warden made a sweeping gesture with her hand off to the right. Tal'Thor went flying through the air, where he collided solidly with a tree. The elf slid down the side of the trunk, landing in a tumble of arms and legs. He did not get up.

"No!" Si'Cara screamed from halfway across the fight. She finished off the orc she was engaged with and then ran toward them, weaving between combatants.

Karus remained focused on the warden. He could see the maddened rage in her eyes, for she smiled at them and laughed as if what she had done was no big thing. She was clearly confident in her ability to take them. That much was clear to Karus.

She held her hand out and Karus knew that she was about to strike. He stepped forward, holding up the sword like he had been told and praying it worked like it had before. The warden saw what he was doing and laughed even harder. A deep-seated dread settled over him.

Karus suddenly had a flash of Si'Cara out of his peripheral vision. She was running toward them. The warden did not see her. Si'Cara slid to a stop and came down on one knee, scooping up her bow and an arrow. In a fluid motion that was incredibly fast, she raised the bow, nocking the arrow, and loosed. Karus expected the arrow to shatter like the others, but as it impacted the green sphere, there was an incredible cracking noise, followed by a deep *crump*. The shield collapsed, and with it, the warden was thrown violently to the ground. At first, Karus could not understand what had just happened, and then it hit him. Si'Cara had used the last penetrator she had taken from the guardhouse.

The warden picked herself up off the ground. Her lip was split, and her hair was disheveled. There was an ugly bruise forming along her cheek and her right arm hung at an awkward angle, clearly broken. Looking somewhat shaken, she staggered a step toward them.

Karus realized this was his chance. Before he could move, Si'Cara nocked another arrow and released. It struck the warden squarely in the side, punching into her torso. Surprise registered on the warden's face, and a moment later the pain hit. The warden screamed as she looked down on the arrow protruding from her side. The scream was both from pain and outrage. Her good hand went for the missile protruding from her side, but before she could reach it, a second arrow appeared, this one driving through her chest and emerging out her back. The warden grunted with the impact. She looked over at Si'Cara, who was lowering her bow.

Si'Cara's expression was cold. And yet a solitary tear ran from her left eye. Whether that was for the woman she had once served or for her husband, Karus did not know. The bow fell from her hand, as did her remaining arrows.

Blood trickled from the warden's mouth and nose. Si'Cara stood and calmly walked over. The warden's face contorted in rage. She raised her hand toward the ranger. It shook violently. Nothing happened. Si'Cara batted the hand away, pulled out her dagger, and stepped in close, as a lover might. In the blink of an eye, she slit the warden's throat from ear to ear, then stepped back.

The warden choked and blinked, looking at the blood running down her chest. The strength seemed to fail her legs. She fell onto her knees, remained there but a moment, and then collapsed forward onto her face. She lay twitching her last amongst the moss and fallen leaves.

Si'Cara gazed down on the warden a moment and then spat upon her body. All around them, the warden's elves gave up a cry of dismay at the falling of their leader. It was almost like they could physically sense her demise. As if at a silent signal, those elves who had been fighting the elven warriors in black backed away and broke off their fight. Then they joined their fellows and turned with a fury upon the remaining orcs. The black-clad elves joined them. No more did elf seek the murder of elfkind.

Somehow, the wyrms must have known the warden was no longer a threat, for two of them appeared overhead, hovering over the fight. From one of the wyrms, ropes were once again dropped to the ground. Orc reinforcements began lowering themselves into the fight raging below. A number of elves with bows began loosing arrows up at the orcs shimmying down. Several were hit and fell, screaming, before the first orc reinforcement reached the ground.

The other wyrm, having already dropped its load of orcs, began lowering itself into the canopy, claws gripping and tearing into the bark of the tree as it climbed down toward the ground below. The trees in this forest were so large, it could not knock them down. It was clear the wyrm intended to join the battle raging below the thick canopy of branches.

As if in shock and sorrow, Si'Cara, ignoring the fight still raging around them, turned her gaze to Tal'Thor, lying in a heap at the base of the tree. An orc rushed at Amarra, swinging his sword down at her. Karus stepped in front of her and brought his sword up, blocking the strike. The two swords met with the ringing clang that set his hand tingling.

It seemed to shake Si'Cara free. She jumped upon the orc's back and drove her dagger deep into the side of the orc's neck. Green blood sprayed over Karus's face. He tasted the copper tang in his mouth.

"Karus, look out," Amarra screamed. He turned just in time to block a sword from skewering him in the side. The orc bashed at Karus with its shield. It connected with his right side, knocking him back and roughly away. The blow hurt, and badly. He shook himself in an attempt to shake the pain off and stepped back toward the orc, meeting its blade once again with another ringing clang.

The orc abruptly stiffened as an arrow unexpectedly emerged through its neck from behind. The creature grabbed at the arrow and snapped the end off, even as hot blood sprayed out into the air. The orc stumbled a couple of steps, tottered a moment, and then fell over on its side.

Karus did not know where the arrow had come from, but he was grateful to whoever had loosed it. He glanced around and saw no more orcs close enough to be considered an immediate threat. Now that they were no longer fighting amongst themselves, the elves were doing a superb job of killing those orcs that remained. The wyrm was almost to the ground. Once it got down, Karus understood the elves would have a difficult, if not impossible, time dealing with the dragon. He could not begin to imagine how to take such a creature down.

The elves were shooting arrows at the dragon. The arrows bounced off the armored hide and seemed to have no measurable effect. Si'Cara ran to Tal'Thor, with Amarra following close behind.

Karus glanced briefly over at the warden. Blood had pooled around her body, seeping into the carpet of leaves and green moss. He was relieved she was gone, finished.

With no one nearby to fight, Karus did not want to go near any of the elves. There was no telling how they might react to the death of the warden. For all he knew, they might try to kill him as the warden had intended. Karus had no idea where Dennig had gone. The dwarf was nowhere in sight. So he followed after Si'Cara and Amarra. He would focus on keeping himself and Amarra alive.

From behind, there was a blast of flame, followed by screams. The heat from the blast pushed back against the chill of the forest air. A roar from a dragon sounded from above. It was different, deeper than the wyrms'. Another gout of flame blasted down. There was a replying scream, but this one of incredible pain.

Karus looked up and saw that the wyrm that had been working its way down the tree was on fire, and burning fiercely. There was a flash of red above the tree canopy, following after the second wyrm that was attempting to flee and flapping its wings madly. A jet of flame blasted over it. The wyrm trailed fire as it flew out of view, with Cyln'phax following close behind.

Karus saw Kordem hovering overhead, just above the burning wyrm. The dragon breathed another long jet of fire down upon the wyrm, which screamed horribly in reply. Burning, the wyrm extended its wings in the tree canopy and began to beat at the air, knocking branches and leaves and bits of wood down to the ground below, which landed amongst the combatants. A large branch, the width of a full-grown oak, slammed down on top of an orc.

The wyrm was trying to gain altitude, to free itself from the thick branches it had climbed down into. The wyrm was succeeding, but at the same time it was burning fiercely. Karus could smell the stench of burning flesh strong on the air. The tree above them was on fire as well. Then the wyrm cleared the tree, but just as it did, Kordem struck with claws and teeth. He tore into the stricken wyrm with a fury. The wyrm gave an agonized cry as one of Kordem's claws ripped apart its right wing.

Stuck in Kordem's grip, the wyrm snaked its head around and opened its mouth with the clear intention to breathe fire upon the other dragon. Before it could, Kordem's jaws clamped firmly down upon its neck and bit deeply. He shook the wyrm's neck, like a dog with a rat. Down below, Karus could hear the rending of flesh and snapping of bones as the neck broke. It sounded like a tree cracking in two. The wyrm went limp. Kordem carried his kill away, up into the air and out of sight. A few moments later, Karus could hear the wyrm's body crashing through the trees, somewhere out of view.

It was suddenly quiet. Karus glanced around. The fighting was over. All of the orcs were dead. Two of the elven warriors in black approached, their swords out and coated both in red and green blood. One of them held up a hand, as if he meant no harm.

"We are friends," the elf said in Common. "Sword-Bearer, we are here to protect you."

The elf made a show of slowly sheathing his bloodied sword. The other did the same, but did not look happy about doing it. He clearly did not want to dirty his scabbard with blood.

"You bear Rarokan," the same elf said, gesturing toward Karus's sword. He took a step nearer and held up his palms toward Karus. "We mean you no harm."

Karus gave a weary nod of understanding, and the two elves turned their gazes outward toward where the remainder of the elves were checking the wounded, including the orcs. They moved amongst them, searching for the living and swiftly killing any enemy that still breathed. In the distance, Karus heard the cry of dragons and knew that Kordem and Cyln'phax were chasing after the last remaining wyrms. He hoped they caught and killed them.

Karus suddenly felt extremely weary, a deep tiredness coming over him. The fighting was over. He had once again beaten the odds. Fortuna had been kind. He heard a sob behind him. A few feet away, Amarra was hovering over Tal'Thor, Si'Cara at his side. Well, Fortuna had been kind to some. He stepped over to them. Tal'Thor did not look good. He bled from multiple places and one of his legs was twisted at an unnatural angle.

"How is he?" Karus asked.

"His injuries are grave," Amarra said, "but I sense he can be healed."

"Please, mistress," Si'Cara begged, tears running down her cheeks. "Please heal him."

"After what he did to you," Amarra asked, "you still want him?"

"We both had sworn soul oaths to the warden," Si'Cara said. "It is no small thing. Still, never did I think she would order something so foul." Her voice caught in her throat. "I might have done to him what he did to me...had the warden ordered it. The thought of it makes me cringe." Si'Cara gave a sob. "The warden betrayed the blood oath that day, freeing us both to offer our services, to go with you as companions."

Amarra said nothing, but continued to stare at Si'Cara, searching her face. Tears rolled down the elf's cheeks, falling onto the ground.

"I love him." Si'Cara gave another wrenching sob. "I love him terribly. Doesn't the High Father teach forgiveness?"

"He does," Amarra said softly.

"Do you think he can forgive us both?"

"I do," Amarra whispered and held a hand out to Si'Cara's cheek. "And he will."

"You can save him, then?" Karus asked hopefully.

Amarra looked up at him and gave a nod. "I believe so. This will take time. Do not disturb me."

"Thank you, mistress," Si'Cara said.

"Thank the High Father."

"I will, mistress."

"High Father." Amarra bent her head over Tal'Thor and laid her hand upon his chest. "This one has sinned terribly. Despite all that he has done, I feel he is worthy of your blessing and redemption. Guide him along the path of forgiveness and rebirth in faith. I ask that you show him your love. Kindly share your healing touch, for I sense he is good at heart."

The staff flared with light, driving back the gloom of the forest. Karus stood there and watched. Nothing immediately happened. Si'Cara was kneeling beside Tal'Thor, holding his hand, her head bowed and seemingly in prayer. She looked up after a time and gasped, staring at the elf standing next to Karus.

"Kol…" Her mouth opened and closed, but nothing more came out.

The black-clad elf who had spoken to Karus earlier gave his sister a pleased nod. He said something to her in their own language. Fresh tears sprang to her eyes as she replied before reluctantly turning back to her husband.

Kol'Cara was tall, blond-haired, and whipcord thin. His face would have been fair, had it not been marred by an ugly scar running from his temple to his jaw on the left side of his face. He had what seemed like an easy manner and a swagger that marked him as a natural and confident leader.

"I guess we found the Warriors of Anagradoom."

Karus looked over to find Dennig. The dwarf's tunic was coated in both green and red blood. His wild beard was stained green and he had a chunk of hair missing. The bald patch bled. It had been ripped out. He also had a shallow cut upon his left cheek but beyond that seemed whole and well. He was leaning upon his axe.

"I guess so," Karus said and glanced around. To his surprise, he found most of the elves gathered around them, watching Amarra heal Tal'Thor.

"It is an honor to finally meet you," Kol'Cara said to Karus. "Perhaps we should step away to talk, for I would not want to disturb the healing process."

The crowd of elves parted, drawing back. As he passed, most bowed respectfully, which was a surprise. Whether it was for him or Kol'Cara, Karus did not know.

"My warriors and I have dedicated ourselves to your protection," Kol'Cara said, once they had passed through the crowd and stepped beyond several yards.

Karus glanced over the remains of the fight. Bodies were seemingly everywhere, elves and orcs. The dead wyrm lay limp, a lifeless mound. The corpse still burned, as did part of the great tree next to it. Shattered limbs and branches lay all around the dread creature.

Kol'Cara gazed upon the remains of the field of battle with a saddened expression. "So many elves lost for a dark and unholy ambition. This day will be remembered amongst our kind with terrible sadness. It pains me that I was involved in the death of my kin."

"I thought your job was to guard the sword," Karus said.

"No," Kol'Cara replied. "You have that wrong. Long before you came to this world, we swore an oath to serve you."

"Serve me?" Karus said. "What does that mean exactly?"

"We have been waiting for you, Lucius Grackus Lisidius Karus," Kol'Cara said and fell to a knee.

Karus wondered how Kol'Cara knew his full name.

"The High Master of Obsidian asked of us to put aside our lives," Kol'Cara continued, "and leave our families for a greater purpose. We sacrificed for the common good, to wait until the sword was claimed by its rightful heir." The elf pointed at Karus. "That is you. We are here to serve you to the best of our ability, to protect and help you discharge the mission our god gave you." Kol'Cara paused. "Karus, revered son of the High Father, will you accept the Warriors of Anagradoom into your service?"

Karus glanced around. Dennig had come up, as had several of the other elves. Those who had recently supported the warden looked on impassively. Karus counted twelve elven warriors clad in black, like Kol'Cara.

"You wanted allies?" Dennig said. "This is an extraordinary offer. Were I in your position, I'd not pass this up."

Karus rubbed his jaw. As Dennig had said, it was indeed too good an offer to pass up. He'd be a fool to do so. Still, something was bothering Karus, warning him to tread carefully. It was his gut again, and the feeling was incredibly strong. It took him a moment to realize what it was that bothered him.

Karus had never much cared for servants and slaves, though he had once owned one. He recalled Amarra accepting Si'Cara and Tal'Thor as companions, instead of taking them into her service. That had happened in the warden's hall. Then it had occurred again on the hill before the fortress's gate. Amarra had accepted Si'Cara's offer of service on the condition that she serve only as long as she desired. No, that was not quite right. Now that he thought about it, the acceptance of service had been conditional... until

Si'Cara felt called to do something else. In essence, Amarra had made the ranger a willing ally instead of a sworn servant. He turned his gaze back to Kol'Cara.

Elves were a proud people. They also considered themselves superior to all other beings. If Karus took Kol'Cara and the rest of the Anagradoom into his service, they might ultimately resent having to serve a lowly human. It might also create hard feelings amongst the rest of the elves. Karus badly needed allies. The arrival of the Horde only reinforced his feeling. He made his decision.

"I will accept you as an ally," Karus said, stepping forward and pulling the elf back to his feet by an arm, "but never as a servant. I also do not require you to kneel to me, ever. We Romans don't kneel, even for our emperor. Will you join me as an ally? Will you fight by my side against the Horde and in the name of the High Father? I would count it a great honor."

Kol'Cara flashed him a broad grin that was tinged with what Karus thought might be relief.

"And so, you pass the final test set by the High Master," Kol'Cara said. "It was one that could not be overcome by magic, but by character...just as was intended. You have freed the Anagradoom to fight alongside you...as allies."

Karus offered his arm, which Kol'Cara clasped firmly. The Warriors of Anagradoom gave up a cheer.

CHAPTER SIXTEEN

K arus and Dennig stood side by side. It was morning on the day following the battle in the forest. They were a short way up the slope of the hill that climbed to the fortress, forty yards above the camp. Their departure from this cursed place had been delayed to give Tal'Thor and two other elves the opportunity to rest after the healing they had received from Amarra. Karus had not wanted to stay, but she had insisted, before falling into a deep sleep herself. And so, despite Karus's better judgment, they had remained the night.

Amarra and the healed elves had finally stirred and awoken with the rising of the first sun. Again, Karus was frustrated by another delay. Amarra had wanted to speak with all of the elves. She had stated it was important that they be given the opportunity to return to the High Father. And so, they had yet to leave.

The two dragons were below, resting for the journey to come. They also had been impatient to leave. Cyln'phax had a number of slashing injuries that raked along her right side. A great many of her armored scales had been torn away. Reddish black blood seeped down her flank and into the long grass.

Cyln'phax had assured Amarra the injuries were not as serious as they appeared and would heal soon enough.

Apparently, the dragons possessed some natural ability that allowed them to heal rapidly. As if in proof of that assertion, overnight some of her wounds had ceased bleeding and grown a fresh membrane of pink skin. Kordem had told Karus the skin would quickly harden and in a few days new scales would replace the ones that had been ripped away.

He glanced over at Dennig. Karus had climbed up to this spot because he had initially wanted some space, and it was something to do while he waited. Dennig had joined him a few minutes later. Since then, perhaps half an hour had passed. No words other than a nod had been exchanged. The two silently watched the activity below.

The surviving rangers and guards had selected a spot one hundred yards to the left, near the base of the hill and just beyond the tree line. They were busy preparing the warden's body and those of the elves who had fallen. The dead would be cremated. The elves had worked through the evening and into the night, gathering and stacking wood for the funeral fires.

"Elves believe that once the soul has left the body, all that remains is a shell," Dennig said, breaking the silence.

"A shell?" Karus asked.

"The shell, an empty husk," Dennig said. "Whatever you want to call it."

"I see," Karus said.

"They don't honor the body, but the person who once inhabited it, the soul, if you will," Dennig continued. "Hence the reason they burn their dead. The soul spark, as they call it, has already traveled onward toward the next plane of existence. They see no need to bury their dead in the ground, constructing a crypt for remembrance or fashioning statues of the recently departed. They honor their dead through memory alone."

It made sense in a way, he thought and gave an absent nod as he scratched an itch on his arm. Thankfully, he was free of the blood and grime from the battle. With the Anagradoom as guides, he and Dennig had made a trip to the nearby river before sunset. There they had bathed, washing away the dust from the fortress, along with the blood, dirt, and grime.

The river had been large and slow-moving, the water ice cold. In a way, it had felt like he had been washing away all that had happened the day before—the killing, the stress, everything. When he'd emerged from the frigid water, skin pink and shivering, Karus felt thoroughly renewed. It also helped that he'd been able to change into his spare tunic. The only thing that would have been better was a Roman bathhouse, a true taste of civilization, and he'd not seen one of those since Eboracum. The baths they had found in Carthum just did not compare to the quality he had known.

Karus had also managed to clean his armor. The tedious nature of the work had afforded him time to think and relax. Dennig had even found a comb. His hair, for the first time since Karus had met him, was brushed, his beard neatly braided. The dwarf looked presentable and perhaps even a little dignified.

Refreshed or not, Karus was tired. He had slept well enough, but the last few days had been hard, both physically and mentally. His body ached something fierce. His side was bruised from where the orc had bashed him with the shield. He walked a little gingerly as a result. Bending over to grab something was a chore and needed to be done carefully. The bruise left him feeling sore and reminded him he did not bounce back as quickly as he once had in his youth. Fifteen years ago, he was sure such would not have slowed him down in the slightest.

"I wish I had been the one to kill that evil witch," Dennig said regretfully. "What was done to me and my boys..." The dwarf paused. "If anyone ever deserved to die, she did."

"I agree with you there," Karus said with a glance over at Dennig, whose cheeks had flushed. "The warden earned what was coming, that's for sure."

"She murdered my legend guard," Dennig said. "Six good dvergr. They were fine boys."

"I'm sorry," Karus said, and truly he was, for good soldiers deserved a better end.

"So am I." Dennig kicked at a small bush and did nothing more than disturb its branches. "When I return, I will owe an explanation to their kin. I fear they will find it lacking." Dennig expelled a hot breath. "It never gets any easier."

"No, it doesn't. We're in a profession that sees many fine boys die before their time."

"Aye," Dennig agreed sourly.

They fell into a silence once again. Karus's gaze drifted over to the fire. Tal'Thor and Si'Cara sat side by side. They were alone. Si'Cara was leaning her head against his shoulder. With the exception of Kol'Cara, the other elves appeared to be avoiding her. At first, Karus that had thought nothing of it. But then he began noticing how the elves went out of their way to avert their gazes when she passed near. This troubled him somewhat, for in his mind she had done a great service to this world in ending the warden. Apparently, the elves did not see it that way.

Thunder rumbled off in the distance. Though they had been spared rain overnight, the air had turned even more humid, almost uncomfortably sticky. Karus knew that it was only a matter of time until it began raining in earnest. There was nothing better than rain to drench one's spirits. Well, that and some mud if you were marching.

"I don't suppose"—Dennig looked up at the menacing rain clouds above them—"that you'd consider delaying until the rain passed us by?"

"I would prefer not," Karus said. "I've been away too long from my legion. Also, the enemy knows that we are here. I fear we have delayed too much as it is…" Karus blew out a stream of air. "No, I do not wish to linger in this place any longer than we have to."

Dennig gave a grunt and then a slight shake of his head. "I would never have thought they'd come by flying."

"I should have thought of such a possibility," Karus said.

"Well, we both didn't think of it," Dennig said. "There is one thing I've learned over my long years of military service. Do you want to hear it?"

Karus gave a reluctant nod, wondering what the dwarf was going to say.

"A leader cannot think of everything. You do your best and then wing it from there. Something's always bound to cock up your plans."

"True." Karus glanced over at the dwarf. He was more than correct. At times Karus had known officers to overthink and plan operations to death. When it came to a fight, such behavior could and often did prove hazardous. It created an entrenched level of thinking that made it impossible for people to adapt or improvise to unexpected changes. A commander could get creative, but it was always best to keep things simple. That way, there were fewer mistakes and unforced errors. It was a lesson Karus had long since learned and taken to heart.

"How do you suppose the enemy knew we were here?" Dennig asked.

"I don't know," Karus said and in truth he did not. That alone troubled him greatly. He could understand the warden knowing, for they had been open and honest about their intentions, but not the enemy, not the Horde. He feared it had something to do with a supernatural ability, like those Amarra was now capable of wielding. Maybe the enemy could even sense the sword. That thought worried him even more. If true, that meant the enemy would know where he was at any given moment.

Karus glanced down at the sword on the side. It was powerful and seemed to have a mind of its own. Since the fighting, it had not spoken another word. Karus had even attempted speaking to it. He had felt like an idiot, but he'd tried anyway. There'd been no reply. He had been warned that it was dangerous, but so far as he could see, Rarokan had only proved helpful.

"There's only one reason why they came," Dennig said, following Karus's gaze and looking meaningfully down at the sword. "They weren't here for me, that's for sure."

"I know only too well," Karus said. "It seems everyone wants this sword."

"Not me," Dennig said cheerfully. "I'll just keep my good old trusty axe."

"Mogan steel?" Karus said.

"Damn straight, son," Dennig said, bouncing on his heels. "That axe is better than any magic sword. My people will envy me greatly when they see it, for it is one of a kind."

Karus said nothing to that as his gaze shifted over to Amarra. She was a few yards from the fire. Most of the Warriors of Anagradoom were clustered around her in a loose circle. There were also six of the rangers that the warden had brought along with her. As one, they knelt down before her and bowed their heads in what seemed like a group prayer. They were too far away to hear what was said, but Karus figured that she was giving a benediction or conducting some sort of service.

In the past, he had always avoided the priests who had loitered about camp at Eboracum. They were incessantly pestering the legionaries for coin, offering sacrifices and other such services should one pay for it. Karus had generally viewed them as charlatans, except just before action. Then everyone and their brother sought out the priests, for one could not ignore the gods at such a crucial time.

Karus looked at things differently now. Amarra had access to powers those camp priests could only dream about. He rubbed his freshly shaved jaw, his thoughts lingering on Amarra. After the battle, the elves had been exceptionally respectful of her, especially so after she had healed two of their number, not including Tal'Thor. He suspected those two had joined her service below them.

Amarra was growing into her role as High Priestess, just as he was at leading the legion. She took to her new responsibilities like a bird to air or fish to water. Karus felt a wave of pride rise up within. She was strong, confident, and unafraid in her faith. He loved her for it, and yet he steeled himself to the terrible reality of what was to come. The days, weeks, months, and years ahead would be hard. Karus was sure of it. What they'd been through had been the easy part. The unknown and unexpected lay ahead on both of their paths. Together, he knew they would face it all, united not only in faith, but also in love.

"Do you still intend to get me back to my boys?" Dennig asked, glancing over and intruding upon his thoughts.

Karus met the dwarf's gaze and held it a long moment. It was time for truth. "Should I call you Shoega? Or do you prefer Dennig?"

The dwarf became very still.

"I've always preferred my first name, Dennig." He paused and cocked his head to the side. "How long have you known?"

"I wasn't sure at first," Karus said. "I suspected the warden wouldn't have kept you alive unless you were fairly important. Though there have been other clues, you also kept referring to your soldiers as your boys. Then there was the legend guard and leadership lesson you just gave me. I figured there was a good chance you were him."

Dennig gave a vague nod.

"So, what now?" Dennig asked. "What will you do with me?"

"Do you think I should make you my prisoner?" Karus felt a grin tugging at his lips. "Like the warden did?"

"You don't really expect me to answer that one," Dennig grumbled, "do you?"

"No," Karus said. "I will do as I said I would. I will return you to your people, your army, if possible."

"I am really beginning to like you, Karus." Dennig grinned. "If you were one of my people, I would say you have great legend. But since you are human, I will settle for honorable." The dwarf shook a finger at Karus. "I am taking a shine to you, son."

"Enough so that you might consider working with me?"

"I wouldn't go that far," Dennig said. "Let's not get ahead of ourselves..."

Karus extended his hand toward the dwarf.

"I would be honored to call you my friend," Karus said, "for I believe you are one with great legend. Not everyone could willingly face the dead like you did."

Dennig stared down at the hand for several moments, considering it. He sucked in a breath. "I've never had a human for a friend."

The dwarf said this not in an offensive way, just a statement of fact. That was how Karus chose to take it.

"I've never had a dwarf for a friend." Karus kept his hand extended. "Heck, I've never had anyone but a human for a friend. I didn't even know other races existed 'til we came to this world."

"Aye...friend, then," Dennig said and shook. The dwarf squeezed almost enough to make Karus wince. "I'll be honest, I don't have very many friends, even amongst my own kind. In my position, amongst my people...I can't afford them."

"I will consider myself fortunate, then," Karus said and then turned away, looking back down toward the camp and the two dragons.

They remained silent for several long moments.

"I believe I'm going to talk to our transportation about leaving," Karus said. "Then I will work on Amarra to see if I can jog her along. We've been here long enough. It is time to move on."

"You can say that again," Dennig said.

"Care to join me, friend?"

"Thank you, but no," Dennig said. "I do not know how successful their hunting expedition was...I will not tempt fate by going near those two beasts, at least until I have to and it's time to leave."

"Fair enough," Karus said with a chuckle, for he sensed Dennig was half serious. The dwarf likely wanted some time alone. Karus turned away and then stopped, looking back. "I've been meaning to ask you. What is the family business? You mentioned it in the fortress."

Dennig gave Karus a sour look. "Sheep herding."

"Truly?"

Dennig nodded, looking far from happy.

"That sounds much more exciting than all this," Karus said.

"Don't knock it until you try it," Dennig said, then pointed down the slope. "Aren't the dragons waiting for you?"

Karus laughed and started down the hillside toward the camp.

Kordem picked up his head as Karus neared the fire and swung around to stare at him.

"We will be taking the Warriors of Anagradoom with us," Karus told the dragons.

Amarra told us, Kordem replied. *It will not be a problem.*

Karus was pleased that there was no objection from either of them. They had been strangely silent since the fight, acting almost guilty for not returning in a timely manner.

"What kept you?" Karus asked, voicing the concern that had been on his mind for some time. "We could have used you both a little sooner. It was a near thing as it was."

We ran into a pair of noctalum on the prowl, Cyln'phax said. *We had to avoid them, as they were hunting over this very forest. It took time to work our way safely around.*

We believe it likely they were on the trail of the wyrms, Kordem said.

"Why do you think that?" Karus asked.

They had the drop on us both. Instead of giving chase, the noctalum ignored us, Kordem said. *That was a very strange thing for them to do. They may have been hunting the wyrms or ... something else. We just do not know for sure. However, we think the former explanation is the more likely one.*

"Something else?" Karus asked. "Like what?"

The noctalum are on this world for their own reasons, Kordem said. *There is no telling why they came to Tannis or what they are up to.*

341

"Is there any chance the noctalum will come for us?" Karus asked, searching the sky.

There is always that risk, Cyln'phax said, *which is why we must be on guard and remain vigilant.*

Cyln'phax and I had not anticipated the warden's interference, Kordem said. *We are pleased both you and the revered daughter survived the warden. It is even more pleasing you managed to retrieve Rarokan, the Soul Breaker.*

You have bonded with the dread weapon, Cyln'phax added, *as was prophesied by the oracle. We can sense the link.*

Karus considered the two dragons for a long moment. He knew he did not fully appreciate what the bond meant, only that he and the sword were meant for one another.

"Can you tell me more on this link? The bond between me and the sword?" Karus asked.

We do not completely understand it ourselves, Kordem said. *We do know the link allows you to communicate with the* will, *what you might call the soul and life source, residing within the sword.*

"Soul?" Karus glanced down at the sword. "Life source ... you mean the sword is alive?"

Not quite as we would think of life, Kordem said. *It certainly may think it is alive. It has a mind of its own. Rarokan is but a shadow of true life. You must be on your guard, for the* will *within may try to master you.*

"Me?" Karus said, suddenly chilled. "You mean it could take control of me?"

That is correct, Cyln'phax said.

You are special, Karus, Kordem continued, *as is Amarra, but in a different manner. That specialness is almost unique amongst humans on Tannis. It allows you to channel the* will *of the sword ... to work with it, bend it to your* will *instead of the other way round. The bond, link, whatever you wish to call it, will remain as long as you live. Only in death shall it be severed. As to what Rarokan is capable of... well, that is for you to discover. The sword's power is reputed to be great, awesome, and terrible. That is why the warden desired the blade, as does the enemy.*

"They will keep coming for it?" Karus said, knowing the answer even before he asked.

Our enemy will not rest, Kordem confirmed. *They will seek to possess it and keep after it. That is why the High Master of Obsidian left you the Anagradoom. Only when Rarokan is removed from this world and the Gate is sealed shut behind us... will they cease their efforts, and maybe not even then.*

Karus rubbed his jaw as he considered the dragon's words. They had just added to his already long list of troubles, and in a big way. A thought occurred to him.

"Do you know where the oracle resides?"

We do, Kordem said. *However, I must caution, when searching out answers from her, you don't always get what you ask for. Sometimes you get what you want, other times less and then more than you would care to desire.*

Karus thought on that. Perhaps after he returned Dennig to his army and made it back to the legion, there would prove an opportunity at some point to visit the oracle. At least, he hoped so. He might be able to learn something of use to help guide him in the days to come. The more he learned of this world, the more questions he had.

"If I wanted," Karus said, "could you take me to the oracle?"

We could, Kordem said. *Though you need to be warned, the journey is long and fraught with peril. I am unsure it is worth the effort and the risk.*

"Even more perilous than this one?" Karus asked. Thinking on what they had been through, he was having difficulty imagining a more dangerous journey.

Oh yes, Cyln'phax said. *It would be an extremely hazardous undertaking.*

"When there's time," Karus said, "I would hear more of it and the risks involved."

As you wish. Kordem lowered his head, almost respectfully. Cyln'phax did the same, which surprised Karus. He hesitated a moment, wondering if the two dragons were toying with him. Then he decided they weren't. Had he earned their respect?

"I want to leave, just as soon as we can and Amarra is ready," Karus said. "I intend to prod her along."

"Will you be staying for the funeral of the warden?"

Karus turned to find Kol'Cara coming up behind him.

"No," Karus said immediately, his gaze flicking to the funeral pyres before returning to the warrior. "I will not honor someone who meant us the worst of ills."

"I do not wish to stay either." Kol'Cara turned to gaze toward the funeral preparations. "And yet, I choose to remember the warden when she was a good-hearted person, not who she became."

Karus seriously doubted the warden had ever been a good person. In his scroll, evil was evil.

"Oh yes," Kol'Cara said, his gaze becoming unfocused. "Te'Mava was always a hard, unforgiving woman. But she was also a good shepherd of our people."

"Her name was Te'Mava?" Karus asked.

Kol'Cara nodded. "When we came to Tannis, we were a broken people. The Last War had shattered us, almost to the point of destruction. Here on this world we rebuilt, planted new trees, and reconstructed our home, our culture, which many thought had been lost forever. Without Te'Mava, we could not have done it. She provided the direction, the drive, and the glue that held us together as a people. She forged a bold vision for the future, the clear path ahead. For that, many of us will be eternally grateful, no matter how terrible and misguided she became in the end."

Karus said nothing when the elf fell silent, for he sensed Kol'Cara would continue.

"We thought we had left the war behind. Then the High Master of Obsidian came. He brought with him ultimate power." The elf grew silent again, and glanced at Karus's sword. "It seems Rarokan proved, as the High Master thought, too great a temptation to be ignored. The idea of possessing such power corrupted Te'Mava and turned her heart black."

The silence stretched between them.

"There will be those of power who will desire what you now possess," Kol'Cara said. "They will come for Rarokan."

"Like the warden?" Karus resisted the temptation to look down at his new sword.

"Worse," Kol'Cara said.

Karus gave a nod. It was as he suspected.

"How did you survive?" Karus asked. "The warden said she had dealt with you and your warriors."

"The High Master took steps to mislead the warden." Kol'Cara's gaze briefly shifted to Si'Cara. "In a chamber hidden beneath the fortress, we were put into an eternal sleep that nothing could disturb. We were to rest until the sword was claimed by its intended owner. Though we brought supplies, seed for crops, and tools to maintain the fortress over long, hard years of expected isolation, there had never been any intention to use them. No ... we were going into a long, dreamless sleep ... a slumber beyond the warden's detection and reach. The warden only thought she had dealt with us."

"And if someone else got their hands on the sword?" Karus asked. "Like the warden? What then?"

"We were to kill them," Kol'Cara said, "including the warden. Once the sword was taken, our unnatural sleep ended." The elf suddenly laughed. "We would have found you sooner had not the passage out of our tomb been blocked. It required some amount of excavation to free ourselves."

They both fell silent, turning to watch the preparations. Karus became lost in thought. Everything had been carefully prepared for him, and yet, even with all of that, they had nearly failed. The warden had almost gotten hold of the sword and claimed it for her own. Karus and Amarra had come very close to dying. That alone told him how precarious their situation was... Things could just as easily have gone the warden's way. It was a sobering realization.

He got the feeling that things from here on out would be up to him and Amarra. The planning and preparation that had been done to ensure he claimed the sword were over. They would have to carry the water now. He glanced over at the two dragons and then to the elf before him. They had already gained powerful allies. He would work to find more, for that was the only path he saw that led to success. Going forward, there would be no help but what they provided for themselves. Karus did not know how, but deep down in his gut, he knew this to be true.

"What now?" Karus asked, nodding towards the funeral preparations. "The warden is dead. What will happen to your people?"

"Eventually, a new warden will be chosen," Kol'Cara said. "With elves, decisions like this take time."

"How will the new warden view the killing the previous one?" Karus asked.

Kol'Cara gave a slight shrug of his shoulders. "One can never tell with such things. It matters little to us at this point."

"We deal with it then, eh?" Karus asked. "One problem at a time?"

"You have the right of it," Kol'Cara said, seeming pleased with the response, then changed the subject. "Two of the rangers have requested to accompany us."

"They can be trusted?" Karus asked. A short while before, they had fought for the warden.

"They wish to aid the High Father's cause and apparently have always been believers. I have spoken with them and judge both to be true of heart."

"Gods, we need allies. Even if there are only two, they're welcome to come and fight alongside us."

"They shall prove invaluable scouts," Kol'Cara said. "It is possible that when word of what occurred spreads, more will flock to the High Father's standard."

"You think so?" Karus was heartened to hear that.

"I do."

The group around Amarra broke up. She said a few more words to individuals, then scanned about. She spotted him and started over. Though she had slept deeply the night before, there were heavy bags under her eyes. The healings had clearly taken some toll upon her. Earlier this morning she had gone to the river and bathed.

Despite looking worn and tired, Karus found his heart stirring at the sight of her free of the clinging dust and clean as fresh mountain snow. In anticipation of their flight, she had braided her hair into a single tight ponytail. It exposed her delicate ears and high cheekbones. Karus felt his breath catch in his throat. Even though elven women were perfection incarnate, they had nothing on her external and inner beauty. She was more than he could have ever hoped for, more even than he'd ever desired.

Si'Cara and Tal'Thor stood as Amarra walked by them. They followed after. Amarra shot Karus a wink before turning to the dragons. Her eyes traveled over Cyln'phax's injuries and her expression became quite grave.

"You are able to travel?" Amarra asked the dragon. "You will not aggravate your injuries by carrying us back to Carthum?"

My wounds will not slow me down in the least, Cyln'phax said. *They are minor and will soon heal whether I rest or fly. In truth, I have had much worse.*

She has, indeed, Kordem said. *My mate's wounds are slight.*

Looking them over, Karus very much thought that was an understatement.

Amarra studied the two dragons for a long moment more, as if she were attempting to divine whether or not they were lying. She nodded to herself, almost imperceptibly.

"Shall we go, then?" Amarra asked.

As you wish, mistress, Kordem said. *We stand ready.*

Karus was relieved to finally hear those words. He turned to Si'Cara and Tal'Thor. There was one last matter that needed to be dealt with.

"I am sure I speak for both Amarra and myself," Karus said. He felt the offer had to be made. "You may both return home if you wish."

There was an uncomfortable moment of silence as husband and wife shared a glance. At his side, Karus felt Kol'Cara stiffen. He glanced over briefly at the elf, wondering what was wrong.

"We cannot return home," Tal'Thor said, "ever."

"The warden is dead," Karus said. "Surely you can go home now."

"I will not be welcome in any elven community," Si'Cara said with deep sadness. "The warden died by my hand and mine alone. At best, I am an outcast. At worst, my people will seek justice."

"Sadly, it is as my sister says," Kol'Cara said, "and Tal'Thor, as her husband, shares her shame."

"Shame?" Amarra exclaimed in outrage. "What you did was right. There is no shame in that."

"Oh, but there is, mistress," Si'Cara said. "Amongst elves, murder, whether justified or no … can never be tolerated, or condoned. It will be up to the next warden to decide whether I should live or die. Either way, I shall spend the rest of my days in exile, and so too will my husband."

"You will not spend them alone." Tal'Thor placed a comforting arm around her shoulders. "I accepted you with all of my heart, through the good times and the bad. I will be with you … always … to the end."

Si'Cara's eyes watered as she gave her husband a woeful smile that was filled with a terrible, almost wrenching sadness.

"That wasn't murder," Karus said. "The warden made her bed. It was justice. The warden needed killing and it is as simple as that."

"My people will make no distinction," Si'Cara said.

"What about him, your brother?" Karus asked, gesturing toward Kol'Cara. "He and his warriors killed elves. Does he share a similar fate?"

"We have already accepted our exile," Kol'Cara said matter-of-factly. "We turned our backs on our people when we agreed to go with the High Master. There is no going back for us either. Though in our case, in a way … we are beyond the Elantric Warden's law. My people dare not hold us to account. The High Master of Obsidian saw to that. The Anagradoom do as we see fit in the pursuit of our goals."

Amarra blinked back tears. She stepped forward and embraced both Si'Cara and Tal'Thor, pulling them near to her.

"You are both of the High Father's flock," Amarra said, leaning her head toward theirs. "You shall always have a place with us. You are of our people now, a people of faith. No longer do you answer to the law of the warden, but that of High Father. Do you understand me?"

Si'Cara gave forth a half sob and hugged Amarra back. Her shoulders shook. After a moment, Amarra stepped back from both of them. She leaned upon her staff as if the world were on her shoulders.

"Thank you, mistress. But I fear it will not matter." Si'Cara wiped at her eyes. "If they want, they will come for us regardless."

"Not on my watch," Karus growled. "You both are family now. We look after our own."

"It is as Karus says," Amarra said.

"Thank you, mistress," Si'Cara said.

I really wish you would not encourage this, Karus, Cyln'phax said with a disgusted tone. *You and Amarra are becoming too fond of these elves.*

Amarra shot the dragon an irritated look, then turned to Karus.

"We go now, yes?" she said to him in Latin. "Before the dragon sticks her tail in her mouth?"

Cyln'phax blew out a series of huffs that Karus took to be amused laughter. A little flame shot out. This wasn't the first time Karus had caught them following him and Amarra speaking the language of Rome. Clearly the dragons understood Latin as well. Karus wondered how.

"We can go," Karus said in Common. He glanced back up the slope of the hill. Dennig was still up there, watching.

"We have a dwarf to get back to his people. And then ..." He turned back to face Amarra. "We can go home."

"Home?" Amarra asked.

"Home to the legion," Karus said. "Home to our people."

"Home." A tiny smile tugged at her lips as she repeated the word. "I like that. I like that very much."

Karus turned to Kol'Cara. "Let's get the packs and any supplies you need secured to the dragons."

More elves, Cyln'phax said sullenly. Smoke escaped from the dragon's snout as her breath hissed out. *It would only be worse if there were more dwarves. Can I eat one, Karus? Please? Now that you have plenty, you would not miss an elf or two ... would you?*

Karus was amused to see Kol'Cara's head snap around to look at the dragon. The elf was clearly wondering if the creature was serious.

"I thought you just ate?" Karus played along, though it was a struggle to keep from laughing. "You were out hunting, were you not?"

You are probably right, Cyln'phax said, sounding mildly disappointed. *An elf might spoil my meal of wild teska that's digesting. Well ... maybe if I get hungry later, you will let me eat one?*

Kol'Cara looked over at Karus, suddenly less sure. There was a questioning look to his eyes. It was Karus's turn to give him a shrug of his shoulders. Karus turned away and went to get his packs. The sooner everything was secured, the sooner they'd be away.

Less than an hour later, Karus was once again upon Cyln'phax's back. It had begun to drizzle. Wrapped tightly in his cloak and the blanket that Si'Cara had provided, Karus was hot. He had a feeling that shortly he would be wet, cold, and miserable, something to which he was not looking forward.

Half a dozen elves and one dwarf were riding on Cyln'phax's back. The elves seemed somewhat excited, like Si'Cara had been on her first flight. Amarra and the rest of the elves who had chosen to accompany them were mounted on Kordem. This included the Anagradoom and two additional rangers.

Preparations to burn the remains of the warden, the wizard, and the elven dead had been completed. There was one large pyre for the warden and a series of smaller ones for the other elves. The first of the fires had been set. Smoke was just beginning to swirl lazily upward into the gray, drizzling sky. The elves stood well back, their gazes firmly fixed upon the pyres. It was as if they had turned their backs upon their fellows who were about to fly off on the dragons, which they might have done.

Thunder rumbled off in the distance, a promise of more rain, as Cyln'phax spread her leathery wings. The dragon flexed her wings once, then leapt up into the air and gave a series of powerful flaps that drove them upward. Karus was pressed into his seat. The wind began to blow in his face and the drizzle began to pelt him.

He looked back down at the smoking pyres and the elves remaining behind. He hoped that the next warden would not be as difficult and stiff-necked. He knew he couldn't count on that. No matter how justified, there might be serious repercussions for what had occurred under the cover of the trees below them. Still, that was a problem for another day.

Karus's thoughts drifted to Amarra and her father, the former King of Carthum. Was he still out there? Would they encounter him? Would he prove to be another problem to be faced? He had too many problems on his plate at the moment and would not worry about another one that had yet to materialize. Karus's hand dropped down to the hilt of his new sword. Whenever he touched it, he felt the tingle in his palm. It raced up his arm, then was gone. Though he could not put his finger on exactly why, he found something comforting about the feeling.

As the dragons climbed higher, Karus looked over at the Fortress of Radiance. The keep was nothing but a large mound of stone now. They had done it and successfully retrieved Rarokan. He was coming away with allies and, surprisingly enough, a friend. Now, he needed to not only find more allies, but also figure a way off this world, before it became too late and the Horde washed over his legion like an avenging tide.

"The hard part lies ahead," Karus said to himself.

You have the right of that, Karus, Cyln'phax said to him. *What lies before us all will be most difficult, but faith and determination will get us through it. Now, talk no more. Let me fly in peace, for we have a long way to go.*

EPILOGUE

Krix gazed around at the bodies of orcs lying scattered across the forest floor. The elves had left the orcs to rot where they had fallen. No thought had been given to any funeral rites, no respect offered. To the elves, orcs and most other races were considered lesser species. That irritated Krix immensely. Though he himself was human, these had been honorable warriors. They deserved better.

The body of the wyrm was off to his right. The loss of the orcs he could accept. The loss of the wyrms irritated him further. Four had been lost, all irreplaceable. Yet, what truly enraged him was the opportunity that had slipped through his fingers. If only he had been closer and not off world at the time the fortress's defenses were finally breached. If only he had been able to come himself…If…There were always plenty of ifs to go around.

He clenched his fists, the rage threatening to overwhelm his reason. He fought it down, beating it back, for it never ended well when the monster inside him was released. Keeping the beast locked up in its box was a struggle he did not always win. When it escaped, Krix had almost always regretted it.

"Harak is dead?" Krix asked, turning to face Castor's minion, a twisted, misshapen, ugly thing. He had generally thought Castor's most devoted servants were pathetic creatures. That he had to consort with one bothered him little. Castor was a minor deity in the alignment, yet a steadfast ally. Therefore, the creature was to be treated with due respect. Krix needed the minion and the forces it commanded, a vital component of his Horde.

In truth, he liked this minion. It had proven not only reliable, but also capable in carrying out tasks. Krix valued anyone who had such qualities.

"Yes, Lord Krix," the minion responded. It came out as a hiss. "Harak did not survive. I found his body half crushed by the wyrm."

"That saves me having to punish the fool," Krix said, for had Harak had any brains he would have taken overwhelming force. "The noctalum have been taking too many of our wyrms of late. We can't spare the four Harak lost."

"It is the Knight of the Vass," the minion replied. "The knight drives the noctalum onward in their hunt, encourages them."

How unlucky was he to have a Knight of the Vass trapped on this world? And just to make matters worse, a flight of noctalum, allies of the Vass, were stuck on Tannis as well. Krix cracked his neck. It was maddening and drove him to distraction.

He swung his gaze unhappily around the battlefield, seeing but not really looking. He had toyed with the idea of allowing the knight to escape through one of the World Gates just to get her off Tannis. The gods only knew what trouble the knight would cause on another world. How would such an act come back to bite him with the confederacy and the council? Surely it would. No, he would have to deal with the knight himself...somehow, in some way.

"Eventually, we will have to do something about her," Krix said, "and the noctalum, too. The cost of such a venture is the only thing holding me back."

"Yes, we will," the minion agreed, "and it will likely mean the loss of most of our remaining wyrms. Better to do it sooner, I think, then delay much longer. She grows in strength with each passing day."

Krix gave a grunt. His rage bubbled up, becoming almost uncontrollable. The minion was likely correct, but that was not what enraged him.

"This"—Krix held out his arms—"is not just a travesty, but a waste of an opportunity."

"We believe a good number of elves perished in the fight," the minion said, as if that made their losses more palatable. "And I understand the Elantric Warden fell in battle as well."

Krix looked sharply over at the minion.

"The witch, Te'Mava, is finally dead?"

"I thought that would please you," the minion said, its twisted mouth opening in a sick grin. "My spies have confirmed this. En'Sis'Lith has also passed on into the shadow."

"This wasn't a complete shambles," Krix said, feeling his rage begin to wane just a tad. An opportunity had been lost while another may have just presented itself. Then the rage returned. "Still, we did not get the sword."

"No," the minion agreed, "but we know who has Rarokan and where he will be taking it. That in itself is invaluable."

"Carthum," Krix said. "This Karus, from the cradle world of humanity. He and his legion must be great warriors to have been brought to Tannis."

"That is likely true," the minion said. "We have two columns totaling forty-five thousand within easy marching distance. The humans from Earth are few in number."

Krix gave a nod, but did not immediately reply. The human soldiers occupying Carthum were an unexpected complication. They had inexplicably somehow traveled to

Tannis from humanity's cradle world. Such things were not supposed to be possible. Cradle worlds were sacrosanct, untouchable, and had been locked away by the gods themselves. Someone had meddled, and the thought of it made Krix deeply uncomfortable, for an escalation in the war was now a very real possibility. The gods themselves might intervene more directly.

Tannis had been a relative backwater. But now that these humans from Earth had come, the council and confederacy had become very interested in speeding up the conquest of this world. Assets and additional forces that had been denied in the past were now available and being pushed upon him. Some of those forces, the more troublesome, he did not desire but could not refuse either.

"Those two columns were intended to trap and corner a dwarven war band," Krix said, recalling the strategic situation around Carthum, a land yet to be occupied by his forces. "Is that not correct?"

"Yes," the minion said. "I could divert them to Carthum."

"No," Krix said. "That would allow the dwarves to escape. Destroying a war band is something we cannot pass up. Deal with the dwarves first. Then turn your attention to Carthum. Remember, these humans are from a cradle world. They would not have been brought to Tannis were they not strong, a force that by rights should be considered quite dangerous. We need to proceed with caution, at least until we know more about them."

"I am not sure that is wise, my lord," the minion said. "Already they gain allies against us, refugees fleeing from lands we have overrun. What if they give these broken peoples strength of heart? What if they give them the will to resist? If we allow them too much time, they may assemble a mighty host against us. We should consider turning the full might of the Horde upon them ... before they become too strong and a threat to our plans."

The ifs again, Krix thought as he considered the minion's words. The creature did have a point. He turned the matter over in his mind, attempting to look at it from all angles. The minion waited.

"No," Krix said finally. "Not yet. There are still powerful peoples on Tannis. If they are seeking allies, we must do everything in our power to deny them such."

"What are you thinking, my lord?"

"We need to take advantage of our good fortune." Krix held his arms out about him. "You said it yourself. The elves have lost their warden, and wizard. All they have left is a half-trained apprentice, who will now need to step into the role of the master. They are weak, finally vulnerable. Now, I think, is the time to strike."

"You mean to turn our focus and effort to the elven forests?" the minion said, sounding somewhat but not completely surprised. "Our plan was always to deal with the elves after the dwarves and humans of this world were either defeated or subjugated. Even without the warden and their wizard, such an endeavor will be quite costly, my lord."

"Yes, it will be expensive, but not nearly so much as it would have ultimately been," Krix said, becoming convinced this was the right path to take. "Now is our chance."

"And what of the humans in Carthum, this legion of Rome and Earth?"

"Eradicate that dwarven war band, then send your columns to deal with them," Krix said. "You also have one hundred thousand warriors around Lyre, do you not?"

"Slightly less, but the actual numbers matter little," the minion said.

"You can pull reinforcements from them, say another forty thousand, fifty if you must."

"That army has grown soft," the minion hissed with displeasure. "Too long have they been idle, sitting on pacified civilians."

"Then harden them up with a campaign," Krix said, suddenly irritated again. "Deal with the dwarves. Throw your warriors against this legion. At worst, it will tell us what kind of a threat we face. At best, we remove the threat."

"Yes, my lord," the minion said. "And what of the gnome problem around Lyre?"

"Gnomes," Krix spat. Like the goblins, they always seemed to be a problem, creating a series of endless headaches for him. "We ignore them for now. Leave them to their depths, trouble them not. The elves will be our focus. We need to hurt them before they choose a new warden, who I fear may come to the logical conclusion their only hope for survival is to work with the humans and dwarves. Should that occur, our task of subduing this world will become complicated."

"There is something else," the minion said. "An agent of the High Father has arisen."

"I have not sensed that," Krix said, surprised to learn of this news.

"Her powers are still slight," the minion said, "but they are growing. She was here. I fear her presence is not only tied to Rarokan, but the lost Key. It is the only explanation that makes any sense to me."

"I see." Krix thought that was not good news. For nearly a century, he had been searching for the Key that would unlock the World Gate that led to Istros. It had been hidden well, or more likely lost to the mists of time. Events on Tannis had suddenly become complicated, especially if an agent for the High Father was hunting for the Key.

"She sensed me," the minion said, "and I her."

"We will need to deal with this agent, before she gains her full potential," Krix said.

"Yes, my lord," the minion said, "and I fear that will have to be soon. She travels back to Carthum with the sword bearer."

"That presents an opportunity for you," Krix said. "Don't fail me like Harak. Now, do as I've instructed."

"Yes, my lord," the minion said with a bow. "It will be done."

Krix snapped his fingers, exerting his *will*. With it, the forest faded away. He blinked as the projection ceased and the walls of his office in Krakkaen Keep reappeared. Lien, his chief aide, a fellow human, waited. Lien was someone else who was not only capable but completely reliable.

"Summon the scribes," Krix said. "We have orders to dispatch."

"Yes, my lord." Lien saluted and left, stepping through the door to the headquarters where his clerks worked.

Krix went to the window that overlooked the great keep's courtyard. Below, a wyrm waited. She had been fed, harnessed, and saddled. He rested his hands upon the stone of the window sill. After the orders had been cut, he would travel to the World Gate and step through to Longtow. There he would report in person to the council that the sword had at long last been claimed. Rarokan was finally in play.

Though he had resisted doing so, he would return with the dread sertalum, the noctalum's sister race. Nothing on this world or any other would stop him from ultimately claiming Rarokan for his own. It had been so written.

End of Book Two

Enjoy this short preview of Marc's First book:

STIGER'S TIGERS:

Chronicles of an Imperial Legionary Officer

ONE

Two road-weary riders, both legionary officers, crested the bald hill and pulled to a halt. A vast military encampment surrounded by entrenchments and fortifications took up much of the valley below them in a shocking display. Smoke from thousands of campfires drifted upward and hung over the valley like a veil. After months of travel, the two riders were now finally able to set their eyes upon their destination—the main encampment of General Kromen's Imperial Army, comprising the Fifteenth, Eighteenth, Twenty-Ninth, and Thirtieth Legions. These four legions had been dispatched by the emperor to put down the rebellion burning through what the empire considered her southern provinces.

The awful stench of the encampment had been on the wind for hours. This close, the smell of decay mixed with human waste and a thousand other smells was nearly overpowering. What should have been relief at finally reaching their destination had turned to incredulous horror. Neither of them had ever seen anything like it. Imperial encampments were typically highly organized, with priority placed on sanitation to reduce the chance of sickness and disease. The jumble of tents and ramshackle buildings laid out before them, surrounded by the fortifications, spoke of something much different. It told of an almost wanton criminal neglect for the men who served the empire, or perhaps even incompetence in command.

An empty wagon, the first of a sad-looking supply train, rumbled around past the two riders, who refused to give way. The driver, a hired teamster, cursed at them for hogging the road. He took his frustration out on a group of dirty and ragged slaves sitting along the edge of the road. The slaves, part of a work gang to maintain the imperial highway, were forced to scramble out of the way, lest the wagon roll over them as it rumbled around the two travelers.

An overseer resting on a large fieldstone several feet away barked out a harsh laugh before shouting at the slaves to be more careful. One of the slaves collapsed, and yet both riders hardly spared him a glance. Slaves were simply beneath notice.

The supply train's nominal escort, a small troop of cavalry riding in a line alongside the wagons, was working its way slowly up the hill toward the two officers and away from the encampment. Much like every other legionary the two travelers had come upon for the last hundred miles, the cavalry troop was less than impressive, though somewhat better looking in appearance. Their armor wasn't as rusted and had been recently maintained.

Several empty wagons rumbled by the two, which saw additional invectives hurled their way. They ignored the cursing, just as they had disregarded the wagons and the plight of the slaves. Where they had come from, it would have been unthinkable for someone to hurl invectives at an officer, who was almost assuredly a nobleman. At the very least, a commoner would invite a severe beating with such behavior. Here in the South, such lack of basic respect seemed commonplace.

One of the travelers had the hood of his red imperial cloak pulled up as far as it would go and tilted his head forward to protect against a light drizzling rain, which had been falling for some time.

The other had the hood of his cloak pulled back, revealing close-cropped brown hair and a fair but weather-hardened face, marred only by a slight scar running down the left cheek. The scar pulled the man's mouth up into a slight sneer. He looked no older than twenty-five, but his eyes, which seemed to miss nothing, made him look wise beyond his years. The slaves, having settled down in a new spot, watched the two warily.

As the first of the cavalry troop crested the hill, which was much steeper on the encampment's side, the lieutenant in command pulled his mount up.

"Well met, Captain," the lieutenant said. The lieutenant's lead sergeant also stopped his horse.

The cavalry troop continued to ride by, the men wearing their helmets to avoid the drizzling rain but miserably wet just the same. The lieutenant offered a salute, to which the captain simply nodded in reply, saying nothing. The captain's gaze—along with that of his companion, whose face was concealed by the hood of his cloak—remained focused on the encampment below.

After several uncomfortable moments, the lieutenant once again attempted to strike up a conversation. "I assume you came by way of Aeda? A miserable city, if you ask me. Can you tell me the condition of the road? Did you encounter any rebels?"

The lieutenant shivered slightly as the captain turned a cold gray-eyed gaze upon him.

"We saw no evidence of rebels," the captain replied in a low, gravelly voice filled with steel and confidence. "The road passed peacefully."

"That is good to hear," the cavalry officer replied. "I am Lieutenant Lan of the One Hundred Eighty-Seventh Imperial Horse Regiment. May... may I have your name, Captain?"

"Stiger," the captain growled, kicking his horse into motion and rapidly moving off the crest of the hill, down toward the encampment.

The lieutenant's eyes widened. Stiger's companion, without a word or a sideways glance, followed at a touch to his horse, leaving the lieutenant behind.

The door to the guardhouse opened and after a moment banged closed like it had undoubtedly done countless times before. Stiger and his companion stepped forward, their heavy bootfalls thunking across the coarse wooden floor-boards that were covered in a layer of dirt made slick from the rain. The floor had not been swept in a good long time.

"Name and purpose?" a bored ensign demanded, his back to the door. A counter separated the ensign from any newcomers. He was sitting at a table, attempting to look busy and important by writing in a logbook. After a few moments, when the ensign heard nothing in reply, he stood and turned with obvious irritation, prepared to give the new arrivals a piece of his mind. He was confronted with two wet officers, one a captain and the other a lieutenant.

Stiger locked the ensign with a piercing gaze. The ensign was old for his rank, which was generally a sign that he was unfit for further promotion. Instead of forcing such a useless man out of service, he was put in a position where he could do little harm and perhaps accomplish something useful. It had been Stiger's experience that such men became bitter and would not hesitate to abuse what little power was available to them.

Flustered, the ensign tried again. "Name and purp—"

"Captain Stiger and companion," Stiger interrupted, with something akin to an irritated growl. The captain slowly placed his hands on the dirty counter and leaned forward toward the man. The ensign—most likely accustomed to dealing with lowly teamsters, drovers, corporals, and sergeants—blinked. His jaw dropped. He stood there for a moment, dumbfounded, before remembering to salute a superior officer, fist to chest. Stiger said nothing in reply, but gestured impatiently for the ensign to move things along.

"Forgive me, sir," the ensign stammered. It was then, as the lieutenant who accompanied the captain pushed back the hood of his cloak, that he noticed Captain Stiger's companion was not human. The ensign's mouth dropped open even further, if that was possible.

"Lieutenant Eli'Far," the elf introduced himself in a pleasantly soft, singsong kind of voice that sounded human, but was tinged with something alien at the same time. Eli was tall, whipcord thin, and very fair. His perpetually youthful face, complete with blue almond-shaped eyes and sharply pointed ears, was perfect. Framed by sand-colored hair, perhaps it was even *too* perfect.

"I have orders to report to General Kromen," Stiger stated simply, impatient to be done with the fool before him.

"Of course, sir," the ensign stammered, remembering himself. He slid a book across the counter. "If you will sign in, I will have you escorted directly to General Kromen's headquarters."

Stiger grabbed a quill, dipped it in the inkbottle sitting on the counter, and signed for both himself and Eli. He put down the quill and pushed the book back toward the ensign.

"Corporal!" the ensign called in a near-panicked shout.

The guard corporal poked his head into the guardhouse.

"Captain Stiger requires an escort to the commanding general's headquarters."

The corporal blinked as if he had not heard correctly. "Yes, sir," he said, fully stepping into the guardhouse, eyes wide. "This way, gentlemen," the corporal said in a respectful tone. It was never wise to upset an officer, and even more irresponsible to offend one from an important family, no matter how infamous. "I will escort you myself. It is a bit of a ride, sirs."

The two traveling companions followed the corporal out of the guardhouse. They stepped back into the rain, which had changed from a drizzle to a steady downpour. Eli pulled his hood back up, once again obscuring his features. Stiger left his down. They retrieved their horses from where they had secured them and mounted up. The corporal also mounted a horse that was waiting for such a purpose and led them through the massive wooden gate that served as the encampment's main entrance. Stiger was disgusted to see the sentries huddled for cover under the gate's overhang. Those men should have been on post despite the weather.

Stiger had thought it impossible for the stench of the encampment to get any worse, yet it became much more awful and unpleasant once they were clear of the gate. It made his eyes burn. He had only ever once encountered a worse smell. That had been years before on a distant battlefield, with the dead numbering in the many thousands under a brutally hot sun, rotting quicker than they could be buried or burned.

Massive numbers of tents and temporary ramshackle wooden buildings spread out before them, amongst a sea of mud flowing with animal and human excrement. The three worked their way slowly through the muddy streets with rows of tents on each side. They came upon a small stream, muddy brown and swollen from the day's rain, running through the center of the encampment. The stream was threatening to flood nearby tents.

A rickety wooden bridge, which looked as though it had been hastily constructed to ford the small stream, appeared at risk of being washed away by the growing rush of water. Unconcerned, the corporal guided them over the bridge and to a large rough-looking building directly in the center of the encampment. An overhang and porch had been constructed onto the building, almost as an afterthought, but probably in response to the rain and mud.

Several staff officers on the porch loitered about in chairs, idly chatting and smoking pipes or playing cards, as the three horsemen approached. It was clear this was the main headquarters. A rough planked boardwalk that looked like it might sink into the mud at any moment connected the building to a row of larger tents and other nearby buildings. The porch and boardwalk served the purpose of saving the officers from having to get their perfectly polished boots muddy.

A dirty and ragged slave, ankles disappearing in the muck, stepped forward to take the reins of their horses as the two officers dismounted. Stiger tried to avoid thinking about what was in the mud as his boots sank into it.

"Good day, sirs." The corporal saluted and swung his horse around, riding away before anything more could be required of him. Stiger understood that the man was relieved to be on his way. It was said that bad things tended to happen around Stigers.

"This camp is an embarrassment," Eli said quietly to Stiger. "It is very unfit."

"I hazard half the camp is down sick," Stiger responded in sour agreement. He had never seen a legionary encampment in such a state. "Let us hope we are not detained here for months on end."

The two walked through the mud and up the steps to the front porch of the headquarters building, where they hastily kicked and scraped the muck from their boots. The headquarters building was not at all what one would expect for the commanding general of the South. The finely attired officers on the porch purposefully ignored the new arrivals. Stiger hesitated a moment and then stepped toward the building's entrance, reaching for the door.

"Where exactly do you think you're going?" a young staff captain sitting in a chair demanded disdainfully without looking up from his card game. The man was casually smoking and took a rather slow pull from his pipe, as if to show he was in charge.

Stiger turned to look at the staff captain, who wore expensively crafted legionary officer armor over a well-cut tunic and rich black boots. The armor was highly polished and the fine red cloak appeared to be freshly cleaned and brushed. There was not a hint of mud or dirt anywhere on the officer. He almost looked like the perfect toy soldier. Stiger took him to be of the soft type, a spoiled and pampered nobleman, likely from a minor yet wealthy house. At least wealthy or influential enough to secure his current position. Much like the ensign in the guardhouse, Stiger had also unfortunately encountered this kind of officer before—a bootlicking fool. Stiger's lip curled ever so slightly in derision. The bootlicker, more concerned with his fawning entourage of fellow officers, did not seem to notice. Eli, however, did. He placed a cautioning hand on Stiger's arm, which had come to rest upon the pommel of his sword.

"I am ordered to report to General Kromen and that is what I intend to do," Stiger responded neutrally, casually pulling his arm away from Eli's restraining hand. The elf sighed softly. "Unless, of course, the general is not present. In that event I shall simply wait for his return."

"Oh, I believe the general is in," the captain said with a sneer. "However, you do not get to see him without my personal permission."

Several of the other officers snickered.

"Perhaps you should say ... please?" one of the other officers suggested with a high-pitched voice. The others openly laughed at this.

Stiger's anger flared, though he kept the irritation from his face. The captain was likely an aide to the general, a player of camp politics, working to control access and thereby strengthening his powerbase. He was the kind of man who was rarely challenged openly. He was also someone who would most definitely hold a grudge if he was ever slighted or offended. In short, he was another arrogant fool, and Stiger loathed such men.

Suffer the fool's game or not? Stiger was new to the camp and the last thing he wanted was to get off on the wrong foot. Still, the captain's manner irritated him deeply. The man should have behaved as a gentleman, and yet he had blatantly offended Stiger. Should he continue, Stiger would be justified in issuing a challenge to satisfy honor. Somehow, Stiger doubted General Kromen would approve of him killing, or at best maiming, one of his staff officers on his first day in camp.

"Stop me," Stiger growled. He opened the door and stepped through. The staff captain scrambled out of his chair and gave chase, protesting loudly.

Inside, Stiger was greeted by a nearly bare room. The interior was intentionally darkened, the windows shuttered.

Several lanterns provided moderately adequate lighting. A fireplace, set along the back wall, crackled. The chimney, poorly constructed, leaked too much smoke into the building. A table with a large map spread out on it dominated the center of the room. Three men stood around the table, while another, a grossly obese man, sat in a chair with his elbows resting heavily on the tabletop. He had the look of someone who was seriously ill. His face was pale and covered in a sheet of fever sweat. They all looked up at the sudden intrusion, clearly irritated. Two were generals, including the one who was seated, and the two others held the rank of colonel.

"What is the meaning of this intrusion?" the general who was standing demanded. He had a tough, no-nonsense look about him.

"I am sorry, sir," the bootlicking staff captain apologized, pushing roughly past Stiger and Eli. "I tried to stop them."

"Well?" the general demanded again of Stiger.

Unfazed by the rank of the men in the room, Stiger pulled his orders from a side pocket in his cloak and stepped forward. "I am ordered to report to General Kromen for duty."

"I am General Kromen," the large, seated man wheezed before being consumed by a wracking cough. After a few moments he recovered. "Who in the seven levels might you be?"

"Captain Stiger reporting for duty, sir." Stiger assumed a position of attention and saluted.

"A Stiger?" the staff captain whispered, taking a step back in shock.

The other general barked out a sudden laugh, while General Kromen went into another coughing fit that wracked his fat body terribly.

"Captain Handi," General Kromen wheezed upon recovering, waving a hand dismissively. His other hand held a handkerchief to his mouth. "It would seem," he coughed, "we have important matters to discuss. You may go."

The captain hesitated a moment, looking between the standing no-nonsense general and the seated one before saluting smartly. He left the room without saying another word, though he managed to shoot a hate-filled look at Stiger as he passed.

"A Stiger!" Kromen exclaimed in irritation once the door was closed. "Who is your companion?"

Eli reached up and pulled back his hood, showing his face for the first time.

"Hah!" Kromen huffed tiredly. "An elf. I swear, I never thought I'd see one of your kind again, at least in this life."

"Sadly, we are few in these lands, General," Eli responded neutrally, with a slight bow.

"An elf, as well as imperial officer? I thought you fellows had given up on the empire," the other general stated.

"The emperor granted a special dispensation to serve the one known here as Ben Stiger," Eli answered, nodding in the direction of the captain. The nod had an odd tilt to it that reminded everyone present he was not quite human. Human necks just did not bend like that. "The rank conferred was to help me better serve."

"You serve a human?" the standing general asked with some surprise before turning back to Stiger. "What did you do to earn that dubious honor, Stiger?"

"I, ah..." Stiger began after a slight hesitation, "would prefer not to discuss it, sir."

"The emperor," Kromen breathed with a heavy sigh, steering the conversation away from a direction that Stiger was clearly uncomfortable speaking on. "The emperor and the gods have forsaken us in this wicked and vile land."

Kromen was an old and wily politician. Stiger suspected that the general would not press him, but would instead write back to his family in the capital to get an answer. Information was often more important than the might of an entire legion. More importantly, Stiger knew that Kromen wanted to know why a Stiger, a member of one of the most powerful families in the empire, was here in the South, and that required moving the conversation along.

"Perhaps not...You asked for combat-experienced officers and men of quality. Well...here stands a Stiger," the other general said after a moment's reflection, taking General Kromen's subtle nudge to change the subject. Stepping over, he took Stiger's orders. "Were you in the North?"

"Emperor's Third Legion," Stiger replied.

"The Third gets all of the shit assignments." The general handed the orders over to General Kromen, who opened them and began reviewing the contents. Silence filled the room, and all that could be heard was the pop of the logs in the fireplace and the rustle of parchment as General Kromen read.

"An introduction letter from my good friend General Treim," Kromen breathed hoarsely as he read.

Stiger was familiar with the contents of the letter. According to the letter, the emperor had directed Treim to send a few of his best and most promising officers to the South. Stiger could imagine Kromen's thoughts as the general looked up briefly with a skeptical look. The general was finding it hard to imagine that Treim would release one of his truly outstanding officers. The politician in Kromen would scream that there was more here than met the eye. Perhaps even the general might consider this whelp of a Stiger was actually a spy for his enemies in the senate looking to gain some advantage. Though the Kromen and Stiger families were not actually enemies, they were not allies either.

"Interesting," Kromen said after a few silent minutes, and then turned to the other general. "General Mammot, it seems that our good friend General Treim has dispatched this officer at *our* request. The letter indicates more such officers of quality are on the way. Interesting, don't you think?"

"Very," General Mammot replied dryly. "How long did it take you to travel down here, Stiger?"

"Three and a half months, sir."

General Kromen was consumed by another fit of coughing. He held a handkerchief to his mouth, hacking into it.

"Impressive time," General Mammot admitted with a raised eyebrow and turned to Kromen. "Do you think he can fight?"

"General Treim," cough, "seems to think so." Kromen handed over the letter of introduction, which General Mammot began reading. After a moment, he stopped and looked up, a strange expression crossing his face.

"You volunteered and led not one, but two forlorn hopes?" Mammot asked in an incredulous tone. "Do you have a death wish, son?"

Stiger elected not to respond and remained silent. Mammot continued to read.

"Seems General Treim sent us a fighter, and the elf comes as a bonus." Kromen took a deep and labored breath, having somewhat recovered from his latest coughing fit. He seemed to make a decision. He looked over meaningfully at General Mammot, who paused in his reading and caught his look. "We were discussing a pressing issue ..."

"We were," Mammot agreed.

"Well then...since we are now saddled with a...Stiger, perhaps he might prove of some assistance in resolving this irritating matter with Vrell? Don't you agree?"

General Mammot frowned slightly and considered Stiger for a moment before nodding in agreement. He waved both Stiger and Eli over to the table with the map.

"Stiger," Mammot said, "allow me to introduce Colonels Karol and Edin. They are brigade commanders from the Twenty-Ninth."

"Pleased to meet you, Stiger," Colonel Karol said, warmly offering his hand. "I fought with your father when I was a junior officer. How is the old boy?"

"Well, sir," Stiger replied. His father was a touchy subject with most other officers. He found it was best to be vague in his answers to their questions. "His forced retirement wears on him."

"I can understand that," Colonel Karol said. "Perhaps one day he may be permitted to once again take the field."

"I am not sure he ever will," Stiger replied carefully. Many would feel threatened by such sentiments.

Colonel Edin simply shook hands and refrained from saying anything. Stiger could read the disapproval in the man's eyes. It was something the captain had grown accustomed to from his fellow officers.

"Now that we are all acquainted," General Mammot began, directing everyone's attention to the map on the table, "we have an outpost four weeks' march from here, located at Vrell, an isolated valley to the east with a substantial population." Mammot traced a line along a road from the encampment to the outpost for Stiger to follow. "Specifically, the outpost garrisons one of the few castles in the South. We call it Castle Vrell. The locals call it something different."

"We have not heard from them for several weeks," Kromen rasped. "We have dispatched messengers, but none have returned. It is all very irritating."

"The castle is a highly fortified position," Mammot continued. "There are over nine hundred legionaries defending it and the valley. Vrell is an out-of-the-way place, surrounded by mountains and a nearly impenetrable forest. We think the castle unlikely to have fallen to enemy forces." With his hand, Mammot traced a new line on the map, well south of Vrell. "The rebels control everything south of this line here ... There are no roads traveling to rebel territory from Vrell. Beyond the mountains, it is all thick forest for about one hundred miles to rebel territory. The only road to Vrell moves from the encampment here, eastward, through the Sentinel Forest and terminates at the valley. It is our opinion the enemy has simply cut our communications with a handful of irregulars."

"The garrison commander, Captain Aveeno, has been complaining for months of rebels harassing his patrols and stirring up trouble," Colonel Karol spoke up. "Then suddenly, nothing ... no word."

"The garrison is due for resupply," Kromen added, taking another labored breath. "Normally we would send a simple cavalry escort. However, with the road apparently infested with rebel irregulars, a foot company appears to be the more sensible approach."

"The Third has been heavily involved up north in the forests of Abath," General Mammot said. "We would appreciate your expertise on the matter."

"Sounds like a difficult assignment," Stiger said, noncommittally. "How are the rebels equipped in this area?"

"Poorly." Colonel Edin spoke for the first time. "This terrain presents a very difficult obstacle for the rebels to overcome. We have only ever encountered light units, mostly conscripted farmers … the equivalent of bandits."

"What is the condition of the road?" Stiger leaned forward to study the map more closely. Eli stepped closer as well. The map was a simple camp scribe copy.

"Poor, but passable for wagons," Karol admitted. "Imperial maintenance crews repaired it just three years ago, so there should be no significant problems for the supply train."

"I don't see any towns and villages." Stiger found that odd for such a long road.

"There are—or were—a handful of what you might call farming communities," Edin admitted. "Really the remnants. I personally would be surprised if you discovered anyone left."

"Reprisals?" Stiger asked, looking up at Edin. He already knew the answer.

"That was my predecessor's work," General Kromen answered carefully. "A nasty business, though he did a good job in clearing the bastards out. There should be no one left to support the rebels, at least we think, until you get to Vrell. The valley's population is not with the rebels. For some strange reason, they seem to think of themselves as imperials, or at least descended from imperial stock. That said, they are not exactly friendly, at least according to Captain Aveeno's last reports."

"Captain Aveeno could have sent a force to break through, could he not?" Stiger asked.

"Not very likely," Mammot answered with a heavy breath. "Captain Aveeno, the garrison commandant, is a bit cautious. He likely would have put everyone on short rations and kept them in defense of the castle and valley, rather than take the risk of losing additional men."

"Aveeno comes from a good family," General Kromen wheezed, speaking up in defense of the man. "However, he is a timid sort, which is why he is commanding a garrison instead of leading a line company."

Stiger nodded, understanding what had not been said. General Kromen was likely Aveeno's patron, hence his defense. "A good company should be able to get through, then," Stiger said, looking down at the map once again. "Should the rebel forces operating in the area prove superior, a company will likely be able to get word out or at least fight its way back."

"Excellent," Kromen said, looking from Eli to Stiger. "How would you like the job? I have an absolutely terrible company that just became available. With your experience, you are perfect for working it into shape!"

Stiger was surprised he was being given a mission that would take him away so soon after arriving. Though marching with unfamiliar men into territory overrun by rebels was not a terribly appealing idea to the captain, his initial impressions of the legionary encampment led him to believe that such a march would be preferable to risking an untimely death by lingering sickness. He knew that the command he was being offered was most probably, as the general said, a truly terrible assignment. If the men had been idle for months, as he suspected they had, they would be sick, poorly equipped, and out of shape, and discipline would be lacking. So it all came down to risking potential death from slow, lingering sickness and disease or possible death by sword ... Stiger intentionally drew out the silence, as if he were mulling it over. Surely there were other, more effective companies that could be more readily chosen. The two generals, he knew, were also making light of the assignment so that it seemed too easy ... too good. That bothered

Stiger, and he wanted to know why, but could not come right out and ask.

"I would need to outfit the company for a hard march into the wilderness," Stiger said.

"You can draw anything you might require from supply," Kromen responded, almost a little too quickly, which surprised Stiger.

What wasn't he being told?

Stiger had known that his arrival might be a headache for General Kromen. Stiger's family had influence. His presence here might be viewed as the attempt to place a spy within the Southern legions, a spy who was possibly reporting directly to the emperor or Kromen's enemies in the senate.

"We need to open communications with Vrell," Mammot added. "We can issue your company fresh arms and equipment. I will also assign some of our most experienced sergeants to help you work them into fighting trim."

"Could I meet and approve the sergeants first?" Stiger asked. He had known some pretty terrible sergeants, from ass-kissers to sadistic bastards. Instead of being dismissed from the service, such men were frequently transferred from one unit to another.

"Of course," Kromen said.

"How long until the supply train is ready?" Stiger asked, thinking about the training of his men. He needed time to become acquainted with them and to work them into shape. All legionaries received the same basic training. It was a matter of restoring discipline and finding out how rusty they had become.

"Two weeks," Mammot said. "At least, we hope the train will arrive within two weeks, but certainly no more than four. It is due to leave from Aeda any day."

"Good, that would give me some time," Stiger said. He looked at General Kromen, thinking hard. "I would want to train the men my way, with no outside interference."

"Acceptable," General Kromen said with a deep frown. No general enjoyed being dictated to, especially by a young, impudent captain, even if he was a Stiger. Still... Kromen seemed to put up with it, and Stiger decided to push for more.

"That would involve training outside the encampment and living beyond the walls," Stiger added. "I would need space to prepare the men... construction of a marching camp, route marches, arms training..."

"If you are willing to brave a rebel attack outside the protection of the walls, you can do whatever you flaming wish," Kromen said, his dangerous tone betraying a mounting anger. "Anything else you require, captain?"

"No, sir," Stiger said, pleased at having escaped the confines of the encampment so easily. In all likelihood, whatever he had been set up for would prove to be a real challenge. "I will take the job."

"Very good." General Kromen flashed an insincere smile. "Colonel Karol will arrange to have you introduced to your men. He will also see to outfitting your needs." Kromen waved dismissively, indicating the audience was over.

Stiger saluted along with Colonel Karol. They turned and left, emerging onto the porch with Eli in tow. Stiger found Captain Handi resting in the same chair. The captain shot Stiger a look that spoke volumes. Doubtless Handi would be looking for ways to get his petty revenge. Stiger simply ignored him.

"You have a tough job ahead of you," Karol admitted. "The men I am giving you are in truly terrible shape and have been poorly led. Their previous commander was executed for gross incompetence. His real crime, however, was excessive graft and insufficient... shall we say, *sharing*."

"I have always enjoyed a challenge," Stiger replied softly.

"Let us both hope this particular challenge does not kill you," Karol responded. The colonel glanced to the side at the lounging officers toward Handi, who was aiming a smoldering glare at Stiger. "Captain Handi, be so good as to personally fetch Sergeants Blake and Ranl. They should be working over at my headquarters."

"But, sir, it's raining," Handi protested, gesturing at the steady rainfall beyond the cover of the porch.

"I rather imagine that the emperor expects his legions to operate in all types of weather," the colonel responded rather blandly. "Have them report on the double to the officers' mess."

Colonel Karol turned away and stepped out into the rain. He led them along the improvised boardwalk system toward another smaller ramshackle wooden building with a chimney billowing with soft blue-gray smoke.

"Wouldn't want that spoiled bastard to get his fine boots muddy now, would we?" Karol asked once they were out of earshot. Stiger found himself beginning to like the colonel.

A Note from the Author

I want to thank you for reading *Fortress of Radiance*. I sincerely hope you enjoyed it. Karus and Amarra's journey will continue in 2019! Writing a book like this takes a tremendous amount of time, effort, and energy. A review would be awesome and greatly appreciated.

Important: If you have not yet given my other series—Tales of the Seventh or Chronicles of an Imperial Legionary officer a shot, I strongly recommend you do. All three series are linked and set in the same universe. There are hints, clues, and Easter eggs sprinkled throughout the series.

The Series:
There are three series to consider. I began telling Stiger and Eli's story in the middle years... starting with Stiger's Tigers, published in 2015. *Stiger's Tigers* is a great place to start reading. It was the first work I published and is a grand fantasy epic.

Stiger, Tales of the Seventh, covers Stiger's early years. It begins with Stiger's first military appointment as a wet-behind-the-ears lieutenant serving in Seventh Company during the very beginning of the war against the Rivan on the frontier. This series sees Stiger cut his teeth and develop into the hard charging leader that fans have grown to love. It also introduces Eli and covers many of their early adventures. These tales should in no way spoil your experience with *Stiger's Tigers*. In fact, I believe they will only enhance it.

The <u>Karus Saga</u> is a whole new adventure set in the same universe ... many years before Stiger was even born. This series tells how Roman legionaries made their way to the world of Istros and the founding of the empire. It is set amidst a war of the gods and is full of action, intrigue, adventure, and mystery.

Give them a shot and hit me up on Facebook to let me know what you think!

Best regards and again thank you for reading!

Marc

JOIN Marc's NEWSLETTER

Stay up to date! Care to be notified when the next book is released and receive updates from the author? Join the mailing list! You can find it on Marc's website:

http://www.MAEnovels.com

Facebook: Marc Edelheit Author

https://www.facebook.com/MAENovels/

Printed in Great Britain
by Amazon